Leanbh Pearson (Any) lives on Ngunnawal Country in Canberra, Australia. An award-winning LGBTQ and disability author of horror and dark fantasy, writing inspired by folklore, fairytales, myth, history and climate. Leanbh's judged numerous awards, an invited panelist and avid book reviewer and has been awarded ASA, AHWA and HWA mentorships and 2023 HWA Diversity Grant. Leanbh's alter-ego is an academic in archaeology, evolution and prehistory. A museum devotee, insomniac and photography enthusiast, Leanbh is always aided by canine assistants.

Other Leanbh Pearson titles by IFWG (authored or edited)

Three Curses and Other Dark Tales (dark fantasy/folklore/fairy-tales short fiction collection)

Cursed Shards: Tales of Dark Folklore ((Dark Fantasy/Folklore, anthology of short fiction, edited by Leanbh Pearson)

Ghost Warrior (dark fantasy novel)

"A deep dive into Norse mythology, revealing the trickster god as you've never seen him before."

(Juliet Marillier, author of *Wolfskin*)

Loki: Untangling a Tale

by

Leanbh Pearson

Loki: Untangling a Tale

All Rights Reserved

ISBN-13: 978-1-923382-20-6

V1.1

Internal map created by Leanbh Pearson.

Printed in Times and Morpheus font types.

IFWG Publishing International
Gold Coast

www.ifwgpublishing.com

Loki:
A tangle or knot in Old Norse.

For my mother, who raised me to be a Valkyrie, not a princess.

Author's Note

The content, events and characters are entirely fictitious. There are themes within a historical fantasy context including misogyny, violence against women, homophobia, coercive control, war, murder, torture, gore, and disability stigma, which are themes that still present today, but some aspects of this work might be uncomfortable. Be kind to yourself when reading.

Leanbh Pearson, 2025.

Acknowledgements

There are many people I want to thank during inspiration, research and writing of this novel. Firstly, my family and friends who supported me constantly. To Lisa L. Hannett for her inspirational work *Viking Women*, the Icelandic tour guides who provided historical context and folklore to the amazing country of fire and ice. I appreciate the hard work and efforts of my editors Noel and Steve for making this book shine! Special thanks to IFWG (owner, Gerry Huntman) for believing in this work, and lastly, to my canine companions who were always at my side. To my readers, I hope you enjoy this retelling of a unique Norse mythic figure as much as I enjoyed writing and untangling the story of Loki.

Leanbh Pearson, 2025.

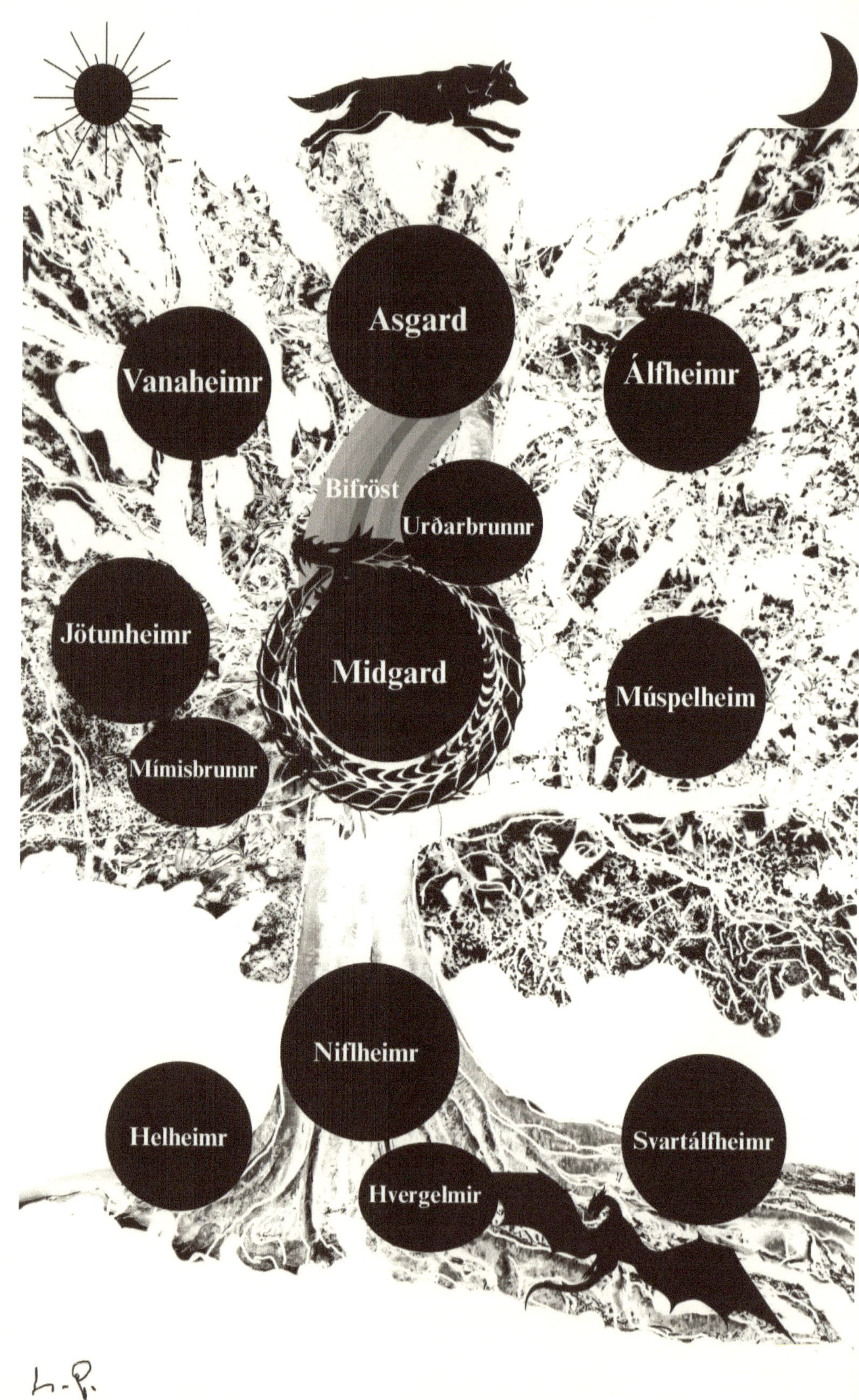
Asgard
Vanaheimr
Álfheimr
Bifröst
Urðarbrunnr
Jötunheimr
Midgard
Múspelheim
Mímisbrunnr
Niflheimr
Helheimr
Svartálfheimr
Hvergelmir

Norse Mythology Glossary

REALMS OF THE NORSE COSMOS

Álfheimr = One of the Nine Worlds in the Norse cosmos and the realm of the Light Elves, the Ljósálfar.

Asgard = One of the Nine Worlds in the Norse cosmos and realm of the Æsir gods.

Bifröst = The rainbow bridge connecting Asgard to Midgard.

Éljúðnir = The dwelling of Hel in Helheimr, one of the worlds in the Norse Cosmos and realm of the dishonourable dead.

Fensalir = Dwelling in Asgard of Æsir goddess, Frigg.

Fólkvangr= Practice battlefield meadows and dominion of Freyja in Asgard.

Ginnungagap = The black void between the fiery realms of Múspelheim and the frosty world of Niflheimr.

Glaðsheimr= the area in the realm Asgard where Óðinn's hall Valhalla is located.

Helheimr = One of the Nine Worlds in Norse cosmos and realm of the dishonourable dead and ruled by Hel.

Hliðskjálf = A chair perched on a stony spire in Asgard which only Óðinn and Frigg use allowing sight anywhere in the Nine Worlds.

Hvergelmir = A poisonous well situated in Niflheimr, source of the river Élivágar which flows into Múspelheim. Situated at base root of Yggdrasil where the dragon Níðhöggr gnaws at Yggdrasil's roots.

Járnviðr = A forest where the witch Angrboða, wolves Sköll and Haiti and werewolves dwell. Járnviðr means 'iron wood' and is located between the Norse realms of Asgard and Jötunheimr.

Jötunheimr = One of the Nine Worlds in the Norse cosmos and the realm of the frost giants.

Midgard = One of the Nine Worlds in the Norse cosmos and the realm of mortals.

Mímisbrunnr = A well of wisdom situated in Jötunheimr beneath a root of Yggdrasil, and guarded by Mimir, who derives his wisdom by drinking from the water of the well.

Múspelheim = One of the Nine Worlds in the Norse cosmos and the realm of the fire giants ruled by Surtr.

Niflheimr = One of the Nine Worlds in the Norse cosmos, an icy, inhabitable realm where no beings can survive. Helheimr exists within Niflheimr where Hel rules over the dead.

Svartálfheimr = One of the Nine Worlds in the Norse cosmos and the realm of the Dark Elves, the Dökkálfar.

Thyrmheimr = the king of frost giants, Thiazi's, hall, and after his death, the hall of his daughter and frost giant, Skaði.

Urðarbrunnr = A well at one of the main roots of Yggdrasil where the Norns nourish the tree.

Valhalla = A golden chieftain's hall in Asgard and communal dwelling of Óðinn and the Æsir gods.

Vanaheimr = One of the Nine Worlds in the Norse cosmos and the realm of the Vanir gods.

Vigríðr = The plain at Ragnarök where opposing armies will battle.

ÆSIR DEITIES

Baldr = Son of Óðinn and Frigg and brother to Höðr. Wife to Nanna and most beloved among the gods.

Bragi = The Æsir god associated with poetry and welcoming the newly slain to Valhalla. Husband to Iðunn.

Frigg = Goddess and ruler of the Æsir and wife to Óðinn, mother to Baldr and Höðr. In Óðinn's absence, Frigg rules Asgard and shares the right to sit on Hliðskjálf. She is associated with the weather.

Heimdallrr = The watchman of the Æsir gods with keen senses guarding edge of Bifröst. At the beginning of Ragnarök, he blows the mighty horn Gjallarhorn to summon gods to Ragnarök.

Hermodr = the son of Óðinn and a giantess, often sent on journeys in Óðinn's place.

Höðr = Óðinn's blind son and brother of Baldr. Unknowingly tricked by Loki into murdering Baldr.

Hœnir = A mysterious and mystical figure among the Æsir gods, often associated with primal magic and animal sacrifice. He is also the god of poetry and frequently accompanied by Óðinn in his travels in the Nine Worlds.

Iðunn = Æsir Goddess and wife to Bragi. Tends to the apple tree that maintains the youth of the gods.

Mimir = A mystical figure in the Æsir became a hostage to the Vanir during the War between the two groups of deities. Mimir was decapitated, and Óðinn preserved the head to consult for advice at the well of Mímisbrunnr.

Narvi = Son of Loki and his Æsir wife, Sigyn.

Óðinn = The gods of war, battle, power and death. Fought a war against opposing deities, the Vanir, before reaching a truce. Æsir dwell in Asgard, one the Nine Worlds of the Norse Cosmos.

Sif = Æsir, goddess and mother of archer-God, Ullr, and married to Thor.

Sigyn = Goddess of the Æsir, wife to Loki and mother to Narvi, known for her sacrifice staying beside Loki during his punishment before Ragnarök.

Thor = Son of Óðinn and the giantess, Jörð. Renowned as a short-tempered giant killer and god of thunder. He is the stepfather of the god Ullr and shared many siblings including Baldr. He also known for this dwarf-forged war-hammer, Mjölnir.

Týr = Æsir god of battle, war and a tactician and renowned swordsman. Loses his right-hand binding Fenrir.

Ullr = Archer and hunting god of the Æsir and son to Sif and stepson to Thor.

Váli = the son of Óðinn and the frost giant Rindr who grew to adulthood in a single day. Born for the sole purpose to avenge Baldr's death by killing Höðr and then binding Loki with the entrails of Narfi, his son with Sigyn.

Vé = One of Óðinn's two brothers who help make the Nine Worlds of the Norse Cosmos.

Verandi = One of the three Norns who dwell at Urðarbrunnr, a well at one the main roots of Yggdrasil and responsible for nourishing the tree. They also weave the fate of mortals and gods.

Víðarr = Óðinn's son by giantess Rindr. He is Óðinn's avenger at Ragnarök.

Vili = One of Óðinn's two brothers who help make the Nine Worlds of the Norse Cosmos.

VANIR DEITIES

Ægir = Sea giant, husband to Rán and father of nine daughters, the waves.

Freyja = Vanir goddess of love and death, the daughter of Njörðr and sister to Freyr. A prophetess and partitioner of seiðr, and a völva, a witch. Her Valkyries ride through the battlefield selecting half the slain for her, while Óðinn takes the other half.

Freyr = Vanir god of spring, brother to Freyja and son to Njörðr. Freyr fell in love with the giantess, Gerðr, and exchanged his giant-killing sword for her servant's help in wooing her.

Gullveig = A mysterious witch who comes among the Æsir and Vanir during the war between the two deities. Gullveig refuses to teach Óðinn seiðr and is thrice burned in Valhalla.

Njörðr = Vanir god and father of Freyr and Freyja. Joins the Æsir after the Æsir-Vanir war and married to giantess Skaði. Dwells in Nóatún, by the coastline.

FROST & FIRE GIANTS

Angrboða = A witch of the Iron Wood, lover to Loki and mother of monstrous children: the giant wolf, Fenrir, sea serpent Jörmungandr and the ruler of the dead, Hel.

Gerðr = Giantess beloved by the Vanir god Freyr.

Hel = The ruler of Helheimr and daughter of Loki and Angrboða.

Hrymr = The frost giant who at the epic battle of Ragnarök will summon the frost giants and steer the massive longship *Naglfar* to bring Loki's host to the shores of the battle plain Vigríðr.

Hyrrokkin = the tall, battle-scarred frost giant rides a she-wolf and is tasked to move the longship *Hringhorni* at Baldr's funeral.

Jörð = Giantess mother of Thor by Óðinn.

Loki = A fire giant from Múspelheim who dwells among the Æsir and is bonded brother to the Æsir god Óðinn. Married to Æsir goddess Sigyn and father of Narvi. Loki had an affair with the giantess and witch, Angrboða and sired three monstrous children: the ruler of the dead, Hel; the giant Midgard serpent Jörmungandr, and the monstrous wolf, Fenrir. Loki transformed into a mare and sired Óðinn's stallion Sleipnir. He is the opposing force in the final cataclysmic battle Ragnarök.

Rán = sea-giantess and wife to Ægir and mother of nine daughters, the waves. Collector of souls drowned at sea.

Rindr = Frost giantess and mother of Viddar by Óðinn who used enchantments to seduce her.

Skaði = Daughter of the former ruler of frost giants, Thiazi who was murdered by Loki's schemes. Marries Vanir god Njörðr after Loki plays a trick on Skaði but she harbours a long-standing grudge against Loki.

Surtr = The mighty fire giant and ruler of the realm Múspelheim, leader of the troops against the Æsir at Ragnarök.

Thiazi = Frost giant ruler and father of Skaði who challenges Æsir to battle when she avenges his death.

Ymir = Primordial giant killed by Óðinn, Vili and Vé. His body created the Nine Worlds of the Norse Cosmos, with Yggdrasil growing from where he had fallen across the void of Ginnungagap between fire and ice.

MYTHOLOGICAL FIGURES AND EVENTS

Æsir = The gods who fought for control against the Vanir. After a truce, hostages were exchanged from both sides.

Brokk = Dwarf responsible for tricking Loki and having his lips sewn together.

Dagr = The male personification of Day who rides a bright-maned horse, Skinfaxi.

Disir = Female supernatural beings that are associated with the dead or fate.

Dökkálfar = The 'Dark elves' a race of elves that are distinct from light elves and dwarfs and dwell in Svartálfheimr.

Einherjar = The warriors Óðinn selects from the slain on the battlefield to join him in Valhalla while the other half are taken by the Valkyries for the goddess Freyja.

Eitri = Dwarf brother to Brokk. The smiths who forged gifts for the gods: the golden bristled boar, Gullinbursti; the golden arm-ring Draupnir; and the mighty war hammer Mjölnir.

Fimbulwinter = Three subsequent harsh winters ushering in Ragnarök.

Gjallarhorn = The mighty horn used by Heimdallrr to summon the Æsir to war at Ragnarök.

Garmr = The greatest of dogs who guards the bridge in Helheimr and is often beside Hel.

Haiti = The wolf who purses Mani, personification of the Moon, across the sky devouring the moon at Ragnarök. Half-sister to giant wolf Fenrir and sister to Sköll, offspring of Angrboða.

Hugin = One of Óðinn's ravens who fly through the Nine Worlds gathering information for Óðinn and whose name means "thought".

Hrímfaxi = The frost-maned horse that Nótt, the personification of Night, rides to bring the bring the evening to Norse cosmos.

Jörmungandr = Monstrously large sea serpent that encircles Midgard, and the son of Loki and Angrboða.

Jötunn = Norse name for "giant", referring to both frost and fire giants with jötnar (plural).

Ljósálfar = The 'Light Elves' a race of elves distinct from the Dökkálfar.

Mani = The female personification of the Moon. The brother of Sól, the Sun.

Munin = One of Óðinn's ravens who fly through the Nine Worlds gathering information for Óðinn. The name means "memory".

Mjölnir = The war-hammer given by dwarfs Brokk and Eitri to Thor to kill giants.

Naglfar = A longship constructed from dead men's fingernails and the greatest of ships ever built. Carries Loki and a host of frost giants to Ragnarök.

Níðhöggr = Serpentine dragon trapped beneath the roots of Yggdrasil which gnaws on the roots and consumes corpses of the condemned.

Nótt = The female personification of the Night who rides a frost-maned horse, Hrímfaxi. Nótt's opposite is Dagr, the personification of Day.

Norns = Female figures who weave the fate of men and gods named Urd, Verandi and Skuld.

Ragnarök = The mighty battle fought between Æsir and giants preceded by cataclysmic winters and moral decay. The destruction of the Nine Worlds and rebirth of a new cycle.

Seiðr = A practioner of prophecy and the magic *seiðr*.

Skinfaxi = The horse ridden by Dagr, the personification of the Day, with the name meaning to "shining mane". Dagr's opposite is Nótt, the personification of Night and her horse, Hrímfaxi meaning "frost maned".

Sköll = The wolf who purses Sól, personification of the Sun, across the sky until devouring the sun at Ragnarök. Half-brother to giant wolf Fenrir and brother to Haiti, offspring of Angrboða.

Skuld = One of the three Norns who weave fate of mortals and gods. Dwells at the well of Urðarbrunnr which nourishes Yggdrasil.

Sleipnir = Óðinn's eight-legged stallion by Loki.

Sól = The personification of the Sun and sister to Mani, the Moon.

Urd = One of the three Norns who weave fate of mortals and gods. Dwells at the well of Urðarbrunnr which nourishes Yggdrasil.

Vanir = The opposing deities who fought against the Æsir. A truce was made through exchange of hostages.

Völva = A witch, prophetess or seeress and usually a female practitioner of *seiðr*.

Yggdrasil = The mighty ash tree that supports the Nine Worlds of the Norse Cosmos.

Prologue
The Beginning

I watched the creation of the Nine Worlds. Some stories now claim it was Óðinn's work alone, but he is the last of those three brothers forged from where fire and ice met. They stood over the slain corpse of the giant Ymir and carved up his body to forge a new cosmos. They were magnificent, these brothers. I crouched in the darkness, hidden from their sight. My own clumsy hands touched the black cavern walls of Múspelheim where Surtr ruled the fire giants. He had no need for me. I was ugly. My hands were barely functional and unable to hold axe haft or pick. Even my feet were contorted, and I shuffled in an uneven gait that would cause everyone who saw me to stare.

There was only the ice realm of Niflheimr, the dark void of Ginnungagap and the fiery world of Múspelheim. Spread across the void of such empty darkness was the body of Ymir, the primordial giant who had toppled between fire and ice. Óðinn walked along the length of Ymir's corpse and watched the boiling blackness of the void beneath his feet.

Óðinn gave a quick gesture to his brothers, Vili and Vé. Vili's craftsman's hands sculpted Ymir's flesh into land and poured the blood to fill hollows and made the seas and lakes, rivers and fjords. Vili carved the giant's bones into rocks and from his lengthy spine, a sapling unfurled. It grew quickly, with roots winding deep along the giant's length. Yggdrasil sank roots beneath the surface of the Midgard Sea to grow tall and strong. Ymir's spine lurched upright as Yggdrasil spread its branches above us. Óðinn held Ymir's massive skull in his hands. He inspected his carving on the inside of the skull and admired the constellations carved within the dome of the skull. He stood and admired Yggdrasil's mighty form before mounting Ymir's skull on the top the tree. From where I stood, the carved constellations of stars were bright glimmers against the darkness inside the vault of the skull. The blood, bone and flesh formed the Nine Worlds nestled into the branches of Yggdrasil.

I crept further from the lava-streaked rock to better see Óðinn. He fascinated me. He shone among the dull and ordinary and cast his brothers into shadow.

"

In Óðinn's blue eyes was a spark of rare intelligence and cunning.

Do these brothers know I'm here? Do they know a monster watches from the shadows? The irony that three children formed by the same primeval meeting of fire and ice as Ymir should take knives to the greatest of them. Vé had been busy while my attention was on Óðinn. He'd crafted the first humans from the bloody clay at Yggdrasil's roots. He breathed life into them and gave strength to these new creations. Óðinn looked upon Vé's humans as if they were his children. In time, they'd become so.

All this I watched, and I longed to be like them. I wanted clever craftsman's hands that could shape clay and bone. I wanted the beauty of form they all possessed. I wanted to have these gifts so I might bring something new, something clever to these burgeoning worlds. Instead, my body was too misshapen to crush rock.

I gathered my courage and crept from the crevice of the black stone and peered across the newly shaped landscape. Where only a small sapling had sprouted from the broken corpse of Ymir, a towering tree now stretched its roots deep into the void of Ginnungagap. I followed the towering trunk straight into the very heights of the sky, where golden leaves unfurled, and nestled among these branches were five sparkling worlds shining with new life. This was the beauty Óðinn and his brothers had created. *Would they now carve them into their own territories?*

"Why do you watch us, giant?"

I started at the voice so clearly meant for me. Óðinn scrutinised me with an expression that was half-curiosity and half-mischief. He waited for me to explain. I glanced quickly behind me. Surtr was nowhere in sight. Óðinn was definitely speaking to me.

I coughed to clear my throat. The harsh language of Múspelheim and my distorted form always made speech difficult. "There is beauty in these worlds you've created from the carcass of the old."

Óðinn took a steady but deliberate step towards me. His brothers, Vili and Vé, stood exactly where they could keep their eyes on me. The ugliness of my form meant they didn't truly look *at* me, but rather their eyes slid *over* me. Unlike Óðinn, their gaze never stayed in one spot for too long. I met Óðinn's gaze. His eyes were the same brilliant blue as the newly formed icy world beneath the roots of the mighty tree. He scrutinised every involuntary twitch of my body, each unintended grimace of my lips and the trembling of my hands. *What am I to him? A curiosity? A malformed fire giant Óðinn adopts for his personal amusement?*

"Does Surtr know you come here while we work?"

I shrugged, but the uneven shoulder of lumpy tissue wrinkled like the rock surface behind me into uneven cracks and crevices.

"He doesn't care for me. I'm useless to him. "

I held up my misshapen hands to demonstrate that a fire giant with only three or four uneven fingers was neither a suitable warrior, nor useful for anything else. I smiled, but my lips twisted into a grimace.

"You find what we have done here beautiful?"

"Is there not beauty in the creation of something new? Ymir was a tyrant, and no one will weep for his demise. Instead, you and your brothers have created light from darkness."

Óðinn half-turned to look back at his brothers. These three giants bore no similarity to the frost or fire giants. They were each unique and magnificent.

"Óðinn!" Vili shouted from the ridge. "Stop talking to that thing."

I lowered my eyes immediately. That *thing*. He was right, of course. Why should Óðinn bother to converse with me? I *was* barely more than a thing. I breathed, but I could do little more.

Óðinn held up his hand to ignore his brother and hold off further argument.

He looked at me, *really* looked at me. His intelligent gaze scraped over the rough surfaces of my body, the uneven tissues that looked like rocky crevices, and then he stared at my hands: the malformed and uneven length of all my fingers. His gaze travelled down to my feet, and I shuffled self-consciously. I was malformed in every aspect of my body. My legs were too short, my arms too long, my fingers too few and oddly shaped, and my feet were large and completely flat. It was as if I had been cobbled together by the last of the lava, which had dried lumpenly to form muscle. I was a being of ridicule and a source of amusement for my fellow fire giants.

"Surtr has no use for one with your intelligence?"

I laughed in my gravelly tone. "Surtr has no use for intelligence. Have you never met fire giants? If I can't hold a sword or an axe, make weapons or wield them, I am of no use in Múspelheim."

"Can you imagine what you and I could make of these Nine Worlds? Surtr may have no use for one with intellect, but I do. I have a great many things left to achieve, and I could use a brother like you."

"You already have two brothers."

Óðinn glanced back at his blood brothers. "They don't share my vision for the future. They don't see the glory I envisage. But I know you do; I know you see more in the future than what we've created here. In that respect, you are more brother to me than those two."

I sensed a trap and slid my fiery gaze to Óðinn's blood brothers. "What do you want in return? You've already killed Ymir and shown your strength. If I am to be beside you, then I ask that you give me a form like your own. I have no place as a fire giant. I want to be rid of this misshapen form you behold that earns me only ridicule. I want a trade. I want to be as beautiful as the rest of your creation."

"You want a body to match that quick wit?"

"I want to be how you see me and not the way others do."

Óðinn nodded once and held out his hand to me. My rough, ungainly fingers clasped his wrist, and we shook on our deal.

Óðinn's piercing blue eyes met mine. He held my gaze but kept contact with my arm. His touch began to tingle and then burn like the worst of the fiery pits of Múspelheim. I howled in my broken voice. Did Óðinn's brothers turn towards us? I couldn't see. My eyes rolled in their sockets, but I caught sight of two bodies crumpled on the ground where they'd fallen. Vili and Vé. Were they dead? Óðinn's searing eyes told me the truth. He'd killed his blood-brothers. Whatever life-force they'd possessed he now wielded to shape me anew. Magic flowed from Óðinn and along our joined hands like fire and ice, and where it met, my body transformed.

I lost consciousness at some point. I woke to a gasping pain that sizzled along every fibre of my being. When I opened my eyes, I saw the perfection that Óðinn had created. I was handsome. The god lowered his hand to me and helped me stand. My feet were light and tingled with a quickness of movement foreign to me. I stared at my well-muscled but wiry arms, the long legs and well-toned torso. Every part of my new body reflected the quickness that had been within me all along.

"The Nine Worlds are ours to take. Do you have a name, fire giant?"

"Loki," I said and grinned. "I'm no fire giant anymore."

PART ONE
BEFORE RAGNARÖK

Chapter 1
The Curse

Óðinn stared hard at Loki, his single, cobalt blue eye assessing, calculating. Although the god had sacrificed the other eye for wisdom in a time when the Nine Worlds were still young, Loki always found the brightness of that gaze unnerving.

"You want to know something?" Óðinn asked. He cast a sidelong glance at the party of Vanir gods standing nearby. "I don't trust them."

The Vanir had assembled themselves in a tight, defensive cluster at the centre of the Hall of Valhalla. Although it was a small envoy, the gods and goddesses present were the most significant in their race. These were the ones Óðinn had tried to crush beneath Thor's brute strength, outmanoeuvre with Týr's skillful swordsmanship and defeat with his own tactical cunning. But the Vanir persisted, not yielding or breaking, and all without a true king among them. Njörðr, ruler of the ocean depths, was the oldest surviving god and was also the father of many of the strangers. But they seemed to be ruled by an older woman—a witch. She was neither intimidated nor frightened by Óðinn's host of warriors. Despite the shield walls of bristling steel and flying arrows, she remained unbending before him and the Æsir.

The Vanir held sway over the mortal men and women of Midgard who gave prayers to the Vanir with a regular devotion that was unparalleled. Naturally, Óðinn saw this inequality of worship as a bartering piece he might use to win the war against them. But Loki, trickster and schemer, knew no matter how many times the mortals prayed to warrior-deities like Æsir, when drought or famine threatened, when there was a need for bountiful harvests or full fishing nets, they'd pray to the Vanir.

"You don't trust them?" Loki asked.

He looked purposefully at the Vanir. The situation reminded him uncomfortably of the giants and, by extension, himself. Óðinn saw the power the Vanir possessed was independent of himself and something beyond his control. He didn't like it.

Óðinn leaned closer, speaking conspiratorially. "There's great strength among them. A power we could use. The witch who leads them is skilled *seiðr* and I doubt she will ever offer it to me willingly. No. Until we bring them to heel, they'll always be a threat to me."

"You plan to destroy them, then?"

"What else would you have me do with such vipers in our midst?"

Loki stared at Óðinn; surely, he must be mistaken. "What you're suggesting is falsehood in your own hall. The breaking of Guest-Laws. It's the worst dishonesty imaginable. It won't solve this situation but only lead to bloodshed."

"And I seek advice from one more skilled than me in falsehood. Are you not?"

"Those are traits of which your kinsfolk accuse me."

"You heard Gullveig speak only moments ago. The wisdom of eons falls from her lips. Think how much knowledge she possesses and how much the magic of prophecy would offer us."

"She won't share such gift with you. What you desire will lead us all into war. Do you need me to repeat that a third time?"

"It's knowledge that's necessary for our survival. If I possessed *seiðr*, I might avoid war at every turn."

"If Gullveig grants this to you, would you stop the violence for those in Jötunheimr, too? The giants have always been your enemies. Would you reserve the *seiðr* for yourself? Allow it only to benefit the Æsir?"

Óðinn frowned. "We must survive above all else, brother."

Loki crossed his arms over his chest. "Of course. I understand that."

He wanted nothing to do with what was being proposed. But they'd pledged themselves as brothers, a bond tying them more closely than many who were true kinsfolk. Yet, the potential of the *seiðr* attracted him, too—the promise of such potent magic they would share.

Long ago, Óðinn had taken him when he was a misshapen, misbegotten giant from Múspelheim. He'd transformed his body into one that was handsome, lithe, and which matched his intellect—like all the Æsir. In gratitude, Loki had bound himself in kinship to Óðinn. He'd follow wherever Óðinn led, even when he waged war against the frost giants of Jötunheimr. But now his brother was proposing to take sword and axe to this witch in his own hall, shedding blood under the truce of Guest-Law. Loki couldn't abide it.

"Where Gullveig is resolute, her apprentice, Freyja, looks more ambitious, don't you think? I might be able persuade her."

Loki ran his gaze run appreciably over Freyja, stopping at the sheathed longsword at her hip. "She looks more like a shield maiden."

"Such warriors are valuable. I've already consulted with Mimir."

"I don't care what counsel Mimir gave you, but I'll have no part in this."

"I only want your presence at my side, brother. Gullveig will suspect nothing if you remain with me. Remember, *seiðr* is the only way we can protect the Nine Worlds."

Loki swallowed the honeyed mead in one gulp, but it seemed bitter. "Óðinn, please reconsider. This isn't wise or just."

"Have you had the gift of prophecy, Loki? Many of your ideas aren't wise or just, and I've never grumbled."

"What makes you certain Freyja even knows *seiðr*? What if you destroy Gullveig and lose the magic of *seiðr* forever?"

"See how Freyja clings to Gullveig's side? She is her closest confidante, a true apprentice and ally. I'll use whatever tactics I need to win this war."

Loki refilled his mead and consumed liberally. "You'll regret this decision."

At the end of the hall, the Æsir and Vanir had broken their uneasy stand-off and now mingled, eating and drinking with each other as they walked along the long tables laden with the bountiful feast. In this instant, there seemed little inclination to fight. *Perhaps Óðinn is right. Maybe without Gullveig, these two races can unite peacefully.*

Loki's gaze flicked to Gullveig, the witch standing tall and proud, her dark hair streaked with silver. She was like a boulder in a river current, separating the stream she stood within, resilient and unmoving, the water passing around her. Loki lounged in his engraved chair beside Óðinn and Frigg's more elaborate thrones. He watched the witch's eyes follow Óðinn, never straying from him. Beside her, Freyja was motionless. She was tall with blonde hair artfully braided, her comely form clothed in the shimmer of chain mail. Loki focused on the long, bone-handled blade she wore at her hip. The sword looked comfortable on her. While he studied her thoughtfully, her piercing gaze fixed on him.

He raised his goblet in a feigned drunken gesture, tipping it back and swallowing more of the honeyed mead. It curdled in his stomach. He wasn't certain Óðinn was right about Freyja. She was undoubtedly the most beautiful among the Vanir, known for stirring men's hearts to passion; she was goddess of love and war. But to Loki, she seemed no more amenable than the witch. Of course, Óðinn would never know how Freyja might react until they removed Gullveig from her side. He slouched and wished himself anywhere else. Even as he scowled into the hearth flames, he barely stirred when Óðinn took a seat beside him. Then, with a single hand gesture, all attention in Valhalla fell on Óðinn.

He smiled like a hunter luring prey to slaughter. "Gullveig, I'm much impressed by the art of *seiðr*. Come, teach it to me. Will you show me it once more?"

Loki stared more intently at the flames. He heard the whisper of movement across the floor as she stepped forward. He held his breath and willed any other course of action, another series of events, to play out this night. From where he sat, he saw her shake her head in refusal again. Tension flooded the hall.

Óðinn stood, his ravens dislodged from his shoulders in a flurry of feathers, and flames erupted around Gullveig.

Unable to flee, Loki cringed in his chair and watched as the witch screamed and burned. He'd imagined the many alternative paths to peace Óðinn had cast aside in pride and arrogance. The unbearable flames persisted, and Loki drank more of the mead which tasted as sour as the dealings in Valhalla tonight. He kept his eyes on Freyja as she stared in horror and outrage, while Gullveig burned a second and third time. Each time, her flesh regenerated, burnt and began to heal anew as the blaze continued. Loki wanted to flee the hall but was transfixed by terror and couldn't force his limbs to move. Finally, Gullveig spoke through charred lips and a ruined throat that was scorched and raw. But the power of the völva was unparalleled and even in her thrice-burned body, she gave Óðinn one last prophecy - an unforgettable lesson in *seiðr*:

> *"The greatest of winters will beset the Nine Worlds,*
> *Brother shall fight brother, kin will slay kin,*
> *In the age of axes, swords, shields, and wolves,*
> *Ravenous Fenrir shall break his bonds,*
> *And in fire, the Nine Words will end."*

There was the thwack of a spear hitting flesh and splintering bone and a final scream, piercing and vengeful before Gullveig died. Loki huddled with his knees to his chest, the prophecy chilling his blood like ice despite the blazing pyre. He couldn't stop staring at the witch's blackening remains as the words of her prophecy echoed in his mind.

Chapter 2
A Surprise Return

I walked swiftly down the steep slope of Bifröst. I felt incredibly lonely. Why would the Æsir not welcome me with the equal sense of brotherhood as Óðinn? When had my place among them been effortless? Never. I'd always fought for my position and respect among the gods. I was only the fiery brood from Múspelheim and not much more than a curiosity Óðinn kept around for his amusement. But it *was* something.

"Black thoughts, Loki?" Heimdallrr asked.

"Dark indeed." I'd left the rainbow bridge of Bifröst behind me and started to trek across the meadows toward Valhalla.

"Don't let the warrior queen frighten you."

"Freyja?" I pretended not to understand.

"I keep my ears alert. I hear the beating of dragonfly wings and the whispers of these growing flowers, Loki. But I also hear schemes."

I stared at Heimdallrr, then shifted my gaze beyond him to the battle-training meadows of Fólkvangr, now gone to seed with wildflowers and further to the forested realm of Vanaheimr where the light elves and Vanir gods dwelled.

"Do you know what Freyja planned? How I became separated from Óðinn and nearly lost in Ginnungagap, that primordial void trying to consume me?"

He shrugged and flexed sun-bronzed shoulders. "I can't speak without breaking pledges sworn long ago. I'm pledged to silence on the many details I hear in Asgard. I can offer you some wisdom, though. Would you hear it, Loki?"

"Go on and tell me," I muttered feigning mild disinterest. I'd been wondering how I'd get the information, and here it was being offered to me.

"Freyja and her brother are the closest siblings in Asgard. You're quick-witted, Loki. It's more than most believe, but Freyja and her brother Freyr share desires and some of them are more delicate than others."

This was gossip I could use. "So, the whispers are true then? Freyja shares her bed with her brother Freyr?"

"Don't exclude other possible desires they share in common. That might include an inclination to curse you."

"Are you implying that Freyja and Freyr contrived together to curse me to Ginnungagap? I hope that's what your convoluted riddle means, and not that Freyja and her brother share carnal desires that include me."

Heimdallrr roared with laughter. "Would you mind if they did?"

"Freyja is a very beautiful woman and her brother is a well-formed man. I can't deny I've never considered such a pleasurable amusement before."

Heimdallrr's raucous laughter followed me as I continued toward Valhalla. It was concerning to think Freyja and Freyr might be colluding to destroy me, and that Óðinn wouldn't learn of it if Heimdallrr was as tightly bound by his pledge of silence as he claimed. Unless, of course, he was only bound from telling it directly to Óðinn?

I crossed the remaining several yards to Valhalla and slipped into the shadows beneath the overhang. The rich smell of roasting meat and mead clung to the shadowy depths outside the open doors. I paused on the threshold.

"Come in, Loki!" Thor bellowed from the room inside. "Stop fretting out there like some bride before her wedding night."

I chuckled to myself and entered the golden longhouse of Valhalla.

The moment my bare foot touched the rushes of the room beyond, the chatter and laughter fell silent. I stood, hands relaxed at my side, letting my gaze roam the assembled Æsir and the few elves carrying goblets of mead and platters of roast meat toward the feasting tables. I smiled, snagging a goblet from a passing elf, and stepped forward to greet Thor.

The god of war and thunder was an impressively muscled man, as all the legends claim. His thick red hair hung in short braids; his neatly trimmed beard framed a huge grin as I stepped toward him. He pulled me to him, clasping my slender forearm, fingers wrapped near double about my arm. He frowned then, peering down at me before booming with laughter and engulfing me in an embrace. Once we'd been like brothers to each other, nearly as close as Óðinn and I had been. When Óðinn was young and I had just emerged from Múspelheim, we had roamed the lands of Asgard, Niflheimr and Midgard together. Then something like age had changed Óðinn, and he'd become more obsessed with gaining knowledge and encouraging others to pursue his goals. Thor had been born to Frigg, and it had become my responsibility to cajole him from ferocious tantrums and, steer him, as a youth, from outbursts of rage and sudden storms. Eternal youth still flourished in Thor, where it had long-since wizened in Óðinn. I still felt the camaraderie with Thor now. Perhaps it seems absurd that the god of trickery feels kinship for the god of battle frenzy. I am certain the feeling is mutual.

"I have long heard the All-Father tell tales of your shape-shifting forms, Loki," Thor said, releasing me and stepping back, gaze roaming my body appreciatively. "I never imagined you'd make such an attractive woman,"

"Ah," I said, grinning in reply. "You should think better of my skills, Thor. Have I not the greatest understanding of womanly perfection of anyone in this room? Must I remind you that even Freyja took me to her bed more than once?"

"It is true! You of all should know a woman's form," he said, laughing, but glanced toward the far door.

I leaned closer to Thor, and he bent conspiratorially toward me. "Are you afraid of Freyja, too?" I asked in softer, teasing tones.

He straightened abruptly, regarding me with shock before laughter rumbled from his broad chest like the thunder of approaching storms.

I twirled the richly engraved silver goblet in my hands and smiled. It was comforting to be among these gods who knew me so well. Heimdallrr and Thor accepted me without question. I glanced behind Thor to where Týr sat in quiet conversation with Ullr. In front of them was a throng of gods and gathered elves, the god Bragi tuning his small harp while speaking in quiet undertones to the twin gods, Baldr and his blind brother Höðr. I smiled to Thor and stepped away, weaving through the throng gathered, noticing Thor's wife Sif sitting beside Njörðr, the god of seafaring.

Týr smiled as I approached, looping an arm about his up-drawn knee. "Óðinn brings you home again?" he asked, eyebrows arched.

I nodded, meeting the steady gaze without flinching, and swept my arms wide and bowed.

I flicked my gaze to Ullr, but he remained silent, absently fidgeting with a leather strap on his quiver lying behind him on the bench.

Týr nodded once. "Don't make us regret the decision to call you amongst us again."

I cocked my head slightly. "Do you speak for Óðinn, then?"

He shook his head, the blonde fringe falling across his eyes. "No, I don't. I speak in fair warning of consequences should you bring ruin upon us."

I smiled bitterly. "These are different times, Týr," I explained, gesturing to my female form. "I am not likely to father any wilful wolves this time."

He smiled at his own foolishness. "You were always quick-witted, Loki,"

"Then you bear me no dire grudges that'll sweep your sword from its sheath?"

A repressed snort. "Not tonight, Loki," he agreed.

"I might survive the evening then," I said cheerfully.

The words had barely left my lips when the double doors at the far end of the mighty hall swung open and the Vanir gods stood upon the threshold to Valhalla. Conversation died abruptly as Ægir and his nine daughters swept into the throng of elves and seated Æsir, the god of the ocean and his progeny moving through the longhouse like the waves they personified. I stood still as Iðunn, the most youthful and innocent of the gods, clung to Baldr's arm like a frightened child.

"You were saying you'd survive?" Týr asked softly, his breath warm against my ear.

"I thought I might," I muttered, watching as Freyr stalked into the room. The giant-killing sword hung in a bejewelled sheath at his hip, golden eyes scanning the room. He was clearly looking for his sister, Freyja, and the Valkyries, the host of warriors that always accompanied her.

Behind Freyr, enetered the Valkyries, women warriors dressed in shining chainmail. At the edge of the shadows, I heard the black horse stamp on mighty hooves and the impatient jangling of its harness. From a deeper darkness stepped another woman clad in chainmail, the white-gold hair framing a pale and youthful face. Freyja had a short axe sheathed across her back as she took Freyr's proffered hand and crossed the threshold into Valhalla.

"Loki!" Freyja shouted, voice like the chill wind across a battlefield.

The blood drained from my face and I willed my traitorous knees not to buckle as I squared my shoulders. Bluffing was the only way to win this game. A restless fingertip tapped on the edge of my goblet, and I feigned nonchalance, stepping into the open space in the middle of the feast hall. I was aware several elves and lesser gods of the Æsir moved clear of me, apparently not excited about the prospect of chunks of eviscerated Loki on their clothing.

"Freyja," I greeted, sarcasm lacing my words, arms open wide. "We were just speaking of you."

Freyja arched a perfect blond eyebrow, a nearly imperceptible glance at her brother. "Freyr!" she snapped.

I flicked my gaze to the left, noticing Freyr had closed the distance between us, hand loosely gripping the hilt of his sword. "Do as your sister commands," I hissed, and returned my attention to Freyja. The silver rings on her fingers glittered in the firelight and her chainmail shimmered distractingly.

"Do you need to polish that ensemble?" I asked.

Her mouth tightened. "Óðinn retrieved you from whatever cesspit you were wallowing in?"

I nodded, fingers tapping a tune along the goblet rim. "As you see."

"I see a woman," she replied.

"A keen observation," I said, glancing again at Freyr to confirm he hadn't moved. "What gave it away?"

She narrowed her eyes and took a step forward, the tap of her booted heel echoing in the silence. "Why are you here?" she growled.

"Óðinn's request." I was irritated, and more frightened than I liked to admit by her intimidation. "Dare you thwart the All-Father's will?"

"No," she said smoothly, raking her eyes over me as if to draw blood. "You do that with no effort from me."

"Óðinn is coming," Thor said softly to Týr, his words heard by all in the heavy silence of Valhalla.

"You'd best flee, Freyja," I said, smiling without sincerity.

She bowed her blond head, the chainmail clinking like jewellery. "I never liked this hall," she said to no one in particular.

"Dreadful memories of burning alive when you wore the guise of that witch Gullveig?" I asked.

Freyja's top lip curled, and she took another step toward me, arm reaching to unsheathe her axe. Involuntarily, I stepped backward, conscious of the close circle of Valkyries hemming me in. Freyr stopped his sister's hand, calmly wrapping his fingers tightly about her wrist. The brilliant gold of his eyes swept over his sister's face. Freyja hissed, eyes like molten silver meeting mine. The silent exchange took only moments, but it felt like eons until Freyr released her, and Freyja's hand fell casually to her side again. The tension in the hall subsided a little then, and the twang of Bragi's harp string echoed in the silence.

"I will come for you, Loki," Freyja said.

"I'll look forward to that," I lied, wincing inwardly at how weak my voice sounded.

Freyr gave me a considering look, his mouth a tight line before he spun, the golden sword tapping against his leg as he strode from Valhalla. I waited for the twelve Valkyries to leave but they paused, hesitating while the shield-maiden Freyja stood at the threshold watching Freyr disappear into the darkness beyond the hall.

"You'll regret you ever left Múspelheim." Freyja stepped into the shadows beyond the door.

Silence hung heavy and threatening in the air as the Æsir waited for the Valkyries to follow their mistress from Valhalla. When at last the sounds of booted feet had subsided, tentative sounds stirred within the hall again. I exhaled slowly, my guts a twisted knot of fear and adrenaline. Freyja would deliver on her threat. I knew her words had been more prophecy than intimidation. In that moment, as I shakily drained the rest of the mead from my goblet, I knew Freyja had convinced the Norns to banish me into Ginnungagap. I still did not know why. Pondering the possibilities of why Freyja might hate me so much, I grabbed another goblet of mead and left sobriety behind.

Chapter 3
Aftermath

Long after Freyja and her Valkyries swept from the hall, the Æsir remained silent. I drained another goblet of mead, my head now spinning, as the hall of Valhalla, the awkward shifting of feet and quiet mutterings around me the only sounds. After what felt like an eon, Óðinn and Frigg stalked into Valhalla, jolting the hall into activity and snapping the tension like the sudden break of a storm. Several of the gods clustered near Óðinn, Frigg and Týr spoke quickly but calmly, no doubt recounting the events during Óðinn's absence. Unsteadily, I grabbed another goblet of mead, tossing the empty silver cup to the floor with the careless abandon of the extremely drunk. I ignored the surprised elf who stooped to collect the discarded goblet before fleeing. I drunkenly scanned the Æsir, the gods and goddesses speaking in hushed groups, their attention darting nervously to me before looking away. Would it sway some to Freyja's argument?

"Come!" Thor bellowed, his voice like thunder. "If the Lady Freyja will not join in, us, there will be more mead for us."

I relaxed and collapsed into a seat behind me, the jovial outburst from Thor clearing the tension. I glanced at Óðinn, whose stony gaze had fixed on the closed doors at the end of the hall. There would be no words of comfort or questions until he mastered his anger. I waited, conscious of the simmering rage that rolled from him like waves. When I could bear his proximity no longer, I shifted in my seat and looked longingly toward Thor, hoping the big man might rescue me. But Thor was speaking with Týr now, slapping the slender man on the shoulder, mead spilling from his cup in another roar of laughter. Thor would not rescue me.

"My love," Frigg said, gliding from the shadows behind me, looping her arm gently around Óðinn's shoulders, drawing him away from me. I had not even noticed he had moved toward me.

I sagged against the high back of my chair, the effects of the mead spinning my head and blurring my vision. I let tension and worry drain from me. Lazily,

I watched Frigg's hand on Óðinn's arm, keeping him at her side. How had I ever thought the fickle Lady of Asgard would arrange for Ginnungagap to consume me? She was conscious of my attention. While Týr spoke with Óðinn, Frigg gave me a wink, and the peal of laughter that broke from her lips easily diverted Óðinn's attention. For Frigg, the stability of the Nine Realms and among the Æsir was paramount. I did not doubt her willingness to have me thrown into a pyre if it benefited the stability of the Nine realms, but she had more wisdom than I'd expected: she understood the fondness Óðinn felt for me. No, Frigg was not my enemy among the Æsir. My worries lay squarely with Freyja and those who might support her.

"Loki," Thor called, raising a cup of mead above the heads of the assembled Æsir. I raised my eyebrows and slid from the chair, weaving between the gods and goddesses, elves and dwarves that had assembled at Óðinn's request.

"Here." Thor pushed a goblet of mead into my hands.

I clasped the goblet, barely avoided dropping the richly engraved golden object on the floor before Thor turned back toward Týr, deep in conversation about some battle tactic they had been discussing.

I drank from the goblet; the mead slipped over my tongue, warming my blood and lifting my courage. The mead was good, the honey and spice rich and restorative. I exhaled in a sigh, the anxiety caused by Freyja's open challenge to Óðinn leaving me. I closed my eyes, allowing the noise of Valhalla, Thor's booming laughter, and Bragi's melodious music to soothe my fears.

"Loki," Frigg's quiet voice came from behind me, and I felt a hand on my arm.

A firm hand on my elbow guided me away from the gathering around Thor. We walked toward the benches surrounding the outer edges of the hall, toward a woman seated alone near an open doorway. My heart stopped in my chest. The woman was young, barely beyond a maiden, her pale golden hair plaited elaborately; secured on top of her head and draped across her shoulders was a thick wolf pelt, the fur white as snow. Holding my breath, I moved beside Frigg as though in a dream and watched her eyes widen. They were beautiful eyes, innocent like a doe's and exactly as guileless as I remembered them. Her slender hand lifted to her mouth as she stifled an exclamation. I could only stare at the hand-fasting ring around one finger, the familiar design of plaited silver. She didn't speak but stood, and with the wolf pelt swirling around her shoulders, she fled the room.

"Sigyn!" I called.

I stood, my hand shaking, mead slopping from my goblet. To mask my embarrassment or bolster my courage, I drank off the rest of the mead. I wiped my mouth with the back of my hand, pausing momentarily to stare at the silver plaited ring on my finger. Wordlessly, I met Frigg's gaze before unwinding myself from her grasp and walking back toward the gathered Æsir.

I strolled purposefully through the mingling gods and goddesses, downing goblets of mead as I walked, replacing empty cups on serving trays before taking others. Thor stood where he had been, the circle of gathered Æsir staring at me from where they'd observed the meeting between me and my wife. In the short distance it had taken to cross the floor of Valhalla, I had consumed several tankards of mead and with the final empty goblet clasped loosely in one hand, I smiled guilelessly at Thor.

"It may take some time for Sigyn to become more adventurous in her choice of lovers," I said, gesturing to my own female form and slipping my arm around Sif's slim waist. "Surely, the Lady Sif is more worldly?" I asked, sliding my hand up from Sif's waist to cup her breast.

I watched Sif's expression change from puzzlement, shock to smouldering outrage.

"Never mind," I replied throatily. "I can teach you."

I heard the indrawn exclamation of the surrounding Æsir and the muttered warning from Óðinn. I was aware of Thor's rage, had been determined to provoke it, and so did not move as he struck me unconsciousness.

In the morning I woke on the floor, head propped on my arm and face buried in the ruff of a hunting hound. Frowning, I opened my eyes, staring at the unfamiliar grey fur of the dog sleeping beside me. How did I get here? I rolled away from the dog, pain lancing through my skull. Clutching my head, I vomited onto the floor rushes. The dog whined, lifting a massive head and looking at me over a powerful shoulder.

"I'm fine," I whispered.

I dragged myself across the floor. I turned away and closed my eyes. I was conscious of the soft, padding paws behind me as I crawled to the hearth. When my fingertips touched the stone border of the fire-pit, I twisted sideways, clenching my jaw against the pain and nausea, before levering myself against the supports. I kept my eyes tightly closed, gently resting my head against the pillars of the hearth, conscious now that I was not alone. Óðinn's gaze was a familiar one but I did not respond.

"Does this amuse you?" I finally asked, eyes still squeezed shut against the dim daylight.

"Not as much as you might expect," he replied.

I opened my eyes to slits, squinting at him. "How bad was it?"

"How much to do you remember?" he asked, hands clasped loosely between his knees.

"I remember Freyja's threat and drinking a lot." I squeezed my eyes shut against the memory. "And I remember Sigyn."

"And?" he asked, leaning forward slightly.

"There's more?" I groaned, burying my head in my hands.

"I'd advise you to avoid Thor for a few days," he said, smiling sadly but with fondness.

I lifted my head, met his eye. "What did I do?" I asked.

"Do you really want to know?"

I thought about it for a moment, weighing the misery of Freyja's hatred, the painful rejection by Sigyn. "No," I finally said. "I don't suppose I do."

"Come with me," Óðinn said, standing up, shaking the wrinkles from his worn clothing. "I have something to cheer you up."

I looked at him, noticing he still wore the clothing from the evening before. "Where have you been?" I asked, frowning at the simple attire. "You didn't stay in Valhalla last night, did you?"

"What does that matter to you?" he asked, peering at me apprehensively.

"Does Frigg know?" I asked, grinning as I climbed unsteadily to my feet.

"No," he replied. "How do you know I didn't sit here all night keeping watch on you?"

I halted, hand against the hearth pillar for support. "I don't think you'd dress that nicely just for me."

He looked at his clothing, inspecting the tidy but not immaculate tunic and leggings. "These are hardly my best clothing," he mumbled.

"I know," I said, wincing as I took a step forward. "Your clothing is neat without exaggerating your status. You dressed to impress but not signify your rank. Who was the lucky woman?"

Óðinn took my arm, ignoring my question, which only made my grin widen. He helped me from the hall. Every step toward the daylight outside Valhalla was fresh agony for my sensitive eyesight. When we reached the main doors, I gestured for Óðinn to stop. Concerned, he let me lean heavily against the doorframe.

"Loki?" he asked, inspecting my face. "Are you feeling all right? You're very pale."

I gestured my impatience, but nausea rolled through me with a sudden vengeance. I felt the wave of dizziness crash upon me, quickly twisted aside but still vomited on Óðinn's leather boots. When the twisting of my guts ceased long enough for me to speak, I hastily wiped at my mouth and murmured apologies.

"How much did I drink?" I cursed.

"A lot," Óðinn replied, glancing at my trembling hands. "I think Thor's hit to your head probably did most of this damage, though."

I closed my eyes. "Why did Thor strike me?"

"You told me you didn't want to know."

"Is he likely to hit me again?" I asked, clutching at my stomach against a fresh wave of nausea.

"If you avoid him, he'll calm down again," he replied.

"Fire and ice," I groaned.

I ignored the unease in my guts, instead clinging to Óðinn as he led me into the meadows outside Valhalla. We paused on the sweet-scented grass, the morning light setting the dew sparkling. I took deep breaths of the fresh air, realising how stagnant the inside of the hall had been. The crisp morning air cleared my mind, and I inhaled deeply, filling my lungs as the nausea subsided.

"What is supposed to cheer me up?" I asked, cautiously titling my head to regard Óðinn.

"A sacrifice," he answered, patting my hand and leading me across the damp grass.

"Not my own, I hope," I muttered, feeling his body tense beside mine.

"A bullock," he said, mastering his unease.

"Ah," I said, nodding sagely. "Nothing improves a hangover like slaughter and evisceration."

I hurried behind Óðinn's long-legged stride as we made our way down the sloping fields outside Valhalla. Towards the distant woodlands on the horizon, I sensed the presence of unseen observers following our progress as I straightened my sleep-wrinkled clothing. I scrunched up my face as I squinted against the morning light. My garments were smeared with residue from the feast, spilled mead and dried vomit. I had indeed drunk myself far from sobriety. Ahead, Óðinn had halted, and I nearly tripped over his foot propped on a stone. I glared up at him while he surveyed the shadowed woods beyond.

"Well?" I asked, aware my tone resonated with complaint.

He arched an eyebrow at me, the cloth covering his missing eye crinkling like the lines of amusement around his mouth.

"What?" I grumbled, again trying to smooth the front of my tunic.

"Do you really think removing the wrinkles will make you more presentable this morning?" he asked, dubious but smiling.

"No," I said, squinting up. "Who are we waiting for?"

"What makes you think we're waiting for anyone?" he asked.

I rolled my eyes skyward. "Were you admiring the view of these woodlands we've seen a million times?"

He chuckled in response, scanning the surrounds one last time. I peered down at my stained tunic again and picked gingerly at the hem.

"Ah, here he is," Óðinn said with genuine pleasure.

"Is this dried vomit?" I asked, not looking up at the man approaching.

"Ah, Loki, my favourite wandering trickster, the speaker of honeyed words and bitter truth."

I met the dazzling gaze of the mysterious Hœnir, who dwelt in the woodlands of Asgard, neither part of the Æsir nor separate from them. This was the god who often accompanied Óðinn travelling through the Nine realms. Hœnir kept many secrets, practised divination, and was the embodiment of higher ecstasies and was, frequently, a poet.

I grinned at his description of me, glancing again at my tunic front. "I enjoyed a few too many of the highest ecstasies last night."

"I would expect no less from you," Hœnir replied, sweeping golden-brown hair from his face and rubbing a hand across his short beard.

"The task for today?" Óðinn asked, turning to Hœnir.

"Already prepared," he replied, gesturing over his shoulder toward the woods.

Óðinn nodded in satisfaction, then walked away, his long stride quickly taking him further from my side. I watched him move across the meadows, a god who often masked his authority with the guise of simpleness.

"Let's go, then," I sighed, glancing up as sunlight poured through the rising fog. "The sooner the divination is done, the sooner I can settle the unease in my guts."

Hœnir's frown deepened as he studied me. I stared into the pale, ice-blue eyes of the god who gained power from the abandonment of self to ecstasy, granting the rarest illumination. A flicker of unease shadowed Hœnir's gaze as though clouds shifting through a pale blue sky, momentarily obscuring sunlight.

"Let's go then," he agreed finally, breaking the tension.

We found Óðinn in a small hollow nearest the edge of the woodlands, the trees clustered close to the meadows like the ranks of an opposing army. Óðinn was softly brushing his hand down the broad face of the bullock, the beast restlessly shifting hooves in the morning light, breath steaming in the cool morning air. A shiver passed along my skin, prickling flesh into goosebumps as a premonition hit me: hands slick with steaming blood that splattered across the dewy grass. Óðinn whispered comforting words to the bullock, his eye meeting the bovine gaze as the knife in his other hand cut deep across the exposed throat. The beast tossed its massive head upward, the blade cutting deeper as sunlight refracted off the curling horns. I watched in wordless unease as Óðinn calmed the beast, continuing to whisper comfort as the bullock lowered itself to its knees, Óðinn bending to the grass himself alongside the animal. I remained on the outside of the ritual, watching as Hœnir approached, chanting softly under his breath, power flowing through the meadow as he drew on the energy of the sacrifice, reaching into the depths of the unknown.

Above me, morning fog momentarily obscured the sunlight, and I glanced quickly at Óðinn. The All-Father faced Hœnir. There was a strange similarity between them which appeared stronger in that unguarded moment. The grass was slimy with blood, the bullock on its side, body without breath. Again, the prickling of my flesh as I watched Hœnir scoop with hands cupped to the slowing wound at the beast's throat. The golden-haired god stood and then, turning to Óðinn, proffered the bloody offering. My stomach twitched in nausea as Óðinn touched his lips to Hœnir's hands, sipping the sacrificial life blood with reverently closed eyes.

The swell of power through the morning was so strong I could never have prepared for it. I tried to resist the magic, the strength of it buffeting me like a storm against the shore, and turned my gaze frantically to Hœnir. Those ice-pale eyes met my own, the brightness in them terrifying as the magic stirred my blood, consuming my will. I think I cried out. Maybe I called for Óðinn before I fell to my knees. Bright, slanting sunlight cut through the fog and I crawled toward Óðinn, my hands and legs covered with blood. I collapsed into the grass, wet with dew and blood, and stared unseeing upward. I heard the call of a horn somewhere. Jubilant laughter broke from my lips and I wondered if the echoing horn was Gjallarhorn and Heimdallrr calling us to battle.

I stared up at the brilliant blue sky, dimly conscious I was intoxicated by the strange magic Hœnir had worked, ecstasy flooding my senses. I blinked against the shimmering sunlight, unable to stop the overwhelming dizziness drowning me with pleasure and felt the sunlight like a warm caress on my skin, heard the breeze like a lover's whisper.

A sharp screech echoed through the meadow and I stared dumbly at the approaching eagle, the giant wingspan momentarily blocking the sunlight from my face. Flooded by the sedative effects of Hœnir's magic, I was slow to understand the threat but rolled to my feet as shouts from Óðinn and Hœnir called from somewhere near me. The bright sunlight returned, and I scanned the sky for the eagle. It turned in the sky and came winging back with talons lowered and beak open in a screech of anger. Instinctively, I raised my forearm to protect my face. I grasped the eagle by its talons with my free hand.

"Loki, no!" Óðinn shouted.

Dumbly, I stared down at the shocked and concerned face of my oldest friend. Without warning, the eagle had lifted me into the sky, its powerful wings beating upward. *Should I let go?* I stared at the increasing distance between myself and the ground, noticing how swiftly the ground surrounding the sacrifice was becoming a smaller area of blood-stained earth. Already Óðinn and Hœnir were tiny figures with arms waving in frantic gestures. The power of Hœnir's magic was fading, the ecstasy slipping away into fear as I realised the eagle I clutched was taking me far from Asgard and south toward Jötunheimr.

Chapter 4
Giant Kin

I watched the meadows and woodlands of Asgard fade around and beneath me as the raptor carried me higher, my feet trailing through the dense mist of the clouds. I wondered at my foolishness for leaping at the eagle. Grasping the feet had been madness. In a single moment, the talons had twisted, grasping my wrists and turning my stupidity into a dangerous predicament. Now, I dangled above the changing landscape, fear burning through my veins as the giant eagle flew north toward Jötunheimr and away from Asgard.

I twisted slightly in the eagle's talons, squinting back toward Asgard. Sunlight cut sharply through the morning, illuminating the clouds with a molten whiteness tinted gold. I closed my eyes against the brightness, the fading magic Hœnir had stirred contributing to my hangover.

Suddenly, the world tilted, and my stomach lurched, nausea threatening to overwhelm me. I gulped in a deep lungful of the cold air, tears streaming down my cheeks as the frigid air struck me. I opened my eyes, gasping as the eagle's massive wingbeats lifted me higher into the sky, the ground disappearing below the clouds, the curved horizon arching dramatically to reveal the bleached bone markers that bound the sea. Here was where Óðinn and his brothers had slain Ymir, the greatest of the giants, and cast his dismembered body into the four corners of Ginnungagap, forming the Nine Worlds.

Beyond the white bones, the darkness of Ginnungagap beckoned. Against the formless void, the stars shone with a remote and foreign light. The peace Ginnungagap offered was complete and uncompromising.

I sighed as I stared at the icy beauty of the darkness, feeling something deep inside me longed for evanescence into the void. The eagle screeched as if in protest to my unspoken desire. Without warning, the eagle folded its massive wings and dropped, heedless of my extra weight, into a spiralling dive through the sky.

The thick mist and dense cloud cover rose quickly to meet me as I fell, plunging after the eagle. The eagle released my wrists and dove alongside me as I plummeted toward the ground. I screamed in defiance and fear as death sped towards me, until the icy air choked my cries into sobs. I wouldn't let Hel take me into her domain without a fight, however useless it might seem. I screamed with quieter, more terrified sounds of my imminent death choking from my lips. I too was a shapeshifter, and in an inate instinct, I flapped my arms in a ridiculous, pin-wheeling motion, hoping to save myself from splattering onto the rocks below. The golden eye of the eagle peered sidelong at me. The scrutiny in that sharp gaze was part-amusement, part-contempt, but I was too afraid to rebuke it.

"Help me!" I shouted at the eagle; my voice immediately stripped away into the atmosphere above me as we fell.

I twisted mid-air, lifting my legs away in anticipation of the fast-approaching ground. The wind was agony against my cheeks, tears freezing on my face as the snow-covered landscape stretched before me. Tall mountain peaks came closer, the black stone crags jutted above the low, clustered clouds, the sharp rock glittering with melting ice as sunlight touched it. I slid my gaze away from potential death by impalement, shifting my gaze instead to the thick cloud that wreathed the mountains.

I whispered prayers to Óðinn, Frigg, Thor, to any of the Æsir who might listen and save me from this ungainly death. The eagle cocked its head as we continued to dive, the dense cloud muffling my screams and sobs. I closed my eyes, anticipating the impact that would shatter my body, releasing my shade from its flesh-crafted shell.

I felt the eagle grip my wrists again. Relief filled me even as the razor-like talons of the bird clamped about my flesh, slicing the skin, rivulets of blood running down my forearms. I sobbed with gratitude to this horrid bird, with the pain lancing through my arms even as I squeezed my eyes shut, tears freezing in the corners of my eyes. How close had I truly been to death? Would these northern snows that never melted have saved me from the jagged stones beneath? I shook my head, still sobbing with relief as the bird lifted again into the sky.

The sudden swirl of freezing wind was sharp and strong. The eagle's wings beat tirelessly as the wind buffeted us sideways, and I swung wildly beneath the bird. I thought of eagles flying to roost with dead prey as I swayed precariously, and I wondered, not for the first time, if the bird intended to gut me once it reached whatever roost it now flew toward. Swinging in the uncaring gale, eyelids closed to protect my sight from the ice chips that formed part of the blizzard, I did not see the cliff face until too late. My shoulder slammed painfully into the ice-covered stone, shards of ice sheet dropping to the ground below me as the winds slapped against me. Air gushed from my lungs and I wheezed a strangled breath through ribs I knew were broken.

The eagle screeched, its annoyance directed at me or perhaps at the strengthening gale. Then, without warning, the bird hauled us through the air, wings striking against the prevailing wind with determination. I sighed in agony, gritting my teeth against the pain as the bird lifted us above the lip of a rocky precipice. It hovered, massive wings fighting the gale before it swayed precariously and I reached, body stretched, toward the cliff. Grinding my teeth against the pain, I hooked my feet over the ice-rimed ledge, letting the next gust of wind push me toward the cliff.

A raw scream broke from my lips as the eagle released my arms and, using the impetus from the wind, I flung myself onto the icy precipice. I fell with limbs outstretched and flailing, gracefulness abandoned, onto the stone. My face hit the cold rock with a slap and my nose broke beneath the force of my fall. Hot blood wet my cheeks and chin, quickly beginning to freeze, already crusted with ice. I remained motionless for a moment, flat on the ground, exhausted beyond belief, before I forced my feet to scrabble against the icy rock. I needed to get myself upright, find shelter, or I would die here. Groaning in pain, fatigue and cold, I struggled to my hands and knees and crawled away from the edge of the precipice.

In the far corner of the ledge, the lashing ice had not penetrated far under one overhang and, scrambling behind a large rock, I huddled with my knees against my chest. I gritted my teeth and ignored the savage complaint from my broken ribs. Wearily, I rested my forehead on my knees and exhaled shallowly. I knew where I was and that for now, the eagle would not feast on me. It had deposited me for its master— and I was now captive and a long way from Asgard, deep within the territory of Jötunheimr. For this storm-ravaged mountain was Thyrmheim, the fortress of the frost giant Thiazi. For now I must wait, conserving my energy until Thiazi decided what to do with me.

Hoarfrost crept across the ice that covered the rock, my leather boots frozen to the ice sheet. I could do nothing about my hands except push them into my armpits and curl in on myself, keeping small to retain body heat in my core. Would Thiazi come? Would the resentment between Thiazi and Óðinn be strong enough for me to be offered as a symbolic punishment for crimes committed by the Æsir? My lips twitched in a smile. It was probably something the Norns would find amusing, those bitter old hags. I considered the idea further, turning it over in my mind, the sharpness of it as biting as the cold. I would die here on this ledge, I realised bitterly. Óðinn was not coming to save me. Thiazi would not offer a last moment reprieve. I was going to be a sacrifice for a grudge shared by the Æsir and giants, a hatred forged from the beginning of the nine realms.

The oldest of the giants were like Thiazi, giants of frost and ice who, like their kin in Múspelheim, giants of fire and flames, shared origins with the elements of chaos, of which the first giant, Ymir, had been the mightiest when

Óðinn and his brothers cut him down, carving his corpse to fashion the nine realms and the all beings who dwelt there. Óðinn was the oldest of the Æsir to walk the creation he'd created from the blood and bones of the giants. Not surprisingly, the giants only felt rage toward Óðinn and desired nothing more than to quench their vengeance with the destruction of the Æsir. It was ironic, then, that I would be the offering for retribution. I was not as ancient nor powerful as Thiazi, but I was kindred to the giants. It felt offensive to pay for Óðinn's crimes with my blood. I wasn't recognised among the Æsir any more than I was among the giants.

I was dimly aware when the heavy stone door behind me opened, sending snow gusting and swirling around the small ledge. A firm hand grabbed the back of my shoulders and dragged me from the icy prison. I could not feel my feet or legs, so it didn't matter how roughly my captor dragged me across stone floors and down steps. He tossed me into the centre of a large room, onto a rough fur hide covering the floor; it seemed like the softest of wool against my ice-burned skin. Burrowing into the meagre warmth it offered, I shivered and my eyelids fluttered as awareness returned to my body. I realised how close to death I'd been out on the ledge with the blizzard nearly stripping life from me.

A large hearth was behind me, and firelight danced across my skin. I heard another log thrown onto the fire, embers and flame roaring with the extra fuel. A wave of warmth rolled toward me, caressing my frozen limbs and awakening a fire within them. If I had considered the moments before frostbite as painful, the return of blood to my frigid hands and feet was excruciating. I writhed on the floor. Then electric pain flooded my body. It was intolerable and I thought I'd go mad before it'd stop. Bucking my spine and dancing my heels across the stinking floor covering, I gnashed my teeth, screaming obscenities into the air. I longed for the sensation of the cold, the numbness that had been peaceful only moments before, now stripped away and replaced with outrage and agony.

Absently, I noticed an amused chuckle from the other side of the cavernous room, a cruel voice that bit into my mind like the blizzard that had caused this pain. I hurled a string of insults from my stuttering lips, cursing Thiazi with every obscene and horrendous offence I could imagine.

"Do you think that can really be done?" Thiazi inquired from beside the hearth.

"I'm inventive," I stammered, still writhing on the floor. "Come closer and let's see if I can shove your balls up your nose."

He laughed with genuine amusement that only made me snarl more obscenities.

After an unendurable length of time, the agony of my body subsided to burning pain. I still twisted on the hearth rug, flapping my limbs uselessly as nerve endings sparked like lightning bolts through my flesh. Slowly, the sharp jabs of pain became less frequent, and my insults lost the wrath that had fuelled my outrage. I became more aware of my surroundings, noticing the large room carved completely from the inside of the mountain, rough-hewn stone still visible on the walls. Thiazi sat in a massive carved stone chair, furs and pelts draped across it, his legs spread wide, hands loose in his lap, but pale eyes fixed on me, the thick beard obscuring most of his face except the braided sides around his thin lips. I snarled something at him and twisted in pain once more before falling still, panting from the exertion. A tall blonde woman strode into the room and stood behind his chair. She was pale like snow but had blue eyes bright as a glacier and just as harsh. A quiver was still slung across her leather jerkin. She was beautiful and remote. Her eyes hardened as she regarded me.

"I appreciate the offer, Thiazi," I said, laying still in a moment of respite. "But I doubt I have the energy for such amorous activities right now. To be offered such a woman, though, is an honour."

The woman's eyes narrowed, her lips twisting in anger. I smiled despite myself, knowing I'd hit the mark as intended. As expected, a bellow of rage broke Thiazi's composure and he shot to his feet, a massive fur-clad boot kicking me in the ribs, sending me rolling toward the hearth. Another rib broke and I gasped with the sharp pain. Suddenly laughter broke from my lips and I half-sobbed, half-laughed beside the fire.

"Your daughter, I assume," I chuckled, gasping in air. "She's ravishing."

"Skaði," Thiazi growled in a warning to his daughter as she advanced toward me.

The woman halted immediately; fists clenched together tightly as she glared at me. I glimpsed the brilliant blue eyes and the icy sparks of fury within them. She was as beautiful and deadly as these frozen mountains. Thiazi might be prone to fits of fury that were easily provoked and quickly subsided, but Skaði was more calculating and colder. Her anger would be remorseless and unrelenting when provoked. It is always useful to understand the limits of your enemies, and Thiazi was more easily managed than his daughter.

"What do you want with me?" I finally asked, meeting Thiazi's glare.

Thiazi loomed over me, roughly dragging a hand across his thick blonde braids. "You are kin."

I raised my eyebrows. "Since when did all giants regard me as kin?"

"You are a child of Múspelheim," Skaði said.

I flicked my eyes toward her briefly. "I am. But the frost giants of Jötunheimr have never claimed kinship before."

Thiazi crossed his massive arms over his chest. "Giants are one, Loki. We don't squabble for power among ourselves like the Æsir and Vanir."

I nodded solemnly at his words. "Then the children of fire and ice are all equals? Sounds harmonious."

"Don't mock me."

"Forgive me. The irony has obviously escaped you both. I am a child of Múspelheim and yet, even as you claim kinship with me, you keep me your prisoner. If there is *any* sense of equality, it's not clear right now."

Thiazi growled low in this throat, a long stride bringing him closer to me. Despite myself, I slunk backward and away from the threat of violence.

"What do you want then, liar and trickster?" Skaði demanded, stepping forward to place her hands on the back of her father's empty chair.

"I want the truth," I said as calmly as I could. "What do you really want from me?"

Thiazi met my gaze directly. "I want the Æsir's sweetest fruit."

I frowned. "You want Iðunn?" I guessed.

Thiazi nodded. "Your life in return for the sweet one."

I thought of the guileless young woman who had danced so merrily at the feast, celebrating my return. Could I really give her up to this brute? Frantically, I thought of how I could extricate myself from this frozen fortress. Óðinn could not reach me here. Even Thor was not strong enough to challenge Thiazi in the lands he ruled. The giants drew power from the lands they ruled, just as Óðinn drew power from Asgard. I knew Óðinn well enough to understand the calculating leader he was and that such a risk was not in the best interests of the Æsir. Óðinn might be my oldest friend, we may be bound like brothers, but Óðinn would always place the safety of those dependent on him before risking everything for an individual. I accepted the altruism required to hold Óðinn to his promises, but I could never understand it. I was a child of chaos. The strength of my power was in my survival. Here, Thiazi was right: I was kindred to the giants, and no matter how I enjoyed walking among the Æsir, I would never be like them.

I knew I walked a thin sliver of danger now. If I refused Thiazi, he would end me without compunction. The giants were only interested in how they might survive, and the hatred of the Æsir ran deep. I was more a traitor to them for living among the Æsir than I was kindred to the giants.

I licked my lips. "I can bring you Iðunn."

CHAPTER 5
Iðunn

Anxiety roiled through me as I walked from the dense woodlands of Vanaheimr, stepping into the meadows of Fólkvangr. Even as I walked, hands slung casually in the folds of my now tattered tunic, I was conscious of being watched, the never-sleeping elves that dwelt in the forests of Vanaheimr observing my return. I knew without a doubt that Freyr was aware of my return, and soon his sister would be, too. Stepping through the wildflowers of the meadow, I was conscious of the quickening that shivered through Asgard, the network of communication between all living things passing information toward Hliðskjálf. The sound of the light footsteps sweeping across the long grass caught my attention. My suspicions as to the identity of the approaching god was confirmed by the familiar stride. I looked up to see Óðinn approaching in some haste. He was wary, but I'd find out if he truly trusted me, as he claimed. The thought of my impending betrayal seemed justified in that moment as Óðinn's eye narrowed and he slowed his gait. I loosened my shoulders and raised a hand in greeting.

"I am so grateful to be home," I said with genuine pleasure. Already the warmth of the morning sun was easing the bitter frostbite I had sustained in Jötunheimr.

"How far did the eagle take you?" he asked, a smile crinkling the lines on his face.

"Far," I said, stepping up to embrace him.

His muscular arms wrapped around my slender form, and he stiffened slightly and he held me a moment too long and I let my arms loosen about his broad shoulders.

"Is there something more you wanted?" I asked huskily, my hands smoothing the muscles of his shoulders.

Abruptly, he let me go, stepping back to regard me cautiously.

"Don't you think that embrace was becoming more than a little too familiar?" I asked mockingly.

He laughed, tension evaporating. "So, where have you been?"

I rolled my eyes skyward. "By the time the eagle got low enough for me to jump, I was on the border of Jötunheimr." I gestured to my torn clothing and waggled my frostbitten hands at him. "Next time you and Hœnir decide to have another event like that, exclude me."

Concern warred with amusement, transforming his features with conflicting emotions. "Jötunheimr?" he asked.

I nodded. "That was a massive eagle. Why was it here, do you think?"

His lips were a thin line. "A spy, I imagine."

"The frost giants can certainly hold a grudge," I agreed. "When I leapt into a snowbank, the bloody bird dived after me, talons and beak scratching my arms to shreds. I threw some rocks and eventually it flew off. It's a long walk back, though," I mumbled.

"Hm," he agreed, clearly lost in thought.

"Can I get some dry, clean clothes?" I asked hopefully. "Maybe some food?"

"Of course," Óðinn said, slapping my shoulder and making me stumble. "How inhospitable of me."

"It's fine," I muttered, falling into step beside him. "I doubt Frigg will be pleased with your hospitality, but I'll suffer it for some warm bread and mulled ale."

He laughed again, but I could tell his thoughts already raced through various scenarios, planning investigations into what threat the giants now posed.

We arrived at Valhalla and Óðinn threw open the massive wooden doors, sunlight lancing into the dim interior of the hall. I could hear the sharp smack from the loom in the back room, the soft singing while Frigg weaved. Óðinn's gaze skirted the open space of the hall, instantly drawn to the song. He strode through the space, weaving around the central hearth and spit, following the sound of his wife's song.

I stood in the doorway, staring at the slim figure motionless beside the hearth. Iðunn's dark eyes met mine and her features transformed with a youthful brilliance. I shivered, a thin breeze cutting through my torn clothing. Iðunn clasped her hands in front of her before moving toward me, skirts swaying with her lithe movement. My eyes roamed across the curve of her hips, a slender narrowing of her waist, tracing upward to the gentle swell of her breasts.

"Loki?" Iðunn asked, voice sweet and vibrant.

"Did you know there's another tree with apples, just like the ones you pick?" I asked, meeting her dark eyes.

"Where?" she asked eagerly.

My smile faltered, noticing Iðunn's hands clasped together like an excited child.

"Let me show you," I answered, grinning. "I'm sure it is exactly the same type of tree. But I thought the one growing at the base of Hliðskjálf was the only one."

"I always thought so too," she said excitedly, bobbing her head in agreement.

I walked away from Valhalla, Iðunn hurrying to keep pace with my swift stride. Iðunn kept up a quick flow of conversation, thoughts tumbling from her lips as she considered various options. I added little to the flow of her questioning, muttering noncommittally to her conversation. Instead, I kept my awareness on the passing meadows of Fólkvangr and the approaching dense woods of Vanaheimr.

"Where are we going?" Iðunn finally queried when we stood at the fringe of the woods. Dappled light scattered across the faint path winding through the forest.

"I found the tree in a small grove through here," I answered, smiling back at her. "I hardly knew the grove was even there, it's so forested."

I hesitated on the fringe of the woods, a moment of fear drenching me in doubt. What I was about to do was wrong and I hated the idea of Iðunn in Thiazi's hands, his brutal force against her innocence and defencelessness. I remembered Óðinn's narrowed gaze and the suspicion darkening his thoughts as he considered my story about how I returned to Asgard. He did not trust me still. Anger sparked in my heart, fire momentarily lighting my eyes. I clenched and unclenched my fists, swallowing with outrage. Óðinn had a traitor in Asgard and he still considered me as the greatest threat to him.

"This way," I said with a smile, gesturing to Iðunn to follow the path into the woods.

She gave me an excited smile before preceding me along the path, half-skipping down the steep slope covered in loose leaves. I glanced over my shoulder toward the sunlit meadows of Fólkvangr and the distant, curling smoke from Valhalla. I nodded once, a silent acknowledgement of the wrongs Óðinn had committed against me and the likely consequences of my actions.

I had been so certain the bond between myself and Óðinn was tight, inscrutable, and unbreakable. Yet when the eagle had taken me to Thiazi, Óðinn had not followed. None of the Vanir or Æsir were there to rescue me. Óðinn had left me with Thiazi and to whatever mishap I might endure, or however I might extricate myself. Iðunn was the only way I could extricate myself from Thiazi's prison. There had been no other option available to me but to follow Thiazi's demands.

The forest grew darker, wilder, and the trees more gnarled, branches reaching toward the path like grasping hands. Iðunn glanced back uncertainly at me, the slightest flicker of doubt in her gaze.

"Just up there," I assured, pointing ahead to where a small clearing opened in the dense forest.

"I see it," Iðunn answered with relief.

I watched her run ahead, noticing for the first time she carried the pouch of apples. The woven bag bounced against her hip as she stepped over the slight incline and dropped from view into the clearing below. Genuine fear broke through me. It was one thing to hand Iðunn over to Thiazi, but I had not realised she carried the fruit with her. Iðunn's magic was not only caring for the sacred tree that grew at Hliðskjálf but to nurture the fruit that sustained the immortality of the Æsir. Until I could organise a rescue for Iðunn, I'd expected the Æsir would manage a few days, boosting their strength by consuming the apples she had already picked. Now I realised Iðunn carried those apples with her. Once Iðunn was gone, the Æsir would quickly sicken alongside the tree she normally tended and the weakness that would grip the gods would be incurable, save from Iðunn's return and her care of the tree. What had I done? What horrendous mistake was I making?

I opened my mouth to cry out, but Iðunn's surprised scream filled the forest instead. I shut my mouth, the warning going unspoken, and instead I rushed to the incline and staggered down the slope, coming to a halt at the edge of the trees. Ahead, Thiazi already gripped the willow-slender woman in his big hands. A victorious smile on his brutal features quickened my heartbeat, fear tripping along my nerves.

"Accept my gratitude for the ripe fruit you gift me, Loki," Thiazi grinned.

I opened my mouth to speak, but the words died on my lips. I closed my mouth again as I met Iðunn's wide eyes, her terrified stare pleading with me.

"You've fulfilled our bargain," I nodded jerkily to Thiazi. "Best you leave before Óðinn notices she's missing."

He grinned at me, hands pawing at Iðunn's body. "Such a beauty," he murmured.

I turned my back, disgust and horror at my own foolishness threatening to turn my knees to water. I held my composure and walked away through the forest, hoping my step was steady, and attempted a swagger. Even after I heard the screech from the eagle and a terrified scream as Thiazi lifted Iðunn into the sky, I kept silent.

I stumbled back through the dense undergrowth of Vanaheimr, tripping on tree roots that snagged my feet, scratching my face and hands on protruding twigs. If I'd not been so terrified of what a foolish deal I had just made, I might have wondered why the forest was so aware of me. But I didn't stop to think, and continued toward the open meadows of Vanaheimr, blundering into fallen branches in my haste.

I glanced at the sky, noticing how late the afternoon had become and wondering how long I had been gone from Valhalla. Would anyone have noticed yet?

Were the gods already searching for Iðunn? I glanced again at the sky visible through the network of branches. Had I lost my way? Where was that path that led from here? I staggered as my heel slipped on a hidden, moss-covered log. I recovered, my foot landing in a shallow hollow, and lurched awkwardly, arms outstretched as I tried to recover my balance. My ankle rolled beneath me and the forest canopy tilted wildly. My hands groped for a hold on the surrounding tree trunks. I caught a flash of movement in the periphery of my sight. I twisted mid-fall, foot sliding further from beneath me. The forest floor rushed to meet me, the nauseating scent of mouldering leaf litter filling my nostrils. I gagged, coughing and swearing as I clambered on my hands and knees into a sitting position.

Rich laughter trickled through the forest, sending shivers through me. This was not good. I glowered at my ankle, the muscles already swelling where I had strained it. I heard the snuffling of wild boar nearby, the squeals from the piglets as they rooted through the undergrowth.

"You really shouldn't be here," a melodic voice spoke from behind me.

"I know," I grunted, wincing as I touched my sprained ankle.

"Did I hear Iðunn's voice not so long ago?" the man asked, slipping from the forest gloom to stand near me.

"It's been a long time since either you or your sister graced the halls of Valhalla," I replied, glancing suspiciously around me. "Where is Freyja, anyway?"

"She's gone to aid Óðinn," he chuckled, a sound like rain on leaves. "The Æsir grow weak already, but I suspect you know why."

"Freyr," I growled, losing patience. "You and your sister can play whatever nasty little mind games you like afterward, but I need to get to Óðinn now."

"Oh, I don't think Óðinn wants to see you right now," he said.

"I am at your mercy. My actions have seen that Freyja has whatever ingredients she needs to poison the Æsir against me. But just help me back to Óðinn now."

"Why would I do that?" Freyr asked, tilting his head to regard me quizzically.

"Because if you don't do that," I hissed under my breath, "you'll rue the day you stood against me."

The bright green eyes held mine a moment too long. I slid my gaze away, realising he would not offer any aid to me. I noticed then how his long fingers curled reflexively about the golden hilt of his sword. Freyr was the god of forests and abundance, but he was also a god of war, the blade he carried edged with sunlight.

"You genuinely hate me, don't you?" I queried, sounding more surprised than intended.

"Yes," he replied simply.

"I always thought Freyja's hate for me was what fuelled your own," I replied, shaking my head ruefully.

"We may have come from the same womb, gifted similar strengths, but we are different, Loki," he said. "Freyja is as much the warrior as Týr and would kill you without hesitation. I am less forgiving to offer you a quick death."

I stared at my hands, flexing my fingers to marvel at the long scratches and thin cuts marring my skin.

"As fascinating as this talk has been," I said, wiping my hands across my dirt-smeared pants and tunic, "I need to go now."

Freyr gave a solemn nod, a strangely courteous gesture. He did not move to help me stand, but watched as I struggled to my feet, testing my weight gingerly on the injured ankle.

"Until next time," I called, waving cheerfully to Freyr as I hobbled toward the sinking sun on the western horizon.

"Freyja will destroy you, Loki," he called after me.

"Until then," I snarled in reply. "You boar-loving weakling," I muttered as I lurched from tree to tree, finally seeing a path clear from the forest. Or rather, when Freyr finally released me from the forest.

Chapter 6
Immortal Fruit

The sun was setting behind the imposing form of Hliðskjálf when I stumbled across the fields of Fólkvangr, moving as swiftly as my limping gait would allow toward the hall of Valhalla. The torches were just being lit as I approached Valhalla and even from this distance, I could hear the conversation from inside. I nodded mutely to the elves who moved silently around the dooryard lighting the outside torches and braziers. The lowing of cattle from the stables added a melancholy note to the darkening twilight and rising commotion from inside the hall.

I stood on the threshold and stared at the unusual sight. I threw the double doors open to the gathering night, the braziers in the dooryard sending showers of embers against the growing shadows. Exhaling, I gathered my nerves and stepped into the fire-lit interior of the main hall.

The central hearth was an empty pit; no shoulder of boar or hindquarter of stag roasted above a fire, fat dripping and spitting into the flames. The lack of a feast filled Valhalla with an eerie emptiness, as though the Æsir had already faded. I stared dumbly, mouth gaping as I registered all that was wrong here. No young maidens moved through the crowd, tankards of spiced ale in their hands, no harps or whistles poured music through the hall. In the corner by the far hearth, Bragi had stopped playing. His gnarled hands, held towards the fire for warmth, but these were no longer those of a harpist and skald. Instead, those long-fingered and dextrous hands showed the swollen-joints and extremities of an old man.

"Then where is Loki?" Freyja challenged, voice ringing above the arguing gods.

I turned my head, searching the crowd for Óðinn. I knew he was aware of my presence. The pledge that bound us tightly also linked me to him in a way I never understood.

"He is here," Óðinn replied, countering Freyja's accusation with stern civility.

"Then make him explain," Freyja snarled. "If Loki is as innocent as you claim, let's hear it from him."

The crowd grumbled. A few curses and insults shuttled back and forth among the gathered gods. Emotion was running high and tempers fraying fast. I doubted Óðinn could keep them in check this time. I muttered a curse at Freyja as I stepped closer to the crowd, straightening the remains of my jacket, still shredded and stained from the forest.

"Loki knows what Iðunn's gift is among us." Týr was speaking, the calm and rational tone to his voice soothing the crowd. "He would never harm Iðunn, knowing it would destroy us all."

"Loki has never been one of you," Freyja spat, her tone venomous but stirring the doubts among the gods.

I flinched, halting in my effort to push into the outer circle of the gathering. There was a murmur of agreement with Freyja's words among the gods and those voices growling louder. I heard the shout of Thor as he bellowed for me to explain myself if I was truly present. The doubt among the gods was growing with every snide insinuation Freyja threw to them. I knew she hated me, but I had never really understood why. There. The smallest of seeds planted in my mind that she resented my bond with Óðinn and the protection that afforded me. Could it have been Freyja who was so jealous of my position among the Æsir that when she'd been known among us as Gullveig and first came to Valhalla, I had witnessed and been neither Æsir nor Jotnar and done nothing to intervene in her torture and murder? Had Gullveig lived on with the glamour of Freyja? Had her prophecies to Óðinn only germinate into fear and mistrust among the gods? Could Freyja really be Gullveig? The crowd grew more discontent. The shouted demands grew louder that my betrayal be punished. The shouts for Óðinn to punish me and soon those calls outnumbered the pleas for calm. If there was one thing Freyja had learned from her time as Gullveig, it was how easily the Æsir were manipulated by fear.

Thor's massive hand gripped the back of my jerkin, dragging me to the centre of the crowd. He tossed me like a discarded pup at Óðinn's feet. I landed on hands and knees, so close to the central cooking pit that soot-smeared grease covered my palms. I scooted backward from the edge of the pit, away from the charred remnants of previous feasts. I shuddered, aware that if the fire had been lit tonight, I would have fallen on the coals.

I lifted my eyes to Óðinn and felt my breath expire in my chest. He had aged beyond comprehension. The proud bearing of the All-Father was still there but collapsed inward on itself. He sat straight in the tall-backed chair, hands resting on the arms, but he was a shrunken, ancient husk of the man I knew so well.

"Loki," Óðinn said grimly, the single cobalt eye fixing mine but a slight film now dimming the intense gaze. "Is what Freyja says true?"

I glanced around the assembled Æsir. All the gods and goddesses were ageing quickly. I licked my lips, mind spinning through possibilities of how I might explain my actions so they would understand. The pause between Óðinn's question and my response stretched into an endless silence, where the future of the Æsir hung on my answer and Óðinn's reaction.

"Of course it's true. He's betrayed you before." Freyja's slender frame was tall and regal among the weaker Æsir.

"How is it you and Freyr aren't affected like the others?" I asked and gestured to the aged bodies of the gods.

"Were you hoping we would be too?" Freyja countered, dark eyes glittering beneath her golden fringe. "Not all have fallen to your tricks and betrayal."

"It seems so," I muttered, not having the time to consider whether Freyja knew she would escape the fate of the Æsir.

"You have threatened us all," Óðinn sighed, voice sounding tired beyond endurance. He leaned back in the chair, bodyweight resting heavily on the wooden frame like I had never seen him do before.

Thor moved through the assembled crowd, the confident stride of his boots on the stone sending shivers of anticipation through me. Thor was the strongest of the Æsir and if anyone could challenge Thiazi, reverting the tragedy of this situation, it was Thor.

I heard him stop a few paces behind me, the bellows of his great lungs heaving in the air as he struggled to constrain the rage consuming him. Thor had never been good at controlling his anger. I tensed, expecting the surge of magic that preceded his fury. As it always did, that wave crashed against my senses but half the strength I had expected. I half-turned in surprise, noticing the grey streaking his red hair and beard, the wrinkles at the corner of his eyes and corded muscles in his hands. Thor had aged. The strongest of the Æsir would be no match for Thiazi in this state. I felt the blood drain from my face with the realisation I had doomed us all. My reaction was answer enough for Thor and, although his strength was not equal to Thiazi, the blows would be more than sufficient to pummel me into the stones. I wheezed a startled cry before the first blow sent me face-first into the flagstones at Óðinn's feet.

The beating might have lasted moments or years. I only noted the passage of time in the brief moments before another blow, the splattering of my blood across the stones, the heaving gasps of Thor as he meted out my punishment. I rolled and crawled, anything to evade the blows and kicks that always found my unprotected sides or the areas already bruised and broken. When I could no longer shout in protest, when my cries dwindled to wheezing gasps of pain and then to sobs for mercy, I finally made no sound at all. In the brief moments of consciousness between the blows, I understood only pain and someone dragging of my broken body across the flagstones.

I woke to the rattling intake of breath. It paused, then another shallow gasp. I tried to open my eyes, but blood had crusted my eyelashes shut. I listened to another wheeze, the pause, then a rattle of exhaled breath. Was it my own? I was not aware of my chest rising and falling, barely conscious of anything but the harsh breathing beside me.

"Get up," a voice commanded, cracking through the stillness like a thunderclap.

I forced one eye open, wincing at the residue that gumming my left eye shut.

The Æsir surrounded me, a stooped and ageing hoard of gods. I saw the hall of Valhalla through a bloody film, the red haze obscuring none of the animosity toward me. Óðinn leaned over me, the cowl of his hood thrown back to reveal steel grey hair, deep lines that marked his face, the long-fingered hands that gripped the hilt of his sword gnarled with age.

"Loki," he commanded quietly, anger burning beneath the surface of his voice, "you will make repayment for the damage you've caused us. Lure Thiazi back here and let us deal with him."

I parted my split lips, fresh blood dripping down my chin. "You're not strong enough," I began.

"No, we are not," Óðinn hissed, cobalt eye glittering with malice. "Thiazi will be weaker away from Jötunheimr. Bring him to us."

"How?" I whispered, thinking of the mighty frost giant.

Thor hit me hard, my head snapping sideways, pitching me again onto the blood-splotched stones.

"Find a way," Óðinn snapped, resuming his seat. "Return Iðunn, and we might have a chance."

I lifted my cheek from the stone floor, surveying the Æsir who regarded me with bitter hatred.

Weakly, I pushed myself from the floor, the burning pain of cracked ribs, broken fingers and the agony of my smashed face igniting into a fury of hurts. I lost consciousness, the blackness swooping upward to swallow me.

I yelped as icy cold water was poured over me. I shivered, crying in shock and pain as the elf placed the wooden bucket on the ground with a sharp *clack*. I stared at my blood running freely in rivulets across the stone floor. Thor had beaten me badly. I was certain these injuries would prevent me from making the trek to Jötunheimr and, even if I did, I couldn't do it in time to save the Æsir. The only way I could travel to Thyrmheim to rescue Iðunn was in another form. As a wolf, I could run over the rough terrain, but it would still take days. I wasn't even sure if my injuries would allow me to change form. I hung my head as the cold water dripped from my bloody hair, my cut eyebrows and cheeks.

"Freyja?" I asked, not looking up from the stones.

"What?" the imperious voice replied from somewhere behind me.

"I need your aid," I said, the words leaving my lips reluctantly.

The stillness that hung about Valhalla was palpable. I wet my lips, tasting blood.

"Please," I whispered, hating how she made me beg.

I heard her sharp intake of breath, the quiet tread of leather boots across the stones. The sweet scent of meadow wildflowers surrounded me, dizzying and arousing. I silently cursed myself. They might beat my body beyond endurance, but it still responded to the ardent sexual desire Freyja awoke in me. I lifted my head as she knelt beside me. The heady scent of her so close near broke me with desire. I was conscious of the embers burning in my eyes and knew she understood the hunger she roused within me.

Freyja leaned closer, lips parted slightly as she gazed at me. "What do you need?" she asked, her tone suggestive despite the simple words.

I licked my lips, determined to focus. "I need to transform," I said. "I'm too weakened to do it alone."

"Ah," she replied, an eyebrow arched at me, pale lips still slightly parted. "Would you have me help you?"

"Yes," I sighed, my traitorous gaze falling to the swell of her lower lip.

"Beg it of me," she breathed.

Freyja's magic surrounded me, engulfing the air between us, the heavy scent of wildflowers warmed by sunshine, the taste of honey on lips and the touch of silken skin.

"Lady Freyja," I whispered, voice breaking on her name. "I beg aid of you."

She straightened, the seductive magic suddenly absent like the disappearance of a lover's touch. I leaned toward the space she'd occupied, but it was cold and empty. My lips parted, eyes burning with desire and need. I exhaled a shaky breath, turning to follow her steps across the flagstones.

A few paces from me, Freyja stopped. The swaying cloak of fox pelts swirled about her long legs as she turned to face me and the words she spoke were rich with an old magic, ancient and found only among the Vanir. It was the magic Freyja had first used when she came to Óðinn in the guise of Gullveig and spoken the prophecy of the destruction of the Nine Worlds. Óðinn was right to fear her.

I felt my body change beneath Freyja's magic, my senses sharpening as her power settled across my skin, warmed by sunlight and shimmering like firelight. The expanse of Valhalla seemed to grow, the wooden chairs in which the Æsir were seated elongated and became finer. I moved my head, the keen eyesight of the hawk now mine. I shifted not broken arms but healed and powerful wings. I unclenched my taloned feet and opened my razor-like beak, snapping the air with a sharp click.

"You don't have long for my magic to bind your form," Freyja said solemnly to me. "Your kind are not like ours, and my powers have an unpredictable hold."

I bobbed my hawk head and opening my wings. I lifted effortlessly into the air, swift wingbeats carrying me out of Valhalla and toward Jötunheimr.

Chapter 7
Rescuing Iðunn

I flew over the deep forests of Vanaheimr, swift wingbeats carrying me across the stone chasm that marked the border between Asgard and Jötunheimr, and followed the narrowing chasm north, tracing the river to where it transformed into an icy glacier. I dove through the low cloud, soaring across the expanse of dark forests, buffeted by the strengthening winds as the woods grew wilder and the snow-dusted forests climbed toward the foothills. Steadying my outstretched wings, I braced against the crosswinds and turned, towards the snow-packed foothills and into the mountain range in the distance.

The winds buffeted me as I circled the mountain peaks glittering encrusted icy crowns. The keen eyesight of the hawk revealed the fine detail of the black rock and where glacier blue cut through the fissures. I hovered a moment, to marvel at the harshly beauty of Jötunheimr. These lands were not my own, but I felt a kinship to the frozen harshness that Asgard never drew from me. I let the wind carry me backward, then with strong wingbeats I lifted higher into the sky.

Exhaustion and terror during my previous journey to Thyrmheim had prevented any observation of the frozen landscape, but now I circled above the rising mountain peaks, the lands of Jötunheimr laid out below me like a map. At last, I spied a familiar sharp crag, the black rock jagged and clothed in hoarfrost. I folded my wings, diving toward Thyrmheim, the hidden hall of the frost giant Thiazi.

The strong northern winds swirled around Thyrmheim as the speed of my dive became erratic, caught by the crosswinds surrounding the mountains. Unfolding my wings and forced to control my flight as the gales tossed me closer to the cliff face, I appreciated the strength of the eagle form Thiazi had taken last time as I struggled to lift the body of the hawk above the chaotic gales. Caught between the crosswinds and carried toward a narrow black stone ledge, I scrabbled with my talons against the stone, gouging the rock until I found purchase. I sheltered for a moment, considering how I might approach Thyrmheim without dashing the frail hawk's body into pieces on the stone. Movement on the periphery of my sight me caught my attention. I swivelled my head, keen gaze searching for the slightest shift in light that meant movement.

Iðunn stood on the opposite side of a sheet of blue ice, hoarfrost decorating the outside surface. I cocked my head, looking beyond her slight frame, silhouetted against the firelight behind her. The chamber was empty and no movement beyond except the flickering firelight. Could Thiazi, in his arrogance, have left her unguarded? A plan started to formulate in my mind.

I lifted my wings wide, and they were immediately taken up by the wild, erratic gales that that tossed me closer to Thyrmheim. Instead of trying to fly against the wind, I let it carry me as it would, my fragile body tossed like a leaf in a gale. Would this work? Would the wind actually deliver me where I needed to be? Or would they smash me into the jagged black rock? The gamble paid off: I was swept behind the mountain peak and, nearly thrown off course, I steered myself back into the main current. The opposing wind current caught me and as I tumbled chaotically through the squall, my claws found purchase on a wide, smooth rock ledge. I hopped across the stone, talons tapping loudly against the sudden silence closer to the mountainside and to safety.

I perched on the wide stone expanse where Thiazi had first dropped me to freeze. Surveying the thick pile of snow against the stone wall, I noticed a slight chink in the rock, light slipping onto the ledge. Nearing the gap in the stone, I realised it was the edge of the massive doorway Thiazi had used to trap me outside. Last time I had been a prisoner here, the stone surface had been seamless. If I hoped to undo some of what I had done, I would need to change my form to rescue Iðunn from this point onward.

Closing my eyes, I drew on the magic buried deep within my body. My strength was a feeble thing. The beating Thor had delivered and the flight to Thyrmheim had taken much from me. If I did not return with Iðunn and restore the balance of power to the Æsir, my strength would be as forfeit as my life. I felt the shiver of magic along my limbs, the power dancing through feather and talon, urging my form back into that of a man. Even as I drew on those fragile reserves, I envisioned myself standing tall and strong. I envisioned myself in the masculine form I had borne through Asgard before Ragnarök.

When the magic deserted me, fatigue heavy on my shoulders, I opened my eyes. I noticed immediately the absence of the keen eyesight the hawk had provided and, peering at the slash of light between stone, I lifted my hands. My fingers were still long and graceful, but now had a distinctly masculine shape. I flexed my hands, no longer talons, and reached toward the chink in the otherwise smooth stone.

Gripping the narrow cleft in the black rock, I prised my fingertips deeper into the gap, hauling backward with my bodyweight as I did so. Even as a man, I had never been muscular like Thor or Týr, but I had a wiry strength that belied the slender form. Gripping with fingers and toes on the icy rock, I ignored the sharp pain of cold burning my naked skin as the stone slab slowly inched aside.

Leaning my arms against the black rock, I sighed, sweat freezing on my skin as frost dusted my pale flesh. Exhaling deeply, I hauled backward on the stone slab, feeling the mechanisms that allowed it to swing, finally give way with a tearing groan of icy protest. The sudden absence of opposing weight was a shock, throwing me off balance. I stumbled backward a few steps but, keeping focus and I staggered inside the mountain hall. The outside granite door swung shut behind me with an ominous echo throughout the corridors that couldn't fail to alert anyone to the presence of an intruder…

I drew another shaky breath, ignoring the stabbing pain of torn muscles as I walked toward the warmth of the hearth. Absently, I was conscious of Iðunn standing in the doorway to her chamber I had seen from outside. The searing agony of frost-burned skin and torn muscle consumed my attention and, limping to the hearth, I let the fire warm my injuries.

"Don't," I said to Iðunn, holding up a warning hand to stop the question on her lips.

The slender young woman abruptly shut her mouth and nodded obediently.

The pleasure of warmth offered by the small hearth fire soon became a rising torrent of torture. Why is it that pleasure and pain are always opposing sides of the same coin? The return of sensation into my frozen limbs was welcome, but quickly turned sour. The quiet curses I spoke became whimpers of outrage before blossoming into angry shouts and prayers for numbness to return.

Iðunn sat beside the hearth, feet propped up and off the flagstones, big eyes watching me as I cursed and sobbed in many languages. If I had been the compassionate sort, I might have been ashamed of my foul language near an innocent like Iðunn. I was not burdened by such concerns and so curses and many imaginative insults poured from my lips.

"You said that one already," Iðunn announced from beside the fire.

I stopped, raising an eyebrow at her before kicking another pile of thick blankets across the room. "What do you know?" I snarled.

"Loki," Iðunn said, smiling, "are you here to rescue me?"

I nodded sharply. "I'm not very good at it, am I?"

She shrugged, breaking the tension of my tantrum.

"This is my fault," I said, gesturing to Thiazi's hall.

"Yet you're here to make amends," she pointed out.

I exhaled, near sobbing with the effort. "I deserve none of your kindness," I said.

She stared at me. "My kindness is mine to bestow," she answered. "Now, do you have a plan to get us away from here?"

I looked about the sparse room, conscious of my nakedness now. Glancing about me, I realised there was nothing in this hall except for the pelts covering the flagstones near the hearth and the massive black stone slab carved into Thiazi's throne. I turned as Iðunn held out the warm, woven cloak she had been wearing. I smiled a little self-consciously but took the proffered clothing, fashioning it quickly into a skirt, leaving my chest bare.

"Did he touch you?" I asked Iðunn, gesturing to her bruised face and, more vaguely, to the rest of her.

She shook her head sharply, blinking back tears that caused me more pain than the frostbite had. I turned away, hastily wiping the back of my hand across my face.

"Good," I said gruffly, scanning the room for any useful items. "There's not exactly much here, is there?" I asked, turning to her with a smile.

"The giants aren't known for their civility," she answered, recovering her composure.

"True," I agreed, smiling reassuringly. "Myself excepted, of course."

Iðunn startled, realising her unintended insult, and stammered apologies.

"It's quite all right," I reassured her. "They're not truly my kin."

I prowled around the confines of the room, glancing down the dark, silent halls that branched from this main room. There was nothing here. Wherever Thiazi might keep weapons or supplies, they were far from this chamber.

"How long since he left?" I asked, conscious now that the giant could return any moment.

Iðunn looked at the hearth, judging time by Thiazi's absence and the amount of wood brunt in the hearth. "There's only one log remaining. He'll return soon," she whispered, fear quickening in her tone.

I nodded, the plan already in my mind as to how I might rescue Iðunn and return her to the Æsir. Even severely weakened, I knew any more magic would drain whatever resources I had left to me. I prided myself on always being a rationalist, choosing between irreversible damage and self-preservation. There were a few choices here and none were good. I could leave Iðunn here and endure the weight of her inevitable misery on my conscience and likely be pursed to my death by the Æsir if they survived. I could use whatever magic I had left and return Iðunn to the Æsir and hopefully save them. If I was fortunate enough, my actions might warrant some reprieve from certain death.

"Stand here," I said to Iðunn, indicating the space immediately before me.

She frowned but came to stand trustingly in front of me. "What are you doing?" she asked.

"Something foolish," I sighed, kindling to life the magic within me.

Iðunn stared into my gold-flecked eyes, making me self-conscious of the embers of fire now stirring within their depths.

I flexed my long fingers, gently placing them on Iðunn's shoulders, noticing how she flinched slightly at my touch. *My fault*, I reminded myself. Exhaling steadily, I blew gently across Iðunn's face, moving along her shoulders and down her torso, the magic sparking like tiny embers in the air.

In only moments, Iðunn had vanished, her lithe form replaced by a small, golden nut that lay on the bear pelt on the floor.

I bent to pick up the nut, staggering to my knees as I did, the room spinning awfully with my exhaustion. Nausea rolled through me, crashing inside my guts like waves in an ocean. I steeled myself, determined not to vomit. Carefully, I scooped the golden nut into my trembling hands.

"You'll be all right now," I promised her.

I struggled to my feet, my body aching now with fatigue and the memory of my last beating at the hands of Thor. I cast Iðunn's cloak aside, moving toward the frozen ledge on the far side of the room. I pushed my shoulder against the black stone slab, and it moved ponderously as I heaved my bodyweight behind it, shoving fresh snow and ice from its path.

I stared at the scenery before me, the ice-encrusted mountain peaks, the fading sunlight as twilight approached. No time to admire the view, I reminded myself. Crouching on the icy ledge, I placed the golden nut amid a shallow snow drift and called upon my magic once more.

Transformations were always the hardest. Shifting matter from one form to another was the most strenuous of magic and the type not common among the Æsir. The Vanir, like Freyja and her brother Freyr, possessed this magic in abundance, but it was stronger still in the giants. I was from Múspelheim, where the fiery current of energy seemed strongest. This was a magic I used with ease, but not tonight. Beaten near-death and having already given much of my power to transforming Iðunn, I was weak. I hadn't known how the secret of her connection to the apple tree that grew in Asgard. Yet unlike the Æsir, she had the eternal youth like the Norns. If Iðunn was kin to whatever the Norns truly were, they would set their hatred of me and their wrath for what I'd done in stone.

I felt the shiver of magic answer to my will. The twitching and prickling of my skin as warmth flooded me, the frigid cold of Jötunheimr abating as the power of Múspelheim kindled into flame within me. The itching of my skin became unbearable, and I closed my eyes, not wishing to see the feathers that were likely breaking through my skin. My feet arched in agony, talons forming where a human shape had been, and my hands clawed uselessly at the ice as they stretched into wings.

When the transformation was complete, I remained still for a moment, reorienting my mind inside the perception and keen senses of the hawk I now resembled. The magic now complete, I was weary with exhaustion and agitated with the hawk's desire to be in the sky. Controlling myself, I spread my wings slightly, testing them for flight against the strong northern winds. When ready, I stepped forward, one talon gripping the pale-golden nut before I spread my wings wide and launched into the icy gale that took me higher into the sky above Jötunheimr and closer to Asgard.

Chapter 8
Like All Giants

It seemed the entire might of the north wind blew against me, and I struggled to open my wings against it. Buffeted by the gale, I spiralled off course, and was nearly thrown against the black rock of the mountain, expecting the fragile hawk bones to be dashed upon the sharp, icy crags. Spinning downward, I kept my wings half-closed until a savage gust tossed me behind a rocky spire, the momentary shelter it provided giving me the time I needed. I twisted mid-air, opening my wings, and with three steady upbeats, I turned again, moving through the crosswinds that surrounded Thyrmheimr and aided in keeping the mountain fortress so impregnable. Allowing the innate consciousness of the hawk to guide me, I carried the small nut in clenched talons, lifting higher into the predawn sky, pirouetting and twisting through air currents and channels determined to dash me into the mountain.

After what felt like an age of aerial manoeuvres, I broke above the crosswinds protecting Thiazi's kingdom and felt the smooth air high above Jötunheimr. I hovered momentarily, casting the keen hawk gaze across the snow-capped mountains and the bright eerie glow of glaciers. No movement. Satisfied I might have entered and escaped Thyrmheim without notice and hoping my rescue of Iðunn might be successful, I gently spread my wings wide and glided toward the distant forested realm of Asgard.

I flew steadily with even wingbeats, spending no more energy than I needed. Although I could see the tempest of winter storms brewing above Thyrmheim, I was not such a fool to imagine Thiazi would leave his fortress entirely unguarded. I worried pursuit would follow at any moment, and I needed whatever energy I had to ensure Iðunn returned safely to Asgard.

I focused on the passing snow-covered landscape below me, alert for any movement. The astonishing eyesight gifted to me with the body of the hawk was a constant source of fascination and distraction. I was conscious of every slight movement on the snowy ground below me, from the twitch of a rabbit's ear, the subtle shift of a hunting fox, to the rapid escape of a hare. Nothing escaped my notice, but still I waited in fear for sounds of raised alarm from Thyrmheim, or the giant wingbeats of Thiazi as an eagle, ready to swoop from above. I crossed the forested threshold between Jötunheimr and Asgard in the fraught moments during dawn. I was almost unaware of the passing of time until the golden brilliance of the rising sun lifted above the eastern horizon.

I focused only on the singular stone peak of Hliðskjálf and, flying closer, I noticed the solitary figure beside the wizened tree at the base of Hliðskjálf. Freyja glanced up at me as I circled above Óðinn's throne. I uttered a sharp cry of relief and wearily folded my wings, diving toward Iðunn's tree.

Exhaustion had so completely claimed me that even though I aimed to perch on the curled branches of the tree, I toppled through the canopy, branches snapping with my fall. I released my grasp on the nut, opening my talons as I struggled to prevent myself from plummeting into the ground.

I landed with a soft thud in the dewy grass at the base of the tree. Startled by my headlong fall, I remained motionless on the ground, perceiving only the slow tumble of the nut as it rolled into a nearby depression in the grass. Concussed, or perhaps worse, I hardly noticed when a pair of leather boots filled my eyesight. I wasn't sure if I could move, if I was alive. I watched as long-fingered hands scooped up the nut.

"Safely home again," Freyja whispered to the nut.

I squawked out a brief protest, conscious of the broken bones within the frail hawk's body.

Freyja did not respond but continued whispering in a soft murmur to the nut. I watched from my vantage point on the ground as Freyja returned the nut to the grass. The goddess murmured quietly and golden flecks unfurled from the nutshell, consuming the air above the husk. I saw Freyja's enchant surrounding me engulf the space and nut with her deep magic. The Vanir goddess might despise me for her own reasons but in that moment, I knew how similar the actions were to my own. I secreted this a fascinating nugget of knowledge away and weakly flapped a wing.

"Óðinn says I must save you," Freyja explained before ruthlessly adding: "He never said I must do it quickly."

I remained in a motionless heap of feathers and tangled wings at the base of Iðunn's tree while Freyja worked her powerful but subtle magic. Iðunn returned to her true form, the lithe body of the maiden, beside Freyja.

"Loki," Iðunn shouted, dropping to her knees beside me.

I felt the sharp rebuke of pain as Iðunn cradled me in her hands, tears falling on my feathers.

"Can you heal him?" Iðunn asked as she turned to Freyja, voice lit with naive innocence.

"He doesn't deserve it," Freyja replied gravely, but took my battered body from Iðunn.

Fear flowed through me as Freyja held me between cupped hands. Unable to escape, I panicked, pecking uselessly at her fingers, but she only held me more firmly. A moment of hesitation caught me, and the rapid racing of my heartbeat echoed in the silence. Freyja spoke into that vacuum of sound, her words a whisper. I stilled, the quickening beat of my heart suddenly faltering. Freyja spoke once more, her words commanding but emotionless as her fingers wrapped more firmly around me. I struggled feebly before the darkness engulfed me, robbing me of sight and sound.

When I woke, it was to daylight and the soft grass beneath my cheek. I was in my human form and with it, the absolute agony of broken bones. Freyja had transformed but not healed me, other some rudimentary healing to what should have been fatal injuries. I still had many broken bones. I inhaled, readying a curse on my lips. It died in a hiss of agony when pain blossomed through my chest. I kept my eyes closed, snarling wordlessly to take shallow breaths instead. Curse that conniving witch. Curse you Freyja. Thinking it was enough to ease the bitterness in my heart.

Sharp pain ignited in my abdomen. My eyes flew open with the shock of it. I stared up at the late evening sky, twilight already falling across Asgard. I was aware then of the cold pressure against my stomach, an inch below my sternum. The glint of a golden blade rested against my blood splattered skin.

"I don't know why she saved you," Freyr drawled, regarding me with contempt. "You're like creeping rot that spoils the harvest."

"Nice," I wheezed, hissing in pain.

"You nearly destroyed everything," he continued, placing an infinitesimal amount of weight against the blade that made me scream in agony.

I tried to twist away from the blade, grinding my teeth together as tears leaked from my eyes.

"I don't understand Óðinn," Freyr continued with disgust. "I don't understand what worth he sees in you."

The pain was blinding, stopping the breath in my lungs and keeping every insult behind my lips. I heard the clamour of shouts and hasty conversation from the near distance. I wanted to cry for help, but the memory of Thor's last beating and Óðinn's resigned sorrow kept my cries to muffled sobs.

"Where is he?" I heard Óðinn's commanding voice and determined stride.

"He's severely injured," Freyja was saying, her tone admonishing.

"He's a fool," Óðinn snapped.

"He is," Freyja agreed, voice closer now. "I left him with Freyr."

At the mention of his name, the Vanir god straightened, the slight shift of his body moving the sword in his hands. Pain erupted in my guts, and I writhed sideways, screaming as my eyesight blackened. I heard nothing but the thundering of blood in my ears as I pressed my hot cheek against the cool grass.

"We need him," Óðinn said, his practised hands efficiently but gently noting my injuries as they roamed across my feverish skin.

"You think Thiazi is stupid enough to attack Valhalla?" Freyja asked.

"He's a giant. They're all stupid," Thor said.

Bright pain sent red lights dancing across my vision, but I heard myself laugh, the sound distant and hysterical.

"We need to heal him," Óðinn decided. "The internal bleeding, broken bones and infections are ravaging his body."

Freyja did not immediately reply. Her silence hung heavily and met with the quiet shuffling of boots.

"I do this because Iðunn cares for him," she finally answered. "I owe you nothing further."

"Agreed," Óðinn answered. The agreement to save my life struck between them and binding Freyja was to heal me.

I was conscious Freyr stiffened in anger at me, his body radiating outrage at his sister's decision to save my life. Evidently, whatever manipulations Freyja was embroiled in did not warrant her brother's opinion. It displeased Freyr, and he stepped away from me, spitting on the ground near my cheek. I was too exhausted to move and just hoped the spittle hadn't landed in my hair.

A cool hand touched my cheek, and I flinched, unaware time had passed. The space surrounding me was quiet, empty except for Freyja now. I shivered in the deepening twilit chill, my fever running dangerously high. Even if I was kin to the giants of Múspelheim, this body wasn't designed for the fiery heat of the fire-giant form I naturally took. While Freyja cleaned my naked and broken body with a sweet-scented wash, I realised she was going to save me. I had expected her promise to Óðinn to be a ruse and that she would let me die beneath Iðunn's tree, surrounded by the fruit capable of rejuvenating the Æsir, but its power never working for me. It would have been an ironic death, and the symbolism was too strong for Freyja to let pass. Yet she had pledged to Óðinn that she would heal me. While she whispered healing prayers above my broken body, the magic of the *volva* almost tangible in the air between us, I considered that Óðinn now owed Freyja a debt and I worried about what she might expect in return.

I stretched the cramps from my limbs, my awareness returning with the slow movement of my body. In the hawk form, my body had been a strange assembly of wings and talons and my consciousness had rapidly adjusted to that physical form. Now, restored to my human form, I struggled to regain the subtle control of my limbs, the precise flexion of fingers and expression from the many muscles of the face. When I thought I could stand, I climbed slowly to my feet, nearly overbalancing and pitching myself forward. I recovered, a scarred hand grasping the tree trunk immediately in front of me. The apple tree. It was Iðunn's sacred tree, fertile and healthy, I realised, carefully craning my neck to gaze. Dusky red apples hung from the upper branches, the lower canopy already harvested. Iðunn had restored the Æsir to their powers and saved my life with the same effortless benevolence.

I walked a few steps around the tree, hands ready to grasp the trunk if I faltered and nearly completed the circle of the tree but stopped at the south-western point. The shouts of men and annoyed bellows of oxen drifted from the woodland fringe. I started towards the dark woods of Vanaheimr, walking like a doddery grandfather. The thick grass fields and meadows of Fólkvangr soon gave way to the wilder forests, where the woods formed an imposing wall of ancient trees along the southern border. They had cleared a wide path into the forest; the woods echoed with the sharp ringing of axes and clang of tools from the stonemasons. I staggered at a half-run along the track. The passage of several oxen carts and teams had scored deep imprints on the soft soil. I followed these and the familiar sound of Thor's raucous laughter drawing me into the clearing carved from the forests of Vanaheimr.

I stood on the fringe of the woodland, not yet in the clearing but neither among the wilderness of Vanaheimr. I could not understand how Freyr would allow such destruction and the sacking of his lands.

"Loki!" Thor bellowed in greeting.

I flinched despite myself, recalling the savage beating Óðinn had allowed him to give me. A brutal beating that should have taken my life. I hesitated, staring at Thor and the welcoming gestures he gave me.

"He thinks you might beat the life blood from him again," Týr explained, noticing how Thor's confusion was quickly turning to anger.

"Those events are in the past. You returned Iðunn to us," Thor replied, still gesturing me closer. "And now the All-Father will punish Thiazi for his audacity to strike so hard at us."

"What?" I stammered, noticing for the first time the repairs to the Giant's Wall that encircled Asgard, the pyre being constructed at the base of one stone corner tower. "What is Óðinn doing?" I asked.

Thor swept his massive arms wide to encompass the scene. "A trap," he answered proudly.

"A trap?" I asked, hoping Thor would elaborate.

"A trap," he confirmed, grinning like a madman.

I raised my eyebrows, turning slightly to Týr. "A trap?" I repeated.

The tall swordsman of the Æsir nodded, stepping away from the massive pyre. "Óðinn thinks Thiazi will attack us here," he said, quirking an eyebrow at me. "Somehow he thinks Thiazi knows of these woods in Vanaheimr."

I crossed my arms over my bare chest, meeting the unflinching blue stare of the taller man. "Interesting," I agreed.

"Óðinn thinks we could lure Thiazi into acting rashly with the right incentive."

"Absolutely not," I said, interrupting him.

"Don't think your life is so precious to Óðinn," Try reprimanded.

"It's not that," I said, shaking my head. "I thought you meant to use Iðunn as bait."

"No!" he snapped, his voice remote like a glacial wind. "You might prefer those tactics, Loki, but Óðinn is not so corrupt."

I rolled my eyes. "So, Óðinn wants me to be the bait to lure Thiazi into this trap you're crafting?" I asked, ignoring Týr's offer to defend myself and invite his wrath.

"When Thiazi realises the trap, we remind him that the giants have no right to walk in Asgard."

"Sounds wonderful," I glowered, waiting for Thor to realise he'd offended me in the same stroke as Thiazi. The silence grew too long, and I wondered if Thor had meant the insult or if he truly was more stupid than I'd ever noticed.

"What shall I do then?" I asked in a falsely cheerful tone.

I shifted into the hawk form once again. The sharp pain of stretching ligaments and feathers pushing through skin was almost familiar to me now. There had been a time before when I had frequently shifted forms, preferring the grace and power of a wolf to the wiry but fragile human body. I had never been that keen on birds and, even though the hawk shared the predatory instincts of the wolf, they shared nothing more than that and I found the intense focus of the hawk to be restrictive. As a wolf, I had always kept more of the human intellect and processes that I prided myself in possessing. In the hawk, these traits had faded into only the basic drives of my memory.

When the change of form was complete, I shook the feathers now covering my body, adjusted the wings along my side and swivelled my gaze to meet that of Óðinn. My mentor, friend and brother stood solemnly beside the pyre, a single cobalt eye fixed on me.

"Find Thiazi and bring him as close to us as you can," Óðinn said, his tone deliberately simple for the hawk's attention.

I bobbed my head and stepped along an outstretched piece of timber that jutted from the pyre, and met Óðinn's stare with the unblinking gaze of the hawk before flexing my talons against the wood. Tilting my head directly upward, sharp gaze finding the faint clouds above the forest canopy, I let out an unearthly cry and opened my wings to their full span and propelled myself upwards into the air.

The hawk was swift. In only a few strong wingbeats, I was above the forest canopy, tacking toward the south and the frozen mountain ranges of Jötunheimr. I flew steadily, gaze sweeping the ground below for any movement, ignoring the tiny shifting shadows of fleeing prey beneath me.

In moments, the sharp cry of an eagle split the sky. I darted sideways, just avoiding the raking talons as the eagle dropped from above me. Twisting in mid-air, my wings beat furiously at the crosswinds, carrying me away from the eagle, but too slowly. The eagle climbed higher in the sky again, the greater wingspan giving extra power against the shifting winds. I propelled forward and narrowly missed another attack by the pursing eagle. It was Thiazi. I couldn't explain how I knew, but the kinship shared by the giants told me this predatory bird was as false as I was.

I shot forward in the sky, wingbeats pulling me ahead of Thiazi and closer to the shadowed woods of Vanaheimr. I saw the bright light of a bonfire below me in the clearing and knew keen-sighted Heimdallrr had prepared for my next action.

I folded my wings, dropping from the sky like a stone through water. I dove toward the darkened wood and the rapidly increasing pinpoint of light. Even as I twisted aside from another attack by Thiazi, I felt the concentration he required to pursue me. Unlike the forms taken as men, these predatory birds had little concern for traps. Everything focused on the hunt.

When the ground was only a hand's breadth from my talons, I spiralled aside, cannoning toward the bright flames of the bonfire. I was a child of Múspelheim and knew the flames would never harm me. Thiazi was a giant too, but claimed kinship with the icy mountain halls. Flying without thought but enjoying the pure, reckless speed of the moment, I passed through the fiery touch of the bonfire, feathers burning and dissolving into ash as I passed. I heard the intake of startled cries around me even as I emerged from the bonfire, hawk-form obliterated into ashes while my human skin freshly blushed with the warmth of flame. I paused as I took several more steps away from the bonfire, frowning at the silence reigning among the Æsir. *Why isn't Ullr sending arrows after Thiazi?* I slowly turned around to stare at ashes and remnants of charred feathers still floating toward the ground beside the bonfire. Thiazi hadn't diverted away from the bonfire. Instead, he'd tried to follow me into the flames, and it had killed him.

"Well, I wasn't expecting that to happen," I said into the silence.

Chapter 9
Freyja's Sight

The echo of my words hung in the air as the assembled Æsir were motionless, staring in shock at the drifting particles of the former frost giant. A thick tension curdled the air before Thor began laughing, his massive voice booming above the exclamations and shouts from Týr and Ullyr. I suddenly shivered, immediately aware I was stark naked, the air rapidly cooling as Night drew closer. I whirled, barely hearing the approach of one of Óðinn's slender Ljósálfar attendees. The tall being quirked an eyebrow and proffered a thick woollen tunic. I nodded grudging, gratitude overcoming my concern at how silently those creatures moved within a forest. I knew the Ljósálfar were the protective beings of the Vanaheimr woods, but even as I accepted the clothing, I warily watched the dappled forest light absorb the form. Repeating my fears aloud, I pulled the tunic over my head and cinched the belt. These woods belonged to Freyr, and I trusted the Lord of Álfheimr as much as I trusted his sister.

I moved toward the shadowy fringe of the woods, desperate to flee the magic that crawled across my skin, prickling and chill. I needed to flee whatever magical response Thiazi had elicited when breaking the faith and invading Asgard. A power kindled in Asgard that was no friend to the giants.

I hurried through the dense understorey of the forest, pushing away the reaching vines and stepping over tree roots. Despite my haste, I moved near-silently. I rolled my shoulders, anxiety increasing with the knowledge unseen beings were watching me. The fabric of the garment rubbed against my skin, warm and uncomfortable. I wanted to lose this form and run faster and more keenly through these woods, to flee toward safety.

I stopped beside an ancient oak tree, massive, gnarled branches reaching toward the sky like upraised arms. I quickly pulled the belt from my waist, the leather feeling constraining, and looped it about a branch. Heartbeat quickening with the fierce desire to change, I stripped the tunic off, casting the garment into the tree where the Ljósálfar could retrieve it later.

Standing naked once more beneath the dappled forest light, I flexed my fingers and toes, feeling the earth beneath my feet, the air against my fingertips. I tilted my head and rolled my neck to ease the tension and the tight muscles in my shoulders. Exhaling, I lowered myself to hands and knees upon the forest floor and drew in a sharp breath, arched my back and released the ancient power the giants shared with Freyr and his sister. The power to transform the body into another was not a blessing the Æsir had received, but it was a power I commanded with ease.

The change of form was swift and painless. At the moment between exhale and inhale, I lowered my arched back, releasing the power with a sigh. I trembled, muscles clenching tightly before I willed my body to assume the form I desired. Muscles lengthened, becoming lax as body shape changed as fluidly as glacial ice melting in sunlight. In the briefest of moments, the transformation was complete.

I dug my long claws into the moist earth, lifted my muzzle to the air and inhaled the forest scents. I had known I was not alone, aware of the Ljósálfar even as a man. Now possessed of the keen senses of the wolf, I could see and scent the Ljósálfar easily. I met the gaze of a woodland elf, the form curiously wizened like tree bark. The liquid black eyes blinked in momentary surprise or acknowledgement before resuming an unashamed observation of me. I sneezed and shook the ruff of my pelt, bearing the tips of fangs in quiet warning before I loped away through the underbrush.

I did not travel far, but moved swiftly and much more silently through the woods. I drew near the woodland fringe above Vanaheimr. A small mound crested with trees overlooked the meadows of Fólkvangr and the solid bulk of Valhalla. Glancing up at the towering peak of Hliðskjálf, I heard the steady rhythmic chanting from just below the mound. I cocked my head, listening to the familiar voice of Freyja as she chanted and trying to determine where she was. The faint wisp of smoke drifted past my sensitive nostrils and I realised the mound must have a shallow cavern at the rear. I considered fleeing and returning to Óðinn's side, not wanting Freyja to know I had overheard any of her sacred rites. For although Freyja was a goddess among the Æsir, she was as much a witch as anything else. The rites she practised were those of the *Volva* and the sacred nature of them was well known.

I was about to withdraw into the dense undergrowth of the forest when Freyja's chanting suddenly stopped. I froze, hackles raised on the wolf pelt, body quivering with the need to flee or fight. From the opposite side of the clearing, Freyr stepped into the small grove, an entourage of the Ljósálfar flanking him. The Lord of the Álfheimr greeted Freyja and then approached her. I halted, curiosity warring with sensibility as I heard the hushed tones of the siblings below in the meadow. I should run as fast as the wolf could manage through the forest, but I waited, then crept forward, belly to the ground. Near the edge of the overhang, I stopped, nostrils filling with the scent of Freyja and Freyr below. The Ljósálfar that had accompanied Freyr was invisible to my senses. They had either vanished into the realms between this one and wherever such beings existed, or they cloaked their presence from me. I did not focus on this now but turned my attention to the conversation between the siblings.

"Are you certain?" Freyr asked, alarm in his tone.

There was only silence, then the dry clattering of bones across a stone surface. "I am certain," Freyja coolly replied, as though angered her sibling would doubt her.

"Will you tell Óðinn?" he hissed.

"Better that Óðinn is warned and ignore my advice than I be seen to withhold knowledge."

"The Æsir do not respect your knowledge," Freyr scoffed. "Why would Óðinn even care if you withheld knowledge?"

Freyja sighed. "There are many games afoot, Freyr. I don't expect you to understand them all," she said unkindly.

He sucked in a breath and hissed a curse at her, but said nothing more.

"Don't be petulant," she reprimanded. "I must go to Óðinn and warn him of Skaði's vengeance."

Soft leather boots crunched on soil and I saw a shadow block the mouth of the grotto.

"You have few allies in this world, Freyja. Don't be foolish enough to treat me with disrespect again. If you wish the Æsir undone and blood truly paid at Ragnarök, be kind to your brother."

Freyja snorted, her boots echoing purposefully toward the cavern opening. There was a sharp scuffle, and I edged slightly closer to the overhang, hanging my muzzle in the air to catch the scent of what occurred below. I could smell anger and lust, the rough sounds of Freyr as he pressed himself upon Freyja. There had been many rumours that the siblings were often lovers, but such incestuous claims never truly known. As I pressed my belly closer to the mossy earth, ears flicking and nostrils flaring, I learnt all the knowledge I might require to claim such rumours were true.

When I was certain the couple were more engrossed with each other than aware of their surroundings, I inched backward from the overhang and disappeared into the dense forest once more. There were many things I could accuse Freyja of being but a witch was one of the least concerning. If I had understood Freyr's accusations of his sister, Freyja was involved in a plot seeking revenge upon the Æsir at Ragnarök. I wondered again if she had been involved in my near-demise in Ginnungagap.

In wolf form, I loped through the quiet forest, pushing heedlessly through the dense bracken and thick undergrowth. The trills of small birds and the distant noise of startled prey were constant sparks of interest to the wolf's senses, but I tried to focus my mind. There was nothing in this world or any of the worlds that came without drawbacks. Everything needed equilibrium. Negatives must balance all positives. Using animal forms was not any different and so I borrowed the strengths of the wolf but must accommodate the weaknesses too. The wolf was a silent and swift master of the forest, but it was also a skilful hunter and so distractions bombarded my senses as I moved through the woodland. Around me, I was aware of the shifting shadows and silent movements of the Ljósálfar and the other beings of Álfheimr. I paid them no heed, picking up the pace as I hurried to reach Óðinn with my warning about Freyja. I knew she would inform him of Skaði's approach, but I feared her machinations might be too subtle for Óðinn to realise until it was too late.

I thought I knew why Freyja might seek to bring the Æsir to their knees. If I was correct, it explained why she sought to cleave me from Óðinn's side. I recalled those events from Valhalla when Gullveig had offered her skills and warning to the Æsir and how they had persecuted her, how Óðinn had destroyed that form, burning her upon the hearth for daring to oppose him. In those days, I had feared his actions were wrong and blind to what Gullveig could offer him. Óðinn had been younger then, proud and determined to master the Nine Worlds, and he resented the knowledge Gullveig obviously had, which he did not. Ever since that moment, Óðinn had sought knowledge, as if he could prevent the warnings Gullveig had uttered that night. I alone had recognised Gullveig for what she was, a powerful *völva*, the words she spoke upon the hearth three times the weaving of a curse. Instinctively, I think Óðinn knew the power behind those words, and it terrified him. Since then, he'd strived to learn everything that might prevent the curse Freyja had laid upon him.

Ahead, the forest broke into the wildflower meadows of Fólkvangr and I slowed to a trot. I continued across the plains, the shoulder-length grass hiding me from the view of the gods gathered around the mighty hall of Valhalla. I knew only Heimdallrr would know of my approach, for his senses missed nothing, and so it did not surprise me when the god gave a shout of challenge and greeting. Carefully, I approached the watchman of the Æsir, eyeing him cautiously, noticing the knives and axes strapped to his bulky form, the leather breastplate adorned with finely wrought gold that glittered in the evening light. Heimdallrr watched me skirt slowly around him, the broad-shouldered god smiling and crossing his massive arms over his chest. In response, I gave him a lop-sided, wolfish grin before continuing to the cluster of gods near Óðinn's hall.

Thor held a massive beaker of ale, shouting a challenge to one of Óðinn's chosen warriors. The warrior, for all his impressive bulk, glanced a little nervously at the ale before nodding and shouting his acceptance to Thor. The red-haired god boomed with good-natured laughter and thrust the skull-sized goblet at the warrior. I skirted the assembled gods and warriors, the boasting and drinking likely to continue well into the evening. The bonfires had been lit, already throwing sparks and spirals of embers high into the dark sky.

I finally found Óðinn and Frigg seated a little apart from the festivities, the two leaders of the Æsir, in hushed conversation. I wove through the clustered groups of revellers, seeking the shadows where I might quietly shift my form but felt Óðinn's bright gaze on me as I disappeared into the darkness beyond the great hall, conscious of him speaking a quiet word to wolves beside his seat. He knew I had returned and would seek him out.

Around the opposite side of Óðinn's massive hall, I found the deep darkness I needed. The shifting of form from man to wolf was relatively effortless, but I could not say the same for reverse transformation. I lowered my head, focusing on the form I wished to assume, allowing the power to flow into my limbs. A soft growl rumbled through my broad chest, lifting my lips in a snarl as the magic arched my spine, pulling muscles and tendons as my limbs assumed an upright stance. I panted heavily, the wolf pelt disappearing patchily to reveal human skin between shortening hair. Another growl and snarl broke my lips, muzzle shortening and flattening as sweat broke across the skin, exposed to the cold air even as my paws lengthened into hands and feet, fingers and nails replacing claws.

The power within me surged, completing the transformation, and I staggered across the thick wooden planks of Valhalla. I stood there, sweat chilling on my bare skin as trembling shook my body. I fought to regain control of my form and my senses as a human understanding of the worlds returned to me. That was when I realised the commotion from the nearby festivities.

I ran from the shadows, the sudden demand to use my human form causing me to lurch and stagger uncertainly across the open space toward Óðinn. I saw Freyja's golden hair adorned with glittering jewels and the stamping host of mounted Valkyries in the field behind her. Was I too late?

"Óðinn," I shouted, my voice gruff and uneven.

The one-eyed god turned, lifting a shaggy eyebrow to regard me without comment.

"I think I preferred you as a wolf," Freyja said sharply, gaze roaming unnervingly across my naked body.

"We all know what you prefer," I snapped, ignoring her. "Or, should I say, who you prefer?"

She rolled her eyes, long nails tapping a faster beat against her chain mail-clad arm. "Why do you keep him around?" she asked Óðinn.

Óðinn shrugged, placing a hand reassuringly over Frigg's where it rested on the arm of her chair. "He's amusing."

"Hm," she replied, unconvinced. "He nearly cost your life and those under your protection. You have a strange idea of amusement."

Óðinn shrugged again, patting Frigg's hand in a way meant to tame her notorious anger and hatred for Freyja.

"You think Skaði would be so foolish to invade Asgard to avenge her father?" Óðinn finally asked, reclining back in his seat.

"I know this to be true," Freyja replied, glacially. "The power of a *volva* has always been mine to command."

Óðinn made a noncommittal harrumph and returned his shrewd attention to me. "What did you want, Loki?"

"She's speaking the truth," I blurted, eyes widening in shock at what I had instinctively said. "I saw her practising the arts of *seiðr*."

"Hm," he replied, considering the best course of action against the giantess. "Skaði might be her father's daughter, but she is untried in battle. I don't think she could match us even if she desires to bleed Asgard until it rains out blood in Niflheimr."

"What do you propose, then?" Freyja asked crisply.

"We see what demands the new Lady of Jötunheimr makes of us."

"Wait," I shouted, reaching imploringly toward Óðinn.

"No," he snapped, blue eye seeming to spark with rage. "Freyja is right. I have not yet forgiven you for the treachery you showed us. I may never forgive it, Loki."

I let my hand fall, standing mute and uncomprehending as Óðinn strode away from me. Of the gods who followed, only introspective Týr gave me a backward glance.

Chapter 10
Skaði's Vow

I stood outside Valhalla until full dark clung to the uneven hollows of the meadows and an owl in the forest cried in victory of prey caught. I shook my limbs, awakening myself to the chill evening wind plucking at my naked flesh. I could not understand how Óðinn could be so blind to Freyja's machinations. Did he think Freyja at odds with her former beliefs when she used the name Gullveig and came to Valhalla as a witch pronouncing doom to the gods? Surely he did not imagine everything in the Nine worlds was malleable to his will? I spluttered in laughter, teeth chattering with cold. Of all the beings less malleable to Óðinn's will, Freyja was at the top.

Forcing my stiff limbs to move, I shuffled toward the big open doorway to the hall. Already the scent of roasting meat, stew and warm mead was tantalisingly close. I staggered toward the doorway, grasping one of the support posts to keep my numb feet from pitching me into the dirt.

"We really should consider making some clothing compulsory," Baldr drawled from the cluster of men near the doorway.

I met his bright gaze. "Then you won't mind providing suitable attire for a fellow traveller?"

Baldr scoffed. "In return for what?"

I bowed my head in feigned gratitude. "In return for the humble storytelling skills I might offer. A few amusing tales to inspire laughter and keep darkness from this hall?'

Baldr shivered as though a chill breeze had brushed him. His brother Höðr bent closer and whispered something inaudible. I cocked my head to regard the blind god, the only god among the Æsir who was without any sight. Baldr glanced at me and shoved Höðr's arm in jest, a playful smile on his lips.

"My brother says you may take what clothing you can win from those assembled here tonight. If your stories please us, we will provide you with an item from our person."

I grinned, knowing the fact that the blind god couldn't see me didn't seem to matter. "A deal."

In the hours that passed from when I entered Valhalla, I sang songs and spun riddles for the gods. It was near midnight when I had claimed enough clothing to be almost fully dressed.

"What is the bet?" Óðinn raised his tankard to salute me.

I bowed my head, bare chest still covered in a shimmer of sweat after performing acrobatics for a set of fine daggers Týr carried at his hips.

"More!" Thor bellowed above the musicians and raucous behaviour of the hall.

I glanced quickly at the open doorway, a sliver of precognition warning me of approaching danger. I made to move forward but Thor's massive arm shot out and blocked my path, his dark eyes fixed on mine.

"I said *again*," he whispered in deadly seriousness.

"Oh," I breathed, bowing my head in fear and a small part annoyance.

"Let me ask a question," Óðinn said softly from his high-backed chair.

I inclined my head slight, knowing I was exempt from the laws binding the Æsir to always speak truthfully when answering a direct question. Did Óðinn know this? Did he perhaps only suspect it?

"Why do you insist Skaði will seek vengeance?"

"The giants are a proud race," I whispered. "You know better than any of us gathered here. The giants and the gods have gone to war in the past for much less than this situation. The strongest of the giants has been killed by our hands. This will not be well accepted in Jötunheimr."

"You sound like you claim kinship with them," he said quietly. "But you renounced ties with the giants when you walked upon the fertile lands of Vanaheimr."

"Do not question my loyalty," I snapped. "I owe my gratitude to you, Óðinn but I am still kin to the giants, no matter how I might wish to renounce it sometimes. They are an uncouth rabble," I smiled.

Óðinn inclined his head. "You do owe me, Loki," he agreed, gaze remaining wintry. "I am prepared for Skaði."

"Oh?" I asked.

"Yes," he smiled. "Your kin always want what they do not have."

"Which is what?" I asked, frowning.

"Exactly what you sought from me," he said, a mirthless chuckle. "Beauty."

My lips flattened into a line, but I bowed my head, acknowledging Óðinn had beaten me. There was a dangerous note that thrummed beneath his words, a warning that his anger and suspicion were raised against me, and I'd best be careful lest I become impaled upon them. If he would not hear my words, then I could not save him from the snare Freyja was tightening around him. I held Óðinn's gaze a final time, then gave a jerk of my head and sauntered to an empty corner of the hall, prepared for Skaði's arrival.

The howls of Óðinn's wolves echoed through the evening, silencing conversation in the hall. I looked up from my steepled fingers to regard Óðinn. The god gave me a smirk, not pausing in his stride to open the main doors of Valhalla. The gods gathered closer to the central hearth, whispering quietly, a few elbowing each other with subdued chuckles. I watched Thor step to his father's side, shifting his massive frame to block the doorway completely. I could hear Óðinn's voice from outside, his words dramatic but laying the rules for Skaði's presence in Asgard. The laws of host-guest relationships were held with great pride among the Æsir. I glanced at the flicking firelight from the central hearth as I recalled the one time their laws of host-guest relationship had been broken: The night the witch Gullveig walked into Valhalla and laid the curse upon Óðinn.

I shifted in my seat, still unable to see anything around the gods crowding the hall. Sighing, I stretched and began my slow progress through the press of bodies, sidestepping conversations and gestures that threatened to toss mead on me. When at last I manoeuvred my way to the front of the hall, I lingered behind Thor, his massive bulk hiding me from view. I waited, observing Skaði while she could not see me. If Freyja was correct, Skaði was here to claim revenge for the death of Thiazi. I had been the one to betray an oath with her father and I would answer for his untimely death.

"Loki?" Óðinn asked, a chuckle barely disguised in his voice. "Loki is not a killer."

I peered behind Thor to stare at Skaði. She was a tall woman, long-limbed with muscular shoulders and a body that was accustomed to wielding a sword. Her white hair was long, not braided, but hung loosely down her back. Her sharp blue eyes were glacial pools as, unsmiling, she regarded Óðinn.

"Loki is as much a killer as you and I," Skaði said quietly. "I will have his head."

Óðinn pursed his lips together. "Loki's treachery must be paid to us first."

Skaði straightened her shoulders. "I will not leave without Loki's blood."

I sighed and stepped out from behind the shelter of Thor's arm. I heard Skaði hiss in her breath, lips parted like a cat finally seeing the prey.

"I am rather attached to my head," I said, grinning. "I can spare some blood— but not much. You can't be greedy when Óðinn has claim to some as well."

My words were carefully spoken, to offer Skaði reasons to negotiate with Óðinn and remind Óðinn that our bonds had been made in blood many eons ago.

A cobalt eye met mine. "I do have prior claim," Óðinn said to Skaði, spreading his hands in a helpless gesture. "But let me offer you recompense?"

Skaði arched her eyebrows. "There can be little recompense other than the vengeance I seek."

Óðinn shrugged. "Then let me offer you the comfort of my hall according to Guest Laws. Let us negotiate our prices for vengeance in comfort."

"How charming," I snarled, glaring at Óðinn.

The god ignored me and opening his arms, ushered Skaði toward the brightly lit hall. The smell of roasting meat and spiced mead filled the large room. Seated at his usual place by the hearth, Bragi plucked the lyre, the music drifting like a haunting promise.

Skaði glanced back at her troops. I noticed the mass of giants waiting silently in the cold night air. The giants from Thiazi's fortress were beings of frost and ice and looked neither troubled nor uncomforted by the cold night air. The wind tore at the thick pelts they wore about their bodies and rattled the ice-encrusted chain-mail armour.

"Thor," Óðinn bellowed, one hand beckoning his son forward as he simultaneously led Skaði indoors. "See Lady Skaði's troops are attended. Tonight, we will discuss recompense among our races and let justice be done."

"Justice at my expense?" I asked loudly, hesitating near the doorway.

Óðinn's eyes narrowed slightly and I thought for a moment he might renege on our ancient pact.

"You owe me and Skaði equally," he reminded me.

I glanced to the open ground stretching across the dew-covered meadows of Fólkvangr. I could flee. If I changed, I could probably outrun Óðinn's wolves. Behind me, Thor growled, and his massive hand tightened around my upper arm, gripping me with crushing efficiency.

"Let us negotiate," Óðinn called, taking Skaði's arm and leading her among the assembled Æsir. I struggled weakly in Thor's grip until he shook me, his slight movement causing my limbs to flap like boneless rabbits. Rattled, I only recovered my senses when Thor dropped me into a hardbacked chair, seated immediately beside Óðinn, Skaði on my left. Without comment, Thor slid into the chair on my right, stretching his long legs toward the hearth. I regarded the Æsir without comment, massaging my many bruises and my pride.

Óðinn did not speak, and Thor continued to watch the hearth flames as though the answers to all problems were within them. The corners of my lips twisted as I considered that for Thor, this might be the case. The god was often ridiculed among the Æsir and giants for his willingness to make combat a resolution to any issue. From the corner of my eye I watched him, considering how his famous fiery temper was so similar to that of the giants of Múspelheim. Thor may claim hatred of the giants but without us, the god had no skill among the Æsir. He was prized only for his absolute strength in battle; not having the skill of Týr nor the strategy of Óðinn, Thor was a berserker without comparison.

I let my gaze slide beyond Óðinn, conscious of how he watched me without obvious intent. Instead, I turned my unguarded attention to Skaði. The frost giant sat straight in her chair, hands dangling from the armrests with feigned casualness that was belied by her erect posture and grim face. Skaði was a huntress and never known for her joyful abandon but in Valhalla tonight, she looked foreboding. I shivered, as if touched by the sorrow and thirst for vengeance that consumed her. How did Óðinn hope to turn this woman away from battle? I recognised in Skaði the resoluteness I had seen in Freyja when she led the Valkyries. The power of the shield-maidens was calm and remote, so contrary to the frenzy and rage of berserkers.

Óðinn continued to stare into the hearth flames before he spoke quietly. "Skaði, it does the Æsir and giants no good to wage war. Will you not join me and seek a truce?"

Skaði's features did not soften as she turned her pale blue gaze on Óðinn. "What could you offer me that blood will not repay?"

I momentarily tensed, then forced my body to relax, hunching my shoulders and sliding down in the high-backed chair to make myself less of a target.

Óðinn's cobalt gaze held the ice blue as he considered her words. "Bloodshed has never ended our grievances before."

"I do not seek an end to our disagreements, only to settle the current one."

Thor stiffened beside me, and I stole a furtive glance at the war-god. His features were half-shadowed by firelight, but I could see the anger kindling in his eyes. He would gladly take to the battlefield to shed the blood of giants and if Skaði wished blood payment, Thor would make her pay it.

I sighed and yawned extravagantly, reaching my arms wide and purposefully slapping the back of Thor's head as I stretched. As I intended, my movement broke the tension growing between the huntress and the All-Father. I smiled languidly at Óðinn and tilted my chin toward Bragi, who continued to pluck at the lyre, his posture relaxed beside the hearth. Although he was beyond earshot of our conversation, I had noticed the quick glances he stole toward Óðinn and Skaði when he thought he was unobserved.

"Let us bargain for a truce," Óðinn pressed, using my distraction to break the anger that had been steadily growing.

Skaði sighed, regarding the leader of the Æsir as though he were treating her as a simpleton. I did wonder if he had underestimated the huntress from Jötunheimr. Thiazi had been the strongest of the frost giants and held the throne of those icy lands for as long as many had memory. I could not imagine his daughter was a fool.

"What do you propose?" Skaði asked, her tone full of spite as she considered Óðinn. "Will you make me an offer like you made Loki? I lack the vanity where promises of beauty might persuade me to forsake my kin and bind myself to you. Or would you offer me a trade like you once did with the Vanir? Again, I am not foolish enough to think you will trade your best men for those among mine. I cannot think of anything you might offer me that I would accept."

Óðinn nodded, considering her words as he chewed upon his lip. "In all those cases except for the pact with Loki, the trade has been unfairly made," he conceded. "What if I offered you a fair trade?" he asked.

Skaði lifted her brows. "I am not a fool," she snapped, offended and already gathering the edges of her cloak tighter about her.

"Wait, Skaði of Jötunheimr," Óðinn called, halting her movement as she made to stand. "I offer you the choice of a valid truce, a pact made between the giants and the Æsir, an equal sharing of our lands and strengths bound by marriage."

Thor had abruptly ceased the restless fidgeting with his knife blades and now glared at Óðinn. "What?" He stood, and his features darkened with anger.

Óðinn continued to Skaði, ignoring the outburst. "Does my offer interest to you?"

Skaði's cool gaze assessed Óðinn before she spoke. "What are the finer details of your offer?" she asked.

Óðinn leaned back in his chair and was silent while he pretended to consider. I knew Óðinn better than any of the Æsir in Valhalla and I understood his pause was strategic only. He had manoeuvred Skaði into this bargain and he knew exactly what he would offer her. I think Skaði understood the actions but Óðinn was a master of strategy, moving people like game pieces.

"It was Loki's deception that resulted in your father's death and as Loki is under my protection, I have wronged you," Óðinn said, smiling sadly while Bragi's music drifted through the hall. "You may choose any of those here as your husband."

Thor pursed his lips, but I felt the rage radiating from him, noticed the tension in his shoulders and the stiffness of his features as he turned, and without further comment, strode away from Óðinn.

CHAPTER 11
TRICKERY

Skaði met Óðinn's gaze and nodded stiffly. He smiled, and the lines on his weathered face crinkled but no emotion reflected in his cobalt eye. I watched the exchange between the leader of the Æsir and the new leader of the frost giants with a sinking heart. Whatever game Óðinn was playing with Skaði, I knew her youth could not match the skill of his experience but there was an unbending quality to Skaði that was terrifying. The giantess had been manipulated by Óðinn and I understood she'd expected such an event. There was an ageless wisdom in her decision not to attempt an out-manoeuvring of Óðinn, a logical realisation such an effort was a wasted expense. Skaði was like the glaciers that surrounded her fortress home of Thyrmheim, she was unyielding and unhurried in the way she pressed her attack on Óðinn. Here was a leader of the giants who was unlike the predecessors. Skaði was more dangerous than I had ever realised. Did Óðinn grasp the danger of this enemy? I had no doubts he'd try to manipulate Skaði, turn his offer into a win for himself. I had fears that such an event would make a permanent enemy of Skaði: her trust, once broken, wouldn't be regained.

Suddenly, Óðinn stood and with a nod to Skaði, he clapped his hands together and in response, an immediate silence fell upon Valhalla. The warriors seated at long benches paused with goblets raised, about to toast to the continued fortune of those favoured by Óðinn. Even in the uncertain silence that blanketed the hall, I repressed the desire to laugh. The command Óðinn had over the assembled Æsir, the Vanir and even the host who had travelled with Skaði, was complete. Finally, I could not help myself and belched into the silence, the noise echoing in the vacuum of sound with an irreverence that delighted me. Frigg stared at me from the opposite side of the hall and Thor's brows drew tightly together with anger. Óðinn only grinned at me with shared amusement. In that singular moment, I found some relief that the god I had bargained with many worlds ago was still the leader of the Æsir tonight.

"Tonight, I welcome Skaði of Thyrmheim into Valhalla and extend the honour of my hall and rights of host and guest laws to her," Óðinn began in a quiet voice that carried through the silence. "I take responsibility for the wrongs committed by one of my own, such an act that took the life of one of hers and took a father from a daughter."

I lounged in the high-back chair, feigning nonchalance at the whispers and insults that passed about the hall, the very mention of my betrayal a fresh wound to the proud Æsir, and I knew many were disgusted that Óðinn still considered me among them.

"I extend my regret to the giantess Skaði and offer to make reparations for the actions of our own," Óðinn continued, lifting his voice above the furious whispering of the assembled gods. "I offer Skaði the choice of any husband among those assembled here."

A stunned silence replaced the respectful silence of earlier and even I still struggled to come to terms with what Óðinn proposed. The only previous attempt to unite the giants and the Æsir had failed with me. I could not console how my actions could be forgotten. In light of my recent betrayal, Óðinn's proposed terms for reconciliation seemed utterly absurd.

Óðinn turned to Skaði and bowed, hand over his heart as he spoke so everyone in Valhalla could hear. "You have the right to choose a husband from any assembled here," he said with solemnity. "There is but one condition I place as my right as host."

Skaði quirked her brow. "What is your condition?" she asked, clearly unsurprised.

Óðinn smiled mischievously. "You must choose your husband only by viewing his feet."

Skaði pursed her lips, but if she was confused or surprised by the oddness of the condition Óðinn requested, she made no comment.

"Do you accept my law as host?" Óðinn asked, eye glittering with challenge.

Skaði nodded simply. "If I may make a request under the Guest-Law?" she asked and when Óðinn nodded his assent, she continued. "I will abide by the host-law if you meet the condition I place under the Guest-Law."

"What is your demand?" growled Thor from somewhere near the back of the assembled gods.

Skaði turned her remote gaze toward the impetuous god. "If any assembled here can take the sorrow of my father's death and make me laugh, I will fasten my hand willingly to an Æsir."

The silence that followed Skaði's proclamation was heavy. The giantess was known to have little mirth within her and I could not think of a single moment I had ever heard stories of Skaði's laughter. I was not sure she could laugh. I sunk deeper into my own thoughts as absently I heard Óðinn agree to Skaði's terms. I hunkered down in the high-backed chair and wondered, if a glacier could laugh, would it sound like cracking ice or be sweet like the first meltwater?

I watched from my position beside the central hearth as Óðinn clapped his hands. There had been no conversation, whispered or otherwise, since Skaði had issued her own challenge. I smiled ruefully at the giantess who dared challenge Óðinn in his own hall. I would have been more interested in the outcome of who Skaði selected as a husband if I knew such a venture was never going to occur. If my own death was not likely to be called for when Óðinn and Skaði failed to meet an agreement. I glanced toward the doors leading from the hall, but they were secured and barred. Two of Óðinn's chosen warriors stood on either side of the massive oak doors just in case I somehow managed to slip the sturdy bar from its place. These measures seemed extreme even to me and I wondered if Óðinn had gone so far as to lock the doors. Did he carry the keys on his belt? I glanced surreptitiously toward the All-Father, trying to see if the glint of the large bronze keys shone at his hip. His belt was a cluster of leather pouches, mead horns, blades and empty sheaths. If a set of keys were contained within the assortment of items, I could not easily see them. Sighing in frustration, I scrunched down deeper into my chair, willing the shadows to engulf me.

On the far side of the hall, Óðinn had assembled the Æsir and Vanir alike. He spoke quietly to the host, gesturing to the unmarried men among them to separate themselves and stand apart. Despite my intention to ignore the proceedings, my curiosity was piqued, and I watched Skaði's eyes follow Baldr with keen interest and undisguised lust. It seemed Óðinn was right that the giants craved beauty in a way we could not deny. Petulantly, I flicked a piece of sawdust into the rushes at my feet. One of Óðinn's wolves looked up from where it had been dozing to regard me curiously before returning to doze beside the fire-pit.

I muttered beneath my breath, choice curses and nonsense as Óðinn playfully asked Skaði's permission to bind her eyes. He gestured grandly to the men assembled beside the hearth and made elaborate jokes about his own blindness. Skaði barely smiled but allowed herself to be blindfolded briefly. In the moments Skaði was blindfolded, Frigg ushered from the shadows Sif and Sigyn, a long-woven cloth between them. They stood in front of the assembled men, blocking from Skaði's view everything of Baldr and the other men, all but their feet. Grumbling, the men kicked off their boots and stood barefoot upon the rushes.

"Choose your new husband," Óðinn cried to the applause of the assembled Æsir.

Skaði pulled the blindfold from her head, shaking her blond locks free of it and stared with deepening frown at the dark woven cloth, impenetrable as fog at night. I smiled a little, marvelling at the skill Frigg had taken to weave the cloth in such a short time. My amusement died as I watched Skaði's features shift from an almost-smile to a darkening frown, her brows drawing together in growing displeasure. The giantess had no way of knowing which of these feet belonged to Baldr, which belonged to the man she really wanted as her husband. It was a cruel joke, as cruel as Óðinn had ever devised, and it stung me a little to consider his words to me about how the giants prized beauty above all else, the thing which we did not possess. That one thing which I had craved many worlds ago when I first saw Óðinn in his youthful glory and saw the majesty of the Nine Worlds. I had wanted to move among that beauty and be part of it. Óðinn had gifted it to me, binding me to him with what seemed like kindness at the time. Now, I wondered if it had been a jest all along.

"Who do you choose, Lady of Thyrmheim?" Óðinn was magnanimous, as if he offered Skaði a fair bargain.

She scanned the choices before her from the dirty and callused feet of one man, the bronzed and smooth feet of another, to the scraped and pale feet of the third. A slight smile, barely a whisper on her lips, signalled she had made a decision and felt confident in her choice.

"The golden feet are by far the most beautiful and can only belong to one man," Skaði said with triumph. "I choose him."

Óðinn's smile broadened and he clapped his hands in loud applaud. I felt my heart constrict for I knew the truth before Frigg let the magic weaving of the cloth dissolve. I closed my eyes as the cloth disappeared into fine mist to reveal Skaði's new husband. Skaði drew in a hiss of shock that sounded like the air accompanying an avalanche. Baldr smiled apologetically and shrugged his pale feet back into boots, and even Heimdallrr seemed to cast his eyes downward as he pulled boots over his calluses, Njörðr looked embarrassed, the god of the sea glancing at his feet momentarily and then at Skaði with what might have been a shameful apology.

"We have a final bargain to be fulfilled before our feud is settled," Skaði reminded Óðinn, voice foreboding and chill.

I stared at Óðinn for a long moment, observing the All-Father while he contemplated Skaði. The long moment of silence drew into several, stretching endlessly as the Æsir began to shift restlessly. I continued to hold my unwavering gaze on Óðinn. What was he planning to do now? How did he think to escape the impending battle between the giants and the Æsir? A thought came unbidden to me, the chill of it far more deadly that the frosty smile of victory that tugged at Skaði's lips, making them twitch slightly. Did Óðinn actually plan to escape this feud? Or was this entire spectacle a melodrama for his own enjoyment? I decided I did not care. Grumbling, I pushed myself upright, heaving my body upright. Óðinn might desire battle but I wanted to keep my head firmly attached to my neck for as long as I could.

I sighed dramatically. My abrupt movement and the explosive sound of my frustrated sigh echoed louder than I'd intended and drew the attention of the Æsir and Skaði alike. I stood a moment, awkwardly caught mid-stretch. I rolled my eyes, completed the stretch with exaggerated effort, flexing my torso to reveal taut muscles.

"You didn't see my feet," I said, waggling my eyebrows at Skaði. "Want to take a peek?"

Thor snorted from somewhere in the background, the sound dispelling tension in the hall. "If we got away with just seeing your feet, we'd consider ourselves lucky," he said, pouring another cup of mead.

"Consider yourselves unlucky then," I replied, bowing to Skaði and turning slightly to address Óðinn. "Might I accept this challenge on your behalf?"

Óðinn's bright eye held mine. "You have always been counted among us," he reminded me.

I spun theatrically to face Skaði. "Let's make you laugh," I said, and gestured to Bragi beside the hearth. "Then we can organise the hand-fastening."

"Wait," Skaði called, voice cool and commanding. "You have not succeeded yet."

"True," I said, grinning slightly. I gestured toward the two warriors standing beside the barred doors. "Fetch me a goat."

"A goat?" one of the men stammered, looking to Óðinn for reassurance.

Óðinn merely shrugged. "Whatever Loki requires," he answered, gesturing helplessly.

"Hurry up then," I snapped, flapping my hands after the confused warriors.

"Where exactly is this going?" Óðinn asked me as I began to tug off my tunic.

"Consider it my debt repaid," I snarled, hopping around in a circle as I pulled off one boot and then another.

Skaði watched me warily, uncertain and clearly unsure if she was being made a fool. When I stood barefoot in only my breeches, I looked at my long toes buried in the rushes and wiggled them for effort. Skaði raised an imperious eyebrow at me.

"I am not so stupid as to treat the giants like fools," I replied quietly as a protesting goat was dragged into the hall by its horns. "I am stupid enough to treat myself like a fool, though," I explained.

The warriors stopped a few paces from me, warily staring at me half-dressed and untying my hair from a leather thong. I smiled broadly at the warriors, men who had died valiantly in battle but were clearly uncomfortable around me.

"Loki," Óðinn began, stepping toward me and reaching out a hand.

"Thanks to you, All-Father," I whispered, balancing my elbow in his outstretched hand as I shrugged out of my breeches. There was an audible gasp from the room, a loud snort of laughter from Thor and a muttered curse from Freyja.

"I understand that I am the epitome of masculine magnificence," I began to a chorus of mixed chuckles and giggles. I walked forward to the goat that eyed me suspiciously, the long leather thong I used to tie my hair uncurling in my hand. I kept talking to the crowd, speaking with perfect ease as I mocked myself and offered platitudes to Skaði. I looped the end of the thong about the horns of the goat and patted the beast on the head.

"You couldn't have got one with smaller horns?" I asked the warriors.

Both men looked startled and glanced quickly to Óðinn, again for reassurance. I watched Skaði while I spoke, trying to gauge which tactics of humour best came close to breaking her closely guarded heart.

"Don't look at Óðinn," I shouted at the men, making them jump, and saw Skaði's lips twitch toward a smile.

My own grin deepened at that sight and I knew what I needed to do. It wasn't going to be pleasant, or even amusing, for me. It was the discomfort and uncertainty of these warriors and even the Æsir that Skaði found most amusing. Perhaps it was even the fact that a child of Múspelheim created such havoc and chaos in their sense of order that only Óðinn could provide relief from it. I would take the risk. And risk it was.

I sucked in a breath, trying to calm my shaking hands and think of something else, like a beautiful woman. No, that could be disastrous. I kept my mind blank, looped the other end of the leather cord around my exposed scrotum and lifted my face to regard the warriors.

The two men stared in dumbstruck disbelief. I winked at the warriors and tapped the goat on the rump slightly, but it only rolled an eye at me in annoyance. I kicked the beast more firmly with my bare foot, hoping to make it move slightly. The goat stared belligerently at me, tossed the massive, curled horns of its head and backed up. The pain was sharper than I'd imagined. I moved like coals had been tossed at my back, following the goat as it retreated across the open space of the hall.

Glancing up from the goat, I realised it was making a steady line for the warriors who had brought it into the hall. I considered it probably hoped the men would release it from whatever insane torment this was and silently promised to feed the goat warm oats after its ordeal. I held my arms outstretched toward the warriors who visibly paled, not wanting to be part of this jest either.

"Mighty warriors," I called, arms outstretched to them as I made whimpering gasps of pain, following the goat as fast as I could. "Óðinn's most valiant warriors, rescue me?"

The raucous amusement of the gathered Æsir immediately subsided into choked laughter when I spoke. The warriors halted, clearly caught between desperate desire to flee from me and insecurity over what Óðinn might demand of them.

"Will not Óðinn's proudest warriors rescue one of his own?" I cried in hopping gasps toward the men.

Óðinn was laughing into his mead goblet, Thor doubled over with tears running down his ruddy cheeks, glistening in his beard. Even Freyja laughed, her beautiful face lit with amusement as she clutched at Freyr's arm for support, her other hand holding her side from obvious spasms of laughter. I turned to Skaði, seeing her smile genuinely for the first time, her eyes bright like the melting ice I'd imagined.

"Lady Skaði," I cried, entreating the giantess. "What say you?"

Skaði laughed then, a short but melodic laugh like the cracking of glacial ice and the first fall of meltwater. She wiped at an isolated tear on her pale cheek. "I say rescue him," she shouted.

The Æsir surrounding Óðinn lifted their goblets in a shout of agreement. The two warriors looked uncertainly at each other before Óðinn nodded and they stepped toward me. I pushed them away but made certain they held the goat while I untied the thong. I glanced at my swollen manhood and considered it was not the swelling I was accustomed to. I cursed and gestured for one of the useless warriors to collect my breeches. I wasn't certain if I could walk without wincing, wasn't sure I wanted the audience to see just how high the price of their amusement was this night.

I remained in the shadows, gingerly dressing myself and ignoring the congratulations offered to Skaði and Njörðr. None could forget Skaði had chosen Baldr as her husband and Óðinn denied her by trickery. I'd helped Óðinn escape another feud which would have drenched Jötunheimr and Asgard in the blood of both races.

Skaði met my gaze with an icy stare. She'd not forgiven my role in her father's death nor did she forgive my trickery to secure no bloodshed between her and Óðinn. I tipped the contents of the goblet down my throat and hoped I'd gain the wisdom Mimir had promised came with time.

Chapter 12
Forging Resentment

Óðinn arranged the hand-fastening of Njörðr and Skaði to be performed before the sun set on Asgard. I continued to drink heavily, trying to numb my newly acquired injuries, both physical and mental. I had long considered Óðinn my closest companion and trusted him without doubt, but lately it was only doubt that filled my thoughts. I remained near the hearth, nursing my mead and wounded manhood. Baldr approached me, walking with spine straight and shoulders squared as though he went to face a host in battle. I tipped back my head, downing the mead in a single gulp and glowered at him.

"What do you want?" I asked, slurring my words. I wasn't that drunk yet but I accentuated my level of intoxication by squinting up at him.

Baldr stopped a few steps away, uncertain whether to pursue whatever course of action he had been charged with. The occasions when Baldr had willingly sought my aid could be considered rare. Whatever forced him to seek me out now was not his own volition.

"Spit it out," I growled, half-turning away from him. "The Æsir might piss themselves to be close to you, their most beloved one, but I've never seen any reason for it."

Baldr glanced back toward the far side of the hall and I saw Týr give an encouraging punch into the air. I sighed, wondering what horrendous thing was going to beset me now that was so awful Týr had sent Baldr to ask on behalf of the Æsir.

"The hand-fastening ceremony has begun outside," Baldr began, glancing again to Týr for more encouragement. "The fresh evening air is very rejuvenating outside. We wondered if you might not enjoy it while the hall is prepared for the feast?"

I glared at Baldr. "Skaði still bears me ill-fortune," I snarled. "I'd sooner cut off my ear and eat it than displease her by attending this feast," I conceded, climbing wearily to my feet.

Baldr looked relieved that I had agreed to remove myself from the hand-fastening without offering further insult.

"You might be a good man," I agreed, slapping Baldr's broad shoulder as I walked unsteadily around him. "Certainly, you're naive and stupid, but possibly well-intended."

Baldr muttered a half-curse under his breath as I staggered away, weaving unsteadily toward the twilit sky visible between the oak doors open at the farthest end of the hall. Once out of sight from observation by the Æsir, I moved stiffly but without hesitation, throwing aside my feigned intoxication to resume the steadier calm of sobriety.

I prowled the edges of the fields, kicking at clumps of wildflowers with my soft leather boots. The toes would be scuffed and ruined by morning. I sighed and walked deeper through the darkness, drawn to the forest fringe. The half-lights that winked between the trees were a constant curiosity to me and I followed them, my mood darkening as I left the merriment behind.

I was about to step across the boundary of the field and into forest when I heard the soft whine of Óðinn's wolves behind me. I had not realised the two had followed me...*tracked* me? I shook my head. No, they had not tracked me, they had been following me, Óðinn had bid them keep a guard on me. I might choose to shift form into wolf and I had an affinity with the wilder ones; Haiti and Sköll found pleasure in the chaotic hunt just as I did. I turned, meeting the green eyes of Óðinn's wolves watching with an intensity and intelligence that was wolf-like and something more.

"Would you try to prevent me crossing into the forest?" I asked them, lifting an eyebrow.

The closest wolf lifted a lip, a low snarl rumbling from his chest to escape between his sharp teeth. That seemed answer enough. If I tried to do anything Óðinn considered beyond my allowance, the wolves would take me down. I did not doubt Freyja might be called upon to minister to my injuries but it would not prevent Óðinn from maiming me in the first place.

"Fine," I growled, my own voice more feral than any wolf's.

The two wolves lifted their lips at me, snarling in unison before some silent exchange between them broke their challenge. I suspected Óðinn travelled with his wolves tonight and offered his famous guidance. I doubted the wolves appreciated the intrusion to their pack, but they were Óðinn's wolves and perhaps shared his mind as freely as he shared theirs. Shrugging, I turned slowly on my heel and began to walk the perimeter of Fólkvangr, my gaze drifting to the bonfires and celebrations outside Valhalla.

I had not intended to walk all night, but I allowed my thoughts to drift, considering how my return to Asgard had felt so true. I kicked another bunch of wildflowers and missed it entirely, kicking a clod of soil. I stared as the disgorged plant landed near the embers of a bonfire. I stopped, looking about and noticing the landscape for the first time since early evening.

Dawn light was beginning to touch the eastern rim of the sky, Himfraxi long-since vanished from the sky and now Haiti must surely be in pursuit of Sól. The morning was fast approaching, and it had been many hours since the hand-fasting celebrations would have dwindled. Muttering to myself that no one had thought to check on me, I stalked toward the shadowed outline of Valhalla, the rising sunlight behind making a silhouette of Óðinn's hall.

I paused on the threshold. No guards remained on the doors, and an entire army from Jötunheimr could have descended on Valhalla and none of the Æsir been prepared. I smiled at the thought, rubbing my numb hands together with some demented glee as I stepped inside. The hearths were not much more than embers, half-consumed haunches of roasted meat still hung on the spit, and leftover mead and empty goblets and a few discarded loaves of bread remained on the tables. I moved among the sleeping forms of the revellers, where the Æsir and Skaði's host now lay entwined in half-forgotten passion or sprawled in unconscious heaps.

Filling my cold hands with bread and scooping up a discarded knife with a hunk of succulent pork still attached, I prowled around the outskirts of the room. When I had eaten the pork, I stopped beside Thor, his wife Sif's golden hair a shining mass across her husband's broad chest. They had all assumed I would keep them safe, that I would guard these lands while they celebrated the triumph of the clever Æsir over the stupid giant folk from Jötunheimr. Thor was their greatest warrior, feared by the giants and Æsir alike. I squatted beside him, listening to his thunderous snoring and wondering how Sif could sleep through such noise. I wiped the greasy blade on my shirt and smiled. They should never take their security for granted, never forget the gifts I'd offered them and how I had saved them when Skaði's forces could have destroyed Asgard with the Æsir so recently weakened.

I moved the knife blade, quickly grasping Sif's hair. She startled, jerking awake, her elbow digging into Thor's ribs as she sat upright. I used her movement to my advantage, noticing her wide eyes as I held the blade still. I did not cut Sif, nor draw a drop of blood. Sif was a kind woman, a goddess who gave the gift of bounty and summer to us all. I let the blade cut through her golden hair, then tossed the hunk of it onto Thor's lap as I met his enraged gaze.

"Never forget me," I snarled before he hurled me bodily across the room.

I hit the opposite wall of the hall, bouncing off a massive support beam for the upper storey, before landing in a sprawl on the floor. My limbs were a tangled mess, my breath a fiery warning of the broken ribs as I struggled to get upright before Thor could cross the room. I had no hope to recover in time, but I tried. Around me, the room broke into sudden activity and movement. Shouts of alarm warred with outrage, and I heard Óðinn's name called more than once. I squinted one eye open, the room spinning with startling shards of light. I scrabbled to get my hands beneath my chest, spitting blood from my mouth as I heard Thor's heavy footsteps approach. The bellow of rage that erupted from him shook Valhalla, the ground and air trembling with the echo of his anger. Instinctively, and despite the imminent danger, I froze on the floor, unable to move. Thunder growled above Valhalla and Thor stood, legs apart, visibly shaking with rage as he cursed me.

"Thor," I wheezed, reaching a hand toward him as blood dripped from my split brow, trailing down to the end of my nose.

Thor kicked me, his booted foot connecting with my jaw. My head snapped backward and the force of the blow nearly flipped me. I twisted with the impact, turning awkwardly to land on my side. I screamed as my broken ribs impacted with the floor. Darkness consumed my vision but I felt the following kicks tumbling me across the ground. I slid into a chair and lay for a moment, too stunned to move.

"Thor!" Óðinn commanded, voice snapping through the hall, allowing no argument.

I heard a scuffle to my right and turned my head. The dizzying movement made me vomit. I lost consciousness briefly, regaining awareness when Týr dragged Thor away from me again. I stared at the worn boots in front of me, shielding me from another attack. Óðinn's boots, I thought with grim satisfaction. I may have laughed; the idea of Óðinn protecting me from a beating he had willingly let occur only days before seemed funny to me.

"He's like a mad dog," Thor snarled, and I realised he was talking about me.

I laughed more, tears cascading into the cuts on my cheeks, stinging as they mingled with the blood. The throbbing in my skull worsened and I realised dully that Týr was crouched beside me, speaking with the patient voice he used for training hunting dogs and horses. *And mad men,* I thought. I squinted at him. Although his lips were clearly moving, the deepening frown on his face suggested I couldn't hear him. I gestured to my own ear, intending to only touch my ear but smacking my hand into the side of my head. The impact sent another wave of horrible nausea and momentary unconsciousness through me. When my vision and senses returned to me, I was staring at my hand, bright blood on my fingers where I had touched my ear. That probably explained my inability to hear Týr and the awful nausea.

Týr reached beneath my armpits and hauled me to my feet. The hall lurched and swayed horribly. I vomited and dry retched as Týr struggled to keep me on my feet. I could barely determine which way was up. I doubted the roof beams should be where the floor normally was. The sensation was so disconcerting that more tears sprang to my eyes and I regretted my stupidity in cutting off Sif's hair. What had made me do that? Sif was nothing but kind to me, the equality with which she treated me had always been something I cherished. I had intended to anger Thor and cause insult to the greatest warrior among the Æsir. Why then did I choose the hurt Sif in my attempt?

In that moment, the room stopped spinning and the nausea vanished. The horrendous ache in my head suddenly disappeared. I held my hand against Týr's chest, trying to steady myself. Frowning, I looked about the hall, noticing the broken chairs, blood splatter, vomit and discarded items. Those things weren't uncommon after any celebration in this hall but the mark of extreme violence that clung now to Óðinn's hall was unusual. I glanced over Týr's shoulder, also seeing the pale and frightened faces of the Æsir who stood in tight clusters, staring at me with shock and confusion. I saw Óðinn through the half-closed door to Valhalla, watched the broad sweep of his gestures as he spoke to Thor, who paced angrily back and forth outside. I hung my head against Týr's chest.

"Come on," Týr grumbled, not unkindly, shouldering my weight as he manoeuvred me toward a chair. It was one of the few carved, high-backed chairs to remain upright in the hall. He sat me down and regarded me carefully.

I diligently avoided his questioning gaze, seeing Sif standing beside the open doorway to Valhalla, her worried eyes on Thor. She half-turned, conscious of my attention on her now. A slight smile touched her lips, the bright gold of her horribly hacked hair like rays of sunlight as they spiked unevenly around her scalp.

"I will make amends," I promised her. "I will find you such a treasure, finely woven gold-like hair, ringlets of a brilliant lustre until your hair grows back."

CHAPTER 13
SONS OF IVALDI

Breathing quickly, I hurried across the meadows of Fólkvangr, intent on the towering peak crowned by Hliðskjálf and the hidden passages within. I wanted to put as much distance between myself and Thor as I could in case the Æsir changed his mind and decided he'd rather beat me to a pulp after all. Wasting no time, I dashed up the steep incline, soft leather boots slipping on the dewy grass. Ahead of me, the mountain twisted into the sky, Bifröst arching overhead like nothing was amiss.

"Stop, Loki," called Heimdallrr, stepping out from the shadows and dense shrubs where he had been concealed.

"I'm in a real hurry," I explained, trying to side-step the watchman of the gods.

"I can't let you pass," he replied, grasping my wrist in a single, deft movement.

I sighed dramatically, staring at my arm. "I really am in a considerable hurry," I said.

Heimdallrr smiled, relaxed, but the easiness belied the talents of the god. I knew his prowess in battle was equal to any of the Æsir, except perhaps Týr and Thor. "I have no words from Óðinn that I am to let you pass."

I rolled my eyes. "If Óðinn were awake this morning instead of sleeping off the mead and enjoying whatever comely women he bedded, he'd know how desperately I need to move quickly."

Heimdallrr's smile faltered at my slander and his lips tightened into a thin line. He did not reply.

I laughed despite myself. "You truly are comical," I said with merriment, slapping Heimdallrr's shoulder. "When Ragnarök comes and giants attack Asgard, it won't be jokes that we need, anyway."

Heimdallrr's eyes glittered with restrained anger but he still did not speak. Instead, he dragged me toward the hidden passage I had been intending to find.

"Where are you taking me?" I asked, lifting my voice in false concern. "I thought you were doing Óðinn's bidding this morning?"

Heimdallrr glowered at me and pulled aside the tangle of vines that partially covered the narrow fissure in the cliff face. Without further comment, he shoved me toward it. I overbalanced in genuine surprise, tripped on a concealed rock and smacked my forehead into the rough stone surface. Growling in protest, I pushed myself away from the lichen-covered rock and turned to glare at Heimdallrrr. I frowned. The watchman of the gods was gone. I looked quickly about myself, unsure if the repeated blows to my head had caused more than concussion this morning. *No,* I thought, *Heimdallr really has gone.* I rubbed at my wrists, the imprint of his grip still visible, and decided not to challenge the fortunate opportunity offered to me. If Heimdallrr wanted me gone from Asgard and I actually needed to leave, then two events were conspiring to send me on my way this morning. It was the first time in a long while. Without further thought, I squeezed my shoulders through the narrow stone fissure, slipping inside the belly of the mountain, and began my trek into the passageways that would lead me into Svartálfheimr .

I hurried along the dank tunnels that led through the mountain and into the deep, twisting passageways that ran through Yggdrasil, and where caverns opened in the mountain depths, some led into the connecting fissures through the Nine Worlds. Few knew these fissures as I did, and I moved through them with practised speed and familiarity.

At each juncture in the network of passages, I paused and considered my way, the dry and cold air that crept from below drawing me lower into the colossal system of tunnels. These were the caverns and tunnels I had once explored before spying Óðinn beside a glacier-fed spring. I had been fascinated by the young god from that instant when I saw him, spattered in blood from his recent battles with Ymir, the marvellous creation of Midgard surrounding him. There had been beauty and chaos in his actions and I was irresistibly drawn to it and in doing so, I was aware some part of Óðinn recognised its twin in me. In the newly crafted glory of Midgard, covered in the blood of his defeated father and brothers, Óðinn had sculptured my features to reflect the inner beauty he saw in me. Since that moment, with each battle of Ragnarök and the ensuing twilight of the Æsir, I have wondered what might have been if Óðinn had never taken pity of the misshapen giant from Múspelheim.

I negotiated a particularly damp tunnel, slimy water dripping from the sides of the stone as I squeezed my shoulders through a narrow cleft in the rock. Pushing through the crushing pressure of the rock, its closeness and jagged surface, I felt the frigid tendrils of cold air and knew I was very close to Niflheimr. I needed to leave the tunnels here or I would find myself lost in the twisting, chaotic mass of passages, easy prey for the pale dragon Níðhöggr. I shuddered at the thought of the dragon. The sharp claws and rancid breath were enough to turn my stomach but the memory of the pale eyes, nearly translucent, sent uncontrollable panic through my system. There was a bitter, icy touch to the air as I nearly ran through a long stretch of open corridor before stopping suddenly at the far end.

Beyond the narrow expanse of light offered by the tunnel opening waited a solemn rider, mount chewing the bit anxiously. The horse tossed its proud head, white mane like icicles, and its muscled body speckled with hoarfrost. The rider turned her pale face toward me, the battle-axe slung across her back glinting in the dull light. I did not understand why one of Freyja's Valkyries was within the realm of Niflheimr but it sent a shiver through me. I backed away from the tunnel, away from the scrutiny of the Valkyries, and fled. I'd be more willing to meet Níðhöggr than any forces Freyja could have hidden in waiting for me.

At the end of the spur-tunnel, I turned right, hurrying deeper into the darker caverns, the black rock chipped away by axe and by time itself. The tunnel grew narrower as I ran, until the twisting passageway pressed close against my shoulders. Ahead of me, golden light flickered, blossoming brighter, casting the uneven stone at the passage mouth into sharp relief. As I inched closer to the end of the tunnel, shadows stretched toward me like menacing spirits. I stopped, heart hammering as I remembered the Valkyrie on her pale horse. Had Freyja somehow designed this entire scenario as a trap? No, I thought, shaking my head, I was letting fear master me.

I moved hesitantly through the narrow mouth of the tunnel, stepping into a bright cavern illuminated by a massive hearth at one end and populated by many smaller fire-pits. Torches in heavy sconces were secured to the surrounding roughly hewn stone walls.

Immediately I stopped, blinking and dazed in the sudden light. From the other end of the long cavern, I heard a muffled grunt and some heavy piece of metalwork was placed as quietly as possible on stone. I remained unmoving and dazed in the light, letting my senses follow the soft footfalls of a man at the other end of the cavern moved barely audibly. I heard the slight clink of metal as a weapon was lifted from wherever it had rested. I tensed, alert to the sound even as I willed myself to relax, loosen my muscles and be ready to fight, or run if necessary. My eyesight adjusted to the light as the dwarf stepped toward me, heavy mallet held comfortably in his hands.

"Son of Ivaldi," I called, and raised my hand in a gesture of greeting.

"Loki," the dwarf replied gruffly, eyes not wavering from me, the mallet still held ready.

I held my hands up. "I came to make an offer to the greatest of the smiths, the sons of the legendary Ivaldi. But perhaps I am mistaken," I began, glancing about the chamber at the half-completed weapons of finely wrought steel, silver and gold. "This does not look like the work of the greatest of metalsmiths."

"Insult us again and we will smash your skull like a nut," a dwarf threatened from the shadows behind me.

I turned slowly, raising my eyebrows with exaggerated surprise. "There you are," I said with a smile that showed my teeth.

"What do you want, traitor of the Æsir?" the first dwarf growled.

"A tragedy has befallen Sif, and our lady who grants such bountiful harvests weeps for the loss of her wheat-coloured hair. I boldly told Thor that I knew who could shape a magic to replace Sif's hair with natural gold. I told him only the sons of the mighty Ivaldi could create such masterful metalcraft," I explained, my lips twisting with the challenge. "But I shall return to tell Thor I was wrong."

The brothers started forward in unison, their stocky bodies surprisingly swift. I held up my hands, placating them a moment and halting the murderous advance.

"Do the heirs of Ivaldi have the skill to shape such fine magic and metal into a single piece?" I asked.

"We have," the brothers answered.

"I can promise you the enduring gratitude of Thor and his lady Sif in return for your skills," I replied smoothly.

The dwarf lurking in the shadows behind me suddenly strode forward, brushing past me without comment. A hurried conversation ensued between both men. I frowned, realising I could not tell the brothers apart. They eyed me cautiously, glancing my way with quick looks and hurried whispers. At last one of them turned to face me.

"We accept your offer, Loki," the dwarves said, bowing deeply from the waist.

"On one condition," the second brother said, freezing the smile on my face.

"What condition?' I asked, tentatively.

"That you take all the gifts we bestow upon the Æsir to them," the other said in return.

"All the gifts?' I asked, puzzled.

A nod. "Let them not forget Ivaldi's sons so easily. There are many things we can offer the Æsir."

I nodded with a smile. "You have my word," I replied, smiling as I turned. Before I had even left the cavern, the dwarves had stoked the massive hearths, firelight chasing any shadows further from the massive stone chamber as the metalsmiths began their work.

I found a narrow fissure in the stone tunnels not too far from the cavern, but still far enough away from the rhythmic pounding of hammers and the impossible noise and heat of the forge. I settled myself against the rough wall of the tunnel, the stone naturally warm from the constant heat provided by the fiery lands of Múspelheim. These passages led between the Nine Worlds, like veins twisting through the giant form of Yggdrasil, linking the lower and upper worlds. The constant heat of Múspelheim warred with the eternal cold of Niflheimr but somehow the heat permeated throughout the Nine Worlds, a constant where the cold was not. I let the naturally warm stone take the aches and bruises from my muscles, relieve the pain of Thor's recent beating. I sighed, relaxing against the rock, almost longing to visit the fiery depths of my homeland. Almost. There was a reason I had left Múspelheim when Óðinn offered me adventure and a physical form that was not a grotesque parody of the giants. It was no lie that I had desired the beautiful forms of Óðinn and the mortals I watched. The lovely limbs that were graceful and strong, supple like the ash of Yggdrasil itself. My own body had been a thing composed of volcanic rock, black and misshapen. I looked more like the ugly stones that covered the landscape of Midgard than anything else. The misshapen rocks that mortals claimed were trolls who had become caught by sunlight, forever made rigid in stone. I was one of the Jotnar from Múspelheim and we were not beings of solid form. When I had tried to take a physical form in Midgard so I might speak with Óðinn, my fiery nature had become rigid against the air. Óðinn had taken pity on me. A kindness I was certain he regretted on some level now.

I slept a while, warmed by the stone, pain leeching from my body with my worries. I woke much later, head rolled to the side. I opened one eye, surprised by how quiet my surroundings were. The distant sound of hammering from the dwarves had stopped. I could hear nothing from the forge, either. I flicked my gaze around the darkness, still not daring to move in case I was being watched. When I was certain I was alone in the tunnel, I straightened and stretched. The stiff muscles of my shoulders and back complained but then relaxed. I swung my feet from the stone ledge I had propped them against, and flexing my toes inside my soft leather boots, I walked back toward the main chamber where I had first encountered the sons of Ivaldi.

When I stepped into the well-lit cavern, the fire-pit in the central hearth was still burning high and the dwarf brothers were adding the final touches to their pieces. My gaze was drawn instantly to the marvellous creation that lay upon a central stone slab, a delicate coiled net of gold, the metal crafted so finely it really did resemble hair. The piece made for Sif was a masterful mesh of interlocking golden chains, held together at the sides by finely wrought coils of the same metalwork that made the delicate curls. The dwarf brothers were adding the final inscriptions and details to three other items they had made for the Æsir.

"You have clearly outdone any expectations the gods may have had," I said, admiring Sif's headdress. "This is beautiful."

"It is more than just beauty," one of the brothers said, glancing away from his work momentarily. "When the Lady Sif wears the headdress, the magic we have instilled inside will allow the golden chains to grow as if they were her real locks."

"Let the proud gods never forget the power of Ivaldi's sons," I said with a lopsided grin.

"We offer this for Freyr," the other brother said proudly, gesturing to the gold and silver pieces on the stone slab beside him.

"It is very fine," I began, staring in confusion at the jumble of gold, thin lines of silver runic script covering their length, but apart from fine craftsmanship, there seemed no object with which these pieces could readily be identified.

"This is Skidbladnir," the brothers then said in unison. "When needed for battle, the ship will be large enough to hold all the Æsir and always carried by swift winds. When not needed, our magic makes it as small as the god Freyr requires. So small, he might place it in his pack."

"That is indeed useful," I agreed with genuine appreciation.

"To Óðinn, the greatest god of battle, we gift Gungnir, an unrivalled spear that will never miss its mark."

"I am certain the All-father will find such a weapon useful," I replied, eyebrows raised in surprise. These were mightier crafts than I had supposed the sons of Ivaldi would so freely offer the gods.

I gratefully accepted the mesh of fine gold for Sif, the dismantled ship for Freyr and the long spear for Óðinn. I promised the sons of Ivaldi that I would intercede on their behalf and make certain the gods understood the magnitude of the gifts they were being given. I left behind the bright chamber and the residual heat of the forge, walking once more into the darkness of the tunnels. Burdened with the awkward gifts I carried, I stopped frequently during my ascent through the twisting passages. When I was near the entrance to the shaft of tunnels that opened into Midgard, I stopped. I shifted the awkward weight in my arms, considering my options. There was one more pair of master metalsmiths belonging to the ancestral dwarf families from Svartálfheimr . I could make one more bargain tonight and gain more influence with the Æsir and have two dwarf families owe me their allegiance. I considered my actions carefully, paused in the junction of two main passageways, shifting the awkward load from one arm to another. At last, I nodded and turned right, continuing down the darker, narrower passage toward Midgard and away from the more direct route back toward Asgard. Thor and Sif could be patient a little longer if it meant I might get what I hoped from this bargain.

Chapter 14
Gifts of Resentment

I was relieved the passage into Midgard from the vast network of tunnels within Yggdrasil was wider than the other leading from Svartálfheimr into Niflheimr. I juggled the awkward hoard of objects Ivaldi's sons had gifted, shifting them from arm to arm as I squeezed sideways through the gap in the rock face. The passage may have been relatively wider than the one where Ivaldi's sons had established their territory, but the length of Óðinn's new spear was still impossible to fit comfortably through the fissure in the cliff face. Twisting this way and that, I dropped Skidbladnir, the golden pieces of Freyr's enchanted longship clattering to the stone floor with an astounding amount of noise. Though I'd been hoping to pass quietly back into the open air, it was pointless now. Sighing in frustration, I kicked at the longest shining section of Skidbladnir. Immediately, I yelped in pain and hobbling backward, began cursing extensively at the surprisingly solid gold piece. When my outrage was simmering again, I glared at several pieces of the ship I had dropped during my rage. Grumbling, I collected them again into my arms and hurled them one by one out the opening of the stone passage, caring neither that some opportunistic mortal might steal them as they appeared on the grass outside the narrow cavern, nor whether they were somehow damaged from my mishandling. Finally, holding Sif's enchanted golden headdress before me, I dragged Gungnir using one arm, the long, slender spear trailing in the moist soil behind me.

Emerging from the darkness of the stone passageway, I stepped immediately into the bright daylight. Squinting against the midday sun, I stared about the steep wooded slopes of the valley into which I had emerged. There was no movement, no sign of human presence. I pulled a sharp knife from my belt and, leaning casually against the cliff face, I began idly picking at my nails with a blade point. The breeze stirred the canopy above my head, rustling in the nearby undergrowth resumed and a doe emerged on the opposite side of the narrow valley, stepping cautiously from a copse of trees. I waited, unhurried and enjoying the warmth of the sun. I wasn't sure what made the daylight in Midgard seem brighter, but the world seemed somehow more alive. I know mortals spoke of Asgard with reverence, the luminescence of the world overwhelming their senses. For me, Midgard was more alive. Here was a world where time itself was measured in heartbeats and breath. Nothing could be more precious, more exhilarating. I suppose for the mortals trudging with frozen feet through the snow and hunting for prey amid quiet and dangerous woods, the sentiment was lost of them. Confident that I was not about to be ambushed by those very same mortals who would gladly teach me what survival truly meant, I collected my awkward armload of dwarf treasures and began down the valley slope.

By the bottom of the valley, I was practically running, the heavy load in my arms propelling me with increasing speed down the steep slope. Careful not to trip myself up, I skipped across the half-hidden network of tree roots that covered the valley floor and congratulated myself on surviving. Before me, a small brook meandered through the thick cluster of water plants, buttercups crowding its banks. Heaving in a shaky breath, I tried to balance my careering speed before launching myself into the air. My jump cleared the brook, which was narrower than it had looked, and I landed on the other side, just shy of the water plants that gathered in the deep shade of the overhanging cliff on this side of the valley. I landed cleanly but momentum still drove me forward and I stumbled a few steps, unable to use my arms to curb the trajectory of my unwieldy body. I tripped on my own feet, slamming one shoulder hard into the rock surface of the opposing cliff, dropping the armload of golden pieces that formed Skidbladnir. I cursed a one hit my foot. I staggered backward a few steps in sudden outburst and the impossible length of Gungnir tangled my legs. I fell on my backside, staring at the open cavern mouth that led into the territory of the other dwarf master smiths.

"You make enough noise out there to raise the dead from their slumber," the shadowy figure of a dwarf complained from the cavern entrance.

"It's these stupid things," I complained, gesturing with my left hand, brushing my right across my thigh to remove the small pebbles lodged in my palm.

The dwarf made a non-committal snort and stood up from where he leaned against the stone wall.

"What do you carry with you, Loki?" he asked, noticing the bright glimmer of gold in the sunlight.

"Oh, these?" I asked. "Just some gifts for the Æsir from Ivaldi's sons," I said, feigning nonchalance.

The dwarf stepped into the light, inspecting the craftsmanship of the items I had dropped on the valley floor near his own door. "These are very fine," he commented, straightening.

I shrugged. "I told the Æsir I would bring them the finest treasures in the Nine Worlds," I explained, gesturing again to the precious goods. "Then I thought, surely Brokk and his brother could make something finer than these."

"What would you stake on such a wager?" Brokk called from the shadows inside the passageway, his steps echoing as he strode toward me.

"I would stake my head, of course!" I said with a cheerful smile, then frowned. "I mean, surely Brokk and Eitri are superior metalsmiths to the sons of Ivaldi?"

Brokk crossed his muscular arms over his chest, regarding me with cool consideration. He nodded once but did not speak.

"Then it is settled," I said gleefully, climbing to my feet. "Let the Æsir judge who makes the more superior gifts for them," I said happily. "I offer you the same promise I gave Ivaldi's sons, of course."

"What promise is that?" Brokk asked, narrowing his eyes.

"If you make these three items for the Æsir, I will ensure you have the aid and loyalty of the gods should you ever need it."

Brokk considered my words. "Done," he agreed, smiling and clasping my forearm with a surprisingly brutal grip. "Eitri," Brokk called, not releasing my arm yet. "Go start the forge, we must work swiftly to make such masterpieces for the gods."

Eitri frowned at the strained smile on Brokk's lips, perhaps noticing the unease on my own face. Finally, the younger dwarf brother shrugged one muscular shoulder and walked down the tunnel, into the belly of the mountain where the two brothers had their workshop.

"You had better not lie to me, Loki," Brokk said quietly, voice venomous. "If you try to trick me, I guarantee you will be worse off for it."

"You wouldn't be the first to try." I smiled broadly.

Brokk waited outside the underground tunnels that led into the workshop, his careful gaze never leaving me as I lounged beneath a wild fruit tree, its branches hanging heavy with ripe fruit. I ignored Brokk's gaze as it grated over my skin, his observation of me relentless, as though I might suddenly show a sign of deliberate deceit or ill-intent. Leaning casually against the trunk of the tree, I tipped my head skyward and bit into another ripe stone fruit, the juice running down my chin as I sucked at the flesh. Brokk made some noise of disgust and shifted his weight uncomfortably.

"Are you going to help your brother?" I asked from the deep shade, already reaching for another fruit from a branch.

"Why?" Brokk demanded, eyes narrowed.

"Well," I began, without looking at him. "I promised the gods I would return by sunset and Sól is getting closer to the western horizon the longer you stare at me."

Brokk muttered something unpleasant toward me and glanced toward the cavern mouth.

"I assure you I have no particular dislike of rabbits, but nor do I have any sexual inclination toward them," I said in response to his insult.

Brokk rolled his eyes and stalked into the passageway, following the audible sounds of the forge and hammer as his brother began work. I sighed with satisfaction and leaned back against the tree trunk. I would not have much time to rest, of course, but for the moment, I could enjoy the ripe fruit. In moments, Eitri hurried out toward me, brandishing a full horn of mead. The dwarf grinned with triumph as I took the proffered drink and sipped appreciatively.

"What's this for?" I asked, taking another mouthful of the mead and relaxing back against the tree.

"While you wait," Eitri said with a broader grin. "Let it not be said we were poor hosts."

"Of course not," I replied, raising the horn of mead and taking another mouthful.

Eitri bowed his head with acknowledgement before dashing off into the cavern again. I took another, smaller mouthful and considered what an odd little thing the younger dwarf brother was. I had discounted many of the tales that dwarves were made from maggots after Óðinn and his brothers had killed and carved the giant Ymir into the earth. Now, as I watched the retreating form of Eitri, I could not be so certain.

When the afternoon was drawing nearer to its end, I opened my eyes from my feigned sleep. Stretching with exaggeration, I yawned with genuine effort and climbed to my feet. I squinted at the sinking form of the sun as it slanted close to the western horizon and walked toward the cavern's opening. Eitri hurried from the passageway faster than I had anticipated, a look of harassed annoyance on his features. He nearly collided with me, and I grabbed the muscular dwarf by the shoulders to stop his movement knocking me from my feet. Instead, I was propelled into the nearest clump of undergrowth, saving myself from landing face first in a holly bush by pure luck. I spun away from the spiky shrub, grasping again at the dwarf to steady myself. This time, Eitri grabbed at my flailing arms.

"Oh, Loki," Eitri said with genuine shock. "I didn't see you approach,"

"I guessed as much," I said, brushing leaves from my tunic where I'd collided with the undergrowth.

"I was bringing you some more mead," he explained, brandishing another full mead horn.

"Ah," I said, feigning good cheer. "Exactly what I wanted."

I accepted the mead and let the dwarf lead me back to my camp beneath the fruit tree.

"Are you and Brokk nearly finished?" I asked, nodding my head toward the sinking sun.

"Oh yes," Eitri said with an overly bright smile. "Brokk has just one item to finish: a mighty war hammer for Thor."

"For Thor?" I asked.

I shifted my body against the tree, again reminded by the deep bruises Thor had given me earlier that day how these events had befallen me. The darker part of myself hungered to ruin the gift for Thor, clamouring that he receive the gift he justly deserved.

"I must hurry to apply more fuel to the forge for Brokk," Eitri said with an apologetic smile, already taking a few steps back toward the tunnels.

"Then you had best hurry," I said, gesturing my gratitude for the mead and indicating the approaching sunset.

Eitri nodded and turning, ran quickly down the dark passage into the mountain cavern. I waited a few moments, trying to quieten the insistent inner voice that tempting me to take my vengeance on Thor. When I could resist the pull no longer, I climbed to my feet. Carefully, I placed the horn of half-finished mead on the ground beside my belongings and stepped soundlessly to the stone passage leading inside the mountain to the dwarf workshop.

I pulled my own magic around me, felt the familiar shiver of it play across my skin. This was a power that the Æsir did not possess, which only the Vanir shared with the giants. Even so, the magic that shimmered across my skin was unlike that held by either the Vanir or giants, and the ease with which I shifted forms was something mistrusted and feared among both sides. I let the power of air consume my magic and let my physical form shift, discarding one body for another. In the moments between my decision to act and the discarding of my human form, bright insect wings buzzed with impossible speed, keeping my tiny body aloft.

I manoeuvred with the easy grace of all flying insects and darted down the dark passages of the mountain tunnels. I allowed the senses of this new insect form to take possession of my focus, drawing me closer to my prey. Darting through shadow and light, avoiding the brilliant flare of firelight from the forge, I circled the room briefly. I noticed where Eitri stood beside the central hearth, tossing another large log onto the fire, the sparks and flames erupting into the darkness. The vision of this tiny insect was imperfect but the heat radiating from the flames was different to the intense need that pulled me closer to the other bright form in the room.

Brokk stood above the object he was hammering. The bellows of the forge were his to control. The insect mind did not care nor understand the bellows and the forge, but I retained enough of myself to know if Brokk did not get air to the forge, the heat would be too low and the hammer he was creating for

Thor would ruined. I restrained the tiny insect mind a moment longer, feeling the unbearable need rise within the body I now inhabited. It craved the blood pumping hot through the dwarf at the forge, but I waited, barely controlling the hunger threatening to overwhelm me.

Suddenly, Brokk barked some command at Eitri and the dwarf nodded and, turning on one heel, began to walk away down the passages. He was likely going to collect me from where I should be languishing beneath the fruit tree. I realised the gift offered to me the moment Eitri was gone. Brokk could not keep the forge hot without the bellows and the end of the hammer lay within the heat still. I drove forward with improbable speed, the insect wings a blur of movement and precision. I circled around Brokk's forehead as he bent to the bellows. I attacked, diving toward an eyelid and bit, allowing the insect hunger to be satiated as Brokk roared in complaint, a massive hand coming to slap me away. I dove up and to the right, moving quickly between the downward sweep of his hand. Angling the insect body again, I dove for Brokk's right eye, alighting on the eyelid and again allowing the insect to satiate itself. Brokk roared again, his eyes swelling and blood dripping from where he had swatted at the wounds.

Conscious of my timing, I hurtled my insect body away from Brokk's blind and flailing attempts at swatting me. The bellows forgotten in his outrage and momentary blindness, Brokk cursed and shouted as the metal tip of Thor's hammer grew cooler and darker in the forge. I picked up the speed I knew the minute insect could achieve and hurtled down the passageways, seeking the brightness of the outside world. I flew past Eitri as he continued along the passage; he had still not yet reached the opening where he needed to find me beneath the fruit tree. Using the last of the speed, I zoomed through the tunnel opening, out into the fading sunlight of early twilight. I had only moments to change my form but I managed, my eagerness to beat Eitri outside causing me to overshoot the fruit tree. I shifted back into my human form, weak and exhausted, I half-stumbled to my knees. I realised, then, I was several yards from the fruit tree, crouched naked in the water weeds.

"Loki?" Eitri called from the tree, turning a slow circle in confusion.

"What?" I grumbled, hauling myself upright, body smeared with mud and a bit of blood.

"Are you all right?" the dwarf asked, brows furrowing.

"I was planning to take a quick bath," I explained, gesturing to my nakedness and the few scrapes and bruises visible from Thor's earlier beating. "Did you want to join me?" I teased with a lopsided grin.

"No," Eitri answered, awkwardly shifting his weight with growing uneasiness. "The pieces are ready to show you."

"About time," I said, dropping to my knees to quickly dunk my head beneath the water.

Chapter 15
Wagers With Dwarves

A short time later when I emerged from the brook, Eitri was gone. Water streamed down my bare skin, which was now hot with fever from Thor's earlier beating and the sustained use of magic. The bruises blossoming on my chest suggested my ribs were broken. I squinted at the fading sunlight as Sól slipped from the western horizon. Already, the brilliant light shining from Skinfaxi was fading, Dagr drawing that golden horse to a halt and the day to a close. I shivered in the twilight as a breeze brushed my exposed flesh as if to remind me night was fast approaching, the giantess Nótt bringing shadows in her wake as she spurred the frost-maned stallion Hrimfaxi across the sky. I needed to return to Asgard before twilight turned to full night and Mani cast his silvery moonlight through the darkness.

I pulled the loosely woven woollen tunic over my head, thrusting my feet into boots and belting the knives at my side with haste. I quickly threw the cloak over one shoulder, my boots unlaced as I jogged into the tunnels that led deeply into the mountain halls and smithies of the dwarves. I had the end of my belt between my teeth, trying to cinch it around my waist when I turned the corner into the massive cavern where Eitri and Brokk had the smithy. I nearly tripped over my unlaced boots, stumbling to a halt as I stared at the newly wrought objects.

Eitri was smiling broadly as I stared dumbly at the gleaming offerings displayed on the massive slab of stone before me. The bright metal caught my attention, embers of the forge reflected on the golden form of a boar, the tusks and bristles so finely wrought it seemed alive, and I waited as though it might snort in challenge at my blatant stare. I relaxed my shoulders and let out a shaky breath.

"Magnificent," I pronounced, taking my eyes from the boar to meet Brokk's intelligent gaze.

The boar suddenly moved, the bristles shimmering with light as the tiny eyes glinted with malice. I staggered backward, nearly dropping the objects

Ivaldi's sons had gifted me. The boar stepped toward me, lowering its massive head in obstinate challenge. I glanced quickly to Brokk, hoping he had some power over the will of his creation. The dwarf shrugged as though to suggest the boar had good sense to dislike me.

"This is Gullinbursti," Brokk said proudly. "For Freyr this boar carries his own light and can't be overtaken by any creature in the Nine Worlds. He is swift, strong, and he will shake the very earth."

I tried not to stare at the boar as it snorted, head raised in consideration, deciding whether I was worthy of confrontation. After a tense few seconds, the boar snorted derisively and tossed its massive head, golden tusks glinting in the light before it returned to a motionless stance that made me uneasy.

"I am certain Freyr will be impressed," I said quickly to Brokk, turning my attention away from the boar.

Brokk scratched absently at his bushy black beard. "Hm," he agreed noncommittally and turning to his left, gestured to a large, elegantly carved golden arm ring. "This gift is for Óðinn. It is Draupnir, a ring of significant weight and importance."

"It is very finely crafted," I agreed, marvelling at the skilful engraving that was woven around the outside of the ring. I turned the object over in my hands, admiring the gleaming metal.

"There is more to it than mere craftsmanship," Brokk said, berating me. "Every ninth night, eight more rings of equal weight as this original will fall from it like rain."

"That is an amazing gift," I said, raising my eyebrows with genuine surprise and appreciation.

Brokk pushed out his chest with pride and I stepped further to the left, moving us to the last object on the stone table. I frowned as I looked at the meticulously engraved war-hammer, the finely crafted steel and edged gold and silver filigree superb. It would have been an object of marvellous craftsmanship if Brokk had been allowed to finish the hammer without my interruption. Instead, the war-hammer was oddly shortened; the haft of the massive steel head suddenly stopped a hand shorter than expected for the size and weight of the object. I peered curiously at the hammer, pretending I did not understand that the short haft was unintentional.

"What does this do?" I asked, tilting my head to one side as I turned to Brokk.

"This is Mjölnir, a war-hammer for Thor," Brokk said, a little stilted, glancing angrily toward Eitri. "The strength and speed of this hammer is unsurpassed in any of the Nine Worlds," he explained, frowning slightly as he stared at the short haft, fingertips caressing the scoring mark where the metal had been moulded into the slight grip for a hand. There was no way that Thor's huge hands would allow Mjölnir to be carried and swung with the ease or grace of any war-hammer in Asgard, let alone the entire Nine worlds.

"Why is Mjölnir so short?" I asked, raising my voice as I propped one hip against the stone slab.

"Mjölnir is not just any war-hammer," Brokk explained, a blush nearly visible beneath his thick, curly beard. "Thor can throw the hammer and it will return by itself with ease, slaying any who challenge it as though it were an arrow piercing men on the battlefield."

I nodded gravely. "I think the Æsir will be very impressed with these gifts," I said, pretending not to notice that Brokk had not truly answered my question.

"I will come with you to the Æsir," Brokk announced, not meeting my gaze.

"Why?" I asked, a chill running up my spine and snarling my thoughts with questions of whether the dwarf was trying to betray me or the Æsir.

"You are well known for your trickery, Loki," Brokk announced easily. "I want Óðinn and the Æsir to know that my brother and I offer our services and good faith to them and not with any attachments to you."

I frowned. "It would be easy to take offence at that," I said, not smiling.

"Good thing you are not an easy man, then," Brokk replied without mirth, his eyes a deep glacial blue.

I nodded my agreement. "Help me carry all this then," I grumbled, gesturing to the assortment of new objects Brokk and Eitri had just wrought and the golden objects held loosely in my arms that Ivaldi's sons had crafted. "Let the Æsir judge which of the dwarf smiths is the most skilled."

I turned on my heel, wincing at the pain that radiated at my spine and branched across my broken ribs. I stalked from the cavern toward the fading twilight outside the mountain tunnels. I did not wait for Brokk to follow me nor slow my stride for him to keep pace with me. I needed to hurry back to Asgard if I wanted to be certain to meet my agreement with Thor. My wellbeing and my life depended on arriving at Asgard before moonrise, I could not allow myself to be delayed.

Brokk grumbled as he hurried up the steep slope of the valley, the treasures he and his brother had laboured all afternoon now slung into a pack across his back. Before we departed, Eitri had crafted a similar pack for me, the treasures made by Ivaldi's sons carried on my own back, the pieces of Skidbladnir and Sif's headdress. I still carried Gungnir in my hand, the slender spear sharing no magic enchantment like Freyr's longship and so I used it as a walking staff as I imagined Óðinn probably would anyway.

I moved swiftly through the narrow fissure in the mountainside, the cleft in the stone easier to navigate unencumbered by an armload of dwarf treasure. I did not pause or wait for Brokk but continued down the dark tunnels, a faint glimmering light in the pitch black the only indication that the embers I had left still burned. My feet were sure and moved near-silently, my senses tuned to the darkness, and I smiled with satisfaction as Brokk stumbled and cursed in the unfamiliar blackness behind me. The dwarves might be lords of the mountain passages but they were only invincible in their own territories. I stored that information away, burying it like a precious nut for a cold winter when such knowledge might be useful.

I reached the sharp bend in the tunnel we followed and stopped. I knew Brokk had slowed his pace but still blundered in the unfamiliar dark of the caverns. My eyes shone with the reflected embers of the fire I had stored in the crevice. My nimble fingers picked up the torch and, cupping the glowing coal, I touched the dry torch to the fledging fire and encouraged it to life. The flame leapt toward the torch, catching the dry moss and loom castoffs. The natural oils in the discarded fleece before it was woven made excellent torches which lit easily and burned slowly.

In the immediate light cast from the torch, Brokk halted, blinking in momentary confusion at me. I grinned and gestured toward the right fork in the branching tunnel ahead.

"We go right here…unless you seek to visit Níðhöggr?" I asked, grinning as his face paled at mention of the dragon's name.

Brokk followed me down the right passage; the tunnel sloped steeply down and then took a sharp bend left. I paused at the corner of the bend and adjusted my pack, waiting impatiently for the dwarf to catch up.

"From here the slope is long and steep," I told him. "I'm not waiting for you."

Brokk's scowl darkened, and he cursed me softly as I walked away.

I was not long-legged like Óðinn or Týr, and I did not share the muscular power of Thor to make the ascent to Asgard with speed. Instead, I walked with steadiness, my even stride consuming the distance of the climb as my lungs heaved in oxygen. I could hear Brokk cursing me more loudly as I drew further away from him, the complaints and insults becoming quite imaginative as he slowly dropped further behind me. I did not want to wait for the dwarf, but I wanted to assure safe passage for him and me into Asgard when we arrived. Heimdallrr would guard Bifröst with a dedication I never understood.

I turned a sharp bend in the dark tunnel, my feet sure on the uneven ground as the path sloped suddenly down, the path dropping almost vertically into a crevice. Easing myself through the cleft in the mountainside, I emerged into shadowy realms of twilight in Asgard. Squinting after the long passages of blackness and flickering torchlight, I waited while my vision adjusted to the familiar shapes of the hills surrounding Valhalla. I was conscious of the towering peak behind me where the stone seat of Hliðskjálf overlooked the Nine Worlds.

"Loki," Heimdallrr greeted with a solemn nod, stepping quietly from the shadows.

"Heimdallrr," I answered with feigned casualness. "It is a lovely evening for stalking unwary travellers,"

The god cocked his head like a predatory bird. "You are many things, unwary is not one of them."

"True," I agreed, sighing. "The dwarf lord Brokk bears gifts for the All-Father and the Æsir. He follows me through the passages from Midgard but I must go ahead and announce his arrival. Will you let him pass?"

"I can do that," Heimdallrr nodded with a grin. "Does he have gifts for me?"

"You'll have to ask him," I answered, returning the grin.

CHAPTER 16
SOWING VENGEANCE

Heimdallrr boomed with laugher, slapping my shoulder hard and sending me staggering forward. I recovered my balance and gave the watchman of the gods a genuinely amused grin as I gestured rudely at him and dashed into the darkness, dodging his raucous insults. Heimdallrr may have loyalty and an over-zealous commitment to guarding Asgard, but he was good man and I liked him. Even so, I would never test his friendship too far because I knew his loyalty was to Óðinn before any other. I did not dally on the fields of Fólkvangr but hurried across the deepening shadows of the plains where Freyja's Valkyries and Óðinn's Einherjar sparred every dawn and dusk. The well-trodden fields passed beneath the soft leather of my boots as I cautiously approached the brighter torchlights of Valhalla.

Óðinn's hall was a shining beacon in the darkness of the evening, torchlight flaring out into the shadowy courtyard. Bonfires had been lit around the perimeter of the hall and the usual large guards had been posted on the fringes of light and darkness. I cautiously slowed my approach, hugging the pack of dwarf treasure closer to my chest. My body tensed at memory of Thor's recent beating and I knew the stakes from my current wager were possibly too high for me to win. What if the Æsir decided Brokk and his brother hadn't crafted finer metalwork than the sons of Ivaldi? Brokk would have my head, for I had given him my word.

Swallowing my increasing anxiety, I wet my dry lips and stepped into the courtyard. The guard nearest to me startled at my sudden appearance from the shadows immediately brought up his sword. I felt the cold metal touch my bare skin beneath the open neck of my tunic. I swallowed my fear and gave the man my usual cocky smile. A thick beard obscured most of his features and I could not tell if the tightening around his eyes was a scowl or smile.

"Óðinn is expecting me," I explained, jerking my head toward the hall. "Go and tell him Loki has returned as promised."

The guard grunted something, possibly an agreement or a sign of resignation.

I was not sure but watched the big man pull the heavy oak doors of the hall aside and step inside. I braced myself while waiting, carefully arranging my features into a relaxed but confident expression. I waited only a few moments before the bear of a man returned and shouted another unintelligible command at me. I rolled my eyes to no one but silently cursed Thor for hiring brute strength over intelligence. I passed the giant of a guard and stepped cautiously into the well-lit expanse of Óðinn's hall beyond, the massive oak doors swinging closed behind me.

Inside, Óðinn was seated near the central hearth, one arm wrapped around Frigg's waist, the other hand loosely holding a drinking horn. A guarded expression hid most of his thoughts from me, but I knew Óðinn well and understood he wanted me to succeed because if I defied him again, he would be forced to let Thor take his vengeance against me. I gave an imperceptible jerk of my chin, letting Óðinn know I had something planned and I would not let my misdemeanour destroy me so easily. Óðinn seemed to settle more comfortably in his high-backed chair as I approached the central hearth, his fingers stroking the mead horn as casually as he caressed Frigg's hip.

"Loki," Óðinn said gravely, cobalt eye meeting my own as I stopped beside the flames of the fire-pit.

I bowed my head in supplication and recognition of his authority.

"You gave Thor your word that the damage wrought at your hand against Lady Sif could be repaired," Óðinn began, his bright eye piercing my own. "If you have not kept your pledge to Thor, your life is forfeit to him."

I bowed my head, hiding my expression behind the shadows of my lowered face. I swept my arms out in a slow but melodramatic gesture, spinning carefully on my heels as I did so and meeting the stares of the gathered gods surrounding me.

"I see many of you had assembled tonight hoping that Thor might have the opportunity you longed for," I commented, "the option to dispose of the giants in your midst with Óðinn's blessing." I stopped my circling, then suddenly spun, pointing at the far door. "I am afraid I must disappoint you."

The massive oak doors at the far end of the hall opened only a small crack, the darkness beyond a thin ribbon against the torchlight before the doors closed again and Brokk strolled down the length of Valhalla, the pack of treasures slung casually across his back. I leaned against the slender shaft of Gungnir, grinning with unexpected relief and pleasure to see the dwarf.

"May I present the dwarf lord, Brokk, one of the master craftsmen among their kin."

Brokk halted beside me, a wary glance at my wide grin before he bowed sombrely to Óðinn and Frigg. "Óðinn, the All-Father and seeker of knowledge," he began, bowing deeper still and pivoting at the waist so this gesture of respect encompassed Frigg. "Lady of the Æsir and weaver of storms."

"He speaks very prettily," Frigg observed with a wry smile, arching her eyebrow at me.

"The dwarf lords are perhaps not as uncultured as you might imagine," I said softly, smiling slightly.

Brokk straightened and looked at me expectantly.

I reached around into the pack I carried and pulled the golden headdress free with an exaggerated flourish. I bowed deeply, dropping to one bruised knee as I held the glittering cap of tightly woven gold out for Sif to inspect. She moved forward eagerly, ignoring Thor's attempt to grasp her elbow and slow her advance. I kept my eyes lowered but peeked at her reaction from beneath my lashes as her eyes widened, taking in the glorious beauty of the metalcraft.

"Before I explain the gifts my people offer the Æsir," Brokk began earnestly, drawing attention from the golden headdress to himself again. "Loki made a wager with me and my purpose travelling here is to see the outcome fulfilled."

"What wager?" Óðinn asked quietly, raising his eyebrows.

Brokk's smile was calculating and sharp. "He bet that my brother and I could not craft metal beyond the skills of Ivaldi's sons. The price of the wager was his own head."

"Truly?" Óðinn chuckled, glancing at me in surprise.

"I have travelled to make certain Loki cannot deceive us from the promised allegiances with the Æsir."

Óðinn smiled, showing teeth. "Come then, let us see these mighty treasures you offer on behalf of your kin. We shall choose the mightiest gift and proclaim Loki's fate."

I glared at Brokk as the dwarf gave Óðinn a sharp nod of agreement. He swung the heavy pack from his shoulders and placed it at his feet. Brokk straightened and looked at me, then gestured grandly with his arms.

"Will you show the gifts Ivaldi's sons offer?" Brokk asked me. "Explain their might while you may still talk, for afterward, I will have your head."

"You seem very judgemental of me," I answered, quirking my brows before opening the pack I carried. "I've done you no harm," I muttered quietly, withdrawing the golden pieces of the longship.

I held out the shining sections of Skidbladnir, the gold glinting in the torchlight inside the hall. The Æsir assembled around the central hearth and, as I produced the first of the gifts from Ivaldi's sons, the gods crowded closer, jostling for better positions.

"This is Skidbladnir, made by Ivaldi's sons for Freyr. These few pieces of finely crafted gold transform into a longship capable of carrying warriors into battle and blessed by an ever-constant wind filling its sails."

Freyr made an appreciative noise. "Ivaldi's sons offer me a masterpiece," he said with gratitude.

I stepped forward, brandishing the slender spear, then bowed my head, holding the shaft across my palms, offering it to Óðinn. "This is Gungnir," I said, solemnly. "An unrivalled weapon that never misses its mark."

Óðinn stepped forward, lifting the slender spear from my hands, marvelling at its fine craftsmanship and the length which I knew was perfectly matched to his height and reach. It was a masterly wrought weapon, and I could not hide the smile upon my face to see Óðinn admire it so openly.

"The sons of Ivaldi have my gratitude," Óðinn spoke softly, bowing his head to Brokk and a quick, uncertain smile toward me.

I hesitated a moment, uncertain what to make of Óðinn's response. I had no time to ponder the meaning, though, as I gestured next to the golden headdress crafted for Sif. "This headdress for Sif was crafted by Ivaldi's sons, a gesture of their mastery as metalsmiths and kindness. Where I enacted my vengeance against Thor upon his innocent wife Sif, Ivaldi's sons restore her magnificent hair with dazzling gold." I lifted the headdress higher so the Æsir could admire it, the tiny locks and ringlets perfectly wrought in fine links of gold. "When placed upon your head," I said, gesturing briefly to Sif, "the magic imbued within this headdress allows it to grow like natural hair and it is so finely crafted you may change the length and style with just a thought. No need for maidens to tend this headdress with the shears. My petulance was a foolish and awful act. I have only this humble apology and offer this gift from Ivaldi's sons until your own locks can rival these of precious gold."

Sif bowed her gracious head and stepped away from Thor's reaching arms. She came toward me and gently brushed her lips to both my cheeks, accepting the headdress from my hands. I watched in silence as Sif and Frigg placed the headdress upon her shaved head. In moments, the tiny links of gold began to extend, forming ringlets as the patterns increased in complexity, weaving a fine chain and network of gold about Sif's head until the headdress surpassed the beauty that had been her natural hair.

Smiling, I gestured for Brokk to offer his treasures to the Æsir, certain that nothing could be more impressive that the gift offered to Sif.

Brokk gave me a sidelong glance and cleared his throat, taking from the cloth pack the golden statue of the boar. The gold was high quality and the form of the boar engraved with runes I had barely noticed before.

"For Freyr I offer Gullinbursti, a shining boar that creates his own light and has greater speed than any creature in the Nine Worlds."

"Is it not a little small?" I asked, frowning at the sculpture of the boar.

Brokk stiffened at my accusation, a ripple of subdued laughter passing through the gathered Æsir. "Gullinbursti is forged with magic like Skidbladnir and its challenge shakes the very earth."

"It is a masterful gift," Freyr said with gratitude, bowing his head in thanks.

I nodded, pretending to consider, then shrugged. "It's not original though, is it?"

Brokk growled a low warning. "For Óðinn, we offer Draupnir, a mighty ring that for every ninth night, eight more of similar weight and quality will fall like rain."

Óðinn bowed his head in appreciation. "Such skill and craftsmanship is unrivalled."

"My last offering is Mjölnir," Brokk said, turning a wide grin toward me. "A war-hammer worthy of the ferocity Thor is known for and crafted from the strongest steel so it cannot break. Lightning has engraved the runes that cover its surface so that when thrown, it will return only to you, for it is bound to the god of war and storms."

A whisper of appreciation spread through the crowd of Æsir and Thor stepped forward to take the war-hammer from Brokk. I watched as the massive god of war and storms plucked the weapon from the squat figure of the dwarf who was unconcerned by Thor's imposing bulk.

CHAPTER 17
WITCH OF THE IRON WOOD

"Well?" I asked, looking about the gods as they jostled to get closer to the treasures the dwarves had made.

Only Óðinn remained seated beside the central hearth, the spear between his knees. He met my gaze with curiosity and gestured me closer. I glanced at the gods, conscious that any moment they could proclaim the outcome of the wager I had made with Brokk. I understood the odds of the wager I had made and I knew well enough that these were not in my favour this time. I longed to shift the human skin from my body, flee the wretchedness of this existence and escape as a wolf into the forests surrounding Valhalla. I tensed, gaze shifting toward the massive oak doors at the end of the hall. To my surprise, the doors were firmly closed and barred, a large guard posted at either side. Óðinn knew my mind as well as I knew his; perhaps we knew each other better than ourselves. Sighing, I shook my head vigorously as though I were a dog shaking off water and sauntered over to Óðinn's seat. I leaned against the high-backed chair, chin propped on one ostentatiously engraved section.

"They seem awfully fond of the war-hammer," I remarked.

"Hm," Óðinn agreed, not taking his eyes from the gods as they began calling for Thor to test Mjölnir's might.

Thor obliged as I could predict he would, throwing the hammer lightly but with far greater force than any mortal man could achieve. The war-hammer whooshed through the air, clearing a path between the massive, unlit tapers of beeswax at the far end of the hall before neatly returning in a semi-circular path toward Thor. The god opened his hand and Mjölnir fit comfortably into his palm.

"He has rather short hands, doesn't he?" I complained, frowning.

"That is probably one of the oddest criticisms I've heard you offer about Thor," Óðinn said, half-turning in his chair to regard me.

"It just lost me a wager," I sighed. "If I'd noticed earlier, it would've been helpful."

"Hm," Óðinn said again, pressing his lips together as he turned to face the celebrating gods. "Brokk," Óðinn called, voice carrying through the shouts and jeering.

I watched as the dwarf stepped from the gathering of gods and goddesses, his face a mask, inscrutable and unreadable as he approached.

Óðinn considered the celebration surrounding us and the gods clustered around Thor as he threw Mjölnir again. "Brokk," Óðinn called, voice cutting through the excitement in the hall, causing all the gods to pause and turn to regard him. "You have won the wager. Mjölnir is the mightiest gift."

"But the handle is too short," I complained. "Not even a mortal craftsman would make such a weapon with so glaring a fault."

Óðinn raised his eyebrows. "Loki," he warned, "you said yourself that Mjölnir fits Thor's grip perfectly."

"That wasn't what I said at all," I shouted, stepping back from his chair.

"It doesn't matter what you said about Thor," Brokk growled, turning to face me. "You wagered your head if you lost. You'll speak no lies again."

I started toward the doors, prepared to fight my way from Valhalla if I must, but I'd travelled only a few steps when Thor's massive hand clamped around my neck, dragging me backward. Spitting and cursing, I was dropped onto the floor at Óðinn's feet.

I glared at Brokk. "I wagered you had claim to my head, no other part of me," I said, scrambling backward across the floor until I hit the solid and unmovable form of Thor's legs against my back.

"Well then," Brokk answered, grinning victoriously. "If your head is mine, I can at least stop your lying lips from oozing more poison."

Glaring at Brokk, I tried to shuffle away, but Thor's massive hands clamped on my shoulders, holding me firm. "You would not dare," I snarled.

Brokk pulled a long blade from his belt, considering the point as he then yanked the thong from his hair a sinew wider than what was normally used for sewing. I blanched as the dwarf approached and tried unsuccessfully to dodge the blade. Brokk was fast, the tip of the blade nicking my lip but only drawing blood, not sharp enough to sew as an awl might be. I swivelled my gaze wildly around the gathered gods, who seemed amused at my predicament though some averted their eyes from my pleading stare. In horror, I noticed Freyja pass a bone awl to Brokk and felt Thor's massive arms clench my shoulders. Then the pain began.

I screamed until the sinew grew taunt and movement of my lips only increased the pain. When I could no longer scream, I howled in rage, my throat growing hoarse with the effort. Around me the gods jostled each other, drank from horns of mead and ate from the slabs of roast ox on the spit. Through the pain and humiliation, I endured. I buried my consciousness and torment deep within myself so much so that I wasn't aware when the transformation to wolf begun. I only heard the startled cries and shouts from Thor and some of the other Æsir as I slipped from his grasp, his big hands clutching snatches of wolf fur. I snarled in rage, my feral eyes promising the vengeance I would deliver.

I pinned Freyja within my sight, spittle hanging from the corners of my mouth and gaps where the large canine teeth protruded between the stitches. The witch still stood behind Brokk, far enough from me that she would never be attacked during any transformation. Of all the gods assembled, Freyja knew more of shape-shifting than any of them. Through the haze of pain and rage, I wondered if she and Óðinn knew the full strength of my capabilities. Óðinn had long sought to master the abilities of transformation, but some gifts of magic were beyond a price.

I lunged toward Brokk, taking savage pleasure as the dwarf leapt from my attack. Even though the stout metalsmith might be fast, the raking claws on my front paws slashed deep gouges down his belly and legs. Blood scented the air and the wolf instincts of this form overcame my own. Weakened from the torture I had endured, I had little control over the beast within this form. The pain of injury, tang of fresh blood and rising panic in the confined hall, combined to madden the wolf.

Óðinn climbed to his feet, ash staff in one hand, the spear Gungnir in the other. I prowled restlessly toward him, then circled back along the edge of the gathered gods, pushing them closer to the walls, creating more distance between Óðinn and me.

Saliva hung in bloody strings from my jaws and I growled a low, warning threat in my throat as Óðinn took a step closer. The cobalt blue eye met mine and held, unblinking. Behind Óðinn, his two wolves, Geri and Freki, flanked him, lips pulled back from ravenous jaws ready to devour. Óðinn flicked his wrist in a quick gesture and I started, snarling and growling, but he did not attack or move. His wolves remained tense but poised behind him.

The heavy oak door to Valhalla swung open with a groan and cold night air gusted into the hall. I skirted the gods, trotting purposefully toward the exit, never letting my gaze leave Óðinn's or his wolves beside him. Above, Hugin and Munin circled, cawing with anticipation of slaughter. I scented the frost-touched air and bounded into the darkness, the swift feet of the wolf enveloping the space between Valhalla and the dark woods of Álfheimr beyond. The memories of humiliation and betrayal were a small flame compared to the burning promise of vengeance I kindled in my heart. I fled into the dark woods, following the hoarfrost into the icy forests.

When I could run no more, I lay where I had fallen, sides heaving with breath as I tried to pant through sewn lips. I whined, desperate for water, surrounded only by deep snow and frozen forests. I thought I knew where

I was, and it was a long trek from Valhalla. I had run far, the speed of the wolf carrying me deep into the wild winter forests of Jötunheimr. I whined again, the frigid cold beginning to bite through the thick pelt that had sheltered me from many severe storms in the past. Exhausted, I climbed slowly to a sitting position, noticing how silent the winter woods were. It was an eerie quiet, not just the forest drawing breath in the presence of a predator like a wolf. I scanned the stiff, icy boughs, watching the thick cold mist weave through the trees, and realised with a little trepidation I had almost fled into Niflheimr. These were the haunted woods where even the mightiest of the jötnar dared not tarry. I pricked my ears, eyes watching the woods for any sign of movement beyond the thickening mist. I could sense very little, the mist obliterating sound and sight, providing the perfect trap for the one who hunted in these lands. I had been a fool.

I remained on my haunches in the deep snow, keeping an alert but untroubled gaze on the shrouded forest, and waited for my hunter to catch me. There seemed very little else I could do. I forced my will into the senses of the wolf, every fibre of the animal wanting to flee or fight, to do anything but sit meekly in the snow like a rabbit. I held my nerves in check and forced the stiff muscles of the wolf's powerful body to feign a relaxed stance.

A sudden movement, so slight it could have been a trick of the shifting fog and light, caught my keen vision. I swivelled my head, eyes scanning the mist for any other indicators of movement. There were none. I whined anxiously in the cold, the tension becoming unbearable. It was nothing more than shadow and light, I realised, shifting weight back into my haunches and relaxing slightly. Nothing more than that.

A strong hand gripped the ruff of fur behind my ears and held. I twisted, snarling and growling, trying to dislodge and face my attacker. The sinews that bound my lips pulled painfully taunt in my efforts to defend myself and one canine pierced the stitches. Blood oozed from my torn flesh, enraging the wolf. I growled, red-stained spittle splashing across the snow and hoar-frost. The hand that held me used no more effort than was required. My wild struggles proved useless as I was expertly flipped into the air, black branches and white snow reversing momentarily. I landed with a hard thump in the icy snow, wind knocked from my body in a hollow whoosh. It took me less than a few seconds to recover but I was already securely fastened, my four paws strung together in a complicated knot. I tried to run, my sudden movement propelling me forward then sharply into a snowbank as the rope pulled taunt.

The long-fingered hand splayed against my ruff as the woman leaned close to my ears.

"The Æsir send me a gift already nicely muzzled," the witch crooned.

I growled, struggling to free myself but she held me fast to the ground.

She let me move an inch, then pinned me again to the snow so I might meet her gaze.

The witch Angrboða was no ally or friend to the Æsir, nor to the giants. She was very tall, her body long-limbed and supple, a long sweep of dark brown hair hung in a plethora of dreadlocks from her scalp, each plaited with tiny beads and bones. I snarled my dislike of her and she cocked her head and bared her own teeth, the mannerism more animal than human. I quietened, realising on the very logical and more primal level that she had complete control of me. I could do nothing unless Angrboða permitted it.

"Loki?" she asked, eyes widening with recognition even though she asked me.

I snarled in response, blood flecking the ground around my muzzle.

"Did Óðinn do this to you?" she asked me, touching a gentle fingertip to the broken stitches at my lips.

I did not bite but growled another warning and her hand withdrew.

"You were trespassing in my lands, did you know?" she asked conversationally. "I normally make a stew from such grievous affronts to my territory. But you are more my kin than I think you realise."

I snarled again, not wanting to end up in her cookpot but not wanting anything to do with her. Angrboða was the one giants and gods alike called the witch of the Iron Wood. If she inspired such fear in warriors like Thor and Óðinn, in the giants like Thiazi and Skaði, I was no match for whatever games she wanted to play with me.

"Come, Loki," Angrboða cooed, picking up my trussed body as if a full-grown wolf weighed nothing at all. She slung me over her shoulder, the rich scent of her fur cape barely smothering a darker scent. I shifted uncomfortably but she clutched the ruff of my neck still as though I were an ill-behaved puppy. "Let me take care of you."

I whined as Angrboða steadied herself through the snow, the long, curved staff sinking deeply into the snow drifts as she walked. The strange fog seemed to curl about the witch as she walked, her arched antlers decorated with moss and tiny talismans. A tiny empty-eyed bird skull hung directly in front of me and I hoped my fate would not prove the same as Angrboða abducted me from the woods.

PART TWO
THE UNRAVELLING

Chapter 18
A Monstrous Brood

I woke to a suffocating room, the air heady with burning herbs, stale air and sweat. Frowning, I rolled my head to the left, trying to recall where I was. Where was I? The dwelling was unfamiliar, the single room cluttered with a sleeping pallet, central hearth and a mound of fur blankets in the corner. I groaned, reaching to touch my brow, a pounding headache beginning to form. I needed water.

I threw back the heavy fur robe, wrinkling my nose at the stinking sweat-stiffened state of the thing and pulled my cramped legs from the tangle of pelts. No wonder I was too hot. Sweat marked my body, as though this was not the first time I had woken from a similar state. I needed to bathe. I longed for cold water.

I staggered to my feet, nearly crying out as my calves spasmed with the effort to hold my weight. I stumbled slightly, grasping the rough central pole that supported the roof of this miserable hovel. Shuffling to the sliver of muted light I could discern surrounding the doorway, I pulled the stiffened hide from the door and stepped outside in the crisp morning air.

I inhaled deeply, greedily drawing in lungfuls of the fresh air until I felt dizzy with the joy of it. My muscles still protested painfully but I continued my shuffling steps a few more paces, desperate to get beyond the hovel. There was something dark and horrid about the place I wanted to forget, and yet I still had no idea how I had come to be here.

I walked a few more steps around the side of the small hut, following a well-trodden path through the dense bracken and shrubs that covered the forest floor. Tall trees arched overhead, boughs full of spring leaves, freshly budded and newly leafed. The air was crisp and smelled strongly of flowering trees and the awakening forest after winter.

Movement ahead of me caught my attention. I stopped suddenly, the reflex nearly toppling my weakened body to the ground. A young girl, almost a woman, sat beside a well, the end of the long rope beside her. She was playing with a large black wolf pup, the two so completely absorbed in each other they did not seem to notice me. I coughed politely, hoping to not startle them. The girl looked up, her face still half-turned toward the pup. She whispered something quietly to the wolf who sat, lips bared slightly in a small snarl. Neither seemed surprised by my presence.

I realised I was completely naked and still desperately dehydrated. I wet my lips and rubbed roughly at my face, realising with a grimace I badly needed to shave.

"Water?" I croaked, my own voice startling me with its guttural growl.

The wolf pup put its ears back, lip lifting in a snarl, the hackles raised along its spine. I answered by way of reflex, drawing my own lips back to growl at the pup. The wolf regarded me curiously, yellow eyes widening before he lay down on the ground, subservient to my authority but not happy about it. The girl watched our exchange with curious gaze, then climbed to her feet, her simple white gown hanging loosely about her as she moved. She looked too thin, showing less gracefulness possessed of a willowy youth and more the emaciation of the starving I thought, watching her draw water from the well.

I approached carefully, my stumbling steps assuring even me that this starving girl and half-grown pup could easily evade me.

When I was only a step from the girl she turned to me, a wooden cup proffered in her thin hands. Automatically, I reached and accepted the mug, shock stealing any deliberate action from me.

"Father," she greeted quietly, her large eyes downcast as I swallowed the cold water.

Speechless, I stared at the girl, her unblemished features of a maiden who would be an incredibly beautiful one when she grew to womanhood.

"What?" I stammered, unable to think even though images now forced through my mind, filling the missing gaps in my memory with the truth of how time had been stolen from me.

"These are your children," a cold voice said from behind me.

I turned slowly to face Angrboða, my fists clenching while I wondered if I had the strength to attack the witch.

"You did this to me?" I asked, mind spinning to understand the ramifications of me having a child by the most powerful witch in Iron Wood.

She smirked. "You weren't exactly unwilling."

"You drugged me!" I accused, gesturing to the evidence of my wasted and weakened body.

She shrugged one beautiful shoulder. "I couldn't have you running off into the forest while I was indisposed, could I?"

As if to make her point, a low howl issued through the dark forest and a chorus of closer howls answered. I shuddered. The Iron wood was well known as the domain of the witches like Angrboða, but the guardians of these forests were Angrboða's own formidable offspring, packs of giant wolves who shared human-like transformations but always retained more in common with wolves than with any mortal men. There was a dark magic that permeated this forest and it left a stain devouring unwary travellers, the foolish or the mad. Which was I, then?

"What have you done?" I demanded, keeping my tone as calm as I could manage through my rising rage and panic.

"Nothing you did not truly desire," she answered.

I closed my eyes, pinching the bridge of my nose while I fought for control. "Angrboða," I growled.

She laughed, the sound sending shivers of fear up my spine. "Loki," she chuckled. "Don't play the fool. What is your greatest desire?"

I stared at her in horror, knowing well what had been in my heart when I entered into the Iron Wood in wolf form. "To destroy the gods," I said without emotion.

"Then our desires simply aligned in the most pleasant of ways," she said with a coquettish smile that was chilling.

"So, this is the product of our desires?" I asked, indicating the girl beside the well.

"One of them," Angrboða answered.

"One of them?" I repeated, feeling the blood drain from my face.

The witch smiled with satisfaction. "We've had a very extensive time together."

"The others?" I asked.

Angrboða gestured to the wolf pup gambolling at the girl's feet and then waved her hand vaguely at the well.

"What's in the well?" I asked, fearful of the answer.

"Come meet your other son," Angrboða said, moving past the girl and pushing the puppy out of the way.

Gracefully, Angrboða seated herself on the edge of the crumbling wall and leaning down into the well, she called quietly into the darkness beyond. I took another mouthful of the water the girl, my daughter, had served me a moment earlier. My hands were shaking while I waited, the silence heavy with my anticipation and dread. After a few moments, a slender, serpentine form coiled above the rim of the well, the large horned head arching back as the serpent reared back.

"Jörmungandr," Angrboða chided as though speaking to a disobedient child, which I supposed he was.

"Wonderful," I pronounced, sourly.

"This is Hel," Angrboða said, taking the young girl's hand in her own in a parody of maternal affection.

"We met earlier," I said. "At least Hel had the graciousness to afford a guest the respect under such laws."

Angrboða only shrugged. "The Járnviðr is no place for the laws of gods or men."

"Obviously," I snarled, turning away and nearly tripping over the puppy that was playing around my bare feet. "And this one?" I asked, regaining my balance.

"That is Fenrir," Angrboða answered, smirking at my discomfort.

"Now that my imprisonment seems to be at an end," I said, turning to face her, "my stud services are no longer yours to take. I'm going home."

Angrboða tilted her head sharply, the mannerism deliberately unnerving. "Óðinn will take these children," she warned.

"He's welcome to them," I snapped, already stalking back toward the hovel, my limbs still aching, but I was desperate to flee the Iron Wood.

"You won't protect what is yours?" Angrboða asked.

"I didn't want them," I shouted. "I'm not the paternal type."

"Really?" she demanded, following in my wake. "Would your wife Sigyn agree to that sentiment?"

"Sigyn never wanted to marry me," I snarled. "She got forced to marry Óðinn's foster-brother, the notorious liar and giant with aspirations of becoming a god."

"It's almost sorrowful how you actually believe that story," Angrboða said, her laughter cruel.

"It's the truth," I said, reaching the doorway to the dwelling.

I ignored the taunts and insults Angrboða pitched at me while I found some mouldering clothing and pulled it onto my skinny body. I was wasted and had lost what meagre muscle tone I'd once possessed. I dared not let the images of the days and nights Angrboða had abused me, drugged and insensible in this hovel, using me to her own ends. I reminded myself that our compact was nothing targeted toward me, the witch of the Iron Wood meant no harm to me but that I had been nothing more than an opportunity to wage her own war against Óðinn and the gods. I pulled the leather breaches on and tightened the belt and pushed my feet roughly into the ill-fitting boots. I did not consider who these items of clothing had once belonged to before me, it was well known Angrboða and her kin hunted these woods for stray travellers and human flesh was not disdained from the cookpot.

"Farewell, Angrboða," I announced, stepping fully dressed from the stinking hovel.

The witch stood with Hel's small hand in her own, the wolf Fenrir bounding after shadows at the edge of the bracken-covered path.

"Enjoy this idyllic maternal lifestyle," I snarled, beginning along the path.

"I promise you one thing in return for your staying within the confines of this revolting forest," I continued, not turning around. "Óðinn will hear nothing of this from my lips."

Angrboða's only response to my ultimatum was a chilling laughter that echoed through the misty woods, following me as easily as the werewolves who'd tracked my progress with predatory silence until I reached the fringes of the Iron Wood.

At the edge of the Iron Wood, I stepped across the invisible threshold that marked the division of the darker realms of Jötunheimr and the border of Midgard. Half-turning, I looked back into the wall of fog, the shifting forms of giant wolves partially discernible through the shadows. Repressing a shudder, I continued to walk swiftly toward the mountain passages that would allow me quick access into the realms of Asgard.

The scent of sweet wildflowers drifted on the wind when I emerged from the narrow cleft in the rock face and I stood, overlooking the fields of Fólkvangr, Valhalla discernible against the meadows only by the broad expanse of the turf roof. I inhaled deeply as the wind brushed against my body, the air crisp with promises of snow from the distant mountains of Jötunheimr. I shivered slightly, standing still too long with my eyes closed, pressed against the cold rock behind me. I shook myself, mentally trying to dispel the events revealed to me in the Iron Wood. I dared not think what Óðinn would do if he discovered my treachery and the schemes Angrboða had used to manipulate future events. I considered Angrboða, wondering what made the witches of Járnviðr, those less powerful than their mistress, different from Freyja, or the guise she had used as the völva Gullveig when first she came to Valhalla. What powers of prophecy and magic differed between the two? Which one should I fear more?

"Loki," Óðinn called, stepping around the base of the cliff where I stood, dressed in his tattered travelling robes.

"Óðinn," I greeted, a genuine smile of relief relaxing my features.

"What's happened?" my brother asked, squinting at me with concern.

I opened my eyes and gestured to my mismatched and badly fitting clothing. "I was robbed."

"Were you?" he asked, glancing around the empty expanse of the meadows.

"Obviously not here," I chuckled. "Do you think many thieves exchange clothing when they rob you?"

"No, I suppose not," he conceded with a self-deprecating smile.

I pushed off the rock face, trying for my usual lithe step, but slipped awkwardly in the moss at my feet. I pitched forward, arms pinwheeling comically for a moment. The speed of my near fall propelled me into Óðinn but his strong arms caught me and he pulled me into a quick embrace before steadying me on my feet. We stood a little too close and I heaved a shaky breath, looking pointedly at his strong hands still grasping my forearms.

"This is cosy," I said with a weak smile. "But I love you only as a brother, we both know that."

Óðinn did not respond with a conspiratorial grin and I met his stare.

"Do you know where I was before I came here?" Óðinn asked softly.

"I probably couldn't guess," I muttered, disliking the dark tone to his voice.

"You have been missing for a long time," he continued, cobalt eye raking over me, searching me for any signs of deception. "Many were speaking of your anger at how Brokk had treated you."

"Well," I bristled, "you can't expect me to accept torture and humiliation as a justified punishment."

"It was what I deemed a worthy punishment," Óðinn whispered, angrily.

"There's been a lot of that going around," I hissed, glaring at him.

"After you secured the favour of the dwarfs for us, you disappeared into the depths of Vanaheimr and Freyr lost you amongst the woods. I sent Geri and Freki to track you but they were never as fleet as you in wolf form. Neither Hugin nor Munin could spy you in the realms of Midgard or Jötunheimr. I sat for days upon the cold stone of Hliðskjálf searching the Nine Realms but you were hidden deep from all our sight. From the sight of all but one of us," he said with finality. "Can you guess now who I sought?"

"Yes," I snarled, trying to pull away, but he held my arms painfully tight. "You sought Mimir, the wisest of you all, who lost his head for you."

"Mimir was the wisest of us," Óðinn agreed sorrowfully. "He always knew you were both a danger and a blessing to me. You know I preserved his head and seek the wisdom of the one who should never have been sacrificed for us."

"For you," I snapped, anger rising at the unspoken accusations.

"For me," he acknowledged with a small bow of his head. "What do you think Mimir told me?"

"I hope he told you that hag imprisoned me," I growled.

Óðinn nodded slightly. "He told me your role in her schemes was not done knowingly."

I rolled my eyes. "That's a mild way of explaining it."

"What was the result of Angrboða's scheming?" Óðinn asked in a deadly quiet voice.

I paled, thinking of the strange girl-child who had hosted me at the well and the playful wolf pup and even the proud magnificence of the young serpent.

"You already know, why make me speak it?" I demanded.

"Then you do know," he confirmed with a grim smile.

I twisted in his grasp but it did not slacken. "What are you going to do?" I pleaded.

"Those monsters will destroy the Nine Realms," he explained.

"Then don't make yourself a bigger monster and destroy them," I begged.

Óðinn's calculating cobalt gaze met mine but he did not speak

"If you do it, you kill part of me in every sense of the word, Óðinn," I warned. "You who are the wisest leader of us all, the one men call upon to decide the outcome of battle and the one for whom nothing is unknown. Surely you are not afraid of watching three small monsters?"

"Small?" he scoffed, genuinely surprised.

"Hel is but a child, more girl than anything else. Fenrir is a wolf pup and the serpent Jörmungandr lives in a well," I reasoned. "Don't destroy the bonds of brotherhood we made so long ago. Remember when you took pity on a giant from Múspelheim, a misshapen thing that only longed for beauty. You granted me this form that could please the eye, be as swift as the wind and lithe as a wolf."

"I gave you the beauty that matched your intelligence," Óðinn said, considering me as his will waned beneath the onslaught of my pleas.

"You gave me opportunity," I said earnestly, meeting his eye. "Give my children a chance at life."

He sighed, letting go of my arms, and stepped back from me. I shuddered with relief and my limbs felt so weak I reached for the rock face to support myself.

"Thor is bringing them to Asgard," Óðinn finally said. "He will be here soon and I will decide where best to keep watch on your small brood of monsters."

I nodded in relief, gratitude and exhaustion, collapsing my body against the stone surface of the mountain as Óðinn walked away, his tall form already melting into the purpling shadows of twilight as he strode toward Valhalla.

When I caught up to Óðinn, he was already standing outside Valhalla, hand raised to shade his eye from the glare of the fading sun. I followed his gaze, staring into the fading light where Sól had already vanished beyond the western horizon and Nótt was fast approaching on her dark steed.

"You'll keep your promise to me?" I asked Óðinn, surprised at the desperation in my voice. I had never realised how much I cared for the idea of children, of these children, until Óðinn threatened to take them from me.

Óðinn faced me, squinting slightly in the twilit gloom. "Sigyn has borne you two sons. What is so important about these ones? You never consented to these children, you never intended to give them life. Why keep them now? Why risk everything for them, Loki?"

"Do you really not see?" I asked, staring at him, wondering how we could understand each other so well and yet, at times I thought my brother didn't know me at all.

Óðinn returned his gaze to the western horizon, muttering inaudibly beneath his breath.

"Then let me tell you," I said. "I love Sigyn and the sons she has borne me as much as I love this brood of monsters. It doesn't matter if I planned to give life to this one or that, they all share the spark of life that is connected to me. They all deserve the same protection and attention from me, whether they be children of a Vanir goddess, or those of a giant's witch."

"I don't understand why you accept such a risk," Óðinn replied, shaking his head in disbelief.

"Life is life given," I snarled, turning angrily away from him and stalking a few paces into the darkness. "It is not my right to snatch life away because it offends my understanding of the worlds."

I felt Óðinn's anger gather about him like a storm, Huginn and Muninn lifted in unison from his shoulders, black wings spread against the night as they circled him, cawing in outrage. I took an involuntary step backward but before Óðinn could reply or release his rage on me, Thor strode around the bulk of Valhalla, my children clutched in his massive arms.

CHAPTER 19
LOKI'S OFFSPRING

The pale girl-child was silent as Thor swung her down from his grip, depositing her slight form on the dewy grass outside Valhalla. She did not cry or protest, but only clutched her brother, the struggling wolf pup, closer to her chest. Hel was still dressed in the same clean but bedraggled white smock I had seen her in only a few days before. Her her thick, raven-black locks flowed down her back. I steeled myself and met her solemn and singular gaze, fixing me with an inscrutability so intense that nothing could escape her insight. Was it possible Hel had the prophetic gifts of her mother, the magic that ran so strongly in the Iron Wood witch lineages?

I flinched as she took her gaze from me and levelled her calculating sight on Óðinn. I drew my breath in a hiss, taking a half-step toward her as if I could shield her from the outburst I knew was already burgeoning in Óðinn, the affront of this half-giant's child to test her will against his own.

Time seemed to pause, the winds that had been blowing relentlessly all afternoon against the plains of Fólkvangr suddenly stirred again. The twilight hours were gone and night had fallen, the pale god personified by the moon had already cast his silvery glow upon the worlds below him. I longed to protect Hel, to step between her and the power brewing inside Óðinn's barely controlled rage.

"Hel," I called quietly, as one might call to a hound caught teasing a viper.

I did not think she'd react to my voice, but I'd been wrong earlier. I watched as her attention left the locked gaze with Óðinn to meet my anxious eyes.

"This is Óðinn," I introduced him, a nervous sweep of my arm to indicate the leader of the Æsir, the god of war and men and the host of the mighty hall behind us.

"I know," Hel replied, mater-of-fact.

"How would you like to rule a world of your own fashioning?" Óðinn asked her, squatting so he might be at eye level with the young girl.

"Only kings can rule," Hel replied knowingly and smiled, her full lips quirking with pride at her knowledge.

"What do you know of our rules?" Óðinn asked her, seating himself cross-legged on the ground beside her.

She regarded him cautiously before answering. "I know the Nine Worlds are ruled by a king among gods, but he is afraid of what he doesn't know and can't foresee."

I shivered at her words and desperately wanted to grasp the child in my arms, shake some caution into her. Óðinn forgave none for challenging his authority and this barb had met its mark.

"You know a lot about the Nine Worlds then," Óðinn agreed gruffly, wiping his palms on the knees of his breeches. "I would be foolish to disregard such a rational mind. How do you feel about the mortal men and women of Midgard? Have you ever heard the mighty skalds detail the exploits and valour of men in battle? Or the skalds' praise of the virtues of the glorious queens and shield-maidens among the peoples of Midgard?"

"What would I care for the valour of warriors? The ferocity of berserkers? The virtues of shield-maidens or the beauty of queens? I am never going to be among them."

I smiled at Hel's response and was pleased to see Óðinn push backward a little from the girl who regarded him so gravely. If he thought conversations with my daughter were going to be simple, if she would give him a moment of forgiveness or that his clever words could uncoil the distance she placed between them, he was very mistaken. Óðinn seemed to finally understand this too and gave the girl a satisfied nod of his head as though he had discerned her motivations and mechanisations, and not the other way around.

"Loki," he said to me, climbing to his feet.

"Hel is my daughter," I began. Ignoring his raised hand at my interruption, I continued hurriedly: "You gave me opportunity once. I only ask that you give my children the same chance. Or I swear to you, our bond as brothers will be broken."

Óðinn rubbed wearily at his chin, staring at me with bleak resignation.

"Very well," he finally said, turning toward Hel. "Your father intervenes for your life and I will honour our pledge."

I exhaled. The relief flooding through me nearly dropped me where I stood.

"Loki," Óðinn said in a cool tone, "Hel will not reside in any of the Nine Worlds where she may do us harm. I send her to the shadowy realm between Svartálfheimr and Niflheimr, where she will rule in her own hall, Eljudnir. Let her subjects be the souls of the worst from Midgard, for her indifference to virtue and valour make me think them well-suited to her rule."

I bit my lip, unhappy with the coldness in Óðinn's eye. "She is no threat to you except your pride," I snapped, "this child who has more foresight than you like."

Óðinn growled in his throat and behind him, Freki and Geri snarled in answer. I turned, baring my teeth at Óðinn's wolves, which sent them into frenzied growling and snapping.

"Loki!"

I turned too late, saw Óðinn grasp Hel in his long arms as she tried to run away and lift her above his head. Still struggling, Hel's startled expression met mine before Óðinn threw her bodily into the swirling tunnel of mist that had formed from nowhere. Hel screamed, high-pitched and shuddering as I ran forward, desperate to leap after her. Óðinn's powerful hand grabbed me and held me firm, but I dangled over the edge of the abyss, staring in the frozen mists of Niflheimr as Hel bounced down the razor crags of the cliff. Finally she landed in a bloody sprawl at the bottom of the abyss, her white skin torn and bleeding, bruised and already frost-bitten by contact with the icy abysmal ground of Niflheimr.

Óðinn hauled me backward, tossing me behind him onto the wildflower meadows of Fólkvangr but did not look at me. Instead, his gaze moved past me and sought Thor's.

"Bring me the next of Loki's children," Óðinn said coldly.

Thor moved without compunction, holding the struggling wolf pup by the thick ruff of his coat and rolled a large barrel toward Óðinn. The massive barrel picked up speed as it rolled down the slight slope, but Óðinn planted his weight evenly and braced himself against it. Despite being prepared for the impact, the force of the blow when the barrel struck Óðinn's legs nearly knocked him from his feet. It drove Óðinn back a few paces until his boot wedged beneath the barrel, stopping any further progress. Wheezing out a shaky breath, Óðinn met Thor's gaze and smiled ruefully.

"What's in the barrel?" he asked.

Thor shrugged his massive shoulders, glaring sidelong at me.

"You already know, I told you," I snarled. "Just open the barrel and get this over with. Stop playing these stupid games."

"You're hardly in any position to issue orders," he muttered.

I crossed my arms over my chest, ignoring the plaintive cries from the wolf pup as Óðinn gestured to Thor for his assistance with manoeuvring the massive barrel into an upright position. The barrels were awkward and normally were used in Asgard to mature mead, and almost always required two of the gods to move them. I did not move or speak while Óðinn and Thor wrestled the barrel upright again, the oak structure as wide as it was tall and easily the height of Óðinn.

"Loki," Óðinn called, gesturing impatiently to me as he wiped sweat from his brow.

I sighed and rolled my eyes, but walked slowly to their side. After the callous treatment of Hel, I expected nothing good could come for Jörmungandr or Fenrir. I loathed to be involved, and my demeanour was meant to show they shouldn't expect any emotion from me, that they'd wasted their time trying to torture me with such rough treatment. In truth, I suspected that torture had been Óðinn's plan.

"Be careful," Thor warned as Óðinn broke the seals securing the lid of the barrel.

"Unlike you to be fearful," Óðinn mused, brows meeting in thought as he slid the polished lid from the top of the barrel.

"I don't like this one," Thor whispered, as though confiding a shameful secret.

Óðinn nodded without speaking and both gods stood beside the massive oak mead barrel. Twilight was deepening around the plains of Fólkvangr and still Óðinn and Thor did not move. Still, Thor dropped the young Fenrir to the ground where the pup gamboled around Thor's feet and leaping on unsuspecting fireflies. The mirth which had long been buried and deadened within me began the stir at this comical scene, both gods staring intently at a normal-appearing mead barrel, the grimmest of expressions carved into their faces as a wolf pup played at their feet.

The last flare of light from Sól's passage lit the sky, the flaming mane of Skrinfraki sending brilliant embers into the purpling twilight. Jörmungandr rose from the bottom of the barrel, uncoiling his massive form, spiralling upward with such swiftness that Óðinn and Thor leapt back in surprise.

"What can be fearful about that?" I asked Thor, not bothering to hide my smirk.

Thor's bushy eyebrows knit together as he glared at me and muttered a curse under his breath.

"My mother was most assuredly not an indulger in swine," I said, baring my teeth as I smiled.

Óðinn stared at the towering form of Jörmungandr. The glittering scales that covered his form like armour marked him as dragon kin. Óðinn whispered something in trepidation and stepped closer to Jörmungandr, the curved neck immediately bowing and razor-like teeth snapping at the leader of the gods. Hastily, Óðinn took a step backward even as Thor reached for Mjölnir at his hip, the heavy weight of the war-hammer resting in his palm, fingers restlessly tapping the shaft.

"Loki," Óðinn called softly, not taking his eyes from the hypnotically weaving serpent.

"Yes?" I asked pleasantly, not stepping closer.

"Does Jörmungandr have wings?"

"I don't know," I said, thoughtfully. "Didn't you look?"

"Loki," Óðinn growled, keeping his gaze fixed on the weaving serpent in case it prepared to strike.

I sighed exasperatedly. "You expect me to help you? After the kindness you just showed Hel?"

"It was a kindness," Óðinn spat.

I rolled my eyes but took a step forward and gestured to Jörmungandr. Instantly, the mighty serpent hooded its eyes and relaxed its arched frame, tension evaporating as though it had never been. Jörmungandr still watched Thor and Óðinn but he no longer swayed in the eerie hypnotic manner that unnerved me. Even so, the serpent kept his gaze on Thor, eyes lazy and half-lidded as he watched the god.

"Does he have wings? Even the most rudimentary ones?" Óðinn demanded of me.

"No," I answered, watching the serpent and his feigned disinterest in our conversation.

"Then he is a not as terrible a threat as I'd feared," Óðinn sighed with relief.

"Good," I answered cheerfully. "Then let's just move him to a nice lake in Asgard."

"No," Thor interrupted sharply. "That viper will be nowhere near me."

"Afraid of the viper who fits in a barrel?" I teased the god. "You who are feared by even the fiercest of werewolves and the most battle-scarred from Jötunheimr?"

"They do fear me," Thor acknowledged, and then pointed a massive finger at Jörmungandr. "But I fear that one, and with good reason."

"Throw him into the Midgard Sea," Óðinn instructed Thor, not looking at me.

I began to protest but Thor had already moved and taken Jörmungandr by surprise. Before I could utter complaint or counter Óðinn's orders, Thor had firmly fastened the lid of the barrel and hauled it over one muscled shoulder.

"Wait," I spluttered as Thor marched toward another of the swirling misty vortexes that Óðinn summoned from nowhere.

Not waiting for me to argue with Óðinn and the ensuing counterarguments, Thor hefted the barrel higher on his shoulder, halted in the knee-deep fog and threw the barrel into the empty expanse beyond. I screamed, rushing forward after the barrel, feeling as though a part of myself had been ripped from my soul. I could not explain it, but the abandonment of my children into Niflheimr and now into the Midgard Sea pulled at the subtle threads which wove together my understanding of who I was.

I heard the faint splash and the sharp sound of cracking wood as the mead barrel burst apart on touching the surface of the Midgard Sea. Thor shoved me bodily away from the thick, misty vortex and in silence, I sank to my knees. Fenrir growled and climbed awkwardly into my lap, the puppy chewing on my thumbs as I sat numbly, unblinking as Óðinn and Thor beheld the outcome of their latest sin against me.

Jörmungandr did not suffer any injury from being thrown into the Midgard Sea. Fortune seemed to bless this child where it had deprived Hel but still, I watched in numb fascination as the serpent moved free from the splinters of mead barrel. I frowned and then squinted as if what I saw belied what was happening. I turned to regard Óðinn, noticing the thin set of his lips, and understood that he had not anticipated the manner in which Jörmungandr now thwarted him. My son grew impossibly fast, the waters of the Midgard Sea providing some sort of nourishment that had previously been absent. Jörmungandr continued to grow, easily doubly, tripling and then going too far beyond for us to count. In moments, the serpent Thor had tossed away like so much despised filth had swollen to grow beyond the size of the mead barrel that once contained him, but now the Midgard Sea barely contained the massive, curved form of Jörmungandr. I stared with incredulity as my son rested his own head on the tip of his tail and settled against the bottom of the Midgard Sea, one unblinking and lidless eye staring balefully at Thor and Óðinn.

I tried to bury my rage as Thor gripped the wolf pup Fenrir by the scruff of his tiny neck, the pup whining and twisting in fear. Óðinn's cold gaze raked mercilessly over the tiny creature as though he expected it could inflect more damage than Jörmungandr alone.

"Stop this," I pleaded, trying to master my emotions.

Óðinn stared at me with suspicion and disgust. "I vowed to spare their lives but gave no promises beyond that, Loki. I told you my fears and you continue to ignore me."

"Your fears," I spat, losing control of my anger. "Your fears are forever bound to your own interests. What threatens the Æsir the most is you."

Óðinn's gaze narrowed and he turned away from me, beckoning Thor to step closer. The god of thunder proffered the wolf pup to Óðinn, Fenrir wriggling in his grip. Without speaking to me, Óðinn took my son, the tiny black pup fitting into his cupped hands, and closed his eye. I felt the tingle of the magic grate against my skin, the familiar pull of the power of foresight that Óðinn had sacrificed his other eye to gain. The power that came naturally to Angrboða and Freyja, the gift of prophecy that was somehow more a woman's magic than that of a man, was always powerful but never felt so wrong as it did now. I had been by Óðinn's side before when he used this power acquired by his own sacrifice, and it had never felt unnatural but somehow forced. Now I shivered, the magic reaching for me, touching me as though invisible fingers were prying at my soul. Angered, I called my own magic from the fiery depths of Múspelheim and pushed back against Óðinn's invisible touch. I felt him recoil as though I had struck him, saw the startled expression on his weathered face.

"Don't ever do that without my permission," I snarled and stalked forward, plucking Fenrir from his shocked grip.

"What changed between us?" Óðinn whispered, voice soft and perplexed as he stared at me.

"I never changed," I told him, calming the pup with gentle strokes. "I'm not sure you have either, I think we just finally see each other for who we are and not who we'd hoped the other might become."

Óðinn frowned, considering my words as I crooned softly to Fenrir, the wolf pup licking my hands.

"What about the abomination?" Thor asked, gesturing vaguely toward me and the bundle of fur in my arms.

"It's a cute abomination," I corrected, waggling the puppy toward Thor.

"He is the end of everything," Óðinn said calmly, as though speaking of trivial matters. "When Gullveig came into Valhalla and we cursed her for the witch she was, she spoke a prophecy and cursed us. The wolf Fenrir is the devourer of the Nine Worlds."

"We're all going to need to get much smaller for that to occur," I said, squinting at the pup. "Or he's got to get a lot bigger."

"The last is true, I'm afraid," Óðinn sighed, suddenly sounding old and bitter. "Gullveig prophesied that in the final days there will be a mighty battle and, in our twilight, the devourer will howl and break from his fetters, and the three wolves will consume the Nine Worlds."

"Three wolves?" I asked, raising my brows. "Unless this pup has a magical ability to self-reproduce, we only have one wolf born from Angrboða."

Óðinn nodded, pinching the bridge of his nose. "I assume Gullveig warned that Sköll and Haiti will join their brother Fenrir to devour the Nine Worlds."

I nodded, realising now that Sköll and Haiti, the wolves destined to bring darkness when they devoured the sun and moon, were Fenrir's half-siblings by Angrboða. This did not bode well for the gods and how long Angrboða might have been planning their demise. Had I been wrong since my return to Asgard? I had assumed it was Freyja who had wished Óðinn's dominance to collapse, and who had skilfully manipulated me into positions to assure that outcome. Had I been wrong about Freyja? The Norns? Was Angrboða the weaver behind this web of deceit?

"Fenrir must be kept within my sight at all times," Óðinn instructed Thor. "He will never be allowed to run free lest he devour these Worlds, beginning with Asgard. Bind him here and see he never breaks his fetters."

I started with mute shock at Óðinn and then looked down at the sleeping wolf pup in my arms. "Are you certain?" I asked, the disbelief evident in my tone.

Óðinn stared incredulously at me.

"Yes," he finally said and strode away, beckoning for Thor to take Fenrir with them.

Thor stood a moment, obviously as perplexed as I was. He glared at Fenrir as though he expected the small pup to suddenly turn into a giant, slavering monster capable of challenging him. I put Fenrir on the ground, the sleepy pup shook himself then gambolled over to Thor, pawing at his massive boots. The god of thunder glowered at the small harbinger of doom, then stooped and picked him up.

"Look after him?" I pleaded, hating the tremor of fear and hope that ran through my voice.

Thor glared at me from beneath his bushy red eyebrows before he gave a curt nod and strode away, following Óðinn's retreating form.

I remained where I was for several hours, darkness gathering like a cloak around me. Starlight shone bright across the night sky, and I fancied I heard the tinkle of harness from Nótt's mount as Hrímfaxi passed above and the cold evening grew later.

Chapter 20
Dreams And Sacrifices

I watched Óðinn and Thor disappear into the shadows but remained on my knees outside the massive bulk of Valhalla. I remained there while the silent servants kindled the torches around me and lit the hearth inside, the faint sound of Bragi plucking at his harp drifting through the evening. I was lost in bitterness and something like grief, unable to really understand what had passed between Óðinn and me this evening. I did not hear the soft footsteps behind me. A gentle hand touched my shoulder tentatively, and I roused myself. Turning, I saw Iðunn's youthful face framed by the firelight behind her. She smiled at me with a kindness I felt I barely deserved. I had betrayed her, and yet she showed me kindness. I smiled back, unable to help myself.

"Come inside, Loki," she said, slipping a hand beneath my arm and tugging me upright.

I sighed and, with effort, climbed to my feet. I was sore and stiff. My body felt like an old man's this evening, as though every injury I had ever received was a real scar in my flesh and mind. Walking in a daze beside her, I barely noticed where Iðunn took me, and she steered me through the smoky and bright room of the central hall and through the covered sections at the back of Valhalla where the sleeping chambers were. I began to wake then as she led me down the familiar passageways.

"Iðunn," I began, trying to pull my arm free. "I'm embarrassed to say it's a first for me, but I'm not really capable tonight."

She stopped, her wide blue eyes staring at me in shock. "I would never…" she said then fell silent.

"Never mind," I mumbled, pulling my arm free and patting her on the shoulder. I walked the few paces to my own chamber and turned to face her. "I can but hope," I said with a weak grin.

Iðunn smiled a little uncertainly, the shock and insult fading from her features. "Sleep well, Loki."

I nodded and slipped inside the darkened chamber I usually shared with my wife. The chamber was empty, as I'd expected it would be. There was no chance Sigyn would want to be near me after she heard of my indiscretions and that I was now the proud father of three monsters. I laughed bitterly to myself, tugged the rough tunic over my head and dropped it on the floor. It smelled of Angrboða and the heady scent of that hovel. I shuddered and was suddenly desperate to remove all the awful clothing I was wearing. I pulled the ill-fitting trousers from my body and kicked them into the wretched tunic, tossing the frayed belt on top of them. I looked at my hands, remembering them roaming over the supple, pale flesh of Angrboða's thighs and cupping her large breasts. I wanted to vomit. I stared at my hands as though they had betrayed me and immediately kindled the flames that were mine to call. Fire played along my fingertips as I bent and touched them to the stinking, sweat-stained clothing at my feet. The material caught and my chamber was immediately filled with the dancing light of flames and the acrid stench of burning wool. I coughed a little and turned away, staggering the few steps to the large bed piled with rich, embroidered blankets and furs at the far end of the vast chamber. I was asleep in moments, the fire at the front of the room still consuming the clothing stolen from dead men when I fled the Iron Wood.

A disjointed confusion of imagery. The dreamscape of swirling fog of the Iron Wood broken by shattering thunderstorms and the cawing of flocks of ravens. I saw the Norns weaving on their bloody loom, the crack of lightning bolts echoing with the snip of shears as another thread was cut from the loom. I moved through the fog, my feet sure on the path I followed, snout low to the ground and confident that Sköll and Haiti followed me and conscious that we sought another wolf, one who would unite our pack.

I stepped out of the dense mist and stood atop a bluff, the sweeping black cliffs dropping to a churning sea below where Ran and Aegir stood upon the waves, the drowned dead quiet in the water beside them. Lightning split the sky again and I heard the familiar battle cry as Thor threw Mjölnir into the grey sky, the war-hammer spinning past me as Jörmungandr rose from the dark waters to catch Thor's prized weapon in his venom-laced teeth. I turned my head, a flickering brightness catching my attention.

The dreamscape changed instantly, and I stood amid memory once more. It was the fateful night when the witch Gullveig had come to Valhalla and spoken with us all. So many eons had passed since that night and yet I stood in the moment as though it were fresh, staring at the young woman before us, her clothing spun from silken gold, her headdress a masterpiece of gold and silver. I lounged in my high-backed chair and turned my gaze to Óðinn where he sat beside Frigg. His long fingers were loosely gripping the mead horn, his other hand clasped with hers. A smile played along his lips and both his cobalt eyes were fixed on the witch before him. She was glorious and beautiful, temptation perfected, and yet she had an edge that hinted at danger. Gullveig was a challenge to Óðinn's authority and she had walked into his newly claimed Valhalla as though these lands were rightfully her own. She had spoken of arts and knowledge that Óðinn did not possess. I saw him scoff and laugh, deny and belittle the woman in front of him. The gathered Æsir in the hall mocked and challenged Gullveig with equal pleasure but I knew Óðinn better than his own children. I knew that the arts and knowledge in which Gullveig proclaimed proficiency was not within Óðinn's own powers. I saw his glittering eyes turning shaper and the bright sparks of fear begin to shine in them.

I straightened in my chair and lifted my arm casually to draw his attention.

"Gullveig," Óðinn shouted, cutting the merriment and laughter in the room. "We have no place among us for such outspoken pride and dark powers. The prophetic knowledge you claim to wield would surely have warned you how dangerous it is to challenge me."

Gullveig's eyes shone brighter than the gold and silver adorning her headdress. "I know my own danger is nothing compared to the foolishness you provoke."

I tried to shout, to warn Óðinn against his actions, but the God of War moved so swiftly that I couldn't intervene. The spear left Óðinn's hand in a blur and hit Gullveig in the chest between the ribs the blow pushing her backward several paces. She screamed and blood spurted across the floor of Valhalla as she stumbled into the central hearth immediately behind her. Gullveig, recovering quickly, began her curse, and her words were a prophecy Óðinn couldn't circumvent.

I woke with a start, aware of the soft brush of fingertips against my bare shoulder. Perspiration soaked my body, and the soft woollen fabric of the richly embroidered sheets clung to my body.

"It's all right, wake up," Sigyn called gently to me, her fingers caressing my arm.

"I'm awake," I rasped but stayed where I was, body turned away from her, uncertain if this wasn't some cruel illusion. Why would Sigyn be in our bed after all the humiliation I had caused her? No woman would tolerate such an affront to her own pride. I closed my eyes, despising my own foolishness and hating Angrboða with every fibre of my soul.

"Loki?" Sigyn asked, bending over my shoulder, her long hair falling like a golden curtain around us.

"This isn't real," I muttered, squeezing my eyes closed tighter and wishing my body would resist its longing to be touched.

"Are you alright?" she asked, kissing my brow tentatively. "Are you feverish?"

"Nothing is all right," I growled, rolling onto my back and staring into her deep blue eyes. "It's never going to be all right."

Her dark blue eyes were almost black against the pupil, but she bent to me, her lips meeting mine, her weight pressing closer to me. My body responded with the longing I always had when Sigyn was near me. I was instantly angered by my own arousal, and the touch of her breasts against my chest only heightened my need and self-disgust. I shifted beneath her, placing my hands on her hips as she kissed me and gently moved her to my side.

"What's wrong?" Sigyn asked, her lip caught between her teeth.

I frowned. *Did she truly not know what I had done?* Was it possible that no one had not told her yet? I wondered for a terrible moment if she were deceiving me, if this was some malicious game to wound me further. No. Sigyn was nothing like me, which was why I understood immediately that she truly had no knowledge of my betrayal. I swallowed against my dry throat and fought for the courage to tell her.

"Have you and Óðinn had another argument?" she asked me.

I pushed myself upright a little, peering at her intently. "Why do you ask that?"

"In your dreams you were shouting at Óðinn," Sigyn said, laying her head on my chest, fingers tracing meaningless runes on my chest.

"Oh," I said, relieved on one account but also troubled. "We did have an argument of sorts," I explained, brushing my fingers through her long hair.

"Does it explain why you burnt a pile of rags in the middle of our room?" she enquired, titling her face up at me, an amused smile on her lips.

"A little," I replied, reaching up to kiss her. "But probably not in any sensible way."

"Your reasons always seem without sense to me," she teased, returning my kiss.

"I argued with Óðinn about his quest for knowledge. I dreamed of the first night the Æsir and Vanir stood together in Valhalla. Do you remember it?"

"I remember the thrice-burnt witch," Sigyn answered, stiffening in my arms.

"I dreamed how she cursed Óðinn," I admitted. "I remembered how something changed within him that night and he became obsessed with learning how to prevent Gullveig's curse. We argued that night when the rest of you were indoors. I followed Óðinn to Mimir's Well where he had preserved the head of his wisest friend and where he still goes when he seeks council. At the base of the shallow roots of Yggdrasil, Óðinn sacrificed his own eye that night for the foresight it might offer him."

"What truly worries you?" Sigyn asked me, resting her chin on my chest, face tilted upward to regard me seriously.

"I feel a doom is approaching," I whispered, shivering as my perspiration chilled in the night air. "I think none of Óðinn's sacrifices will be enough to prevent the curse that Gullveig laid on us. I think he cannot prevent a curse that is justified."

"You think the twilight of the gods will come?" she asked, daring not to breathe.

"I think we committed a grievance against Gullveig, and no amount of trickery or cleverness can escape the end we deserve."

Sigyn exhaled and took me in her arms, holding me close for a moment as she clung to me. I drifted in her embrace, unable to forgive myself for inaction when Gullveig was tortured so cruelly eons ago and now, unable to forgive myself for actions that would destroy Sigyn and the Nine Worlds. I let myself be absorbed in feelings that were good, in the caress of Sigyn's body against mine and the pleasure she took from me. I buried my regret deeper inside myself as I forgot, for a moment, the doom I had wrought and let the climax of our passion overcome me.

I left Sigyn asleep and stole through the predawn darkness like a lover fleeing from his mistress's bed. Inside the rooms I passed, I heard murmured conversations between couples, no doubt preparing to steal from bedrooms as I had just done. Although I wondered who I might spy leaving a lover's embrace to sneak through the shadowy hallways and seek their marriage bed, I did not pause but hurried through into the cavernous space of the main hall.

Abruptly, I stopped. The tiny hairs on my body rose in warning and I felt the faint shiver of unease as I inhaled the early morning air. Dagr had not yet ridden his proud mount across the sky and the frost-maned Hrímfaxi still stamped the sluggish pre-dawn sky. It was not yet light and power still belonged to Nótt, and under her command all those strange magics best practised under darkness still held sway. I sniffed the air, the crisp scent of morning frost and a slightly acrid tang of an unfamiliar burnt herb.

"Come closer, Loki," Freyja called from the shadows beside the empty hearth.

I started at her voice, recovered quickly but could not shake the uneasiness she always evoked in me. There was a strong power in the Vanir witch that was familiar to me now and reminiscent of Angrboða. I squared my shoulders, preparing to battle her with whatever powers I could muster against her illusions and deceptions.

"I am not like her," Freyja continued mildly, sounding almost bored.

"Your ability to perceive my thoughts before I even think them is evidence enough to the contrary," I said with open hostility.

Freyja's dark eyes regarded me from beneath her auburn hair. She remained seated beside the empty hearth, the burnt remains of the offering still trailing smoke beside her.

"What was done to you was grievous." Freyja was unemotional as if my betrayal was nothing more than one detail among many others.

"I can see it really bothers you," I sneered, crossing my arms over my chest. "You're positively distraught over how I have been wronged."

"Don't confuse my awareness of what happened to you with affection for you," she said, silver eyes piercing mine.

"There's no danger of that happening," I scoffed.

Freyja smirked, her deep red lips marked against the pale skin of her face, her unbound auburn hair framing her face. I felt an irresistible desire stir within me and ground my teeth, fighting the sway of her magic and the betrayal of my own flesh.

"Stop it," I snarled.

"Whatever do you mean?" she asked with a coquettish smile.

I gestured to my obvious arousal and clenched my fists.

"Oh," Freyja cooed in a honeyed tone. "You really are too easily manipulated, Loki."

I rolled my eyes and leaned my back against the wooden pillar behind me. I forced my mind away from memories of Sigyn and our recent passions, refusing to let Freyja stir me into any insensible behaviour I would regret later.

"You remember the night you came here to Valhalla dressed in gold and offered Óðinn a partnership?" I asked, grinding my back teeth together.

"Gullveig came to Óðinn," Freyja said, regarding me icily from beside the hearth.

"Of course," I amended, smiling falsely. "That's precisely what I meant to say."

"What bothers you, Loki?" Freyja demanded, all flirtatious pretence evaporating.

"Gullveig prophesied to Óðinn in such a specific manner," I drawled. "The prophecy was more curse than many believed it to be. Oh, I think Óðinn and I might have been among the few who recognised those words for what they truly were."

"I'm getting bored, Loki," Freyja threatened as she stood up, fingers flexing at her side in agitation.

"I am not as skilful at words as you," I pleaded, holding up a hand for patience. "But that curse had a mighty impact on Óðinn. You drove him to pursue every course of action he might in order to prevent the fulfilment of your prophecy. There was a very sly trick to it, wasn't there?" I asked, watching the tension in her features.

"What trick?" Freyja spat.

"When you strolled into Asgard beside Freyr, you let Óðinn believe you were Gullveig in some other transformation. You let Óðinn think the powers of prophecy were limited to Gullveig. In assuming her identity, Óðinn never questioned there might be not one female seer who shares the magic of the Norns, but entire lineages of witches in giants, the völva who could form an alliance against him."

Freyja's lips imperceptibly twitched, and I knew I had been right. The Vanir goddess and leader of the Valkyries did not reply to my accusation but shook her auburn locks and gave me a tender smile.

"Angrboða did well to choose you," Freyja whispered in my ear as she passed me. "You have quite the stamina, I understand."

"I've heard your brother boasts similar talents belonging to you," I snarled.

Freyja halted, her face close to mine. Her silver eyes pierced me like those of her predatory hawk form before her hand moved lightning fast, long nails raking across my face. I yelped in surprise and stumbled backward a step, smacking my head into the solid wooden pillar behind me.

"Be polite to those more powerful than you," Freyja warned, stepping away from me. "I know precisely what darkness lurks in your soul and what that darkness will make you do. Remember it is not just your body I can so easily manipulate, Loki. You'd be wiser to be kind to me if you wish to survive the coming events."

"What have you and Angrboða orchestrated?" I demanded.

"Only what you and Óðinn deserve," Freyja hissed, and walked toward the open doorway at the far end of the hall. She paused, turning to speak to me over her shoulder. "Remember this last thing, Loki. We will bring Óðinn to his knees, the mightiest god who sacrificed himself upon Yggdrasil for nine nights to gain the knowledge he was too proud to seek in partnership with us. And, Loki, you're the one to deliver him to us."

"I won't betray Óðinn," I warned her, curling my lip in anger.

"You already have," Freyja snorted. "You've known for a while that you're the blade to cut him low. What you don't know is you'll want to do it in the end."

I stared at Freyja, her words sending prickles of gooseflesh over my skin and chill sweat clung to my body. I watched Freyja leave Valhalla, stepping into the dawn light as I fought the bitter bile rising in my throat.

Chapter 21
Betrayal

I fled Asgard in the pale hours after dawn, escaping the memories of what Óðinn and Thor had done to my children, and regretfully abandoning Fenrir for the few days I needed to think. I fled into the vast wasteland territories of Útgarðar, a vague landscape located somewhere between the boundaries of Midgard and Jötunheimr. There I had a small holding of my own, a dank cavern to be honest, but it was my own. So many things had begun to collapse and now they were quickly gathering pace, as though an avalanche was about to carry everything, I knew away from me. I fled like a child seeking shelter to the one place I knew Óðinn would not follow me. This small territory of my own was not far from the mist-drenched Iron Wood, but I would rather take my chances with Angrboða and her kin than stay in the presence of the gods right now.

The cavern dwelling I called home was damp, pale moss decorated the walls, and a thin coating of frost edged the doorway as I entered. I had no servants or slaves to keep this place for me and it looked exactly as one might expect. I sighed, dropping my meagre pack to the cold floor and felt the tension in my shoulders ease. I was completely alone for the first time in what had been many ages.

Smiling to myself, I rubbed my mitten-clad hands together and began sorting the stacked wood beside the hearth, shifting what was driest into the cleared space. I added the tinder I kept beside the chopped wood and flame flared in the twigs. The fire caught. I grinned at the fledgling flames, breathing life into the fire and, when I was certain it was stable, I moved away from the hearth, admiring the light flickering around the single room. This was a far cry from the extravagant dwellings of Valhalla and even the many halls of kings in Midgard, but this single room hewn from rock using my own hands was my own and I cherished it.

Sitting silently beside the hearth, I closed my eyes and listened to the toughened leather across the doorway groaning against the winds outside.

Wearily, I opened my eyes and, nodding in satisfaction that no snowflakes had breached the doorway from the blizzard outside, I lay down before the hearth and finally slept. I needed to think, and my most thorough thinking was always done in sleep. The mind was like the endless passageways of Yggdrasil's roots and it could not be navigated fatigued. To find my way clear of this mess, I needed to think and let my consciousness roam those mental passageways without hindrance of the Æsir, giants, or the intervening Norns.

I finally left Útgarðar when the winter sunlight cut weakly through the morning mist. Although I wore my boots lined with the thickest fur, my feet were numb as I struggled through the heavy snowdrifts, the hoarfrost creating shining patterns on the undulating landscape. I wasted no time crossing the frozen wastelands on the outskirts of the Iron Wood, conscious of unseen eyes following my progress. The region between my shoulder blades twitched under the intolerable pressure of being tracked, and I very nearly scurried like a rabbit across the open, snowy meadows. I knew Angrboða's packs of werewolves lurked beyond the dark trunks of the Iron Wood and the lesser witches of her kin no doubt controlled their hunt. If I dallied too long in these lands today, I might not make it back to Asgard.

I was panting with the effort of forcing my way through the heavy snow when I finally reached the slope at the opposite end of the meadows. I stopped, catching my breath as I stared up at the short stretch of hillside where a path lay hidden beneath feet of snow. The path went through a small section of woodland where the crevice in the cliff led to the passage that would return me to Asgard.

I bowed my head, preparing to rush the woodlands and hoping a werewolf pack wasn't waiting on the other side of the trees. Closing my eyes, I pulled magic around me, pushing my body through the rigorous transformation into wolf form. Although I was vulnerable during the transformation, I poured energy into the process, quickening the shifting of muscles and bones into a different configuration. Somewhere during the transformation, I collapsed onto my side, the excruciating pain driving me to unconsciousness. I woke amid a shallow hollow of slushy snow, in a fever induced from efforts to hasten the change from human to wolf form. The dense fur of my pelt was soaked in wet snow melt that was quickly returning to frigid. I shuffled to my four feet, lifting my muzzle to scent the frigid air, hoping to determine if Angrboða's werewolves were in the vicinity. Although they hadn't taken advantage of my weakened state to launch an attack, I didn't doubt they waited nearby, and while my human mind pondered Angrboða's reason for holding them back, my wolf mind prodded me to escape before they came for me. There was great advantage in the speed and endurance of the wolf-form, and the wolf-mind was useful in evading pursuit. Regardless of whether we were humans, gods or giants, though, we complicated situations by over-thinking them when the simplest of instincts were required.

I remained motionless a moment, then shook myself vigorously, flinging snow melt and icicles from my pelt. Scenting the air again, I stepped carefully from the shredded remains of clothing I had worn. I caught the faint musk of werewolf on the still air; then, without warning, I rushed the heavy snow of the slope before me.

The werewolves broke from the cover of the shadowy forest to my right and left. Hoping to outflank me, the massive beasts howled as their huge claws gained purchase on the undulating landscape of the snowy meadows. I had timed my escape well and the lighter body of the wolf leaped easily up the heavy snow covering the slope before the towering mountains. I bounced easily from the patches of hard packed snow, criss-crossing the slope in quick leaps until I reached the fringe of the forest. I heard the angry snarls of the werewolves as they reached the slope.

I dared not glance behind me but kept the momentum of the wolf's powerful hindlimbs and dashed into the forest. The snarling intensified behind me and the keen hearing of the wolf-form rewarded me with the sounds of scrabbling claws quickly replaced with the slow churning of heavy snow. The heavier werewolves were unable to follow up the slope and instead were forced to use their greater strength to labour through the deep snowdrifts. Even though the pursuing werewolves would be slowed and fatigued through exertion, once into the forest, they could quickly catch me.

I heaved in the frigid air, allowing the wolf-mind to direct my responses as I fled for the safety of the narrow fissure in the mountain ahead. Turning on the icy path, my claws scraped across rotting and frozen leaf-litter and reached for more speed, the long limbs of the wolf stretching into a gallop. Behind me, the howl of the werewolf pack echoed, the frozen trees seeming to shiver at the challenge of the baying monsters pursuing me. Ahead I saw the dark, glassy surface of the exposed rock where the mountain cleaved inward. I raced toward it, the roaring challenge of the werewolves following me as I sped through the narrow gap in the stone, tearing strips of fur and skin from my body on the sharp rock as I fled for safety.

I limped into Asgard, a deep cut to one of my forepaws from the sharp stones. Exhausted and fearful of pursuit still, I was panting heavily in wolf-form as I climbed the rise of the hillock before the craggy peak where Hliðskjálf perched above the meadows of Fólkvangr and the crouched form of Óðinn's hall in Valhalla. Heimdallrr leaned against the smooth stone of the rock face, his eyes half-closed as he hummed a tune beneath his breath. Slowly, his eyelids opened as I limped toward him and he crossed his arms, regarding me solemnly.

"Not a stealthy approach, Loki," the watchman of the gods warned.

I flicked an ear in mild annoyance, continuing toward Valhalla in my shambling gait.

"Óðinn foresaw you would return to us," Heimdallrr continued, following my progress with his eyes narrowed. "I'm not certain much good will come of it."

This time I flicked my tail in irritation at the words and bared my teeth. Even though Heimdallrr could not see my face, the god was renowned for his acute hearing, and he uttered a low chuckle at my anger and insolence. I ignored him, hopping on my maimed paw now, and assumed his legendary hearing could detect even the gentle sigh of my lips parting in a soundless snarl. Not for the first time, I constructed many rude and anatomically impossible suggestions of what Heimdallrr could do with Gjallarhorn. The watchman of the gods might possess superb eyesight and hearing but he was blind and deaf in the obedience with which he followed whatever commands Óðinn issued. I was still mulling over insults for Heimdallrr when I drew near Óðinn's great hall in Valhalla, ranks of the Einherjar and Valkyries forming a tight circle around some commotion in the centre. Immediately, I cast aside all thoughts for Heimdallrr and his questionable intelligence and hastened my three-legged trot, pushing through the gathered warriors who stepped aside in alarm.

When I moved the last of Óðinn's famed warriors aside, I saw the Valkyries and Einherjar had formed a tight rank around a cleared space where a huge black wolf, saliva dripping from its massive jaws, prowled and snapped, testing the boundaries of their legendary courage. I lifted my muzzle, scenting the fear-drenched air, the rage and the cunning of the beast before me. In a moment of shock, I recognised the wolf as kin, a being I shared blood and spirit with and one who belonged to me. Hastily, I stepped back into the crowd of shuffling men, their footsteps crunching the grass of Fólkvangr beneath their boots as they repositioned themselves while Fenrir, my son, again tested the resilience of the battle-hardened troops who contained him.

Once outside the ring of warriors, I awkwardly hurried to the shadows under the overhang beside an outer storage dwelling. There, I forced the transformation upon my body, struggling through the pulling and re-shaping of flesh and bone, the re-configurations of sinew and tendon, mind and form. When it was complete, I lay still for a long time, trembling with exhaustion in the shadows, sweat running down my naked limbs. I did not know what had happened in my short absence from Asgard, but it seemed Óðinn had been correct that Fenrir, the tiny wolf pup last I saw him, would grow as quickly as his serpent brother, Jörmungandr. I imagined all too easily how Fenrir's rapid growth and Óðinn's fear of my children had spawned this monstrous wolf that now challenged the famous combined might of Óðinn's best warriors and Freyja's shield-maidens. The tension in Asgard was near breaking and if I did not contrive some way to save Fenrir, I feared Óðinn would have him destroyed for the threat he perceived. I also had no doubt that the threat was very real to Óðinn and that he had contributed to his own downfall in this way.

I was still lying weakly on the ground when I heard the assembled warriors begin to shout Týr's name. I staggered to my feet and nearly collapsed; the sudden transformation had sapped all my strength. I held a hand out, caught the side of the wood storage barn for support and waited until the weakness had passed. Breathing rapidly, I lowered my head, my face slick with sweat that fell to the ground in salty droplets. I heard the cries of support and clanging of shields again and knew I needed to act—and quickly. Although Thor was the mightiest of Óðinn's warriors, it was Týr who was the most courageous and most respected among battle-hardened warriors. Týr had patience and skill with sword and tactics that was the complete opposite to the fury and speed that was Thor's trademark. If Óðinn wanted Fenrir dealt with, Thor was not the best choice. In the brief moment I had stood before the mighty wolf that was my son, I understood the keen intelligence and physical power that was bound within his form. Týr was the perfect warrior to bring Fenrir to the ground.

I staggered from my shelter, naked and swaying in the sunlight. The focus of the assembled warriors was so entirely fixed on Fenrir and Týr that I had pushed my way through several ranks of men before I noticed any resistance. Even then I did not stop or pause, only shoved harder at the men who began to complain at my passage, heads turning to see what caused the clamour of discontent behind them.

When at last I stumbled into the first several ranks from the clearing, the strong arms of the Einherjar warriors finally grasped me, holding me firm. I stood, watching in horror as Týr approached Fenrir, the wolf half-turned away, keeping his eyes on the warriors at his flanks while he spoke with Týr. The swordsman of the gods stood calmly, a long loop of chain in his hands, his body relaxed and seemingly unperturbed by the tense warriors and threatening bulk of Fenrir.

"Let me try this last one," Týr asked, showing Fenrir the chain he held loosely in his hands.

Fenrir eyed him suspiciously. "Why would I allow you to put another chain around my neck?" he asked, curling his lip with disdain. "Óðinn has already shown he has no love for my kin."

Týr shrugged. "I told Óðinn you would break this chain too, but the All-Father disagreed. He said you weren't strong enough."

"Then let Óðinn come tell me himself," Fenrir countered with malicious glee.

I saw Týr hesitate and scan the assembled warriors. His gaze rested on me for a moment and his lips became a thin line as though my presence decided something in his mind. I had always liked Týr and respected the calm, tactical manner in which he handled any event that threatened the Æsir. I frowned, wondering for the first time if I was now considered among those threats.

"Let us try this one last chain," Týr suggested. "I think it unlikely that even some rare crafted chain of the dwarves can hold you. I offer you a promise of good faith though, to show that I am not threatening you with permanent binding in this chain."

Fenrir snarled and snapped at the warriors nearest his right shoulder; they leaped out of the way as Thor and Ullr strode into the clearing. I bit my lip, fighting in earnest against the stronger arms of the warriors who held me as firmly, as I knew that chain would hold Fenrir if they managed to bind him with it.

"What is your show of good faith?" Fenrir growled, glittering eye on Thor even as he answered Týr.

"I will put my hand in your mouth. If the chain binds you, I will lose my hand for my lies."

"Let us try this chain," Fenrir said, lip curling.

I watched helplessly and began to cry out, suddenly finding that my voice was a near-silent croak in the shouting of the warriors surrounding me. My efforts to transform my body so swiftly in such quick succession had scarred my vocal passages, and strain my voice as I might, I could barely be heard above a whisper. Even if the warriors had not been jostling and cheering for Thor and Ullr as they took the dwarf-crafted chain from Týr, I could not have made myself heard from this distance. I twisted in the arms that held me tightly, searching for anything that I could use to alert Fenrir to the treachery about to be unleashed. I could barely imagine that Týr would sacrifice his own hand for the sake of this foolish task but I could not see an alternative this moment.

Týr stepped toward Fenrir and the wolf obediently opened his massive jaws, the sharp fangs of his canines as thick as Týr's thigh. Offering a nod of acknowledgement and trust to Fenrir, Týr lifted his left hand, moving to place his arm inside the wolf's mouth. Quick as a lightning bolt, Fenrir shut his jaws with a resounding snap and Týr stood, slightly pale against the black muzzle of the wolf, staring at his outstretched but untouched left hand.

"Are you not a right-handed swordsman?" Fenrir asked with quiet malice.

I felt a shiver of pride at the cunning in those words, the clearly disclosed threat that Fenrir was aware of Týr's intended treachery and if fulfilled, the wolf would take his payment in full.

Týr nodded, face still pale, and stretched out his right hand instead. Fenrir obediently opened his mouth, allowing the god's arm within the grip of sword-like teeth.

In moments, Thor and Ullr moved forward, working efficiently and patiently to place the chain over Fenrir, securing the links to the mountainside. I watched with growing unease and something like anger as Thor finally stepped away and Ullr gave a nearly imperceptible nod of his head to Týr. I saw Fenrir move to rise from the half-crouch he had lowered his forelegs to in order to let Týr place his arm within his jaws. The chain tightened and continued to tighten as Fenrir strained against it, jaws closing slightly on Týr's arm as the wolf heaved his body against the dwarf-crafted chain. The chain did not loosen but instead it tightened even more, links disappearing as it magically shrunk in size to secure more firmly to the wolf. I briefly closed my eyes, wary of the treachery and distrust between Óðinn and myself that had led to this senseless action. Fenrir arched his back, pulling Týr forward as he moved his head upward, straining his neck even as the chain tightened and continued to grow tighter as the wolf struggled.

Snarling a resigned sigh, Fenrir stopped moving and still holding Týr's forearm between his front teeth, his dark eye met Týr's implacable face.

"Fool," Fenrir snarled around his teeth and bit down, teeth severing tissue and bone as Týr screamed in agony.

Týr dropped to the ground, blood gushing from his severed arm, the stump now just a meaty red gore against the pale white of his skin. Thor roared in rage and Freyja and a few of her Valkyries stepped forward to quickly recover Týr from beneath the paws of Fenrir. I wanted to vomit as I stared at the smearing blood trail that disappeared into the ranks of Valkyries, the evidence of Óðinn's treachery enacted on his own people. Thor leaped forward at Fenrir, unable to contain the fury that overwhelmed him and using Mjollnr, he beat Fenrir into submission against the mountain side, sweeping another long section of the dwarf-crafted chain around Fenrir's muzzle as he attacked.

In the aftermath of Fenrir's betrayal, I could abide the amusement of the Æsir no longer. I snarled at the Einherjar holding me until they released me, pure wrath setting my eyes ablaze with the fires of Múspelheim. I left the shadowed realms of the cursed lands, stalking toward Asgard as Thor and the other gods celebrated and laughed at Fenrir while he struggled beneath the chain that bound him. I stopped at the far end of the path, turning to look over my shoulder at my once-proud son, now humiliated in fetters. Among the celebrations, I spotted the pale figure of a bloodstained warrior, a tall man holding an amputated arm to his chest. All the Æsir and Vanir were united in celebration, the gathered Valkyries and Einherjar alike laughed and joined in the torment of Fenrir.

Týr, wounded and clutching the stump of his arm, stood aside, alone in his condemnation of the revelry before him and the treachery enacted in Óðinn's name.

Chapter 22
The Road To Hel

I walked the weary path alone that wove through the narrow, shadowy passages from Jötunheimr to Asgard. My head hung low, unkempt hair hanging across my face as I trudged, my heart full of bitter rage for Fenrir's struggle, Óðinn's betrayal of both of us and underneath it all, a poisonous desire for vengeance began to leak into my mind. If Freyja was correct and Óðinn no longer trusted me, if Angrboða's evil machinations were fulfilled and I and my children might overthrow the tyranny that Óðinn now sought to bind the Nine Realms, why should I struggle against the old prophecy of Gullveig? Whether that ancient seeress had been Angrboða or one of her kin did not matter. Perhaps there was no use fighting against such orchestrations of the Norns and their kin, or struggling against my own nature. I was Loki, a child forged from the fires of Múspelheim, and my nature was as volatile and free as those very flames.

I was so focused on my own thoughts, lost amid the heartache and conflict, I barely noticed when my feet touched the insubstantial but slippery surface of Bifröst. I pushed my numb hands deeper into the folds of my tunic, wishing I had thought to ask Sigyn to repair my warmest mittens. My breath came in icy clouds as I walked across the arching bridge of flickering rainbow hues, the magic that stripped glamour and power from the giants when they tried to enter Asgard. It never worked on me and I wasn't certain if Óðinn had designed it with only Jötunheimr in mind. It would be the kind of oversight the All-father might make, thinking all those who were not Æsir, those who were 'giants' must be alike and confined by the same bonds. He was wrong, but I'd never relieved him of his misconceptions, never told him that among those the Æsir called 'giants', the giants of Jötunheimr had different powers, bound by different magic just as those in Múspelheim were different again.

I walked into Óðinn's near abandoned hall, the massive central hearth containing only one boar rotating slowly on the spit above a modest fire. Frigg sat beside the hearth. The clack and thump of her loom as she worked echoed in the quiet room. I glanced about from where I hesitated in the doorway, searching the shadows for Óðinn. He was not present yet and so I hurried across the room, swiping a goblet of mead as a cupbearer hastily approached. I mumbled my gratitude, downed the mead without drawing breath before tossing the goblet back onto the wooden tray. I barely broke stride to drink before continuing around the central hearth, skirting the silent Frigg as she regarded me cautiously from her place beside the fire. I noticed only the firelight dancing off her dark eyes and tight-pressed lips before I was across the room.

Outside, thunder rumbled in the distance as though sensing Frigg's mood. Óðinn's lady was almost as volatile as I was and her moodiness affected the weather with unparalleled ferocity.

"Loki," Frigg called, straightening in her seat, the ladies about her stopping their work to wait in ominous silence.

"Not now," I growled, already turning away from her.

On the opposite side of the hearth, Bragi plucked absently at his stringed harp; the quiet melody felt as though he'd taken the sound directly from my grieving soul.

"I'm going to find my wife," I said to Frigg, meeting her gaze with dark challenge, "and find what comfort she may offer me."

"Don't imagine the dutiful Sigyn will find your abhorrent affair with the Hag of Iron Wood a thing she can forgive," Frigg said, lips tightening in anger.

I scowled and fled the room, ignoring the sharp stab of guilt at the justice in Frigg's words or how her stare lingered on my back, chasing me from the hall.

When I arrived at the spacious room I shared with Sigyn, she was gone. I looked about the empty space, the quarters normally tidy and well kept, the bed usually piled with folded blankets and fur pelts. Instead, the bed was simply adorned, a few plain blankets and pelts lying across the wooden slats of the bedframe. I sat to ponder where she might have gone. I heard a sharp intake of breath and quickly turned, hand reaching for the knife at my hip. I relaxed almost instantly, Sigyn standing a few paces behind me, fresh blankets in her arms.

"Let me help you?" I offered, climbing to my weary feet and holding out my arms.

She hesitated, eyes widening before she gave a small nod of agreement.

I stepped forward, taking the folded blankets from her arms and holding them as she selected one and then another, arranging the more finely woven blankets closer to the top before covering these with several layers of different-coloured bear and deer pelts. When she at last stepped back to survey her work, I took a light step forward, caught her hands and kissed her.

"Let's see if this bed is as comfortable as it looks," I said, pulling her down into the plush pile of furs.

It was several hours later, near midnight, when I woke. Sigyn was awake too, her hand resting on my bare chest, fingers splayed as though to prevent me rising.

"What?" I breathed, searching the darkness for evidence of what had woken me.

The embers of the fire-pit were glowing dimly in the shadows of the room but beyond our securely barred door, I could see the faint but quick movement of lights. In a moment, I realised they were torches hurrying down the twisting passages that led deeper into the other chambers at the centre of Valhalla.

"What did you hear?" I asked, turning to Sigyn in the darkness.

"I heard sobbing," she whispered.

"Someone was crying?" I asked, not certain I understood.

"Yes," Sigyn murmured, and she sounded afraid. "It was Frigg. I heard Frigg sobbing from down the passage."

"Wait here," I said quietly and moved to rise from the bed, but Sigyn's hand clutched at my own. "It's all right, bar the door when I leave."

I wasted no time but pulled on the rough tunic I had travelled in earlier and belted on my blade. I waited until Sigyn had secured a robe about her form and we crept to the door. I kissed her lightly on the lips and then slipped from the room, waiting for the scrape of our door against the frame and the snick of the bar being drawn. When I was satisfied Sigyn was safe, I continued down the hall, moving toward the sound of raised voices further along the myriad of passageways and somewhere in one of the numerous chambers.

It was Baldr's room where the sobbing and wailing form of Frigg sat half-collapsed on the floor, supported by a silent but solemn Freyja. Baldr sat in his bed still, his broad-shouldered frame hung with furs but more discarded on the floor. Beside him, Óðinn was speaking quietly, his tone soothing, but Baldr's eyes were shadowed and haunted.

"What's happened?" I asked Iðunn as I stepped quietly beside the youthful goddess.

She turned to regard me, eyes wide with concern. "Baldr has been having nightmares. This one was very dark, a portent of his death."

I frowned, glancing about the room with some wonder. The Æsir were gathered in tight clusters, arms about each other and whispering in frightened tones. Baldr was the beloved son of Óðinn, the one that no one ever had a disagreement with. I thought for a moment and realised even I had never had a disagreement with Baldr. He was the gentlest, kindest of the Æsir. It seemed that whatever dark portent of death he had dreamed, Frigg and Óðinn considered it a very real threat.

Óðinn gently lifted Frigg to her feet and kissed her, his hands caressing the tension from her shoulders. The moment he released her, though, Frigg lowered to the floor again like a wilting flower, as though life had been drained from her and she lacked the strength to stand alone. Óðinn turned and met Baldr's tormented eyes and gave a grim nod of acknowledgement. The All-Father left the chamber so abruptly I barely had time to follow him and instead had to jog behind for several paces, trying to match his long stride. Óðinn walked so swiftly through the hall and through the darkened spaces outside Valhalla that I couldn't tell where he was going until we entered the dimly lit stables where the stallions favoured by the gods were sheltered from the chill morning air. I watched as Óðinn approached his grey stallion Sleipnir, a horse that was as much my offspring as Fenrir, Hel or Jörmungandr but somehow considered worthy by the gods. I remained silent as Óðinn slung the tack upon his warhorse, the stallion nipping in eagerness to ride.

"What has happened?" I wheezed, leaning heavily on the stable wall for support, but far enough from Sleipnir's reach that the stallion could not grab me in a temper.

Óðinn suddenly whirled, long travelling robes swirling around him. His fierce gaze met mine and the accusation in that eye was almost too much to bear. I shuddered beneath the weight of his searching gaze, knowing well that he sought the truth from me with powers granted only to him. Never before had Óðinn used that magic upon me and it felt like a second betrayal, a cut sliced deeper upon the one already dealt over Fenrir's binding.

"You think this has to do with me, don't you?" I asked quietly. "You who deal in lies to Fenrir and betray my trust, and now you think to accuse me of further mischief? Or of worse, Óðinn? Whatever Baldr has dreamed has such darkness to it that you think the malice lies with me. Explain yourself to me," I hissed, lip curling in sudden anger. "Explain what I have done that merits such mistrust from you, among all of them?"

Óðinn stared at me, his cobalt eye darkening with rage and his lips narrowing into a thin line. He did not speak, did not explain why he considered me capable of such cruelty. After a long moment, he turned and began to lengthen his stride away from me again.

"Tell me!" I shouted after him, my voice pitched high with anger and wretchedness. "You owe me that, at least."

"Baldr dreams of his own death," Óðinn said, still walking away. "I seek answers, Loki, not more riddles."

I uttered a cry, the noise strained and jagged with shock. Did he really think I would kill his son? His most beloved son? I stared, uncomprehending, as Óðinn and Sleipnir were swallowed by the shadows. I leaned heavily on the stable wall and then decided to use the magic that Óðinn did not possess.

If he would not trust me willingly and explain his fears, then I would follow him in secret.

I endured another transformation, shedding my human form more easily now as though the magic was without resistance. I tried not to contemplate why such a thing might occur and tried even harder to ignore the realisation that in no longer denying parts of myself, there was no fight or challenge between my forms. As if to clarify the introspection further, the wolf-mind and wolf-form were not separate as they once had been from my own. Instead, I now shook the winter weight of my coat and began to lope after Sleipnir, my full consciousness integrated with the instincts of the wolf.

I did not lope for long, but let my body stretch across the meadows and rolling hills of Fólkvangr; the aching muscles no longer protested at the transformation, and I easily made the distance to come within sight of Sleipnir. The big grey stallion was swift beyond all the horses, but I was Wolf and even Sleipnir could not outrun me. Still, I cautioned myself and bade my time, slowing to follow further back, lest Óðinn realise he was being tracked.

The road Óðinn took led across Bifröst and arched down steeply toward Helheimr, the worn and dusty path covered with the ashes of the dead. We were going to the domain he had gifted Hel. Of all my children, he considered Hel the most useful to him and rather than completely throw her away like Jörmungandr or bind her like a feral dog as he had done to Fenrir, Óðinn had installed Hel into her own Realm. I had not visited my daughter since and did not know whether she considered Helheimr a gift or the prison it truly was. The girl I had met beside the well in the Iron Wood had been many things and she had understood with a wisdom much older than her physical body suggested. I thought Hel probably knew the truth of what Óðinn had done. She was not bound in chains like Fenrir, but neither was she free.

The road to Helheimr twisted and passed through the narrow gorges and clefts of mountain passages, the chill and frozen winds of Niflheimr blowing stronger as we neared that bitter Realm. Ahead, Óðinn stopped and pulled Sleipnir's reins hard, the stallion rearing in protest at being halted so abruptly. I felt Óðinn's power slide over me and not find me as he nudged the prancing horse forward. I slunk lower to the ground and hid behind an outcrop of large boulders, watching the stallion snort and champ the bit in growing unease. In the distance, at the top of a steep mountain peak, the earth the dull colour of ashes, I saw the large boulder where Fenrir was chained. I watched his body twist against the chain that held him, and the whine that escaped his mouth was ravenous and pitiful. *Óðinn will pay dearly for his grievance against Fenrir.* As if in answer to my eerie precognition, a wind stirred across the plains of Helheimr, whipping tendrils of ash into spirals that collided with each other, breaking apart only to form anew.

Directly ahead of Óðinn lay a steep ravine, and a churning torrent of water moved through the abyss below. Sleipnir tossed his head, eyes rolling in anxiety as Óðinn urged him forward, closer to the narrow bridge, Gjallarbrú, which crossed the dark chasm. I made to rise from my concealment, but Sleipnir suddenly snorted, and Óðinn stopped. A chill howl echoed through the shadowy lands, and I saw the dark shape of a massive hunting dog emerge onto the narrow bridge, held in check by a thin chain wrapped about the delicate arm of a pale woman. She was beautiful, skin the colour of moonlight and dressed in the white robes of a burial shroud. Hel stood motionless upon the bridge, the bulk of the hel-hound at her side. She did not approach but continued to test the tension, waiting for Óðinn to act.

Óðinn bowed his head in acknowledgement to Hel, a solemn understanding that he did not have her permission to enter Helheimr. He swung the mighty grey stallion around and Sleipnir galloped up the steep road before him. I hesitated, observing the motionless figure of my daughter as she stood her ground against the king of gods. I stared in awe at the power Hel commanded before I turned and fled after Óðinn.

Chapter 23
The Seeress

I followed Sleipnir's hoof prints along the ash-covered road as Óðinn galloped away from Hel. Honestly, it wasn't very difficult to follow Sleipnir, the eight-legged stallion made massive gouges in the ground as he passed. I trotted along in Óðinn's wake slowly, hesitantly, as I noticed Sleipnir's pace began to slow ahead of me, Óðinn obviously checking the stallion's speed. Frowning to myself, I followed more cautiously, wondering what Óðinn was planning. He had been furious and intent on gaining answers when he rode from Valhalla, and I did not imagine he would so easily abandon his quest now. In answer to my musings, Sleipnir's hoof prints led from the road ahead, the gouges across the ash-covered landscape proof enough of the stallion's passage. The road disappeared as it curved around a cliff. Thinking Óðinn might know I was following him and planned to ambush me on the blind side of the passage, I hesitated, lifting my nostrils to the breeze. Although I was not in the wolf-form anymore, I had always possessed keen senses. I sniffed at the breeze, scrunching up my face in disgust at the putrid smell of decay that wafted from the marshes to my left where Sleipnir's many hooves had turned over clods of oozing bog. I could not sense Óðinn, neither with my physical senses, nor through the bond that tied us as brothers. Growling low under my breath, I crept toward the bend in the road. Tensed, I placed my hands either side of the grey stone and with one last glance behind me, I drew in a steadying breath. Peering around the edge of the cliff face, I saw the road swept slightly wider around the sharp stone cliff face, barren and unmarked by Sleipnir's hooves. I looked back at the stinking marshland behind me.

Sighing, I turned and eased the tension from my shoulders. I stared at the bogs and foul-looking liquid that stagnated in the pools ahead of me. Why had Óðinn gone across these marshlands? I did not imagine for a moment Hel would offer an easy passage into her realm and I was fairly certain bogs were not the worst torment in her imagination. If an easier path did continue into Helheimr and was not guarded by Garmr the hel-hound or Hel herself, I knew

Óðinn would never find it so easily. The All-Father might be cunning and powerful among the Æsir but he was not as cunning as the giants. Grimacing at the marshes, I stared at my bare feet and was grateful for once that I had no boots to destroy in this journey. The vile stench of rot that emanated from the bogs would never wash from clothing or belongings. I wiggled my toes in the ashen soil and tried not to think about the mud that would soon be squelching between my toes as I crossed this forsaken landscape.

I stepped across the threshold of the marshlands with an expression of horror. There was no reaction from the nearby bogs, no spurting of that revolting liquid, nor belching from the pools of stagnant water. The marshlands remained the same. I frowned in momentary consternation, half-expecting rotting corpses to rise from the depths of these unmarked graves but nothing happened. I halted, one foot held aloft in mid-stride as I realised what Óðinn was doing here in Helheimr. These marshes were the borderlands of those who had been forsaken by Óðinn and Freyja, neither valiant warrior nor shield-maiden. The dead who drowned at sea were in the saltwater depths with Ægir and Rán, while young maidens rested with Gefjun. The dead who were forsaken, murderous and unworthy, were sent to Helheimr. I stared at the marshes, only now realising what Óðinn must have known when he confronted Hel on the bridge. Óðinn sought to speak with a shade, a seeress who had been deemed most unworthy by the Æsir and burnt in Valhalla: the seeress Gullveig, who had cursed Óðinn all those eons and turnings of the worlds ago. *Did Óðinn really intend to raise her shade? Did he imagine she would speak the truth to him?*

I lowered my foot to the soft ground and muttered a quiet curse of my own. I did not want to follow Óðinn, and yet I knew I must. He had lost his trust in me and our bond as brothers was terrifyingly close to being severed. I was uncertain what would happen when the last tattered threads of our bond broke beneath the weight of mistrust, but I wanted to preserve our promises if I could.

The marshes were frigid. The air was cold and clammy against my bare skin. My teeth had begun to chatter in protest against the bitter chill but I had ignored it. I pressed onward, keeping my gaze on the sodden ground and following the clods of broken earth that would lead me to Sleipnir. The horizon was drenched in mist so thick I could barely see further ahead of me than a few paces, and I had no idea how far the Road was from where I now walked. Time seemed meaningless in this pale and putrid realm.

Ahead, I heard the soft rumble of Óðinn's voice. I stopped immediately, lowering into a crouch as I struggled to see through the veil of mist. The stink of the bog was awful this close to the ground and I tried not to retch as I peered into the shifting mist, finally discerning the white bulk of Sleipnir against the wall of mist beyond. Squinting in the poor light, I saw Óðinn slightly to the left of the stallion, hood thrown back and arms raised high as he called into the swirling fog. A dull and muted noise responded, like the cracking of stone or striking of lightning, but as though heard from a great distance. Peering into the mist, I saw the spectral form of a woman rise from the bog like a wisp of smoke, hair improbably long, rotting gown making for a miserable burial shroud.

"Who comes forth to wake me?" the seeress spoke, the filmy white of her sightless eyes sweeping over the marshes.

I pressed closer to the ground as the dead eyes of the seeress scanning the marshy earth where I crouched. Although I was certain the decaying tissue of those eyes could no more see than any corpse, I saw her stiffen in recognition of my presence. A cold, malicious smile widened on the mummified face, her skin pale and waxy with death but stretched too thin, like a wet sail hauled up a mast. I considered crawling away, afraid of this shade Óðinn had conjured and wanting to hear nothing the spectre had to say. Before I could move, Óðinn stepped forward from beside Sleipnir, his robes shifting the swirling white mist that tried to cling to him.

"I have called you forth," Óðinn said in a voice that carried over the chill marshes and drew the complete attention of the shade. "I am a Wanderer, a traveller of realms, and I want to know of Hel."

The shade stared at Óðinn with corpse eyes, her awful smile growing wider. "What would you know of Hel, Wanderer?" she asked as though an ordinary conversation was taking place.

Óðinn pushed his hands into the folds of his travelling robes, I imagine trying to keep the warmth within his flesh. He glanced around the desolate landscape, then returned his focus to the shade.

"I have travelled these Nine Realms, I have seen the marvellous halls in Asgard, the riches and feasting in Valhalla, the furious frosts of the wild mountains in Jötunheimr. I have walked the passages and frozen depths of Niflheimr, seen the dark and cold of Svartálfheimr . I have travelled to the halls of men in Midgard and even seen the fiery chasms of Múspelheim. In all these Realms and even though I have travelled through the passages of the Giant Ash Yggdrasil, I have never been to a place like Helheimr before."

"What intrigues you about these barren shores?" the shade asked, eyes glittering malevolently.

Óðinn looked beyond her as though he could see through the deepening mist to the chasm beyond and the bridge that Hel had stood upon earlier.

"I saw a river not far from here," Óðinn began with quiet wonder, "a furious and flowing thing that poured through the black abyss of stone. Beyond the bridge, I saw a mountain peak, a giant wolf secured therein and beyond further still, there was a desolate shore. An endless ocean seemed to stretch to that shore of ash and all the golden ornaments in the Realms clattered on the floor of Hel's hall when I walked through there. The tables were set with empty plates and empty pitchers waited for mead, the hearth was set for a feast that had not yet come."

Óðinn halted, staring into the mist and I realised he was talking now of Baldr's nightmares of the dark dreams that had disturbed the bright god and the Æsir so deeply. I silently moved positions so I could keep both Óðinn and the shade in sight.

Óðinn lifted his gaze, meeting the dead eyes of the seeress. "What is Hel waiting for?" he asked. "Who is this feast prepared for?"

The shade chuckled with a malicious laughter that sent a cold sweat running down my spine. "Hel has prepared her hall for the mead of the gods, the shades of Helheimr will be joined by the brightest of the gods. The feast is in honour of Baldr and for all the powers and might of the Æsir, and none shall be able to break the weaving laid upon the Loom."

Óðinn ground his teeth, outrage making the cobalt of his single eye burn incandescently in the eerie mist. "Tell me how," he snarled, the mist swirling in an unseen gust. "Tell me, seeress, who will be the one to take Baldr from the Æsir? Who will take Óðinn's son?"

The shade shifted above the bog, the unmarked grave beneath writhing in response to Óðinn's anger. The stench of putrefaction grew stronger and I shuddered, repressing the urge to retch again. "Baldr's life-blood will be drained by his own blind brother, the fatal blow delivered by Höðr."

Óðinn closed his eye momentarily, then stared with cold rage at the shade before him. "Baldr's death must be avenged, for Höðr would never willingly slay his own brother. Who will carry out the deeds of vengeance for Baldr?"

The seeress smiled unnervingly as she met Óðinn's gaze. "Óðinn will lie with another who is not his Lady. There is a giantess of frost and starlight, Rindr is her name. From the broken vows between Óðinn and Frigg, Rindr will give birth to From the broken vows between Óðinn and Frigg, Rindr will give birth to Óðinn's son Víðarr and it is he, a child born of anger and betrayal, who will take Baldr's vengeance and lay his slayer upon the funeral pyre."

Óðinn's face was white with repressed rage, his lips a tight line as he spoke with sharp words. "Who will be the mourners at Baldr's funeral?" he asked in a clipped tone.

The shade laughed, cruel and high-pitched. I pushed myself closer to the ground, trying to block out the horrible noise that threatened to freeze my bones and the blood within my veins.

"I know who you are, Traveller and Wanderer of Nine Realms. I have spoken what you wished to hear, and you will hear no more from me, Óðinn the All-Father."

"You are not wise, seeress," he barked with bitter laughter. "There is a familiar chill to your words that reminds me of another time we met. How is it that the witches of your kin have shared such memories and skills?" he wondered, glaring at the shade of Gullveig.

"Ride swiftly back to Valhalla, Óðinn," the shade warned. "There are many secrets in these realms that you do not yet know."

"I have taken and contained the Three Monsters birthed by the witch of your lineage!" Óðinn snarled. "You can do more harm to mine."

The shade sneered, her lips pulling back in a rictus smile. "Then why is there fear in you, Óðinn? You have no power over me here. None will raise me from these lands again, nor shall I walk upon the Realms once more until Loki is freed from his fetters and joins with the snarling jaws and ripping claws of Fenrir unbound and they both freely combine with the darkness before Ragnarök."

Óðinn did not slow his haste. He flung himself onto Sleipnir's broad back and urged the mighty stallion forward, hooves already thundering across the marshes while the shade of the seeress Gullveig he had called forth subsided back into the boggy depths of her grave, her howling laughter echoing in the mist-drenched landscape. Pressing my hands over my ears, I tried to physically block the echo of Gullveig's maniacal laughter. Swaying unsteadily, I got to my feet and trotted after Óðinn, following the tracks hewn through the bog by Sleipnir's eight-legged stride.

Chapter 24
Oaths And Lies

Óðinn reined in Sleipnir when he approached the open doors of the hall, Valhalla no longer shrouded in the darkness of night but in blazing light, despite the hours until dawn. I trotted cautiously behind, keeping out of his sight and his awareness as I slunk into deep shadow behind the barn. I dropped to all fours, sides heaving with exhaustion in my effort to keep pace with Sleipnir on the return journey. Óðinn's stallion was fast and I had pushed beyond my physical endurance to make certain I wasn't missing when the All-Father returned to Valhalla. The mistrust between us had grown so deep and the roots were rotten, spoiling the friendship we had once enjoyed. I couldn't afford Óðinn's wrath when I was already weak.

While Óðinn took Sleipnir into the warmth of the barn, grunting acknowledgements to the few warriors who waited inside, I drew on my remaining strength, pulling deep from the reserve of power to force another transformation through my body. Even though I expected the change would be hard, I hadn't anticipated how exhausting it might be.

I lay huddled in the shadows of the barn, limbs shaking and slick with perspiration until Óðinn had left. I heard the distant shouts of challenge and greeting from the warriors guarding the door to Valhalla. I remained where I was, muscles cramped with fiery pain that radiated through me. I had pushed my body beyond its endurance and I couldn't take any further straining. Still, I had to get up. I needed to be inside the network of passages that filled Valhalla like a beehive but I couldn't move. My throat was raw from my strangled cries and my breathing came in ragged pants. "Get up," I growled to myself.

I drew in my will and forced myself to stand, stifling the scream that tried to tear free from my throat. My vision darkened and dizziness took me. I stumbled sideways, grabbing for anything to support me. Pain burned hot and furious through my body and I nearly fell, caught blindly at the half-door of Sleipnir's stable. I sagged, my knees collapsing as strength left me. I dropped, weightless and powerless to stop myself.

"Loki?" a quiet voice in my ear asked.

I stirred, half-waking before losing consciousness again.

"Loki?" the man's voice called again.

Groggily, I mumbled something, squinting into the flaring torchlight above. It blinded me and bright starbursts blossomed across my vision again.

"What did you do?" Freyr asked.

I swore, cursing at the Vanir god who cradled me in his well-muscled arms as though I were a weakling.

"Come now," Freyr said with intolerable good humour. "Let's be civil to each other. I can see you need assistance."

"I'm sure you'd love to give it to me," I muttered, trying and failing to escape his grip.

Freyr chuckled again, his strong arms tightening slightly around me, preventing my efforts to struggle from his grip. "I'll take you to Freyja," he said, standing with me in his arms as easily as if I were a child.

"I'm sure you know the route to her bedchamber well," I muttered.

He laughed again, without malice, and I could not tell if he were truly an idiot or my insinuation simply had no effect on him.

"I know the way as well as you," Freyr replied, the slightest reproach in his tone.

"Oh?" I asked, head lolling against his shoulder as he marched across the shadowy open meadows to the rear entrance of Valhalla.

"Of course," Freyr said, using his massive shoulders to push aside the door and we entered a dark passage. "Freyja is my sister. Why you know the way to her bedchamber I can only assume is less innocent."

"I'm not really the kind of man she prefers," I mused, my bare feet brushing along the rough surface of the wall. "She's more attracted to the tall, muscular type. Quite a lot like you, actually."

Freyr stiffened momentarily, his stride catching before he continued, but I knew my barb had sunk deep. I stored that item of knowledge away, certain that what I had witnessed in the cavern in my wolf-form many years ago had not been an isolated incident. These siblings were a lot closer than any of the Æsir would be comfortable knowing.

Finally Freyr halted outside a closed door that was the only chamber in this passage. I deliberately let my head loll sideways, only half-feigning the exhaustion that consumed me. Freyr ignored the gentle press of my breath against his chest and I grinned as he knocked loudly on his sister's chamber door.

Freyja opened the large oak door with a swiftness that belied her slender frame. I knew she was more warrior than most of the Æsir in Valhalla, but she often appeared more ethereal than her battle-clad persona as a leader of the Valkyries.

"I brought you a gift," Freyr announced, holding me draped across both his arms like a husband with a new wife.

"You shouldn't have," Freyja murmured, but stepped back to allow her brother to enter.

I twisted in Freyr's grip and wound an arm about his neck, pulling myself closer to him so I was pressed against his chest. I let my laugh brush the bare skin of his neck as he hurried into Freyja's chamber.

"Will you ravish me here and now?" I asked, my lips against Freyr's neck as he tried to drop me on the floor.

I tightened my arm about his neck, chuckling as he shook his shoulders and tried to dislodge me.

Freyja sighed exasperatedly. "Let him go," she said curtly, closing the bedchamber door.

"I'm trying," Freyr said, flinching as I kissed hungrily beneath his jaw.

"Not you," she replied, instead grasping me by the hair, wrenching my head back to stare into her angry eyes. "Let go. Stop teasing."

I unwrapped my arms and legs from around Freyr and he moved aside. Forced to bear my own weight, my legs refused to hold and I slid to the ground at Freyja's feet.

"How often have you been changing forms?" Freyja asked me, her lip curled in silent disgust.

"Too many," I replied, bowing my head. "Do you think I could have some clothes? I'm sure you're not unaccustomed to naked men in this bedchamber, but I never intended to be one of them."

"A sudden need for modesty after such ardent desire?" Freyja asked, glancing briefly aside at her brother.

"He's worth the desire and discomfort," I said, my gaze roaming appreciatively over Freyr.

Freyr tossed a blue woven cloak to me and I caught it, covering my obvious arousal.

A loud knock against the chamber door shook the solid wooden frame. I glanced at Freyja but she strode toward the door and opened it before I could try to hide.

"Lady Freyja," the handmaiden began, her voice fading as she stared incredulously at me.

"Does the Lady Frigg have need of me?" Freyja prompted calmly.

The handmaiden bowed her head in apology. "Immediately," she breathed, not daring to meet Freyja's eyes.

"Tell the Lady Frigg I will be there in a moment," Freyja answered, closing the door.

Freyja leaned her forehead against the door, pale cheeks slightly pink with outrage. She turned, pointing a finger at me. "This is your fault," she hissed. "So, you will play your part now."

I shrugged my shoulders from where I sat on the floor. "Can you heal this?" I asked, gesturing vaguely to my weakened limbs.

"Those will heal in their own time," Freyja replied, pulling a white fur wrap over her pale blue tunic. "Limit your transformations and you won't cause such damage. For now, your weakened state could be useful to me."

"Happy to oblige," I answered, grinning. "Where do you want me to lie down?"

"You'll come with me to answer Frigg's summons," Freyja replied, glancing at Freyr. "Can you help support him?"

"Will he try anything again?" Freyr asked uncertainly.

I held up my hands. "I'll keep these to myself."

"Hmm," Freyr grunted, hauling me upright. "Keep your ardent desire from growing again, too?"

I threw my head back against his shoulder and laughed.

"Are you both quite done?" Freyja demanded, indignant.

"Lead the way," I said, gesturing weakly.

I sighed, admiring the sway of Freyja's hips as she stepped into the passage and turned, her gaze narrowing as she caught me looking.

"You really are as lustful as they all claim," she muttered.

"If only you knew the truth," I whispered, winking at her.

Freyja's lips quirked slightly before she nodded to her brother, and we walked through the shadowy, labyrinthine passages of Valhalla to answer Frigg's summons.

Freyr half-carried me into the main hall as we followed in the wake of Freyja's stride, her gown swirling behind her. I let my gaze roam across the assembled gods and goddesses clustered about the high-backed chairs where Frigg and Óðinn sat with stern expressions. Freyja paused before Frigg, then bowed her head slightly in greeting. Compared to the manner of bows and gestures of honour that most of the Æsir reserved for Frigg and Óðinn, I was reminded again how Freyja and her brother were constantly outside normal behaviour.

"Lady Frigg," Freyja announced in greeting, meeting the stormy gaze of the Æsir queen. "Excuse my delay. I was entertaining a guest."

The cool stares of the Æsir settled on me with unnerving dislike.

"Loki?" Frigg asked in surprise.

"I was curious to see if the rumours of his sexual talents were true," Freyja replied, lying as smoothly as I might.

"And were they?" Frigg asked with unhidden curiosity.

"An exaggeration. You can see I quite exhausted him," she said, gesturing to Freyr, who was still assisting me to stand.

Frigg's lips quirked. "Interesting," she mused, her fingers looping with Óðinn's in an obvious act of reassurance.

"Loki," Óðinn called, startling the calm of the room. "Did you enjoy yourself?"

I chuckled, letting desire flood my expression as I stared at Freyja. It wasn't difficult: there was something intoxicating about her and Freyr and being this close to them both stirred me in ways I did not understand.

"Yes," I answered, flame flickering in my eyes as I admired Freyja. "She is delectable."

"Then you'd best not let her husband ever hear you say so," Óðinn warned without his usual humour. "And perhaps you owe your wife another apology."

I pulled my eyes from Freyja and whatever spell she had drowned me in. I heard the scraping of a chair as Sigyn stood. Her stony gaze met mine and she stalked from the room, a handmaiden following her in a rush of swirling cloth.

"Obviously," I answered, meeting Óðinn's cool gaze.

"How can I be of assistance, Lady Frigg?" Freyja asked, turning the conversation back to the reason for the summons.

Frigg's eyes darkened, her hand squeezing Óðinn's tightly for reassurance, I thought.

It was not Frigg who answered Freyja, but Óðinn. He patted Frigg's trembling hand, then stood, his cold blue gaze never leaving my face. Finally, he wet his lips and lifted his glacial glare from me.

"Freyja," Óðinn began, the chill of his animosity toward me still lingering in his tone and causing Freyja's shoulders to tighten. "Our beloved son Baldr has been beset by dreams of dreadful darkness, the biting chill of endless winters and screams of the battlefield haunting his waking hours. You know I travelled to Helheimr and sought a meeting with the lady there," Óðinn's voice was barely above a hiss as he finished speaking.

"I do not know the outcome of your travels, though," Freyja prompted, with a significant sidelong glance at me which might have been construed by anyone else watching as reminder of her evening activities but sent a chill of warning through me. Freyja would have words with me later, and they would be done by blade point if necessary.

Óðinn seemed to recover himself, nodding briefly. "Of course," he answered, gesturing vaguely toward me. "Your inquisitive nature found entanglements of another sort."

Freyja's lips tightened and she straightened herself. "How can I aid you, Lord Óðinn?"

Óðinn's gaze darkened at the suggestion. Thunder growled in the distance, and Murin and Hugin cawed restlessly from their perch in the rafters of the hall.

"I was reminded of the prophecy the völva spoke when she first entered this hall, the words of a skald are often curses," he mused, watching Freyja with some consideration.

Freyja sighed. "If you have nothing to ask of me, I will return to my bed-chamber," she said, already turning and indicating to her brother to take me with them.

"Wait," Frigg pleaded, climbing to her feet, her gown formed by a swirling mass of storm clouds. "The shade which Óðinn spoke with was Gullveig, and she foretold Baldr's death at the hands of his brother."

Freyja paused mid-stride, turning slowly around to face Frigg and Óðinn across the narrow distance of the hall. The Æsir were clustered in tight huddles, their faces each a mirror of fear and anxiety.

"Höðr would never hurt his brother," Freyja answered, frowning at Frigg.

"Precisely," the All-Father replied, his midnight blue gaze levelled at me. "I know only one who could sow such chaos and discord among us."

Freyja wasn't listening to Óðinn or even watching him, her attention was fixed on Frigg. "You are the goddess to whom all pray for blessings of motherhood. You know your sons like none other, and you are afraid," she said, stepping forward to take Frigg's hands in her own. "Tell me what aid you seek."

"The witch's shade said Baldr would be killed by an arrow. I see only one way such a thing can never come to pass."

Freyja smiled slightly, meeting Frigg's dark eyes. "I will prepare the necessary items for the oath-bindings you require."

"Hurry," Frigg said, voice shaking with fear and helpless anger. "Baldr's time grows short. I feel it."

"You have my word," Freyja answered, bowing her head to Frigg and striding past Óðinn, her shoulder knocking against his own, forcing the man from her path.

Freyr wasting no time moving us toward the massive oak doors, pushing his considerable strength against them and they parted with a groan. Cold air rushed into the hall and Freyr stood a moment, supporting me awkwardly against his side and waiting for Freyja. She swept past us with an intoxicating scent and billowing cloak and Freyr slammed the oak doors behind us, following his sister into the black night beyond Valhalla's shining hall.

"Is what Óðinn says true?" I asked, struggling to keep pace with Freyr's stride and barely able to see Freyja ahead of us, silhouetted against the starlit horizon.

Freyja stopped, her spine rigid as Freyr continued his steady pace toward her, but I felt the cold reach of her anger. I shifted in Freyr's grip, desperate to escape the wrath I felt radiating from the Valkyrie leader ahead of us.

"What do you imagine you'll gain by killing Baldr?" Freyja asked me, her tone cold and hostile.

"I'm not going to kill Baldr!" I protested.

Freyja's dark eyes reflected starlight as she stared incredulously at me. "Óðinn believes the prophecy."

"Óðinn is angry with me," I stammered. "Everything I do lately is interpreted as an act against him."

Freyja continued to stare at me, her pale face and starlit eyes remote and unsympathetic.

"He craves power and supremacy," I shouted, frustrated at her silence. "He claimed once he wanted nothing but unity and to show me what beauty might truly be. But he never understood those things, Freyja. He only understood beauty that conformed to his design, he only sanctioned unity that was wrought by his hand for his own gain. You of all the beings in Asgard must understand this."

"Why would I understand that?" Freyja asked in a deadly, quiet voice.

My anger rose, igniting the twin fires in my eyes and starlight met flame as I stared at her. "Because you are descended from the skald just as Gullveig was, just as Angrboða and the witches of the Iron Wood. All of you have knowledge and power Óðinn can never possess nor control."

Freyja let her breath hiss between her teeth as she lifted her gaze above my head to Freyr, who stood behind me. "You tread a path of ice so finely wrought it's like dragonfly wings, Loki."

I rolled my eyes. "Óðinn can't continue in this fashion," I said softly. "We are bound unto each other like brothers. I would do him no harm that is not necessary to stop this course he takes us all down."

"I caution you against making Baldr any part of your plans to teach Óðinn a lesson," Freyja said quietly.

I shook my head. "Where Óðinn is leading is too far, Freyja. He's taking us onto an icy bridge where we can't go forward or backward, where melt is trickling from beneath our feet. The Nine Worlds require balance, Freyja. You of all the seeresses should understand why the Norns weave our fates in such a manner."

"I do not presume to understand the Norns," Freyja said, eyes sparkling with anger. "I would think you smarter than to believe you could, too."

"Don't let us be enemies," I pleaded, shoulders sagging with exhaustion.

"You were injured tonight and I was sacred bound to care for the sick," Freyja said, coldly. "But don't mistake my actions tonight for those of a friend. I would gratefully see Óðinn's course be averted but I'd see you ground beneath an axe blade before aligning myself with such a volatile force."

I did not respond but sank to my knees in the meadow of wildflowers, watching as Freyja and her brother continued across the open hills of Fólkvangr, moving toward the cavern deep in the woodlands of Álfheimr where Freyja would work her arts as a skald, the ingredients stored for healing and binding.

Chapter 25
Intoxicating Spring

I stumbled into the central hall sometime in the late afternoon the next day. I ignored the glances, whispered comments and snide asides that followed my progress. Óðinn was not in Valhalla, and I took the opportunity to let the binding of anxiety that had tightened around me whenever in his presence to loosen slightly. Bragi sat beside the hearth tuning his harp, a set of flutes and a small drum on his right. He looked up as I shuffled closer, my clothing still unkempt and my hair mussed from sleep.

"Loki," Bragi greeted with a solemn nod, not taking his attention from tuning the instrument in his lap.

"Tell me something, bard of the Æsir," I drawled, propping one heel against the stones surrounding the hearth. "Where is Óðinn?"

"I don't actually know," Bragi said, glancing momentarily from his work, but he lowered his voice conspiratorially. "Thor said he desired nothing more than to travel to Jötunheimr, though."

I frowned. "To Jötunheimr?" I asked, perplexed. "Why?"

Bragi shrugged, plucking lightly at the harp strings. "Why does Thor ever travel to Jötunheimr?"

"To harass the giants?" I asked, grinning.

"And they accuse you of not being Æsir," Bragi scoffed.

"Do they now?" I asked, my tone darkening with unbidden anger.

"Not me," Bragi continued as if I hadn't spoken. "You made a mistake once with my Iðunn and if not for Freyja it would have cost you your life to save her, but you'd have paid it. I respect that loyalty, Loki."

I regarded the bard as he plucked another few notes from the harp, not meeting my gaze. "You're a rare type," I said, smiling lopsidedly.

Bragi grunted in agreement, twisting a wooden peg on the harp and fiddling with the string. I knew the bard well enough to understand when he was absorbed in his work. I would get no more titbits of information from him today. Sighing, I strolled away from the hearth and stepped outside the double doors of Valhalla.

On the fields of Fólkvangr, the army of Óðinn's Einherjar were testing their skills of swordsmanship, the axemen and archers practising in ranks of warriors that stretched back toward the forest fringes of Álfheimr, the dark woodlands seeming restless and waiting. Thought of Álfheimr led my mind back to the previous night where Freyja and Freyr had disappeared into that deep forest to prepare the magical binding that would save Baldr's life. A thought crossed my mind, darting from my grasp like a wraith, but I dashed after it: a memory of the overheard prophecy shared between Óðinn and Gullveig's shade. The long-dead witch had spoken of Óðinn's son, who would stop Fenrir at Ragnarök. Gullveig had told Óðinn that his son, Víðarr, would be a child no older than a year but a man fully-grown, and she had spoken not of Frigg as Víðarr's mother but of Rindr, the embodiment of frost.

I stood unseeing as the warriors duelled before me, memories and thoughts colliding in my mind as I placed the pieces of the overheard conversation into line. Rindr was a frost giant and even if I had no real proof, I knew she shared some ancient bloodline with Angrboða. Víðarr, who would defeat Fenrir at Ragnarök, would be both a man and child at the same time. I recalled again the speed with which Hel, Jörmungandr and Fenrir had grown. These were things Óðinn knew and could exploit.

I chuckled low to myself as a passing servant gave me a curious glance. Óðinn's lady Frigg was using all her power and those beyond her in the Nine Realms to save Baldr's life while her husband had gone to beget a child with a giantess. The hypocrisy of the actions, the callousness of Óðinn's schemes, made me angry, and with anger came a deep sorrow.

Loud shouts and jeering broke me from my thoughts. I spun about, startled by the sudden noise. I was surprised to find I had been standing near-motionless outside the main doors to Valhalla for some length of time. Afternoon had nearly faded into night and the large torches and bonfires of the evening were being lit.

In the fading twilight, the young men of the Æsir were assembled, the Einherjar clustered around in tight groups, contributing equally to the raucous noise. I saw the bright golden hair framing an equally impressive face and strong jaw. I froze, bewildered and confused as Baldr clapped his blind brother Höðr on the back. For a god who was apparently distraught about his dark prophetic dreams, he looked remarkably good natured.

"Loki." Týr, the one-armed god, stepped silently from behind me to stand at my left.

I eyed the bandaged stump where Týr's hand had very recently still been and remembered with a shudder Fenrir's binding and his malicious amputation of Týr's hand as payment for his betrayal.

"What are they doing?" I asked, ignoring the past and the knowledge that lurked between us like fetid waste.

"I'm surprised Freyja didn't tell you her magics for Lady Frigg were successful," Týr smiled, returning his eyes to the men before us.

I grinned at the sharpness to Týr's tone, which conveyed he knew there was more to my evening with Freyja than the purported intimate activities. "I don't think Lady Freyja was truly that impressed with my stamina," I replied.

"Freyja is hard to please," Týr admitted, a bright glimmer in his eye that left me wondering if he was speaking from experience.

"Then Baldr is saved?" I asked, turning fully to face Týr. "There is nothing in the Nine Realms that can harm him?"

Týr shrugged nonchalantly. "I believe that is what the young Æsir wish to find out."

"Surely they wouldn't," I began, shaking my head in consternation as a huge spear was thrown toward Baldr.

I almost lurched forward, waiting for the awful sound of metal meeting and splitting bone and wet tissue. To my complete surprise, Baldr stood unharmed, grinning with complete abandon as the Æsir cheered and gods rushed to gather more unusual weapons and objects.

The tests and games that the Æsir played lasted long into the evening and even the Einherjar were growing bored and restless when Týr placed his mead cup on the small wooden table beside us. He stood tall, muscular shoulders flexing beneath the constraints of his tunic.

"To the brightest son of Óðinn," Týr called, raising his cup of mead to toast Baldr.

I smiled grimly and lifted my own cup, tasting the liquid now warm against my lips. I closed my eyes, longing for the machinations of the gods to leave me alone.

I woke the next morning to loud banging on the solid door of my chamber. Cursing loudly, I buried my aching head under the blankets. The banging only intensified.

"Sigyn!" I howled, throwing back the blankets and opening my bleary eyes to glare around the bedchamber.

The room was a horrendous mess of tossed clothing, odd boots and a few scattered furs that were heaped near the door. The heavy bar across the door was firmly in place, despite the fists bashing on the other side of the door. The bedchamber was empty, though. Grumbling, I climbed from beneath the warm blankets, yelping at the cold air on my naked skin. I grabbed one of the fur blankets on the floor and wrapped it about myself before hauling the door open.

Týr stood with his usual unruffled clothing, ready to knock again. He frowned at me and lowered his hand.

"What do you want?" I snarled, turning away and stalking back toward my bed.

Týr peered inside the bedchamber as if expecting someone else to be inside. "Are you alone?" he asked.

"Yes," I snarled, throwing the fur blanket to the floor disdainfully. "If you'd like to partake of carnal delights, can it wait until after breakfast?"

"Ah," Týr began, stepping into the room, still glancing about uncertainly.

"I was joking," I hissed, picking up a rumpled tunic from the floor and pulling it over my head. "What do you want? I've got a horrendous headache."

"I see," Týr began quietly. "Where is Lady Sigyn?"

The pounding in my head intensified and I rounded on him, bloodshot eyes laced with flame. "Not here," I spat.

Týr held up his hands in a gesture of hopeless surrender. "Óðinn and Frigg requested your presence to celebrate the success of Freyja's magic."

"Curse Baldr and his brilliant golden hair," I muttered, pulling pants on beneath my tunic, then shoving my feet into a pair of boots.

"Can I make a suggestion?" Týr asked, raising an eyebrow.

"Make it quick, there's a team of dwarves bashing at my skull," I said, wishing my headache would abate.

"At least wear boots from the same pair?" Týr said, grinning.

"Get out!" I roared at him, glaring at my feet and the mismatched pair of boots.

After Týr had left, I considered whether I could flee Valhalla and the wretched celebrations. The very idea of spending the rest of my day with the Æsir was torture, listening to their insipid comments about the impeccable Baldr and his magnificent looks. I agreed Týr was right, though, and looking at last night's soiled tunic, noticed pork dripping and mead staining the front. Sighing, I shrugged off the tunic and walked toward the rear of the bedchamber, already thinking over the catalogue of perfumed scents and oils that might tame the wild ringlets of my hair.

When I had bathed and scented my hair, running the oils through my newly trimmed beard, I coerced my hair into many tight plaits an inch in length. I smiled as I pulled on a fresh tunic and fine-woven pants and, to please Týr, I even selected matching boots. Although the mead from last night was still determined to punish me for overindulgence, I did feel considerably better when I walked into the central hall several hours later.

I was surprised to find half the Æsir host already assembled around the central hearth, servants carrying large platters of freshly roasted meat and baked bread onto the long tables that stretched the length of Valhalla. The warriors from Óðinn's Einherjar and Freyja's Valkyries were seated around the far end of the large hall, already deep in conversation, challenges and boasts.

I snagged a drinking horn from a passing servant, the rich mead sweet as

I wove through the room, a nod of acknowledgement from Týr who stood in conversation with Thor against the far wall. I headed for the central hearth and the roasting boar, fat dripping from the meat as it rotated slowly above the flames. Smiling, I removed the knife at my hip and carved a few hunks of meat from the roast, placing my empty mead horn on a tray as another servant hastened past me. Ignoring the scowl from the elf carrying the tray, I pocketed a fresh bread roll on my passage across the central hall.

Óðinn, Frigg and Baldr were yet to join the celebrations so I leapt nimbly onto the ledge beneath the high window and took pleasure in my pilfered meal. Movement in the periphery of my vision caught my attention and I half-turned, the glimmer of light on pale blonde hair suddenly enticing. Freyja stood in a gown of spring tones, her pale skin the colour of snowdrops as she noticed and moved toward me. Although her gown was simple, the rich hues shimmered with movement, the cloth clinging to her form, two simple brooches pinning her cloak in place. Her hair was decorated with many small flower buds and as she drew closer, I realised I was staring. Wrenching my attention back to my food, I ate another mouthful, chewing even though I had completely lost interest. Freyja stood beside me and watched the room while I observed her, the lovely profile of her form and the pale blue tattoos that marked her skin somehow obscured today.

"You're staring, Loki," Freyja whispered, turning her silver eyes on me.

My mouth was dry, and I sat there like an adolescent bewitched by his first lover. I barely noticed I'd put the bread aside, Freyja's hand caressing my arm, her lips against my throat.

"What have you done?" I asked, a hitch in my voice.

Freyja laughed throatily, sending shivers through my body and I pulled her closer to me, need and desire overcoming all logic.

"Truly," I breathed beneath her ear, hands roaming her slender but strong hips, "what have you done to me?"

"Nothing you'll regret," she whispered, her own breathing fast and excited.

We nearly left the hall before Óðinn, Frigg and Baldr joined the remaining Æsir. I was half-lost to desire, and need was coursing through me with growing intensity by the time Óðinn and Frigg walked through the doors in front of us, dressed in their finest garments. Óðinn wore a midnight blue tunic, silver buttons carved with wolf heads, the spear Gungnir glamoured as a short staff buckled at his hip. Frigg was dressed in a swirling gown woven from summer twilit clouds, a fine shawl pinned with square brooches matching Óðinn's embossed design of wolf's heads. Startled by their regal appearance and flushed with desire, I bowed my head to the rulers of Asgard. I heard the derisive snort from Óðinn as he led Frigg away, no doubt completely aware of my preoccupation. I nearly rushed headlong into Baldr as he stepped from the shadows behind his parents, and Freyja pulled me uncomfortably close, my mind racing through scenarios not hindered by clothing. Despite my hurried breathing, I gazed at Baldr, aware of the brilliance he encouraged in gods and mortals alike. He was tall and broad-shouldered, his sun-blessed form dressed in simple, autumn-coloured garments. I realised with a sudden shock that the white teeth, golden hair and kindness that Baldr portrayed was truly who he was. He was kind, simple and blessed. He lacked the scheming mind and warlike ferocity of his parents and in being everything Óðinn was not, Baldr would always be protected by the Æsir. Before I could contemplate the myriad implications, Freyja pulled me down the narrow passages of Valhalla toward her bedchamber and I soon forgot the shining prospect I had envisaged in Baldr.

CHAPTER 26
·QUEEN ·OF THE ÆSIR

I cried out in ecstasy, hands lifting Freyja's hips with my own, my mouth to one of her breasts, when Sigyn burst into the bedchamber. The heavy oak door slammed against the wall, but I barely noticed: Freyja's movement above me still claimed all my attention as she pushed me toward climax. Her head was thrown back in a groan, long pale hair tumbling about her as I dropped my hands from her hips, crushing the thick furs on the bed as I clenched my fists. That moment, I was close enough to passion to be mad with it, my body aching with a desire and release I imagined was like death. Sweat ran into my eyes and I closed them, shouting Freyja's name as her hips drove into mine and the room seemed to spin.

A savage slap across my face stung me, and the rings drew blood. I opened my eyes in absolute shock, my mind unable to follow the sharp assault. I still felt Freyja's strong and magnificent body around mine, her thighs pinning me in place as I looked straight ahead at her. She smiled a secretive, mocking little smile and tossed her pale hair across one shoulder, covering her breasts nonchalantly. Still struggling to understand, my mind fogged with lust and the afterglow of such a release. Freyja pulled away from me, moving to the edge of the bed, already collecting her discarded robes.

"What?" I croaked, trying to rise to my elbows when another sharp slap rocked my head back against the bed.

I rolled my head to the left, dazed and really confused. Sigyn glared at me, her fists raised to strike me again.

"Oh," I said, vaguely recalling the door slamming open when she intruded on us.

"I endure everything for you," Sigyn hissed, voice low. "Your flagrant disregard for our marriage, constant dalliances, flirtatious overtures and those longer entanglements," she looked sick. "Angrboða, of all creatures!"

"Freyja seduced me!" I exclaimed, pushing myself up onto my elbows.

"Of course, you were such an unwilling partner," Freyja scoffed from the edge of my bed, already dressed.

"She intoxicated me with some seiðr trickery!" I protested.

"Don't lie, you're disgusting," Sigyn hissed. "Óðinn might have made your body attractive, Loki, but your spirit will always be a giant's."

I stilled in the bed, anger turning from fire to ice at my wife's words. "And I have always disgusted you so?"

"I will abide no more," Sigyn shouted, glaring at me. "Were you hoping I'd never know about those monsters you fathered with some giant witch? Or were you thinking you'd carry on behind my back, leave me to endure the snide glances and whispered comments whenever I enter a room? Being married to you was the worst decision of my life."

"What of our sons? Does Narvi disgust you too for the giant blood he shares with me?" I demanded, sitting upright.

Sigyn paled at my words and I felt the flames kindling in my irises. The fiery nature of the Múspelheim giants was never something the Æsir were comfortable with, not even Óðinn, for it reminded them of my true capabilities. I was still a fire giant regardless of my appearance now.

"You know I love them," Sigyn answered quietly. "Which is why our marriage is going to be dissolved. They will take my name and position among the Æsir. They need have nothing to do with your taint."

I turned to Freyja, who had moved to the middle of the room and was tying the sash on her robe.

"What about you in all of this?" I accused. "You wrought this damage for what gain?"

Freyja stared at me as though I had gone completely insane. "I have no gain here but fighting for what Sigyn desires. She has every right to call upon Frigg and request your marriage be dissolved. You have never been a suitable husband and I can attest to many of your manipulations myself."

I stared at her, aghast. "Half of those were your lies and manipulations!"

Freyja turned to leave the room, hesitating at the doorway to look back over her shoulder. "I don't remember them that way at all."

"Get out, Loki," Sigyn said to me, pointing at the doorway where Freyja stood. "You're no longer welcome in this chamber."

I stared at Sigyn, speechless as she glared at me. "You're not serious?"

"Perhaps Lady Freyja will welcome you to her chamber," she said, firmly.

"Sigyn," Freyja began. "Your friendship is worth more to me than his fine body."

"Is that what we are? Friends?" Sigyn asked coldly. "I think you and Loki are better matched than you imagine."

"He is not worth such hatred from you," Freyja answered, head bowed. "I deserve your anger now. When you speak before Frigg, call on me."

"Wait a moment!" I shouted, getting to my feet and hastily pulling on trousers. "You're not just walking away from this ruin," I said to Freyja.

She turned to leave, glaring balefully at me before she swept down the passage in a rustle of clothing.

I looked at Sigyn, who had been my most dependable wife, the one who was always here to return to no matter what disaster befell me. Her face was impassive, her lovely features deliberately unflinching as she pointed at the open doorway.

"Don't do this," I pleaded. "I love my sons. I love you."

I was aware of the effort Sigyn underwent not to bend to me, to show how much this final betrayal too far truly meant to her. A tear beaded on her eyelashes but she held my gaze, unblinking until I walked to the doorway. I stood there, shoulders bowed against the sudden weight of sorrow. I half-turned, spying Sigyn hastily wiping the tear from her eyes before she met my gaze once again.

"Don't come back, Loki," Sigyn said. The hurt and disappointment in her voice nearly broke me as I turned on my heel and walked away. I continued down the passages of Valhalla, the handful of clothes I had gathered off our bed hurriedly bundled into a makeshift pack.

I thought I knew what Freyja hoped to achieve with breaking my marriage to Sigyn. My only formal ties to the Æsir were through my marriage bonds and with those dissolved, the only bond remaining was between Óðinn and myself. It was an ancient pact we had made eons ago when the worlds were young and I had first chosen to leave Múspelheim. When Óðinn had changed my appearance, worked my flesh from the misshapen thing I had been, a thing fire giants regarded as useless and unimportant, Óðinn had made a pact with me. He was the only surviving son of a new race of beings, ones which were not the Vanir nor the giants but something similar to both. We were alike in temperament and both of us were outcasts in the Nine Worlds. We were like brothers, not bound by blood but something deeper. I had remained true to my nature because the giants never change our temperament, our power and nature are derived from the sources of Jötunheimr's frozen glaciers or Múspelheim's fiery rivers. I had an ominous feeling that my bond with Óðinn wasn't enough anymore. He had become too alike those older brothers he'd killed when the Nine Worlds were so very young.

I had one suspicion left and I wasn't sure why its curiosity burned so brightly in my mind. I needed the answer now. If Frigg truly intended to judge my marriage to Sigyn when her own to Óðinn was just as shameful, I needed to know if Frigg was a woman who lied openly or perhaps just to herself.

I left the warm rooms of Valhalla and stepped into the frigid night chill, hunching my shoulders against the cold as I trekked toward Fensalir and where I knew I would find the Lady Frigg.

Vengeance was on my mind as I struggled through the hip-deep snow toward the torchlight in the near distance. Just above the gently rolling hills, a small thicket surrounded a lush garden, stone bridges crossing brooks that ran between a series of small ponds. These were the gardens of Fensalir, the main hall where Frigg spent her days whenever Óðinn was travelling. Tonight, snow hung heavily on the pine boughs draping over the frozen ponds. Shivering in the freezing cold, I slogged up the shadowed slope slightly southwest of Fensalir. If this plan was to work, Frigg could not know who I truly was.

Crawling on hands and knees, I clawed my way to the rise, numb fingers scrabbling against the icy ground. Heaving in frigid air, I surveyed the quiet household, the absence of guards or watchmen, the torches in the main yard already burning low as dawn grew closer.

I closed my eyes, recalling the warning Freyja had spoken often enough about using the powers of shapeshifting too frequently and the dangers that increased when shifting into a human form. I smiled bitterly, thinking also that I was a giant, but none of Freyja's words applied to me, and the witches like Angrboða never warned against changing of forms. I stripped off my sodden cloak and pulled the damp woollen tunic over my head. I kicked off my boots and shrugged out of my pants to stand naked in the snow. Of course, I thought ruefully, Angrboða and her kin weren't exactly above cannibalism so they might have different standards.

"Let's see if you're a liar, Frigg," I whispered, wiggling my toes in the snow.

The magic curled about me, brushing my rapidly freezing body with a warm glow that became increasingly hot. The tingling across my skin began to burn and I started to twitch uncomfortably. Just when I thought I could tolerate the transformation no longer and maybe I'd made a mistake, my spine bent horribly, stooping my back like that of a crone. My flesh stretched, then sagged, my hair curling around my face in an uneven mass of silver ringlets. I looked at my hands, watching the knuckles swell with false age, wrinkles quickly marking my skin with an ever-increasing spread. My vision dimmed with cataracts, and I wished I'd had the foresight to get a walking staff from Valhalla before I left. I had intended to be an old crone, but I'd not really considered the practicalities of what that really entailed. Stooped, swollen with arthritis and nearly blind, I'd be lucky to make it to Frigg's house without getting lost in the darkness and expiring out here. It was also the perfect guise to force Frigg's hand and make her take me in, with the hospitality she would normally show guests—a little further, even, in my case. I needed Frigg to care for me so I might speak with her and not be handed over to one of her lesser servants.

Shivering in the cold, I bent my already stiff and stooped spine further, rummaging through the cloth pack I'd brought with me. I'd thrown a few hasty supplies into my bag before I left Valhalla. I removed a long, loose woollen dress, the type I'd seen many old crones wear before and exactly the type one old crone in particular had worn, before I stole it from her washing line. I pulled it over my head, wrinkling my nose at the smell of aged wool and the silt from the Midgard river where it had been washed. Removing the thin, inadequately fur-lined boots, I tugged these on my swollen feet and tied the laces as securely as I could manage. Lastly, I pulled on the thin, fur-lined woollen cloak and secured the brooches on my bony shoulders. I hurriedly hid my former clothing beneath the low branches of a pine and made my slow, hesitant progress toward the main house yard of Fensalir.

Chapter 27
Frigg Deceived

My progress was slow through the heavy snow outside Frigg's hall but even as I struggled over the waist-deep snowdrift that had accumulated against the low stone wall encircling Fensalir, I thought how unprotected Frigg was from any invading groups of frost giants from Jötunheimr. Óðinn had grown very arrogant and lazy in his protective measures. He'd left Frigg unguarded with only Heimdallrr on guard at Bifröst responsible for the safety of the entirety of Asgard. I wondered when these changes had occurred in Óðinn, how I had missed these crucial points. I slogged through the much wetter snow of the gardens, and despite the stone pathways having obviously been cleared of snowfalls earlier in the day, fresh snow had begun to build its frozen layers overnight. I hurried toward the main doors of Fensalir. Already I could sense Dagr and Sól preparing to make passage across the sky, exchanging places with Máni and Nótt in their eternal race across the heavens. Standing before the main carved oak doors, I lifted the gold door knocked and struck it ponderously against the solid wood.

The echo of gold on oak rang through the large, meandering structure that constituted Fensalir, giving me moments to appreciate the silence of the surrounding forests. It was very isolated here. Finally, I heard the rushing of footsteps and hushed whispers, the snap of an order and then door bar was pulled free, throwing the main doors open.

Frigg stood across the other side of the threshold, thick fur cloak secured about herself. I squinted through the cataracts that inhibited my eyesight in this wizened guise and then peered closer, exaggerating my confusion at being greeted by the lady of the hall. Honestly, not everything was exaggeration.

"Lady Frigg?" I enquired in genuine surprise, thinking to capitalise on the unusual situation.

Frigg's delicate brows knit together, and several other ladies stood hesitantly in the shadows behind her, whispering in nearly inaudible voices.

"Most glorious lady," I stammered, wiping a hand across my wrinkled face, pretending to accidentally dislodge the deep hood of the cloak that covered my thick, silver hair.

"Old mother," Frigg answered by way of greeting, bowing her head slightly in acknowledgement.

I peered at both hulking warriors who stood on the edge of the doorway, hands on the hilts of their swords, eyes fixed on me like I might become the source of their next entertainment any moment.

"This is a mighty hall," I mentioned to no one in particular, staring with apparent fascination at the intricate woodwork and fine, inlaid crystals.

"Forgive my rudeness!" Frigg exclaimed, startling from her poorly concealed shock. "Come inside, old mother. You must be freezing! The winter winds are so harsh that even the frost giants dare not tread out there this night."

I smiled, bowing my head in many quick nods of gratitude as Frigg bustled me into her hall, a wandering crone she neither knew nor had expected but whom guest law dictated she must now welcome and feed from her own supplies. I had timed it to be an imposition and it was clear, from Frigg's initial surprise, it had been exactly that. I was impressed with how quickly Óðinn's lady recovered and dutifully attended to me as though I were any of the Vanir or Æsir ladies come to visit.

Frigg took me into the modest hall to the right of the atrium. A comfortable central hearth overlooked a sprawling garden, now dormant for the winter and buried beneath layers of snow. I knew that in the spring and summer months, that garden was full of lazily nodding flowers, creeping vines and ripe fruit trees. This early in the dawn, the garden was dusted in icicles and looked as remote as Niflheimr.

"Here," Frigg said, gesturing expansively to a wide bench before the hearth that had been hastily stirred to life, the flames now hungrily licking at fresh wood.

"Thank you, Lady Frigg," I replied, bowing my head in gratitude. "It is so kind of one as great as you to take pity on such an old woman."

"We all deserve kindness," Frigg said.

I smiled, peering up at her through cloudy eyes wondering if she truly believed that. The sincerity in her expression only confirmed my suspicions that Frigg lied to herself, and she was unaware of her own blindness.

"It is very gracious of you, Lady," I said again, bowing my head and holding my aching feet before the fire.

Frigg frowned a moment, and I wondered if she had pierced my glamour in some way. She stood poised, unsure, hands held demurely in her lap.

"Have you no fur-lined boots?" she suddenly asked me, staring at my thin leather footwear in horror.

"I am alone in this world," I explained, rotating my ankles stiffly to warm them. "I have no children or grandchildren to provide such things, Lady Frigg."

"Oh," Frigg answered, but knelt at my feet, already hastily untying my loose laces and pulling off the soaked leather boots.

I watched Frigg with genuine amazement, her long, delicate fingers normally used to skilfully weave the weather now massaging my feet, encouraging circulation back into my toes. The muscles spasmed painfully and cramped.

"What brings you to my hall, old mother?" Frigg asked, glancing up as she continued to massage my poor feet.

I shifted in my seat. "I came to see if you had been successful in saving your only son, my Lady," I said. "I live far from other folk and did not know if my vow and those from others around me had proved true. If the god Baldr was unharmed?"

Frigg sat back on her heels, fear shadowing her features. "Your vow was well spoken, old mother. I thank you for your desire to preserve Baldr's life. He is among the brightest and best of us."

I smiled, leaning back in my chair as the spasms in my feet relaxed beneath Frigg's nimble fingers. "Baldr is indeed beloved among the Æsir, my Lady."

"I would have nothing harm him," Frigg whispered, kneading a sore tendon in my foot a little too painfully, making me flinch.

"I heard tell you had every single living creature swear allegiance to you. Is that so, my lady?" I asked, leaning forward with genuine curiosity. "That nothing alive would harm Baldr?"

"That is so," Frigg answered, adjusting her gown modestly and beginning to massage my other foot, sparking new waves of pins and needles. "We do anything for our children."

"That must have been a truly impressive task," I said, shaking my head in wonder. "You had even the smallest things swear allegiance?"

"Yes," Frigg replied with a smile. "Baldr is much loved in these Nine Worlds."

"Did you even ask the mistletoe?" I asked, frowning.

Frigg looked up sharply. "The mistletoe?" she queried. "Of course. The prophecy spoken by the witch's shade proclaimed mistletoe would be the weapon used. All the mistletoe plants were the first to give their pledge."

I nodded, feigning contentment and settled back in my chair. "That is good, my Lady," I answered, arranging my worn skirts about my legs. "All should swear allegiance to preserve Baldr for he is the brightest and most promising of the gods, indeed he is."

"He is," Frigg said with a smile, preparing to stand.

"Did you seek vows from even the youngest plant of the mistletoe growing in the glen near Útgarðar?" I asked.

Frigg paused, frowning slightly. "No," she answered with doubt. "But that mistletoe was barely more than a sapling. No harm can come from it being crafted into any weapon…not yet anyway. Once it is large enough, I will seek its allegiance."

I stared at the shadows of doubt and concern that darkened her expression. "Then all is well, Lady Frigg?"

"Yes," she answered, standing up and shaking the stiffness from her own joints.

"Good," I replied with a smile. "I am much relieved to hear the prophecy won't be fulfilled. I am even more pleased to hear that giant-lover Loki shall not lead us into twilight."

Frigg startled, whirling to face me in a mass of darkening clouds that spontaneously formed to encircle her body like a new dress.

"What do you know of the twilight of the gods?" Frigg demanded. "Who are you?"

I hesitated briefly, considering my options. "Like all those in Asgard, I am on your side," I explained. "Many of us do not trust the giants. I meant only that without the brightest of the Æsir, our lives would be like a twilight before true dark."

Frigg relaxed slightly. "Loki is a vile creature," she confided. "Why my husband tolerates him I have never understood. But even Óðinn is becoming wise to the trickery and malice of that foul giant. I have out-schemed Loki this time and will see him thrown from Asgard. Without the protection his wife Sigyn can offer him, Óðinn will not tolerate his grievances and betrayals," she finished, eyes bright with undisguised hatred.

"We are fortunate for your leadership, Lady Frigg," I replied flatly, unable to feign exaltation at her words.

Frigg smiled and graciously inclined her head in appreciation, but seemed to consider me with unnerving mistrust.

When I had completely warmed myself beside the fire and sunlight glowed brightly across the snowy landscape outside, I thanked Frigg for her hospitality and made my slow progress to the front doors. My questions had stirred some unconscious concern in Frigg and she was barely aware of me when I departed.

I wasted no time. I hurried as fast as the shambling gait of the aged woman could manage, walking only to the nearest copse of trees and shedding the crone's clothing. Shivering in the morning air, I shifted my physical form, biting back the scream of pain that threatened to tear from my throat as muscle, skin and bone reshaped itself.

When at last I knelt naked in the snow, my body in the familiar form and physique restored, I dashed to the hasty camp I had made earlier in the predawn darkness and gathered my items from beneath the pine tree. When dressed again as Loki, I buckled on my knife and strapped the leather shoes that never wore thin to my feet. I needed to travel to Útgarðar, and quickly. Frigg had lied to us all and she had deceived Óðinn. Her deception of Óðinn was not unsurprising to me—their marriage was a volatile arrangement. Her words had kindled the smouldering coal inside me that flared with each new slight and prejudice against the giants. Now, it was time to crush the arrogance of the Æsir.

PART THREE
Beginning Of The End

CHAPTER 28
THE BRIGHTEST ONE

I travelled swiftly to the furthest reaches of Jötunheimr, where the mountains formed a naturally impregnable ring-wall surrounding the fortress of Útgarðar. Within that shadowy realm of craggy peaks and granite ruled the one who remained nameless through all my travels. If Óðinn knew his name, he never spoke it. Perhaps it was from fear or jealousy, because the king of that dark mountain kingdom possessed powers similar to the Vanir and Æsir alike. I often wondered if he were a discarded son, brother or even lover of Angrboða's for the similarity of their powers. Whatever the true nature of the nameless ruler in Útgarðar, I'd heard him confused with my own name often enough to know to avoid him. I'd travelled there once or twice with Óðinn in the early years of our brotherhood, but not since the worlds were young had I returned within the borders of Útgarðar proper.

I passed the twisted forest of the Iron Wood and felt the many eyes of the werewolves and other creatures at Angrboða's command. I did not pause or hesitate as I dashed across the semi-circular line of plain stones that marked the outer border of Útgarðar. I felt the shiver of power that passed across my skin and was conscious of another's attention drawn to me. This was often the case when crossing that near-invisible barrier, and I did not slow down to consider it.

I hurried toward the small grove that was sunk below the plains I had fled across many times before. This grove was as much a place that was mine as any in the Nine Worlds. Útgarðar was as close to my home as any would be, which was why I never corrected any tales that I ruled the mysterious mountain fortress.

My modest hut was certainly not a fortress and the time I had spent away from it now showed in the rundown appearance. The thatch roof needed replacing and the wooden door hung drunkenly off one hinge. I barely spared it more than a glance as I rushed past the ramshackle hut and into the deep, shady grove to the left.

The large trees clustered close to each other, giving the clearing in the centre a claustrophobic sensation. I fell to my knees in the middle of the clearing and ignored the twitching of my spine and shoulder blades alerting me to the many hidden gazes that watched my actions. If I needed to use what I was about to create, it would not matter who saw my crafting here today.

Steadying my breathing, I drew in my will and closed my eyes, my heartbeat loud in my ears, but slowly I bought it under my control. Composed, I opened my flickering eyes. The flames within me that gave power to my magic burning strongly with my need. I reached for the tiny shrub before me, the plant barely more than a sapling still.

The young mistletoe was not much longer than my thumb and had only two curling leaves atop the twining vines of its stubby form. I touched a fingertip carefully to one leaf and pushed my own energy into the plant.

Magic flared bright and hot, flowing from my own body and into the mistletoe. The leaf I touched immediately lengthened, the vine stretching and twisting, thickening and growing woody with age. When the young mistletoe resembled a plant advanced more than a decade, I dropped my fingertip from its leaves.

"Thank you, my friend," I whispered to the plant, unsheathing the knife at my hip. "Your service will be remembered."

I wasted no time, moving the shining metal blade quickly in the forest gloom. The slice of iron through the fibrous branch echoed unnaturally loud in the quiet grove. I bowed my head once more to the mistletoe, re-sheathed my blade and pocketed the plant cutting.

I hurried from Útgarðar and Jötunheimr as quickly as I had crossed their borders, not waiting for the creatures that roamed these woods to become inquisitive or hungry. I also needed to be certain that the course of action already planned in my mind was absolutely justified before I took it. If there were any doubts— and of course, I had plenty of doubt—I needed to dispel them because my place among the Æsir had to truly be nothing more than ashes, for my actions were going to set aflame the battle-lustful gods of the Æsir.

I crossed the meadows of Fólkvangr. The rolling hillocks and wafting wildflower scent of these fields was pleasant in the warm evening. The air was warm and from the vantage point of my greater distance, I could see the Æsir assembled outside Valhalla, large tables and casks of mead carried outside into the summer afternoon. I could hear the roar of Thor's laughter and shouts, the quiet calm tones of Týr as he argued. It appeared they were still testing Baldr's immortality. The foolishness of their games and shouted boasts seemed petty and foolish to me, the stench of stale mead and the clatter of goblets appalling. I wrinkled my nose in displeasure, rounding the corner of the stables. I stopped immediately, retreating into the shadows of the overhanging roof.

Sigyn stood beside an upturned, empty cask of mead, one foot propped against the bottom of the barrel, elbows folded and chin resting neatly on them. It was an image of such pure contemplation and contentment that I wanted to keep the memory of it in my mind forever. She still had not noticed me, so I continued from a slightly oblique angle to her and quietly stepped to stand beside her.

"Loki," she said warily and in warning.

"Sigyn," I began, reaching for her hands as she pulled away from me. "Please," I begged, openly reaching my arms toward her.

"No," she said, vehemently shaking her head, thick blonde hair falling either side of her face.

"Please just let us talk," I begged, arms open still.

"There's nothing to say," Sigyn replied, stepping away toward the open doorway behind her, the shadows of Valhalla waiting within.

"Don't throw away everything we have because I'm a fool," I pleaded.

"That's not why," she said, expression softening slightly. "I can't trust you, Loki."

"I have always loved you. I know I'm unable to settle and I know I'm not faithful to you, especially when I've drunk a lot of mead. You know how easily a pretty pair of eyes, a beautiful smile, can fascinate me. But those are only passing fancies, Sigyn. You are the only one I ever wanted to have children with."

"And Angrboða?" she interrupted.

"I know you don't believe me when I tell you none of that was ever done willingly."

"She shakes her head slowly. " I know with enough mead, you'd screw anything that moved, Loki. Angrboða wouldn't have even needed to drug you."

"Sigyn," I implored, stepping toward her, but she stepped back again. "Why now? Why after everything we have endured, everything we experienced, everything we've enjoyed together? Why make this decision to dissolve our marriage now? I am the same man I have always been. Please tell me what you need, let me please you."

"You're right," she said flatly. "Nothing has changed. You're exactly as you have always been, but I was too foolish to see you. I believed your lies, your promises of never again, those sweet kisses asking for forgiveness. You are the deceiver the Æsir have always claimed you to be. Frigg was right, Loki. I was too blind to see your falseness."

I let my hands fall to my sides as Sigyn turned, and without a backward glance she walked into the deeper shadows of Óðinn's hall. I did not follow. I stood motionless for a long time, fists clenching and unclenching as I stared blankly and time stretched around me. Finally, I turned on my heel and surveyed the meadows of Fólkvangr. The cluster of the Æsir and Vanir were still gathered nearby, the noise of their jests and boasting drifting on the summer breeze.

"Let's see how blind the Æsir can be," I said through a grimace, already striding toward the jovial gods in the distance.

The wildflowers that covered the plains of Fólkvangr bowed their petalled heads against the growing storm that blew from the south. I walked with the wind behind me, the unruly ringlets of my fiery red hair snarling around my head like vipers. I felt the anger inside me burning, knew the golden flecks in my eyes glowed like a stoked furnace. I ground my teeth together, trying to master my anger. I knew it was a losing battle. I longed to unleash my rage and betrayal upon the Æsir like an unconstrained wildfire but I needed to be smarter than that. They had always thought me some curiosity that Óðinn kept beside him like a three-horned goat. I was a domesticated fire giant that could be harnessed and put to work like the oxen and horses stabled in the barns. It was time they all realised I was not their creature to be mocked, beaten like a lesser being. I could do them real harm and sooner or later, they would beg for me to rescue them from their own arrogance and stupidity.

Baldr stood at the top of a slight incline. Fólkvangr never truly reached the height of proper hills but undulated from the forests of Álfheimr to the mountains further southwest leading to Jötunheimr. It was in one of these rolling meadows that Baldr and Thor had set up the latest amusements for the day. Several empty barrels of ale had rolled discarded to the bottom of a narrow cleft between two hillocks, and I stepped around these as I began my ascent to the jeering Æsir on the top of the rise. I moved brusquely past the bored looking cupbearers, two light elves that leaned against a barrel of warm mead, the chill northern wind already cooling the afternoon air.

"What goes on?" I asked one of the elves as I unhooked my own drinking horn and dunked it into the barrel of ale.

"Thor has been challenging any of the Æsir to throw objects at Baldr," one of the elves replied, stifling a yawn.

I quirked an eyebrow. "All day?"

The handsome elf rolled his eyes melodramatically. "All day."

"Easy entertainment for some."

The elves chuckled and returned their gaze to watch Thor as he stepped up to stand before an opening in the crowd ahead. At the far side of the clearing, I could see Baldr standing on a distant hillock, bare-chested and grinning as he slapped his breast and taunted Thor. In return, Thor bellowed a meaningless insult and hurled one of the large carved wooden chairs from the central hall in Valhalla. I watched as the heavy piece of furniture tumbled effortlessly through the air toward Baldr. Ignoring the strong desire to look away, I fixed my gaze on Baldr waiting to see what would happen. The massive chunk of wood shattered around him as though some shield protected every angle of his body, splintering the furniture at his feet. The gathered Æsir roared in triumph and toasted Baldr's immunity with another round of ale.

I moved away from the ale barrels, not wanting Thor to see me here. I did not know if I would truly do what I had planned. Much of my anger had weakened in my walk over to this ridiculous event and the old camaraderie of these gods was refreshing. *But it is false*, I reminded myself, glancing around at the men and women I had called family. These people were not my family. Sigyn had already proved how easily she would throw me aside for merely being who I had always been. How had she never realised who I was? Had all the years of our marriage only ever been an arrangement for her? A thing she must endure until someone like Frigg could offer her the freedom to escape it? No, I thought. These were not my people and never had been.

I tossed my head back, draining the last of the mead from my drinking horn and took out the small branch of mistletoe from my inside pocket. I stared at the cut twig a moment, fingering the uneven wood and glanced briefly at Baldr who stood, perfect and brilliant as always, laughing with Thor. He and Thor were the ones the Æsir admired the most: the children of Óðinn, one whose only talent was smashing things in such an uncontrollable rage as to be useless, and the other who did nothing except smile broadly and tend his beard. If these two were the future of the Æsir, they deserved every wrath that befell them for their stupidity. I took the knife from my hip and standing to the side of the crowd, watched as Bragi struck up another melody with the harp and Iðunn skipped prettily around him, the poetry of the music flowing like honeyed mead. In a few quick flicks of my wrist, I had whittled the mistletoe branch down to a finely tipped dart. It wasn't a huge object nor a sharp axe, but I knew it would have more effect than either of those if Frigg had spoken truly to me. I believed every word she had said last night because she had spoken with the confidence of one woman confiding her secrets to an older matron.

The last notes of the harp echoed over the subdued crowd before Thor bellowed again, calling for more sport. Baldr laughed good-naturedly and with eager steps resumed his position on the opposite side of the meadow. I skirted the edge of the crowd, glancing over the faces of the Æsir who all watched with attention fixed fast on Thor as he threw a double-bladed axe toward Baldr. To no surprise, just as before the invisible shield around Baldr protected him, casting aside the blow of the axe. I saw the slumped shoulders of Baldr's brother Höðr, the blind twin who stood apart from the festivities. *Why is* Höðr, *the brother of Baldr, treated in such a way by the Æsir?* I understood, of course.

I recalled being a twisted, broken creature, a being with a physical form that others considered broken and ugly. I had been despised and Óðinn had pitied me. That was the only reason he had paid me any attention in the first place. He had looked upon this creature of molten rock and fiery form, who spoke with intelligence but lacked the subtle lips to match the wits. Óðinn had changed me, making my form into something he saw as worthy of my intelligence. That should have been my first real lesson in what type of being Óðinn truly was: only the beautiful could be intelligent, only the old could be wise, only the physically strong could be powerful. Those were the same rules under which he had burned Gullveig when she came into Valhalla and cursed him using the foresight only she possessed. It was time Óðinn learned his next lesson, that the crippled could slay the immortal among them.

"Höðr?" I asked as I stood beside the blind man.

He turned, his features a paler version of Baldr's, his smile not broad or radiant, his body seeming neither strong nor virile. In every way, he seemed the shadow of his brother. I felt the pang of pity and the sharper burn of anger toward the gods who could treat their own with such disrespect.

"Loki?" he asked in mild surprise, even his voice soft and mellow, lacking the vibrancy and vigour of Baldr.

"Are you enjoying the amusements?" I asked, keeping my voice light as I jerked my chin toward the answering shouts from Thor and Baldr.

Höðr shrugged one shoulder. "I might enjoy them if I could see them," he explained in a weary jest. "Much of the excitement is lost if you can't see what's happening."

"Ah," I said, letting the silence deepen between us. "Surely someone has been willing to give you a blow-by-blow account?" I asked in sudden surprise. "Iðunn would surely help, let me get her for you."

"No, no," Höðr said quickly, grabbing at my wrist and holding me fast. "There is no need to trouble Iðunn. You're right, she's kindly and would do as you ask. She would be mortified to know I've been standing here all day with not much of an idea of what's going on and no one being my eyes for me. Don't trouble her so now, it's nearly the end of the day, isn't it?"

"It is nearly twilight," I answered, cocking my head at him, wondering how he knew the time of day when he was apparently blind. "But how do you know?"

Höðr laughed slightly, the sound jarring as though he did it rarely. "I am blind, Loki," he explained. "I am not deaf nor lost my sense of smell. I can hear the evening preparations and even smell the boar beginning to roast for the night's meal."

"I wish I had those talents," I grumbled. "I'd be late for meals much less frequently."

"And I wish I had your sight," Höðr laughed.

I looked sidelong at him, judging my anger and desire to wound the Æsir against the kindness I had found in this man. I had never bothered to get to know Höðr well. He often clung close to Baldr; the two seemed inseparable most of the time and I had disregarded him as easily as the rest of the gods. The ease with which I had done it angered me, and with it a colder realisation grew within me. Höðr was maybe not this pale god by choice, he might have been as vibrant as his twin but he had been born blind. In being less than whole, the Æsir and made a place for him in their world, but it was a lesser place than they gave his more perfect brother. It seemed to me that Höðr got the whole intellect of the pair and Baldr got the physical form, but there was a darker truth here. Höðr had let himself be moulded into this pale reflection of who he might have been, he had accepted the place the Æsir had given him, the half-status and neglect they offered him were what he expected. I might have helped Höðr to be more than this weaker version of himself but on the same scale, he had never sought me out, either. He had known my history, for it was as notorious a tale among the Æsir as the many adventures of Óðinn himself. Höðr accepted his lot, and that somehow steeled my heart for what I needed to do.

"Have you had a try?" I asked Höðr casually.

"At what?" he asked, surprised.

"I know Baldr is your brother," I began quietly. "But have you not joined in the jests?"

"I'm blind, Loki," Höðr said, gesturing to his cloudy eyes. "I can't see."

"I know that." I waved away his concern. "I meant has no one offered to help you?"

"To help me?"

"To be your eyes," I said.

"You mean to help me throw?"

"Yes. I can do it. I've done this before, admittedly not with a blind man and certainly a buxom woman, who I showed how to throw a knife."

Höðr held up his hands. "I don't want to be your buxom woman."

"I'd hope not. You're really not very buxom at all."

"I meant," he began, gesturing with embarrassment toward me and himself, "I don't like men that way."

"It's good to share these feelings but I actually meant I've taught someone how to throw a weapon before and *not* bedded them."

"Okay."

"Aren't you tired of not being part of things? This is as much your right as any of the Æsir here. It's wrong that they don't include you in their jests. Let me help you. Let's show how being blind doesn't mean you're not powerful."

"I know how to throw a blade, Loki. You needn't get so close to me."

"Excellent then." I turned on my heel and dragged him up the incline where Thor had left a vacant space.

I glanced around at the Æsir, who had taken another break from the strenuous activities of hurling weapons and random pieces of furniture and farming implements at Baldr. Bragi was seated by the casks of mead again, harp strings filling the twilit meadow with their ringing melody as the cold northern wind continued to strengthen unabated. Thor and Týr were arguing over the next options for possible hurling weapons and in the shadowy gloom, I could just see Baldr yawn melodramatically and swallow another cup of mead in a single toss.

"Stand here," I said to Höðr, grasping him by the shoulders, positioning him into place. I sighted down the stretch of open meadow, the wildflowers waving desolately in the growing wind.

I pulled the small dart I had crafted from my pocket and placed it in Höðr's hand.

"What's this?" Höðr asked, turning the dart over with his fingers, feeling the surface and sharp tip. "A dart?"

"It's not an axe, pitchfork, plough or chair," I admitted, stepping back from Höðr. "But you are blind so let's just surprise them all with a few small things at a time."

Höðr smiled at me. "I appreciate your help," he said, turning back slightly to face his brother across the field.

I grimaced in reply, thinking that of all the things he could have said, his appreciation was probably the one which would wound me the worst. I heard Thor roar with laughter at the sight of Höðr standing there, shoulders slumped against the whipping of those cruel but common jokes. At the end of the meadow, I saw Baldr's bright smile falter slightly as he looked at his twin.

"You're all a pack of carrion crows," I muttered as Höðr threw.

I watched the narrow dart pierce the strength of the cold northern wind, travelling with considerable speed as it crossed the empty distance between Höðr and his brother. I was already turning away, disappearing into the twilight gloom when I heard the sharp indrawn breath of the Æsir, the solid sound of Baldr's body as it hit the ground on the other side of the meadow. There was sudden silence, into which I ran like a coward from the crowd, disappearing into the shadows as Höðr cried out for someone to tell him what had happened. Sound erupted across the fields of Fólkvangr like a great breath indrawn before a shout. I did not wait to hear the outcome of Höðr's throw. I knew the moment the dart had been loosed that Baldr would die. I ran with terror in my heart now because I had wanted it.

Chapter 29
Hel's Request

I heard Frigg's howl of anguish as I disappeared into the shadows of Vanaheimr, the dense woodland creating refuge for me. My hands were shaking. I looked at them numbly, staring as if I could not believe these were my own and pressed them between my knees, lowering my head as the wood tilted dangerously around me. I was breathing too rapidly. What had I done? Why had I done it? I let out a panicked little laugh, the noise jolting me back into reality. I had willingly given the dart to Höðr knowing it would kill his brother. Had I really believed the madness consuming the Æsir, though? Had I really considered the mistletoe dart could be the only thing able to kill Baldr?

"Yes," I said. I exhaled slowly, the acknowledgement settling around me like a weight. I had believed in their fear and I wanted them to feel the same anguish I felt at having kinship ripped away from them. In the dappled forest light, my choice seemed so stark and unconscionable. I had taken Baldr from Frigg because she would take the Æsir from me. I slumped onto the forest floor, pushing my back against a tree trunk. I closed my eyes, dropped my head onto my folded arms and wept.

I could have cried for moments or eons, but I sensed movement to my left and jerked upright, dashing tears away from my face. The forest light looked the same as it had when first I'd collapsed against the tree, but the shadows seemed deeper and longer. I peered into the gloom to my left. Was there anything there? Bright yellow eyes blinked at me. I flinched in shock. My head snapped backward into the trunk.

"Haiti?" I asked tentatively.

The golden wolf slunk from the darkness, the bright strands in her thick pelt catching the last of the day's light. I glanced around the grove for her brother, the pale wolf Sköll. The two were never far from each other.

Haiti circled me warily, head slightly lowered as she kept her gaze on me, but she checked the surrounding woodland. When it seemed she was satisfied I was alone, she sat in front of me, tail wrapped neatly around her forepaws.

Only then did Sköll emerge from my right, advancing from the opposite side where Haiti had been. He was slightly larger than his sister but his pelt had the faint silvery sheen of moonlight. The two wolves stared unblinking at me and I frowned.

"What?" I asked stupidly.

Sköll flicked his luminescent green eyes briefly to Haiti in a derisive glance before fixing his gaze intently on me again.

"To communicate with you both, I need to change my form," I told them. "I just killed a god. The Æsir are probably going to be pretty angry about that."

Haiti and Sköll just stared unblinking at me. They were motionless in the darkening forest.

"Ugh!" I threw up my hands in frustration, shooing the wolves backward with the movement as I leaped into the centre of the clearing.

Haiti bounded forward a few paces, head lowered and tail high, keen for me to challenge her. I ignored her playful stance and instead started stripping off the clothing I wore. It was probably just as well. Once Thor and Óðinn spoke with Höðr, they would have Óðinn's wolves out here and begin searching the Nine Worlds for me. Höðr had right to claim vengeance for his murdered brother and Óðinn for his murdered son. I would soon become the hunted among these worlds. I needed somewhere to hide, somewhere to belong and it seemed Sköll and Haiti still claimed kinship with me.

I tossed my tunic onto the ground and unbuttoned the woollen tights I wore, kicking off my boots as I did. My bare skin was turning bluish in the cold evening air even as I shimmied out of the tights. I began to change my form immediately, conscious that the frigid cold of the early evening could do me quicker harm than Óðinn or Thor.

Lying on the forest floor, warmth floods my body as the magic pulled incessantly on muscle fibres, tearing them and healing them in new shapes. The breaking of bone wasn't sharp or savagely painful, but nor was it comfortable. Bone was reabsorbed and created into shorter combinations, splitting and combining until the structure of the wolf could be properly healed. The process was quick, the physical damage of a transformation brutal beyond imagining, but the haze of magic and pain seemed to drown awareness.

At last I climbed unsteadily to my four paws, head hanging low with fatigue still. The shiver of magic ran through me, and I opened myself to the Wolf, to my other self and the embodiment of who I was.

"Loki?" Sköll asked me, head tilted slightly, ears flattened in respect.

"Yes." I answered in a low growl, lifting my muzzle to stare the younger male wolf in the eyes.

Sköll dropped his gaze obediently but his sister Haiti whined from the shadows.

"Take me where you wanted to lead, Haiti."

The golden wolf yipped with excitement and pounced toward me, her grace and speed belying her true ferocity. I evaded her playful leap, one forepaw swiping her easily aside.

"Where are we going?" I asked Sköll as the white wolf turned away from me.

"Home to Járnviðr."

I thought of the mist-covered woods and the darker creatures, the were-wolves who hunted in the Iron Wood. Had I been requested?

"To Angrboða?" I asked Sköll, still not following him.

"Our mother asks you join forces with us." Haiti said.

I shook myself in agitation, leaf litter arcing around me.

"No," I said, turning away from Haiti and Sköll. "I'm not ready to hunt with you yet. It's not time."

Sköll whined from the darkness of the woods and kept his tail and head low.

"Bring our brother Fenrir when you do join us."

I half-turned, looking over my shoulder at the blue eyes of the golden wolf.

"I will, Haiti."

I bounded up the slope of the forests, long stride swallowing the ground, until I crested the forest fringe and stood on the edge of Álfheimr. Below me, the valley where Valhalla lay among the plains of Fólkvangr looked like a squat, ugly turtle amid the natural landscape. There was something different about the Æsir and it had attracted me. I had mistaken curiosity for kinship, though. On the far border of Valhalla, near the stables, I saw a procession of the Æsir carrying lumber and tools, already beginning to craft the pyre for Baldr. My keen gaze fell on the two gods who lingered beside the stables, the tall, imposing form of Óðinn as he stood beside the massive grey horse, Sleipnir. No one but Óðinn ever rode Sleipnir but tonight, Hermóðr swung into the saddle and the stallion tossed his head in agitation. I watched Óðinn point one long arm across the track that led toward Álfheimr. I flinched, thinking for a moment he had seen me. I then recognised the gestures; even from here I realised Óðinn was explaining the path that Hermóðr must take. There was only one path that led through Álfheimr, and I didn't think Hermóðr would ride Óðinn's stallion to visit Njörðr. No. Hermóðr was riding to Hel.

Curiosity was like an addiction. The moment Hermóðr turned Sleipnir toward Álfheimr, I would follow. *Why is Óðinn sending Hermodr to Helheimr? Do Óðinn and Frigg truly think Hel will bargain with them for Baldr's shade?* Hel had the power and the right to release any shade in her halls. If she decided Baldr was just and did not belong in her halls with the shades of ordinary folk and those of thieves and murderers, it was in her power to grant his shade release from Hel. I flicked an ear back in consternation at the thought Óðinn could be so arrogant. That Frigg could be so arrogant. Óðinn? The man who had been my friend? My brother in everything but blood? I cursed myself for a fool and followed the retreating form of Sleipnir as Hermóðr galloped through the trees and disappeared into the woods of Álfheimr.

The road to Helheimr was dark even beneath the silvery form of Máni, and the moonlight reflected dully off the path. I followed Sleipnir along the twisting road, hoof prints clearly marked on the soil, making tracking easy. Even so, I followed cautiously lest Hermóðr notice me. The dark of the night and closeness of the forest meant Sleipnir moved cautiously through Álfheimr.

When finally, Hermóðr reached the crest of a sharp descent where the road led down into Niflheimr, he reined in the massive grey stallion. Sleipnir snorted and stamped the ground in agitation while Hermóðr surveyed the chasm below. Carefully I loped through the woods until I stood downwind from Sleipnir.

"We can't delay," Hermóðr said, patting the stallion's neck.

Then without warning, Sleipnir reared, and Hermóðr leaned forward, allowing the horse his head. I expected the stallion to throw his rider, but as I watched in silence, it leaped into the dark chasm and dropped from sight.

Bounding forward, I stood on the edge of the steep cliff, searching the darkness below. There was no sign of Sleipnir or Hermóðr . I considered what I had just witnessed. Was there a gateway into Niflheimr here? Had Óðinn told Hermóðr of a secret entrance into the lands ruled by the dark elves? If such a gateway existed, had Óðinn ever told Thor? Surely if he had, all the Æsir and even the dark elves would know.

I trotted back and forth along the edge of the chasm, peering over the steep cliff that dropped into an unknown depth. Darkness swallowed the rock sides of the abyss, and I had no idea what game Óðinn was now playing. I snorted and took the thread of my own Fate firmly in my jaws. I leaped into the air, the shadows of the chasm beneath me.

I did not fall. Instead, my front paws hit a solid surface on the other side. Still, there was nothing but emptiness before me, but I scrabbled for purchase on the hewn stone before the momentum of my leap carried me fully across whatever gateway Óðinn had created or discovered between Niflheimr and Asgard.

Sliding to a halt, I immediately shook the dust from my fur, checking my surroundings as I did. The ice-rimmed mountains to the west marked the entrance to Niflheimr but the stone pillars either side of me formed the gateway to Helheimr. Behind me, a bridge arched over a dark chasm, the icy river Slidr roaring beneath. I watched the bridge sway slightly in the gust of icy air that rushed beneath with the river.

Ahead of me, the road continued up a steep slope, twisting around the grey, featureless mountains of Helheimr. I trotted forward, following the hoof prints Sleipnir had left in the road. The ash-covered landscape was unchanging as I continued along the mountain slopes. I stayed out of sight, always making sure Hermóðr remained a decent distance away. He had only one destination now; he travelled in Hel's domain and I understood the nature of his quest, too.

I had never visited Hel since Óðinn cast her into this realm, and even as I trotted along the well-worn path, I considered how many shades had walked it before me. Hel's world was the final hall for the dead who were not fortunate enough to have died in battle and be chosen by Óðinn or Freyja, nor drowned beneath the waves and joined Rán. Nor was this the final realm where young maidens might be taken by Gefion. Hel's domain was cold and cruel, the shades of the unfortunate: the old, the murderers and the thieves. The landscape looked as merciless as its ruler was purported to be. I had known Hel as a child, intelligent, cunning and ruthless even then, but I could easily imagine how Óðinn's unjust treatment and exile to this desolate wasteland had made her harder than a blade.

It took nine nights to reach Hel's hall. The towering structure carved from the ash-grey rock was brutal and unrelenting. A harsh wind blew off the lake that cupped the shore around the fortress. A series of shabbily clothed figures walked ahead of me toward its massive doors. The ebony wood of the locked doors reflected the dark lake surface below and it was as though I stared into a skull, the shining doors empty eye sockets staring back at me. I shook away the dread aroused in me from sight of the hall of the dead—and hastened into a lope. Ahead of me, Hermóðr had halted Sleipnir outside the doors and was already dismounting.

I saw the shadow slip around the corner of the fortress and creep toward Hermóðr. I was unsure if Hermóðr was unaware of the giant dog advancing unseen. Hel's guard dog was intently focused on Hermóðr so I could get close enough to overhear any conversation.

The ebony doors swung open before Hermóðr 's fist had even touched the wood. He flinched, stepping back as the massive hound pressed its muzzle to the god's unprotected knee. Standing rigidly still, Hermóðr could not move and was forced to wait until Hel strode from the shadows of her fortress.

She was tall and elegant; the pale skin was smooth and youthful but a deathly-pale pallor of a corpse. Her long, raven-black hair shone with health even as the bluish colouring of her lips revealed the damage Óðinn had caused. She half-turned, the one brilliant pale blue eye finding me where I crouched behind rocks. She did not speak but winked at me and turned her gaze on Hermóðr. I was grateful for the speechless guise of the wolf. Had I been in human form I would have shouted my outrage at the sight of her. Óðinn, king of the gods, had thrown her into the depths of Niflheimr and been spiteful enough to leave her to rot. Visible through the thin grey cloth of her robe, bruises and broken bones on her left side but where she'd touched the icy surface of Niflheimr, decay blossomed into rot that had torn flesh from bone, revealing decaying tissue and a red ember where her right eye had been.

"Hermóðr," Hel said.

She advanced smoothly like a predator; gaze focused on the god she had trapped.

"What brings another of Óðinn's sons to my door?"

Hermóðr stared incredulously at Hel as though her statement were the most offensive thing he had ever heard.

"Come inside, Æsir," she said, gesturing toward the open doors.

He hesitated, glancing to either side of the doorway as if he expected an ambush. Hel laughed, the sound throaty but patronising. I watched Hermóðr bristle at her unspoken accusation and the mocking brightness to her eyes. She was enjoying herself, revelling in the ability to hold the Æsir at her mercy. I realised that this was what I had needed. This was the child of my blood. The moment Óðinn had thrown Hel and Jörmungandr away like unwanted pups from a litter, I had lost all respect for the man I'd called brother.

Finally, Hermóðr gave a stiff nod and moved inside the shadowed doorway. Hel glanced to where I remained behind a rocky outcrop. She half-turned and spoke severely to the gaunt servant, Ganglati, who waited inside the doorway. Bowing quickly, Ganglati ushered Hermóðr inside the massive fortress. Without another glance to me, Hel followed inside, the large doors slamming closed with an ominous boom that rattled the glassy black windows, rounded like the orbits of a skull. I huffed out a sigh of exasperation and lay my head on my paws. I was not invited to this discussion.

Hermóðr emerged from the black doors of Eljudnir a short time later. Despite her success as ruler of this forsaken realm, conversation was not one of Hel's talents. Óðinn's son looked pale and shaken, his eyes haunted and lips tight with anger. He glanced behind him again and I saw the pale form of Baldr lingering in the hall, eyes sorrowful and features lacking the customary brightness of the once-mighty god. Hel walked onto the front steps overlooking the infertile lands as Hermóðr swung into Sleipnir's saddle.

"Remember what I have asked," Hel said. "If the conditions are met, Óðinn can have his son back."

Hermóðr nodded gravely and turned Sleipnir. The stallion snorted and fought the bit, prancing across the ashen shores while Hermóðr sat, straight-backed and tall. Hel stood on the threshold, staring out at the churning waters of the river Slidr. When Hermóðr had disappeared from view, she finally turned her gaze to where I still waited, hidden from sight by the bulky rock buttress.

"Father. How pleasant of you to finally visit me."

I slunk from my hiding place but ignored her mocking tone. When only a few paces from her I stopped and shook the thick fur of my coat, ash and fine stone grit was thrown about, covering her. I smiled up at her, the wolfish grin conveying both threat and amusement.

"You want to know what I told him, don't you?"

I sat, curling my tail about my paws and tilted my head expectantly.

"Who's side are you on, Loki?"

Her words reached me in the same clear, psychic speech that Haiti and Sköll used with me. She smiled slightly, the unease I had felt at her wordless intrusion into my mind palpable through this kind of communication.

"Yes, I am your daughter. The blood of your lineage runs as strongly in me as my mother's does. Which bloodline do you think carries this talent?"

"I do not know," I replied. *"I've never been interested in breeding a whole pack to see which carry what talents."*

"A pity. I should like to know."

"Perhaps you should become a broodmare then," I snarled

"Like you did once?" She laughed, then the connection grew frigid between us. *"Certain gifts given to all women were taken from me when Óðinn cast me into this miserable pit."*

I whined, my ears flat against my head.

"Is that pity? It is too late for fatherly concern now."

"What deal did you make with Hermodr?"

"Why would you want to know? Surely you can scamper back to Óðinn and he will tell you. Do you seek to discover if there are any weaknesses in my binding? I'll save you the time: there are none. I am no fool, Loki."

"Then you did not ask Baldr how he came to Eljudnir?"

"He told me his blind brother shot him with a dart."

"He did."

"Why would he do such a thing? Everyone loved Baldr."

"Not everyone."

"You?"

I sensed her surprise through the bond we shared, the slight flicker of shock that trembled through the emotional link.

"Frigg has been plotting to oust me from the bosom of her family. Her family, you see. No room for Óðinn's adopted brother. I should have seen it earlier, never realised the threat I posed to the stability of the Æsir. Frigg was about to see me thrown from Asgard."

"And you killed her beloved son?"

"They were all so tortured over these prophetic dreams he was having. Frigg had an arrangement with Freyja, of all the goddesses, to protect Baldr from all harm. It seemed unlikely that Freyja had been as meticulous as Frigg might insist, and so I sought to prove how Frigg had deceived Óðinn about their son's safety and to show them all how weak they truly were."

"Why Höðr?"

"Well, Baldr is the most beloved of all the gods. They think the light of Sol herself shines from his every orifice. But his blind brother, Höðr, is barely noticed. He's like a pale reflection of his brilliant brother. I thought it might be nice to let Höðr be the one to take the shine off Baldr."

"What you have done is a declaration of war."

"Probably. But you should have seen their shocked faces, daughter. To strike them all where it hurt the most, their pride. After they had lied and bound Fenrir, after Óðinn had thrown you to Niflhelheim expecting you to die. It served them all to understand that they are not invincible nor untouchable. The cleverness they pride themselves upon is easily twisted by one such as me."

"*Clearly.*" The bond between us thrummed with uncertainty and the consequences of fate must have been flooding her mind.

"*Tell me what conditions you have placed upon Baldr's return. I will make certain he stays in these halls.*"

Hel tilted her head slightly as though trying to gauge if my offer was genuine.

"*Hermodr beseeched me, attesting to the sorrow felt by Óðinn and Frigg at the loss of their beloved son. He spoke of how all Nine Worlds would mourn the loss of Baldr's brightness.*"

"*What bargain did you make?*"

"*No bargain, Loki. An exchange of truth was made between Óðinn and myself. I promised the lord of the Æsir he might have his son Baldr returned to his side only if he were as beloved as I was led to believe. Hermodr agreed to the arrangement that Baldr would be released from my halls only if every living thing in all creation shared in mourning his loss.*"

I felt the pleasure of her words flood the connection between us.

A fair exchange. It was a very similar-sounding agreement to the one Gullveig's shade had made with Óðinn in these very lands. "*Do you know what was agreed between Óðinn and the sorceresses' shade?*"

My mother spoke of a prophecy once. Angrboða promised Óðinn would fall to his own pride and lose his beloved son because not everything can be loved equally by everyone in these worlds.

"*Will everything weep for Baldr?*"

"*That would be a terrible truth for Óðinn to learn,*" Hel smiled sadly.

"Truth is often terrible."

She tilted her head in acknowledgement of my words, a smile still twisting the withered corners of her lips on one side.

"I'll make certain there's one who doesn't shed tears for Baldr."

Hel's hand fell firmly upon my shoulders. I froze, wolf instincts in my body disliking the invasion of my space. My lip curled in a soundless snarl as Hel twisted the long, skeletal fingers of her left hand in my thick fur.

"When you're ready for Ragnarök, I'll stand with you on the battle plain of Vigridr."

She released her grip on my fur, but the cold chill of her touch had sunk deep into me. I shivered slightly and without glancing back at her, I fled her stone fortress and didn't slow for another nine nights. I raced through the ashen landscape of Helheimr until I reached the bridge spanning the curling river Slidr. I stared at the huge dog, Garmr, as he howled his challenge to me. I was Wolf and, ignoring Hel's guard dog, I leapt into the air above the black waters of Slidr. Safely on the other side, my claws found purchase on the earth of Álfheimr. Without delay, I pulled myself across the gateway into Álfheimr and stood, shaking with the realisation that I had made my decision long ago. I would bring down the proud Æsir and break Óðinn in the process.

Chapter 30
·Dry Tears

I tracked Hermóðr back to Valhalla. The bright form of Sól was already sinking into the western horizon, but Óðinn stood resolute at the stones marking the boundary to Glaðsheimr. Seeing the solitary figure of Óðinn, I instinctively glanced to the stony peak where the seat of Hliðskjálf was silhouetted in the fading light. I did not see Frigg there. Inwardly I relaxed, ducking beneath the protection the forest could offer. Even as I snuck beneath a thick shrub covered in lush berries, I glanced again toward Hliðskjálf, unable to shake the sensation I was being watched. There was someone sitting in the stone chair. My breath stopped. I hunkered closer to the ground, wishing it could enfold me, sucking me straight to Helheimr and saving the drawn-out process of my death that would surely follow. But it wasn't Óðinn sitting on Hliðskjálf, nor was it Frigg. No one else was foolish enough to use the power of that seat. Or so I had thought. The man in the stone chair shifted, fading sunlight catching the bright gold of his hair. Was that Freyr? Surely, he wasn't so foolish. I watched as the man stood up, the glint of his golden sword confirming that Freyr *was* that moronic.

Óðinn shifted his stance, pivoting from where he waited while Hermóðr approached. He turned to look directly over his shoulder and up to the stone overhang where the seat of Hliðskjálf was now abandoned. But I knew Freyr had not escaped. Óðinn would come after him, demanding recompense for the ultimate treachery. It was interesting to me, that even without my own betrayal, Óðinn had more than enough parties willing to disobey the sternest of his commands.

Hermóðr reined Sleipnir to a sudden halt. The stallion reared, snorting and tossing his head in protest. Eight hooves stamped the ground as Óðinn, and his son discussed the offer Hel had made. I watched with satisfaction as Óðinn's lips tightened with distaste and could only imagine the mocking language Hel had used in her terms.

The final light of Sól had completely faded from the sky and the faint silver blush of his twin, Máni, was already rising in the east. I huffed with the wolf's satisfaction at a successful hunt, the necessary knowledge uncovered.

When I was certain Óðinn and Hermóðr had departed the plains below, I trotted down from the forests of Álfheimr, glancing around me as I did. I would not be caught yet, not when my plans were so close to fruition. In the distance, I saw Heimdallrr standing guard near the shimmering, coloured bridge of Bifröst, but except for the watchman of the gods, only the standing stones observed as I passed into Glaðsheimr.

The following morning was crisp, the blue sky without clouds. I watched from the shadowy woods as Óðinn led the procession of mourners to the shore of the lake. The glacial waters reflected the brilliant blue sky and the inner icy depths as Thor stood upon the shore, admiring the craftsmanship of the ship *Hringhorni* that Baldr had loved. The warship beached on the sands, prow carved with a serpent that resembled Jörmungandr a little too closely for my comfort. I crept deeper into the shadows as Thor approached the ship, large hand tracing the wooden beam and planks as though it were a lover. The scene would have been worthy of ridicule if not for Thor's barely restrained thunderous rage.

Óðinn reached the sand with Baldr's body resting on his shoulder. Höðr, Týr and Ullr and Bragi removed the scarlet cloak that covered the corpse. Gently they lowered the body to the sand and stood staring at the ship on its log rollers. Behind the men, Frigg was accompanied by Baldr's weeping wife. Nanna stood, pale and wretched in the dawn light. Her eyes were badly swollen with grief. I hadn't cared for Baldr, that was no secret, but I felt a pang of regret to see his wife so grief-stricken.

Frigg stepped up before the warship and laid a hand on the smooth wood, whispering a few words under her breath. I watched Óðinn turn to his wife and nod in agreement. Calling orders and organising the gods into a line, shoulders to the prow of the mighty longship, the Æsir began to pour their combined physical strength into a single effort. Still, *Hringhorni* barely moved.

Exhausted, Óðinn stepped back and frowned. He spoke briefly with Frigg before he untied the horn secured at his belt. The summons echoed over the lakeshore, reverberating off the distant mountains of Thor's kingdom. The gods were too grief-stricken to send their own into the water, so one of the frost giants came forth like a servant to do their bidding. Any compassion and misgivings I had about my actions and plans dissipated with that single blow of the horn. None of the giants stood in Asgard to mourn the passing of Baldr. The only one who might be invited to be among them would be present as a servant.

In human form, I rested my head back against the tree trunk behind me and waited. Who would leave Skaði's domain to bother to observe Óðinn's summons? Giants were not beholden to a king or queen like the Æsir or Vanir Instead, loyalty was based on pacts, familial ties and mutual agreements.

A howl of a massive wolf, announced the arrival of Hyrrokkin, an outcast giantess from Útgarðar. She was a battle-scarred warrior and taller than any assembled of the gods here. Hyrrokkin steered the she-wolf she rode as it loped down the slope, snarling at Thor as they approached. There was no love lost between those two, either.

"Hyrrokkin," Óðinn greeted her, and I wondered if he was too weary to hide his surprise and did not bother in such company.

"Óðinn," the giant grunted. She stepped from her wolf and handed snakeskin reins to nervous looking guards. The wolf growled low and threateningly as the men held it on the very end of the length of lead.

"Grief has wearied us and we must ask for your superior strength."

Hyrrokkin glanced at Thor and raised an eyebrow. "All of you?"

Bristling in anger, Thor reached for his war-hammer and his fingers tightened around the haft of Mjölnir.

"Would you aid us to launch *Hringhorni* so we may hold the mortuary rites for Baldr?"

Hyrrokkin nodded in agreement to Óðinn's request but eyed Thor suspiciously. Without further comment, she strode to the longship and placing her shoulder against the wood, heaving with her considerable strength. The ship was heavy. The wooden rollers screeched wretchedly, and Thor stiffened with outrage. Then, slowly, the ship began to move toward the water's edge. Once the bow touched the water, Thor and Týr guided Ringhorn gently into the water, returning some of the solemn observance to the event.

Sighing, I let out a breath I'd not realised I'd been holding and collapsed back against the tree trunk. Freyja stepped closer to the huge longship and stood, gazing wordlessly at the carved dragon upon the prow. Before she could begin the ancient invocations of the mortuary rites, Óðinn fell to one knee beside Baldr's body. Gently, he brushed the bronze brow of his beloved son and began to weep. I wasn't close enough to see but I imagined his tears dripping onto Baldr's smooth cheeks. He was soon joined by Frigg and their tears mingling as she joined her husband. I watched these events unfolding and knew the time to honour my pact with Hel had come.

The branches of the oak trees protected and shielded me from sight while I transformed my physical form. Clenching my teeth, I changed my wiry physique for the taller and more sturdy body of the frost giant. Considering Hyrrokkin was not the only giant who'd assembled on the lakeshore below to weep for Baldr, I couldn't risk being identified as a fire giant from any magical taint lingering after my transformation. I'd taken the form of a middle-aged woman, assuming an older woman who wasn't wise or of child-bearing age would be more likely overlooked among her own kind whether she be giant, mortal or Æsir. It was a plot I'd used many times before, and it was usually true.

I dressed in simple clothing I'd snatched from many different washing lines over the years and kept in supply for such necessities. Wrapping my greying hair in a thick shawl pinned with a simple silver brooch, I walked in stolen boots to the edge of the thronging mourners. I was probably most surprised by how many of the giants had gathered to mourn Baldr with the Æsir. There were many more here than I'd imagined cared for the gods who regarded them so unfavourably.

The crowd pressed closer to the gods at the front of the lake, the beautiful, weeping figure of Frigg the epitome of sorrow. The pale blue of her dress was turning grey in her grief even as Freyja gently pulled on her shoulders, urging her to stand. Baldr's widow, Nanna, knelt silently beside her husband's corpse, Frigg's hand tightly gripping hers. The sight of Nanna's pale blonde hair bound by only a silver circlet and her grief-stricken eyes nearly broke my resolve. *Am I doing the right thing? Isn't there any other way? Did Nanna need to feel the pain of my anger toward Óðinn and Frigg?* It all felt wrong, and yet I could think of no stronger way to strike at Óðinn and Frigg than through the belief they blindly held in their invincibility. The Æsir weren't superior to the giants.

At the front of the assembled mourners, Frigg climbed to her feet. Wiping tears from her cheeks she looked across the Æsir, Vanir and giants alike.

"Hel has given her word to release Baldr from her hall if he was beloved by all living things. Let those who loved Baldr weep for him now. The Nine Worlds without the brightest of the gods are darker and less wondrous for it."

The Æsir began to weep at mention of Baldr's name, hands clutching to other hands in united support. Freyja and her brother Freyr sought each other's hands and held them close by their sides, the twins shedding tears in solidarity with the Æsir. I watched in muted surprise as a few of the giants began to cry quietly, wives weeping alongside their gruff husbands, and the light elves, dwarves and even the dark elves wept for Baldr.

I thought it was going to be difficult not to weep for the pain I had caused and for the loss of life. But as I stared at those around me, the ones who wept beside the Æsir, these gods who would slay them for sport tomorrow, I felt only bitter resentment. My cheeks were dry. The cold air brushed my skin and try as I might, no tears came to my eyes.

"Why do you not weep?" Frigg demanded.

I realised she still knelt over Baldr's body, tears bejewelling her pale cheeks. The crowd around me had parted and now Frigg challenged me directly, horror and outrage in her tone.

I stared back, black eyes meeting her accusation. "Thökk will not weep for Baldr."

Frigg climbed unsteadily to her feet, grey dress slowly shifting into the thunderous purple of storms.

"You condemn him to Helheimr!"

"Let Hel keep what she holds."

Frigg screamed her rage at me but behind her, Baldr's widow stared hollowly at the carved dragon on the longship. Even as Frigg turned, Nanna swayed, clutching at her chest. She half-screamed a shuddering sob, then collapsed onto the sandy shore. In shocked silence, the gods stopped where they stood in the water, arms still loaded with wood for the pyre. Frigg hurried forward, shoving me aside, her hands raking like claws as she glared accusingly at me.

"This death is yours," Frigg hissed, her robes flickering with lightning.

I backed away from the outrage and malevolence in Frigg's eyes, realising properly for the first time how easily she could turn her will to destroying me.

Óðinn and the other gods lifted Baldr's body, wrapped in the scarlet cloth, and placed him against the single mast of the longship, moving wordlessly while Freyja continued her ancient invocation for the dead. The lapping of water and splashing of boots was all that could be heard as the pyre steadily grew around Baldr's corpse. Carefully, Nanna's body had been wrapped and was being carried forward to the longship. I was forced further back into the crowd, and I went willingly to escape Frigg's accusatory glare.

Considering the crowd had gathered for a funeral, it seemed absurd to me they should be so surprised by the observation of one. I had no intention to remain near Frigg and her spiteful eyes. She was not as foolish as some might imagine, and the death of her son cut too closely to her sense of superiority. If she discovered that the reviled giantess Thökk was really the even more reviled Loki, the crowd would probably get three deaths where the expectancy had been one.

The full attention of the crowd had been on Nanna and the weeping Frigg. Since Nanna's sudden death, Óðinn and Thor had climbed from the water, clothes dripping in the chill morning air. I did not wait to see Nanna placed into the longship beside her husband. I hurried back to the safety of the oak grove and, under the protective shield of the dense branches, stripped my clothing and transformed back into my rightful body. Down beside the lake, I could hear the crowd begin to intone the mortuary rituals while Freyja's clear invocation rang clearly above the chanting.

Rolling my stiff shoulders, I stood amid the oak branches and watched as Thor and Týr pushed the bulk of the longship out into the current of the lake, the glacial waters shining pale blue against the flickering flames already consuming the pyre. I sighed. It was done. Baldr would not return to Asgard, and I had all but directly challenged Óðinn's authority. The bonds that had once united us were frayed beyond repair and yet I felt more freedom than I had in eons.

Chapter 31
Betrayal

I did not watch the longship burn on the water of the lake but escaped deeper into the woods of Álfheimr. Even as I ran through the dense bracken and shoved aside the shrubs and clinging vines in the undergrowth, I battled with my decisions and actions. Yes, I felt betrayed by Óðinn, and I was almost certain Frigg had orchestrated my destruction, or thwarted destruction, but it made my actions no less comfortable to bear. They felt sharp against my conscience, the weight and pressure cutting into me each time I considered them. Inwardly, I kept telling myself to stop being so sentimental and realise that Óðinn had always considered me a curiosity, a thing of pity and something he used to show mastery over all things. I was his domesticated giant. It was foolish to believe he had ever thought me anything more than that.

I swiped angrily at a persistent vine; the leafy tendrils caught around my leg and arm as though Álfheimr itself considered my passage a trespass. I staggered backward into a clearing. There were voices nearby. I could hear a muffled conversation as two figures approached from the opposite direction.

"Son of a viper-headed dog," the man said coldly.

I stopped, and breathing heavily, I turned slowly to face Freyr.

The Lord of Álfheimr stood with arms relaxed by his side, shock still plain on his handsome features. The ashen blond curls of his long hair fell to the golden breastplate he always wore. My eyes dropped to his right hip where the golden sword, the tool of my demise, would be waiting. But it was not. I frowned, lifting my gaze to Freyr's equally uncertain expression. I noticed then the graceful young woman who lingered slightly behind Freyr, her youthful, sun-blessed skin turning pale when she recognised me.

"Loki," Freyr said.

"Where's your sword?" I asked, peering around Freyr's broad shoulders to examine the woman hiding there.

"You've betrayed the Æsir. You killed Baldr," he said.

"I did," I said, meeting his gaze. "I also saw you sitting on Hlidskajlf.

Óðinn and Frigg have been very clear lately how they feel about traitors, haven't they?"

"What do you want, you lying coward?"

"Let's make a bargain," I said, spreading my hands wide.

"I won't make such agreements with you. I'll have Thor here in moments."

"But you haven't called Thor, have you? Why is that Freyr? Were you using the mighty seat of Hlidskajlf to spy on your lovely lady here?"

"I wouldn't do such a thing," he said, glancing sideways at the woman in question.

"Of course not," I said, grinning. "How unmanly that would be. Because this fair lady is from Jötunheimr, aren't you?" I asked.

The young woman looked uncertain then smiled with the wit I'd expected from a frost giant.

"I am Gerðr," she said. "My father is king of many lands in southern Jötunheimr. You would be wise not to raise the wrath of the frost giants, Loki. We are kin."

"I am never known for my wisdom," I said, shaking my head slowly. I shifted my focus to Freyr. "She's far more intelligent than you deserve."

"Speak what you want to me before I summon Thor."

I stared at Freyr, reconsidering my options. He was serious about calling Thor, and it didn't seem likely I could dissuade him without resorting to sly tactics.

"I am fairly certain you're not a fool, Freyr," I said.

He glowered at me but remained silent, waiting for me to make my point or finish.

"It surprises me then that you would go against Óðinn's direct commands and sit upon Hlidskajlf. I know as well as you how seriously the Old Man considers strategy, security, and imagines enemies where there are none. What he has never understood very well is emotion."

"Stop dancing on coals, Loki, and get to the point."

"Óðinn prides himself on strategy, intellect and cunning, and emotion has never played much of a role in how he views the Nine Worlds. But he is jealous and prone to passion as easily as all of us and like any man, lust has led him astray before. I can help you explain to Óðinn why you went against his orders and sat upon Hlidskaljf, help you explain it in a manner he will understand."

"I don't need to be associated with you in any way," he said. "I'm calling Thor now and you'll be punished for your crimes among us."

"And how will you explain that you exchanged your mightiest weapon for a woman? Do you think that's a trade Óðinn will agree with?"

"What are you talking about?" he growled.

"Your sword," I said simply. "You exchanged your sword for the hand of this incredibly lovely princess. I know as well as you and Óðinn that your sword is the only weapon that cannot be defeated. Against the frost giants it's certain death and even against Surtr, the Lord of the fire giants, it was merciless. I'm sure Óðinn shared with you the prophecy that spoke of a time when Surtr will venture forth from Múspelheim?"

"Not every prophecy will come to pass," Freyr muttered.

"True, true," I agreed, glancing at him sidelong. "But don't you wish you'd kept that sword now, just in case?"

Freyr glared at me, eyes narrowing before he smiled grimly to me and summoned Thor.

"Shit," I snarled, and glared at Freyr. "Why did you do that?"

He returned my glare. "Because I don't like you."

I rolled my eyes. "Seriously? That's so melodramatic, Freyr. You're really setting a poor example for your new bride. Imagine the brave, bold and undefeated Vanir god she was expecting to marry and instead she's got a sap who's afraid of a sneaky, weaselly giant like Loki. I'd be asking for my dowry back, Lady," I said, turning to the young woman in question.

She sniffed as though she disdained listening to me. I returned my attention to Freyr. "She's obviously used to royalty. That must have been a costly bride price you paid. Are you certain you just *lost* that famous sword of yours?"

"Yes."

In the near distance, I could hear thunder rolling across the sky and the crashing of someone moving quickly through the forest. Thor was coming for me and he wasn't in a good mood.

"Pity you didn't bargain with me, Freyr. I hope she's worth the doom it brings upon you all."

Thor burst through the underbrush on the edge of the grove, cheeks red with fury. He saw me standing alone and unarmed near Freyr and I wondered if he might collapse from sheer joy. There wasn't much point in trying to hide. Even so, with the massive bulk of the red-haired god looming down on me, I forced myself to stand still. Thor did not speak, and he stood over me, face growing redder with unvented rage. I flinched at the murderous intent in his eyes. He wanted to tear me limb from bloody limb, decorate the trees of this pleasant grove with my entrails. His small eyes were feral and mean. For once in my existence, I did not speak. I had plenty of quick jibes and witty retorts that would surely see Thor pound me into mincemeat. But I could not speak for fear as Thor plucked me from the ground by the throat, carrying me like a misbehaving puppy by the scruff of my neck. It did not seem to matter if I could breathe or not, so I let unconsciousness take me as Thor carried me toward my waiting punishment.

Chapter 32
Loki Bound

Thor hurled me onto an ice-slick cave floor. Stone flakes bit into my hands as I tried to cushion my fall, hands bound in front of me. Skidding on my knees, my clothing tore to shreds until I slid to a painful stop at Óðinn's boots. Wincing, I looked up into his merciless eye.

"We were brothers once," Óðinn said to me.

"I should have realised my fate earlier then. Your brothers don't tend to survive very long."

His lips became a thin line. He nodded grimly to Thor and turned away from me, stalking to the other side of the dark cavern.

"You turn your back on everyone eventually," I snarled as Thor hauled me upright.

Kicking and spitting at him, I fought with all the twisting fury I could manage. I was quick and agile, writhing like the snake so many of the Æsir had often accused me of being. But Thor's grip was like iron, his fists incredibly strong as he held me firm, carrying me bodily toward a looming shape behind me. I twisted mid-air, craning my head back to see a large platform of jagged rock had been unevenly hewn from the inside of the mountain. Despite the pervasive gloom of the cavern, the sharp edges of the stone glittered. I yelped and twisted more violently, bending my body away from the rock even as Thor carried me closer to it.

I screamed and cursed. My voice was a hoarse echo off the cavern walls, but it did me no good. I kicked at Freyr as he tried to catch my legs, cursing him with every ounce of power in my being. My magic had never lent itself to curses, but I tried anyway. Freyr did not even pause in his task. He bound my legs to the stone pegs carved hastily from the rock. Arching my back, I twisted near double, but Thor held my arms in one massive hand, binding them to the stone.

I stared at the dark, unnatural bindings on my arms and legs. Thick, viscous blood oozed from my bonds, making my skin slick. The strong iron tang of fresh blood hung heavily in the air.

"You took my son from me," Óðinn said from the other side of the cavern.

I stared uncomprehending at the bloody bindings, my mind refusing to believe what my eyes saw.

"Óðinn," I whispered in horror. "What have you done?"

"What was done to me," he hissed.

The one-eyed god stepped up beside me and slid a short, triangular blade from a sheath at his hip. I felt the cavern room begin to grow darker, faintness threatening to overtake me. He couldn't. Not the man I knew, Óðinn was not capable of such horror. But I knew he was going to. I had stood beside the god when he had walked a battlefield, decided which side might be victorious. I had seen him slaughter Jotun before. Cruelty was not unknown to Óðinn's nature.

Óðinn began to speak, his words transforming the fleshy bindings around my wrists and ankles into hardened metal. As he spoke, he used the blade to carve runes into the hardening metal. When he was finished, my wrists and ankles were bound fast to the rock, and with the rune-carved metal, only very powerful magic could unfasten my bindings.

"Tell me what you've done," I said into the heavy silence of the cavern.

"I killed your son for the son you stole from me," Óðinn said. "My future is bound by the loss of my son; your future is bound by the entrails of yours."

I turned my head, unwilling but unable to not see the iron fetters around my wrists. I had suspected what fleshy substance bound me. I had hoped my suspicions were wrong. But they were not. Óðinn had had used my own son, Narvi, slaughtering him to provide the binding for my punishment. Bile rose in my throat. I did not try to hide my tears or anger as I vomited onto the cavern floor.

A savage slap to my cheek brought me back to consciousness. Groggily, I rolled my head back toward the direction of the blow, vision blurry with the force of it still. Thor glared at me, red beard almost obscuring the thin line of his lips.

"Hit him again," Freyr said from somewhere in the darkness.

"I'm awake," I mumbled, blood dripping from my nose.

I shifted my right arm to wipe it away. My wrist immediately touched the cold metal of the manacles binding me and the nausea returned. I closed my eyes briefly, fighting the impulse to retch again.

I might have hoped this misery was punishment enough, but the Norns had never liked me. I heard the soft footfalls near the cavern entrance, the barest whisper of fur boots on stone. My heart lurched and instinctively, I knew the worst had not yet befallen me.

"I heard you caught him at last," Skaði said from the entrance.

I clenched my jaw, wishing I could grind my teeth until the worlds disappeared.

"To think this sorrowful pile of skin, sinew and bones is what all the fuss was about," she continued, stalking closer to me.

I felt the sharp edge of her fingernail as it traced one of my ribs, sliding down the length of my abdomen and pausing on my hips.

"I expected more," she finished.

"Jealous?" I asked, hiding my revulsion with bravado. "That I'd spend months with the Iron Wood's hag but never touch you?"

Skaði's fingernail dug into the soft skin close to my hip, blood welling up. She hissed at me with viciousness and, as I'd expected, some thwarted desire she dared not name. I closed my eyes on the leader of the frost giants, her glacial blue eyes promising nothing but vengeance.

"I brought something with me from Jötunheimr," she continued, pacing several steps further into the centre of the space.

I had not heard Óðinn speak since the binding; the memory of his words still made my heart ache with the hatred that had rung in them. I heard him clear his throat now, preparing to address Skaði.

"Loki's crimes are mine to punish," he said.

I opened my eyelids slightly, peering at the scene before me. Though I knew Óðinn's vengeance would be exacting, I still clung to the prospect that some remnant of the bonds we shared remained in his heart. I had wronged only him, though, and so it was for Óðinn to dictate the appropriateness of my punishment.

"All-father," Skaði addressed, bowing her head in reverence. "At my father's death, I was an untried leader. Regardless of the many eons I might stand as ruler of Jötunheimr, I could never equal the might of my father's strength. As you recognised yourself, Thiazi was an unrivalled force among the frost giants. In willingness to shed no more blood of my race, I married one of yours in an agreement of peace. Njörðr was a man of the wildest ocean coasts, and I could not forsake the winter peaks of the mountains. Such a marriage cannot be expected to endure and so it did not. I never asked you for the right to seek vengeance of my father's murderer. I ask for that right now."

I sucked in a breath. The noise was a loud hiss in the silence of the underground chamber.

"You seek retribution for Thiazi's murder now?" Óðinn asked.

"I do."

I held my breath. My heartbeat painfully in my chest, a ragged and terrified tattoo of fear.

"I cannot deny you such a right," he conceded, glancing toward me. "But I can't condone the murder of a prisoner, either."

Skaði's eyes glittered like ice crystals. "I do not seek murder, only just punishment."

"Let's discuss it, then," he said, dusting his hands as though to dispel the guilt of his actions. "What do you propose?"

I listened to Óðinn's words, the calmness of his voice and suggestions. I was astounded by the rational answers he provided while debating Skaði over what he would consider a justified punishment for the crimes I had committed against her.

"Would you consider an enduring poison a fitting punishment for the enduring heartache my father's loss has caused to me?"

Óðinn considered Skaði's words and then gave a single, curt nod of agreement.

"No," I wheezed, trying to wriggle away despite the bonds that held me in place.

Skaði smiled, her pale and perfect features shattering the illusion of solemn composure, and she looked every inch the war leader her father boasted she would become. I feared this queen of the frost giants more than I had ever feared her father.

Skaði walked calmly toward me, carefully removing the metallic bag she carried at her side. The glittering links of dwarf-wrought silver shimmered like the scales of the creature I knew dwelt inside.

"You know what this is, don't you, Loki?" she asked me, coming to a halt beside the stone slab to which I was secured.

I twisted away, body nearly bent double but for my wrists and ankles, which I could not slip out of the fetters that held me. Gasping and heaving in air, I collapsed back onto the sharp stone. Admitting defeat, I took a shaky breath and nodded in acknowledgement to Skaði.

"It's a viper from the ice cliffs."

"Very good," she crooned, and bending over me, secured the silver snake above my head. The viper hissed, venom spitting from its fangs as it twisted away from her, rearing backward on itself to stare, unblinking, into her eyes. Skaði stepped back. Beneath the viper, I shifted uneasily, and the reptile's head curved downward in a single, sinuous movement. Venom dripped from its impossibly large fangs.

I closed my eyes and screamed. I knew the stories of the ice vipers. All frost giants told tales of unfortunate relatives that'd been bitten by one of the snakes. No matter what other parts of the stories changed with the telling, only the agony caused by the venom stayed a constant.

I screamed until my voice was whisper of pain. I begged and pleaded, writhed and cursed, but no one came to my aid. Bound beneath the ground, the gods left me alone in the darkness to bear my punishment for eternity.

I finally stopped screaming. Then the only sound was a dismal echo of my own sobs. I drew in another ragged breath, waiting for the next drop of venom to fall, when I sensed someone near me. Warily, I opened my eyes, seeing only a deeper shadow in the gloom, but the presence was familiar.

"Are you to be my final punishment?"

I twisted my face as far from the expected path of the dripping venom as I could get, hoping the viper did not follow my movement.

The woman leaning above me did not answer, just kept her arms outstretched and steady above my face, a stone bowl cupped in her hands.

"Surely you don't want to be *faithful Sigyn* for the remainder of your days?"

She did not answer but I paused, licking my lips. Had I misjudged who stood above me? I heard the now familiar but very faint click as the droplet of venom was released from the viper's fangs and began to fall. I tensed, clenching my jaw so I would not bite my own tongue if I cried out.

My senses were focused so intensely on the smallest of sounds that the splash of the droplet as it hit the surface of the bowl seemed to echo.

"Thank you," I whispered to Sigyn, my body relaxing slightly under the strain.

"I will need to leave you every now and again to empty this bowl," she said. "I cannot ease your suffering in those moments I am gone."

I relaxed a little more, muscles aching with the strain of sustained terror. The stone slab was not smooth, the roughly hewn surface covered in sharp, jagged peaks and uneven troughs.

"After all that I have done to you," I whispered, "why stay now?"

I felt the shift in her stance as Sigyn gently rested one hip against the stone slab.

"Óðinn and Frigg took our son. I cannot condone your actions any more than theirs. If they had killed Narvi to avenge the death of Baldr, I still could see no worth in useless death," she said. "But they tore him apart just to make you suffer. There was no thought given to his or my suffering."

"He did not die well?"

"Can anyone ever die well, Loki?" she asked. "No, his death was not clean nor honourable. Thor tore him apart before my eyes like game meat after a boar hunt. I owe nothing to Óðinn and Frigg after this."

I closed my eyes, unable to free my mind from the horrific images my imagination provided. Narvi had been a humorous boy, neither too troublesome nor talented. He was never a threat to Óðinn or Thor. His savage death served only one point: to make me suffer, both from the degradation of my name and the loss of my son. Sigyn was right, Óðinn and Frigg had never considered her or my son in their quest for vengeance.

"Then here we must stay until the end," I whispered.

"Until the prophecy that Frigg fears so much? The one which Gullveig proclaimed when she cursed Óðinn and the Æsir that night eons ago?"

"What do you know of that?" I asked.

Silence drew close around the cavern, and I feared Sigyn might not speak. At last, she sighed, shifting her feet on the ground, careful not to spill the bowl, and sat on the edge of the stone slab.

"I know the endless winter they call Fimbulvetr has begun."

"Then Ragnarök approaches," I said.

Chapter 33
Fimbulvetr

It grew colder in the underground cavern as the winter raged beyond the mountain halls. True to her word, Sigyn remained by my side, leaving only to empty the bowl when the venom was close to overflowing. If I had been a courageous man, I would have pleaded with her to leave me to my fate. But I am not that man and so I never asked. I needed her company and the solid faith her presence gave me to endure the scorching pain of the venom as it scarred my flesh. I had not always been a handsome man, and I treasured the beauty Óðinn had gifted me all those eons ago. It hurt my pride and self-respect to have that perfect flesh ruined by the venom's scars. If Sigyn had not remained beside me, I would have withdrawn deeper into the ruin of my body. But she stayed, and so I planned my revenge on Óðinn and waited for my brothers Sköll and Haiti to begin the hunt that would signal the beginning of Ragnarök.

I was jolted into full consciousness. True darkness hung deep around the cavern and I assumed it must be night outside. The cavern shuddered, stone dust and chunks of debris scattering to the floor around me. I reached with my senses, searching for Sigyn, who normally lay with her head on my chest, arms outstretched with the bowl held protectively above my face. I could not feel her along my right side, nor my left. I began to panic, realising that she must have gone outside to empty the bowl. My immediate fears of the cave collapsing on me retreated into the background of my mind. I waited, counting heartbeats for the venom drop that must fall. One. Two. Three. Four. I held my breath for the fifth heartbeat. My senses strained, anticipating the pain that would follow. Five. Six. I let out a shakily held breath. What had happened to the viper? Seven. Eight. The droplet fell. Pain blossomed through my mind, obliterating thoughts as a second and third droplet fell in close succession. I screamed as loud as my ravaged voice would allow.

"Shh," Sigyn crooned, brushing my sweat-stained hair from my forehead.

Consciousness returned and I jerked, heart racing as I struggled to re-orientate myself. Had I fainted? What about the cave collapse? Had I imagined it all?

"What's happening?"

"The mountain is shaking," Sigyn said, still stroking my forehead.

"Are you all right?"

"I'm fine, just calm down. The tremors through the earth disturbed the viper. There was more venom on your face than usual when I returned. I need you to be calm."

Sweat prickled my skin, cold and clammy as I shivered in the darkness.

"Tell me what's happening out there."

She did not reply immediately, and I wondered if I needed to press her more firmly for information. I forced myself to focus on the repetitive motion of her hand, soothing away my panic like I was a child afraid of thunderstorms and Thor's wrath. Mind you, any child had good reason to fear Thor's rages, but I let Sigyn calm me and hoped she would tell me what she'd seen.

"Tell me," I pressed when my heartbeat had steadied.

"You mentioned you had brothers once," she began, and sighed with terrible exhaustion. "I saw them hunting in the sky this evening. I knew them for your kin immediately when I saw how similar they were to your wolf form. I know you can transform into anything you wish, Loki, but you always preferred the grey-black wolf. Tonight, Sköll and Haiti have gone hunting as you said they would."

"They will come here for me."

"I expect so. But before you take the actions I know you've planned— don't bother denying it we've been married too long and endured too much for lies now—your true nature beckons now and I know you're waiting until these fetters are gone, then you'll embrace it. There's a battle coming, Loki. I am of the Æsir bloodlines, and I know this as well as you do. I'm not going to stop you."

"Did they chase down their quarry?" I asked, smiling faintly at the thrill of the chase shared between Sköll and Haiti as they hunted through the sky.

"A cold wind blows from the desolation of Fimbulwinter Midgard. I turned to the west, where Sól rode as fast as her golden steed would allow but Sköll ran swifter still, opening his massive jaws and swallowing them both. Shocked, I turned to come back to you when I saw Máni on the eastern horizon, he and his silver horse torn down by Haiti and both devoured. I started to run back to you, but the earth shook, great trembling through the surface as though it would split apart entirely. I regained my feet and took one last look at the sky, the absolute emptiness of it, each star burned out like a campfire doused on a distant plain. Only desolation can lie ahead of us now."

Sigyn finished speaking, voice faint and hollow. I flexed my fingers, a gesture for her hand. She let me hold her wrist and I gently rubbed the smooth skin over the bones with my thumb. Her hands were normally callused with the marks of weaving or threshing, the activities of her days. She lay her head against my chest and began to weep. I wanted more than anything to embrace her, to wrap my arms around her and pull her to my chest. Bound as I was, the only comfort I could offer was the oldest one we shared. I sighed into her hair, continuing to gently stroke the skin of her exposed wrist.

Suddenly, a violent tremor shook the mountain. The cavern shuddered, stone clattering to the ground from the ceiling. Sigyn jerked upright, the bowl nearly falling from her grasp. The venom splashed over the side, just missing my face and shoulder, and hissed, burning into the stone.

"Are you all right?" she asked, panicked as her free hand sought my face.

"It didn't touch me. You?"

"Fine," she said, exhaling shakily with relief.

The cavern shook again, larger chunks of stone breaking from the ceiling, tearing apart the fissures of the mountain. A howl echoed through the depths of the stone, seeming to rise through the rifts in the earth itself. Beside me, Sigyn froze, her hand clutching at my wrist.

"Garmr," I said, in what I hoped was a reassuring tone.

"Hel's dog?"

"Remember what you said about Narvi? What follows will be vengeance for the wrongs committed against him and all who share giant's lineage?"

"You've never been as terrible as I often accused you," she said.

My answer went unspoken as the cavern was ripped apart. The solid stone slab on which I was tied was pulled asunder by the shearing of the earth. Sigyn was thrown from me, her body made a horrible *thwack* as it hit the opposing wall of the cavern. I was tossed backward from the stone, the viper cast into the darkness. I tumbled through the air and collided with the solid rock of the upturned stone slab. Air was pushed from my lungs in a painful wheeze.

I turned my gaze to the middle of the cavern, where my hastily carved stone torture table had stood. The massive black head and shoulders of a wolf protruded from an opening in the earth. Fenrir snapped his mighty jaws, the remnants of chains still hanging from his muzzle.

Quickly, I ran across the cavern, blood dripping from my face where my scalp was cut. Dizziness rushed through me and I weaved awkwardly, bouncing off stone boulders until I found the opposite wall of the cavern. On hands and knees, I searched across the edge of the uneven cavern wall until I touched Sigyn's prone body. I ran my fingers lightly up her leg and torso, feeling for any major trauma. When I reached her throat, I gently pressed my fingertips to the weak pulse of her heartbeat. She would live. I bent carefully over her and half-carried, half-dragged her to the cave mouth and outside. A single large oak tree provided the only nearby shelter. Kissing her gently on the lips, I lay Sigyn on the ground and rushed back inside the cave.

Garmr howled again and I heard Sigyn calling for me outside the cavern. Hoping she would not follow me or search for me, I smiled ruefully at Fenrir as he waited, forepaws on the crumbling edge of the earth.

"Have you ever seen Midgard?"

The massive wolf narrowed his eyes and regarded me. Then he snapped appreciatively at the air and dropped back through the rift in the earth. I glanced back to the cave mouth and saw Sigyn standing wanly in the shadows, watching me. I bowed with a melodramatic flair and, still completely naked, dropped through the earth after Fenrir.

CHAPTER 34
WAKING THE DEAD

I remembered Sigyn's pale face as I followed Fenrir into the darkness. The massive wolf had broken through the crust of the earth, smashing apart rock and ripping free roots from Yggdrasil, tendrils that stretched sideways through the earth now hanging like broken limbs from the freshly carved tunnel. Above in Asgard, the golden cockerel Gullinkambi crowed from Valhalla's roof and waking the Æsir to this new dawn. It would be a time of reckoning.

I hurried after Fenrir. My son had grown terrible and fierce, part of me thought Óðinn was right to fear him. The black wolf was a bulk of darkness in the tunnel ahead of me, the chains that had bound him slapping uselessly at his side, the frenzy to destroy growing in him. Tonight, I wanted nothing more than to join the abandon of the hunt, the wildness and chaos of absolute destruction. And so, I urged my beaten and burnt body to run faster, raising the frenzy inside me. Everything would burn and finally, the Æsir would be forced to acknowledge the folly in thinking the giants were lesser.

Fenrir burst from the tunnel he had created, skidding sideways as he careered off an opposing wall in an older passageway. I slowed, travelling more cautiously behind the wolf, and jogged around the corner of Fenrir's tunnel. Peering down the old passageway, I sniffed at the stale air. Peering at the carved walls, I noticed the pick and chisel marks that ran the length of the arched passage. This was an old construction, the methodical chisel marks were dwarfish in craftsmanship but there were fainter indentations of much older burrowing in this earth. The dark elves had originally carved these passages and once marched these halls. Smiling, I turned to Fenrir, and the giant wolf hunkered low to the ground, ears pressed against the earthen ceiling.

"These halls stretch all the way to Niflheimr. An army could march to Bifröst itself and not be noticed from Asgard until then."

Fenrir's intelligent eyes shone in the darkness and he whined.

"You want revenge on Óðinn and the Æsir?"

Fenrir bared his teeth and snarled. I watched the long strings of saliva drip to the ground.

"Óðinn has always taken great interest in those who rule the lands in Midgard. He often travelled in those lands to sit at firesides and hear the mortals tell tales of Óðinn, the All-father. It seems very arrogant to me now, to travel and hear tales of yourself, embellish a few details here and change several truths there."

Fenrir's eyes glittered with the promise of malice as he watched me.

"He cast your brother into Midgard too. It's time we woke Jörmungandr, don't you think? A family reunion is well overdue."

Fenrir gave a wolfish smile, the beast leaping to his feet, smashing into the passage walls, earth and stones showering onto me. I covered my hands protectively over my head. Grinning, I waved Fenrir ahead of me. The wolf bounded toward Midgard but I waited until the unsteady shuddering in the underground passages had settled before I removed my hands.

I heard a faint crow from another cockerel, the sound echoing through the underground passages from Jötunheimr. I smiled, thinking of Fjalar, that red cockerel in the shadowy woods of Jötunheimr waking the frost giants from slumber, calling them to war. Time was running short now, the forces of prophecy gathering speed and, like an avalanche, nothing could stop the advancing tide of events. I hurried after Fenrir, flexing my fingers as I scented the salty tang of the Midgard Sea. Rounding a sharp bend in the passageway, I instinctively started to slow my pace. Ahead of me, open sky stretched like an endless darkness, and Fenrir's brothers Sköll and Haiti still ran across the sky, devouring starlight in their joyous hunt. Their howls were the call of any wolf, the thrill of freedom and the pleasure of hunting with the pack. I stood on the edge of the abyss that dropped into the ocean below me and, throwing my head back to the sky, I howled into the fading stars. Fenrir returned my howl from the land, his massive jaws wide, embers expelled on his breath. I watched the bright sparks erupt into flame across the nearby thatch roofs and trees, fires quickly spreading through the settlements of the mortals.

"Jörmungandr!" I bellowed into the chaos.

I held my breath, waiting several heartbeats. What if he did not wake? How long had he slumbered since Óðinn cast him into these waters? Then the earth shuddered. I steadied myself against the cavern wall as another great shudder shook Midgard. I exhaled slowly, watching the waves of the Midgard Sea rise higher and higher. Fenrir howled and the earth shivered, then the waves sucked back into the ocean. I held my breath, waiting. The ocean roiled, and a torrent of water with waves the height of mountains rushed towards the land and Jörmungandr rose from the depths of the ocean.

"Jörmungandr!" I shouted again.

The massive head pivoted toward me, spiked tusk-like protrusions curving wickedly from the side of his reptilian head. Jörmungandr stared at me, his gaze full of cunning and feral intent. The eyes of a dragon, I thought with a shiver. I held his gaze even with the knowledge I was probably within striking range of the serpent if he wanted. He reared back on the curled mass of his strong coils, a bony fin running the length of his sinuous body. Opening his mouth, Jörmungandr screamed his rage into the burning sky. Fenrir answered with a howl, followed by Sköll and Haiti, who tore into the screaming mortals on the land. Jörmungandr shrieked again, the sound so shatteringly loud I clapped my hands over my ears but cried my rage in unison with them. Intoxicated by the chaos around me, I howled joyously into the night, mixing my voice with Jörmungandr's battle cry. Grinning, I watched the serpent roll onto the land, snapping and devouring scattering mortals. The massive coils of his body slapped at the water, the ocean roiling and tossing beneath his bulk.

Above the sound of terror and burning worlds, the third cockerel crowed. I whistled to Fenrir, Sköll and Haiti, and gestured to Jörmungandr, then pointed at the massive ship heading toward us across the ocean. This longship, like the third cockerel, was black as the soot raining from the sky. I stood, watching *Naglfar* approach crewed by the dead from Helheimr and Hel's hound Garmr standing proudly at the prow. Grinning wide with the adrenaline of approaching battle, I swung my battle axe over one shoulder and leapt from the shore and onto the deck of the black ship. The grain of the wood beneath my boots felt odd and on closer inspection, revealed itself to be crafted from fingernails. It was garish even for me but I knew my daughter well and Hel would have no compunctions about using whatever resources came most easily. In the infertile lands of Helheimr, I doubted too many trees grew but harvesting the plentiful fingernails of the dead would be simple enough,

The great frost giant, Hrymr steered *Naglfar* against the buffeting winds and tossing waves, the crew of frost giants stood behind me on the deck. Some of the frost giants had joined the ranks of the dead to row with haste. A steady rhythmic beat of the drummer encouraged the rowers forward, but *Naglfar* needed little aid across the sea. The winds were in our favour and even the wash of higher waves from Jörmungandr's passage beside us did little to disrupt the sailing. The crew of giants glanced warily to the silent dead from Helheimr, guarded by Garmr. Hel stood beside me, her dress and robes coloured with the pale grey of grave soil. The long black hair flew about her face; the ravaged half an ever-present reminder of the crimes Óðinn had committed against her. She now rode beside me, not for vengeance but to see it done. Fenrir galloped across the black sky, the once bright light of the sun and moon devoured by Sköll and Haiti, who raced ahead of us.

In the distance, I could see the shimmering arch of Bifröst. The eternal rainbow bridge and solitary gateway to Asgard was unguarded, as usual. Frowning, I wondered why Óðinn had not armed the Æsir and already led the Einherjar to battle.

"Company," Hrymr said gruffly, slowly steering the massive black ship toward the eastern coastline.

I shifted, focusing on the northern horizon to where the leader of the frost giants had long been gazing. A grin tugged at my lips and Hel frowned beside me, focusing her keen eyes on the bright light stretching across the northern horizon.

"Fire giants." I pointed to the north. "Surtr leads them."

Hrymr grunted, hauling on the keel to shift our course, tacking the mighty warship at a tighter angle to the coastline. Turned broadside to the land, I stared at the arching height of Bifröst, still impossibly shining in the darkness. Suspended above, the mountains of Thor's kingdom and fortress overhung the ragged cliffs we now steered toward.

"How did you come to lead the giants?" I asked, scanning the shoreline ahead of us.

Hrymr smiled grimly, his broad features scarred by blades, fists and arrow heads. He kept his dark blue gaze fixed firmly on land, holding the keel against the waves, but his dark blue eyes glanced briefly to me, the colour reminding me of brittle ice. I let my fiery eyes slide over him, roaming his frost-rimed hair and muscular arms as he strained against the sea.

"Skaði made many enemies when she sought personal retribution for Thiazi's death over the honour of the giants. In joining with the Æsir to punish you, she betrayed us. I was chosen as our Chieftain in her place."

I nodded but said nothing, turning my attention back to the growing army to the north. The forces from Múspelheim were enormous. Surtr's army stretched the full length of the northern horizon, the fire giants armed with fiery swords, war-clubs of volcanic rock and flaming arrows. In the black sky above them, the twisting forms of dragons were just becoming visible as they advanced on Asgard.

I was wondering why Heimdallrr was so slow in raising the alarm when I heard the thunderous hooves of Sleipnir as Óðinn galloped from Asgard. The All-father clattered across the shimmering arch of Bifröst before Sleipnir increased speed, disappearing into the darkness beyond.

"Well?" Hyrm asked, considering the shoreline ahead of us.

"Óðinn will seek advice from the mummified head of Mimir before he does anything."

Beside me, Hel made a face, her features twisting in outrage and something very close to anger.

"A problem?" I asked, quirking an eyebrow at my daughter.

"Keeping the dead from the Halls is despicable."

"Still wish to abstain from battle?"

"All will die, I need seek no vengeance."

I frowned at her words; the bitter note of prophecy hung upon them like a rancid smell. I was about to question her further when I finally saw Heimdallrr standing at the edge of Bifröst, barring entrance to Asgard. A single Æsir standing alone against the advancing army of Múspelheim looked absurd. On my right, Fenrir prowled the open sky, snarling at the sight of the solitary Æsir. As I watched, Heimdallrr raised the golden curved horn Gjallahorn to his lips and blew.

The echo of the famous battle horn rang across the Nine Worlds. The water in which Naglfar sailed appeared to instantly calm, the waves pausing mid-curl as the echo reverberated. Then Jörmungandr raised his horned head from the grey water and shrieked in response, spurts of venom issuing from his long fangs. Fenrir responded with a shattering howl and loped forward, head lowered for the charge.

Across the other side of Bifröst, Surtr raised his flaming sword and bellowed a challenge. The army of Múspelheim answered in a thunderous roar, charging toward Asgard.

"Your eyes became flame at Surtr's words," Hel said, her mismatched eyes on me.

"Blood of the fire giants can't ever be concealed."

"Nor should it." Hrymr steered Naglfar toward the narrow bay ahead of us. Further above on the grey cliffs, I could see a long, wide plain.

"They won't breach Bifröst," I said.

"What?" Hyrm asked between issuing orders to his crew.

"We'll fight there," I said, pointing at the uneven ground, jutting stone and treacherous looking ground of the wide plain above the cliffs.

"How do you know that?" Hel demanded, grabbing at my arm.

I did not answer her. Above us in the sky, the rainbow bridge of Bifröst shattered beneath the first wave of the fire giant army. The giants of Múspelheim who still stood on the safety of the approach to Asgard from Midgard roared in outrage as their fellows tumbled back to the ground. The thunderous crack from the broken bridge still sent shockwaves through the atmosphere.

"I just know," I answered Hel.

Above us, the battle for Bifröst continued unseen as *Naglfar* disappeared beneath the overhang of the cliffs and Hyrm steered the warship into the bay, and we prepared to land.

CHAPTER 35
BATTLEFIELD OF VIGRIÐR

The forces of the frost giants led by Hrymr, their hulking forms standing with weapons at rest, with rows of battle-axes and massive swords of glacial ice stronger than steel, assembled behind me. Together, we stood in the still moment before battle, a cold wind gusting across the Plain of Vigridr. Behind us, Jörmungandr reared above the cliffs, his massive, coiled body towering over the plain and fangs dripping venom in anticipation of battle.

Beside him, Fenrir paced, saliva hanging from his massive jaws as he snapped and snarled with eagerness. I exhaled slowly and shifted my grip on the battle axe, the wicked edge of the black volcanic-wrought metal catching the light of the flame that leapt through the upper branches of Yggdrasil.

Beside me, Garmr growled low, hackles raised as he stared with focused intensity on the one-handed swordsman Týr. It seemed a bond had developed between Hel's hound Garmr and my son Fenrir. While Fenrir paced with growing agitation, gaze fixed on Óðinn, Garmr calmly watched Týr and, I suspected, planned to claim vengeance on behalf of Fenrir.

Above me, the dragons of Jötunheimr, bodies armoured with scales like hoarfrost but stronger than shields and teeth as long as broadswords, wheeled across the sky. I nodded grimly to Hyrm as he hoisted the massive battle-axe onto his shoulder, readying himself to charge.

To my right, the fiery armies of Múspelheim flickered and sparked in the darkness, their brilliance reflecting off the frost and ice armour from their compatriots of Jötunheimr. My own eyes burned with the flames of the fire giants, and I bowed solemnly to acknowledge Surtr in his armour of volcanic rock with the flaming broadsword held high.

I stared across the battlefield to Óðinn. He sat astride Sleipnir, the stallion stamping the ground and tossing his head. The great army of the Æsir stood behind Óðinn, the loyal Einherjar occupying the front ranks, the Valkyries waited on their wingless mounts, exposed sword blades across their thighs. Behind Óðinn in a tight cluster were Týr and Thor, Ullr and Heimdallrr. At the centre of the apex of Valkyries, Freyja sat astride the massive boar, its long tusks exposed but armour protecting its huge shoulders and bristling back. Freyja wore a helm adorned by curving steel tusks that shared the same wicked gleam as her mount. Beside her, Freyr rode his massive golden boar, the beast covered in thick bristles I knew were sharp as blades and the tusks protruding from its mouth were twice the length as those of his sister's mount.

I glanced at Surtr, blunt and blackened features as unreadable as the molten rock he resembled. His red eyes focused on Freyr, and I thought he smiled when he noticed the absence of Freyr's mighty broadsword. The one weapon in Óðinn's army that could never be defeated by Surtr was absent this Ragnaork. Surtr laughed and the sound was a deep rumble like an earthquake.

From the sky above me, two fiery red dragons swept toward the Plain of Vigridr, spewing flame onto the earth, scorching several of Óðinn's Einherjar who were too slow to escape the torrent of flame. To my left, the werewolves of Iron Wood howled in challenge. I smiled grimly, then charged into battle.

I sidestepped a swordsman, veering toward the edges of the fighting as the main front of the armies clashed with a thunderous crash of shields and weapons. In the sky above, dragons circled, scorching the earth only to be met by a stream of arrows from the light elf archers behind Óðinn's main ranks. I turned, swinging the axe as I moved, keeping Óðinn in my sight as he galloped Sleipnir straight toward Fenrir. Týr ran behind Óðinn, the great swings of the broadsword slicing apart any giants who stood in his path. Týr had always been a masterful swordsman, and the loss of his right hand had only meant he must learn with his left. A shield was strapped to his right arm, which he used with vicious efficiency, knocking down any who withstood the onslaught of his attack before the blade finished their lives.

I had moved to the edge of the battle and now held ground near the path we had taken from the bay. Below me, waves crashed against cliffs, but *Naglfar* remained high on the shore where Hyrm had left it. Scanning the battle, I saw Óðinn level his long spear, Gungnir, toward Fenrir as he spurred Sleipnir forward. Fenrir snarled in challenge, opening his jaws and destroying swathes of the Einherjar, Óðinn's chosen warriors who harried the wolf from every side. The Einherjar were no match for Fenrir and he smashed men aside with his clawed forepaws, biting and snapping others until the carnage surrounding him formed a low wall of corpses. Still Óðinn cantered Sleipnir around Fenrir, spear levelled at the wolf to keep him at range. I wanted to shout to Fenrir to be careful, to warn my son about Óðinn's mastery of battlefields and manipulation of troops, which he commanded like game pieces. Fenrir was hemmed in by bodies and the shining silver point of Gungnir kept his jaws just beyond reach of Sleipnir.

I caught movement to my left and swung, axe blade cleaving one of Óðinn's

Einherjar in half. There seemed to be more of them than I'd ever realised, as though Óðinn had collected them in anticipation of a battle when he would need countless troops. Swinging the black axe blade in double-handed blows, I moved forward on the warriors, meeting swords and shields with my own strength, kicking and stomping on unwary men when it suited me. I wasn't a skilled warrior like some of these men had been in life, and I certainly didn't uphold the valour of battlefield tactics. If stomping on an enemy's foot got me an advantage, I'd take it.

Garmr howled and I dropped to one knee, swinging my axe in a low sweep to push my enemies backward. I took a quick glance at the fighting in the centre of the battle, watching as Týr drew closer to Fenrir from behind, Óðinn keeping the wolf's attention. Garmr howled in warning and leaped across the battlefield, using jutting stones and the massive, randomly placed boulders. Hel's hound launched himself at Týr from behind. In surprise, the swordsman spun, bringing up his blade. It was too slow, and the blow glanced off Garmr's shoulder and the hound cannoned into the Æsir. Cursing beneath the snarling weight of Garmr, Týr screamed, and there was the sound of tearing flesh.

The Einherjar began to harass me again and my focus narrowed on the small group of warriors. I could not aid Garmr or Fenrir right now. Fate would decide the outcome of their battle; I needed to assure my own survival. I screamed my annoyance at the Einherjar surrounding me, charging forward with a series of wild and furious blows. Shocked, the warriors staggered backward against the ferocity of my onslaught. When I had beaten them back enough, I looked at the corpses lying in a circle around me. Only a few wary warriors remained, carefully scrutinising their next movements.

I turned to check on Fenrir just as Garmr struggled to his paws, shaking gore and blood from his black coat. Týr lay motionless on the ground, throat and chest a gnawed horror. Garmr staggered several steps toward Fenrir, then dropped to the ground, sword wounds gaping in his side. The hound did not rise again and neither did Týr. I needed to get to Fenrir before Óðinn drove the ferocious wolf into an ill-considered attack.

I had gone only several paces when more shining swords of Óðinn's cursed Einherjar attacked. From where I was, battle raged around me but I could closely monitor Fenrir and I slowly pushed the warriors and the fighting in the direction I wanted to go. Fenrir's howl of outrage echoed through the battlefield as Óðinn charged, Gungnir levelled straight at the wolf's heart.

In a massive leap, Fenrir escaped the horrendous confinement of the corpses. Landing almost on top of Óðinn, Fenrir's paw smashed into Sleipnir, raking open the stallion and throwing both horse and rider to the ground. Óðinn rolled with the impact but Gungnir had been thrown from his hand. Roaring with triumph, Fenrir prowled toward Óðinn where he lay pinned beneath

Sleipnr's heavy bulk. The stallion was dead and even as Óðinn struggled to free his trapped leg, it was a useless effort. Fenrir leaped like a wolf on a rabbit, jaws crunching bone and muscle. He shook his massive head, spraying gore and breath of fire across the battlefield before tossing Óðinn aside like discarded meat.

The warriors around me had stopped fighting, staring in shocked disbelief as Óðinn was thrown to the ground. The All-father hit the battlefield and rolled before sliding to a stop in a bloody smear. I saw the brightness of his cobalt eye and knew he still lived, but not for long. Fenrir howled and opened his huge jaws toward the earth, consuming the corpses of the fallen Einherjar, leaving only a faded blackness in their wake. With Óðinn removed from the battle, the ferocity with which the Æsir's armies fought began to fade.

I pushed forward through the chaos of the battle, my axe cutting down any who obstructed my path. I was only several paces from Fenrir when I saw Víðarr take to the field. He was like the shade of Óðinn as a youth, the image of a dead god as I recalled him. I had no time to scream warning to Fenrir. Víðarr charged forward, shield raised against impending blows and longsword ready in his hand. Fenrir caught movement from the periphery of his vision and whirled as Víðarr leaped. The sword in Víðarr's hands reflected the fire, frost and battle around it. Víðarr's blade struck Fenrir's lower jaw, cleaving it off in a single blow. Dropping to the ground, Víðarr spun and brought the sword blade to meet Fenrir's enraged attack. The massive wolf snarled as Víðarr buried his blade up to the hilt in the wolf's chest. Fenrir slammed into the ground, blood and gore splattering his fur. I screamed my rage at Óðinn's son and charged toward him across the battlefield.

Even as I raised my battle-axe against the shield wall of the Einherjar who stood to defend Óðinn's son, a shrill challenge from behind me slowed my advance. Jörmungandr had reared back against the dark sky, flames from the upper reaches of Yggdrasil lighting the sky, his narrow-horned head thrown back, long fangs exposed. Below, on the edge of the cliff, Thor waited, Mjölnir balanced in his hand. His fingers flexed with unnerving casualness against that ridiculously short haft of the war hammer. Thor was never calm in battle. His was a contained fury, like a dog maddened by the scent of blood before it attacks. He was motionless.

"Jörmungandr!"

My voice echoed through the battle but was buffeted back by the furious gust as the serpent struck at Thor. Fangs exposed and spewing venom, Jörmungandr dived with incredible speed toward Thor, the curved horns of his reptilian head hitting the ground, pincering Thor between them. Thor was not idle, and for his many faults, his furious fighting style was legendary for good reason. He bellowed in response, striking Jörmungandr against the skull with

Mjölnir. Hissing, Jörmungandr pulled backward, chunks of stone dislodging from where his horns had pinned Thor to the earth. Even as the giant serpent withdrew, Thor struck again with Mjölnir, hitting Jörmungandr with several quick and powerful blows to the eye sockets.

Jörmungandr swung his head sideways in quick movements as Thor clung to one of the curved horns. The sharp jerk of Jörmungandr's head threw Thor to the ground. Blood poured down Jörmungandr's scaled face, his eyes now bleeding freely. He tasted the air with a forked tongue and like a true dragon of the air, found his prey with scent alone. He struck, diving for Thor with incredible speed and ferocity. Thor tossed aside Mjölnir and struggled for his short sword even as he tried to run. But with mouth open and fangs already dripping venom, Jörmungandr hit Thor, one sword-length fang piercing through Thor's thigh. The god screamed with agony as Jörmungandr reared backward again, carrying Thor with him, speared upon an upper fang.

I watched in amazement as Jörmungandr continued to rear out of the water, body coiling tighter and tighter, preparing to consume his prey. But with shaking hands struggling to work against the shock and venom flooding his body, Thor unsheathed his shortsword. Grasping the serrated edge of Jörmungandr's fang, Thor screamed in agony as he hauled himself upright and plunged the blade into the roof of Jörmungandr's mouth.

The serpent shrieked in sudden pain, coiled body spasming mid-air. The waters in the Midgard Sea suddenly rose in a flooding wave as Jörmungandr began to fall toward the land. I screamed in rage at the loss of another son and began to stalk toward the cliffs, preparing to attack Thor when Jörmungandr finally collapsed. The Einherjar offered no resistance to me as I hit them aside with shield, cutting others down with axe blade. I continued toward the toppling serpent, the massive bulk now falling almost slowly as Jörmungandr wavered from side to side. Feet apart, I hefted my axe, ready for what must come. Somehow, I felt the final moments of my son as Jörmungandr lurched to the left and crashed onto the cliffs. Blood soaked the ground in a growing pool around his head, the damaged eyes now staring blindly at me. I walked slowly and calmly to the left, around the massive open mouth to where Thor now staggered from inside.

The god was smeared in blood, his hands shredded to the bone. Jörmungandr's poison had burnt the flesh from arm, face and chest, and his right leg, which had been pierced by the fang, was broken. My shock at seeing Thor so beaten in battle was brief as the god struggled toward me, dragging his already rotting leg. Thor's red hair, which was not scorched by Jörmungandr's acidic venom, was plastered with blood but his lips twisted with hatred as he saw me. I readied my axe, willing to dispatch him to join his father, even if it wasn't the most courageous of battle victories. Thor staggered the ninth step from Jörmungandr's mouth and collapsed. I lowered my blade, staring as he convulsed once and then was still. I turned my gaze to the ruined body of Jörmungandr, the once mighty serpent—now as motionless as the god.

"Betrayer!" a voice shouted from behind me.

I spun, raising my axe to face my accuser. The rage of war burned hot in me, and I knew my eyes would be the same colour as the fiery embers raining from the sky.

"Heimdallrr," I growled, and leapt toward him, axe held high.

Chapter 36
Ragnarok

Heimdallrr blocked my attack, raising his shield with ease as he gave ground beneath my onslaught. Each strike of the heavy black blade reverberated up my arms, and my shoulders ached with the fury of continuous, unrelenting pounding of my axe. Heimdallrr kept his shield up, fending off blow after blow, but was losing ground as I pushed him back into the chaos of battle. I clenched my jaw, grinding my teeth with the rage that poured from me. I may not be able to strike Óðinn down myself, but I could crush his army.

I cursed Heimdallrr but he remained unaffected, his brilliant white smile irritatingly persistent. He continued to block the axe blows, deflecting strike after strike as though I were an annoying training partner.

"What is wrong with you?" I shouted, swinging the axe low toward his waist.

Heimdallrr merely smiled, skipping lightly backward from the range of my blade.

"I told you once I have the sharpest senses of all the Æsir."

"Except for wits," I snarled.

"Perhaps," he agreed jovially. "But I still easily evade your blows. I hear and see what is coming before any others."

"I can fix that."

I swung the axe with savage intensity, keenly watching him for any indication that he was making use of his preternatural gifts of hearing and sight.

As I expected, Heimdallrr shifted his weight almost imperceptibly before my axe came into his sight. His hearing was very acute. His sight was just as extraordinary, catching the slightest shift in my stance before I would even swing my axe. I paused, holding my next blow and as I expected, Heimdallrr caught my hesitation as easily as he had observed all the other subtle changes in my movement. I could not defeat him using any of the skills or even tricks I knew.

I lowered my battle axe, meeting Heimdallrr's smug smile.

"You brought about this chaos," he accused me.

I shifted the haft of the battle axe in my hands, glancing across the battlefield.

"But you knew it was coming."

Heimdallrr's features twisted in anger, and he lost the seemingly impenetrable calm. He stepped forward, shield raised on his left arm, the right swinging the longsword in quick strokes. He forced me backward and I struggled to keep him from gaining within my range. The double-handed battle axe was a weapon for brute force and lacked the easy manoeuvring of the longsword. Despite the speed of the sword, its length kept me from stepping within Heimdallrr's guard. Unless, I thought, planning my next attack while deflecting several rapid volleys from Heimdallrr…unless I could get upset his calm long enough to get within his guard, where his longsword would be useless.

I pressed my attack, forcing Heimdallrr to lose ground with a series of quick blows, axe head shining darkly in the firelight. I frowned, realising it had become much brighter in the last moments. I stole a quick glance to my right. Nothing except plumes of smoke, hordes of Valkyries charging their smoke-grey steeds across the battlefield. Where was Freyja in all this? She was the leader of the Valkyries, where was she? And where was her brother? My shoulder-blades itched with the sudden realisation I'd not seen Freyr since before Óðinn charged. Of all the warriors the Æsir could have fielded, Freyr was one of the most imposing. What if he was just waiting behind me? If Heimdallrr was deliberately toying with me until Freyr could sweep my head from my neck with his golden sword?

"What's wrong, Loki?"

Heimdallrr's tone was a sneer, the strong sweeps of his longsword suggested he was enjoying my momentary discomfort.

"Is there suddenly a lot more fire than before?"

Heimdallrr used his shield to shove me forcibly backward, taking a step toward me as he quickly glanced around the battlefield. There was momentary hesitation as he noticed the massive branches of Yggdrasil above us were wreathed in flame. He almost paused in his shock, registering what I had noticed only moments before; these were the branches that supported Asgard and Álfheimr.

I was naturally cautious but when risks must be taken, I never dally. I lunged for Heimdallrr, stepping within the range of his longsword, surprising him with the sudden attack. He moved quickly, swinging the sword around in a backhanded arc. But he was too slow. And so was I. The curve of my axe blade cleaved into Heimdallrr's unprotected side, the shield on his left arm easily pushed aside with my body as I followed through with the momentum of the axe. Even as I shoved Heimdallrr's shield away, felt the axe blade sink into flesh and catch on the bone of his spine and hip, I knew I was too slow.

Heimdallrr went down on one knee, screaming in shocked pain. The axe blade had wedged between the thick bone of his spine and pelvis. Balancing his weight on the left knee as blood flowed down his side and legs, Heimdallrr continued the arc of the longsword. The blade slashed through my abdomen, slicing intestines and cutting muscle. I folded with the blow, clutching uselessly at my wound.

Beside me, Heimdallrr collapsed forward. Blood pooled around him, the haft of my battle axe protruding at a horrible angle above his right hip, still wedged in his lower back. He coughed once, blood gurgling through his lungs and running freely from his nostrils.

I clawed my hands toward my hip, searching for the long knife I kept sheathed there. Hot pain burned through me and with shaking hands I gave up the search for my knife. Still clutching at the long wound across my abdomen, I screamed as I rolled onto my back. White hot pain overwhelmed me. My vision dimmed, faded, and I succumbed to the waiting darkness.

Embers rained down around me as my eyelids fluttered open. For a moment, I thought they were fireflies. Then the stench of scorched flesh and burning ash tree returned me to reality. Ragnarök. The battle. The plain of Vigridr. I twitched, sending pain scorching through my body. Reflexively, I touched the surface of my abdomen, gasping at the greater pain there. I let my fingers fall away and I tried to calm my breathing. Too sharp, too shallow. I'd pass out again if I didn't calm down.

My hearing buzzed and threatened to fade. I closed my eyes momentarily, hoping the pain would rescind with my sight. A sudden crash of metal on metal nearby startled me. I jerked, screaming in pain with the sudden movement. I couldn't move. I couldn't escape.

On the periphery of my eyesight, I saw the flaming sword slash upward at the sky, lopping another branch from Yggradsil. The great limb from the Ash Tree fell with a crash and the smell of charred wood. Surtr was here. Where was Freyr? Had he abandoned the battle with his sister? I recalled both of them seated on the golden armoured boars but knew I'd not seen them since Óðinn charged into battle.

Distantly, I heard a shattering roar as a black dragon flew across the sky, its large scales looking like a crazed pattern of molten rock. It spewed fire across the darkness as Yggdrasil burst into fresh flame. Somewhere beneath the earth, a horrendous crack echoed, and Yggdrasil lurched perilously. Níðhöggr had gnawed through the roots of the Great Ash and now Surtr's flames were spreading into what remained.

A bellow rumbled through the battlefield somewhere ahead of me. I felt the concussion of hooves upon the scorched plain and I saw Surtr stand taller in the centre of the melee.

A bright golden boar bellowed another challenge and lowered its mighty tusks, charging toward the hulking figure of Surtr. The Lord of Múspelheim calmly turned, casting aside enemies with a single sweep of his fiery sword.

I watched the bright streak approach Surtr and recognised Freyr's engraved helm and shield. Even though he did not grip the mighty weapon, he thundered beneath Surtr's guard, ducking below the sweep of the flaming sword. Surtr roared in outrage, striking at Freyr and knocking him to the ground. Surtr's sword fell with fatal precision, cutting off the pained squeal from Freyr's golden boar.

Despite the solid armour of molten rock which formed impenetrable plates over Surtr's body, Freyr rolled to his feet, blade in hand. He stood, dwarfed by the imposing bulk of Surtr as he advanced, flaming sword held slightly to the side. Freyr was a master swordsman and he danced away from Surtr's powerful blows, moving easily over the scorched and chipped battleground. But without the prized golden sword that allowed Freyr to defeat any foe, he could not win this battle.

The duel between Freyr and Surtr might have lasted hours or moments, but I watched in the timelessness of the burning battlefield, the screams of dying gods and giants around me. I stared at Freyr in his brilliant armour and waited. Perhaps Surtr had envisioned a similar plan. The lord of Múspelheim was the oldest of the giants and he kept his combat to a minimum, striking only in defence with little need to actively attack Freyr.

I saw the clever trick before Freyr realised it. Even if I could have cheered in appreciation for the ruse Surtr had delivered, I wasn't sure I would have. Freyr skipped back lightly from another bold swing of the fiery sword. Behind him, a low burning branch from the massive canopy of Yggdrasil hung uncertainly above the plain. Surtr feigned an attack, then suddenly side-stepped and lopped the burning branch free. Freyr looked up, shocked as the branch plummeted toward him. He darted to the right and straight into Surtr's sword blow.

There was a sudden hush across the Plain of Vigridr, as though Freyr's death had been felt by all things. Another tremor ran through the earth and the crust broke apart, sending splinters of rock and corpses into the darkness. I stared at the freshly carved fissures in the earth, imagining the pale dragon Níðhöggr who feasted on the dead below. I shuddered, suddenly chilled.

Surtr lifted the flaming sword high into the broken dome of the sky. Tendrils of fire spread across the remaining canopy as the highest branches of Yggdrasil ignited. Where the fissures of earth had opened through the plain, the Midgard Sea now poured torrents of salt water into the dark below. What did not burn would be swallowed by the waves. We had won. The Æsir were nothing but corpses, while only remnants of the giants remained on the battlefield. It was a hollow victory.

EPILOGUE
MY NINE LAST BREATHS

Waves slowly consumed the ashen shores of Helheimr, the water thick with salt as though the world wept tears of sorrow. As I bled onto the sand, I turned my head to look at the grey cliffs ahead, my gaze lifting over the battlefield strewn with corpses: giants, Æsir and Vanir alike. A bitter, blood-tinged chuckle escaped my lips to see Óðinn's proudest warriors. The Einherjar were now discarded like butchered meat, ripped apart by Fenrir's jaws. In that moment, I realised how cruel the humour held within the Norns had been, how twisted the weaving on their loom.

The vast number of bodies surrounding Fenrir were unfathomable. I found it somewhat amusing, dying on the shores of my daughter's realm, while Fenrir, my son, had wrought such destruction that not even Óðinn could withstand it. Behind me in the waves, the bodies of Thor and Jörmungandr left bloody smears on the sand. I had given life to these children, these monsters as they'd been called. The Æsir had feared only what they would bring upon them all.

I lifted my gaze to a bright flickering of fire in the blackening sky. When Surtr had fallen to Freyr, his fiery sword had lit the branches of Yggdrasil and now the cosmos burned. I felt no regret while my blood leached into the sands of Helheimr. I tried to move. I was cold even as tendrils of flame encroached closer on the mounds of bodies near me.

I could not feel my arms. I turned my head but the movement was stiff and sluggish. The corpse of Heimdallrr lay beside me where he had fallen. His ever-smiling face had slackened, and the once-bright eyes were now dull. My axe was still embedded in his broad chest and my outstretched arm unable to grasp the haft. The fatal slice across my abdomen felt icy, as if the touch of Niflheimr were already within me. I shivered at the thought and recalled my earlier vow upon the prow of *Naglfar*. I had promised an ending in Ice. How ironic if this was what the Norns now proffered—a twisted offering, wrapped in their own cruel humour. I laughed despite myself, and a sharp lance of pain ravaged my body and choked my mirth.

I looked over at Óðinn's corpse and imagined the cobalt eye focused on me. He was quite dead. He lay beside his son and avenger, Víðarr. The young man was slumped across his father's body, the sword he'd used to avenge Óðinn still wedged between Fenrir's jaws.

"Loki?"

I looked up blearily into Freyja's face. Her battle armour was clean and unblemished by blood or gore. Where was she during the battle? She'd unsheathed that bone-handled sword. Where had she been during our greatest need against Surtr? The Valkyries had taken to the fight, but I'd never seen their leader among them.

I ignored Freyja and lifted my gaze to see Yggdrasil ablaze. The Great Ash that had arched its canopy above the Nine Worlds was fully aflame. Burning embers fell like leaves in autumn as it shuddered. A tearing noise filled the cosmos and the aftermath of Ragnarök with new sorrow.

I was dying. My blood flowed toward the sea, where it mingled with the salt water to froth against the beach. The steady slap of waves against the sand moved the carcass of Jörmungandr closer. Another of my children, the Midgard serpent, was now one of many casualties in this avoidable battle. While more blood seeped from me and the Nine Worlds faded, the tide rose. I focused on my dimming eyesight, forcing my final conscious action to bear witness as Yggdrasil burned.

I tried to ignore the seductive pull on my consciousness as Ginnungagap grew impatient. *It took all branches back to that singular moment of unblinded sight as though I had been a practitioner of the seiðr*, I realised, thinking aloud to myself. *The misbegotten child of Múspelheim.* The Æsir were no more my kind than the frost giants of Jötunheimr had been. Both were as different from me as I was from them. Now in sorrow, I knew when Óðinn broke faith with Gullveig and she cursed us, her protégée with Valkyries at her side, was more a danger to us than we'd ever realised. I relinquished consciousness and let thought and memory flow uninhibited into the void of Ginnungagap.

Even dying on the Plain of Vígríðr while the Nine Worlds burned around me, I took satisfaction that Óðinn, for all his arrogance and tyranny, could never defeat Gullveig's curse. Nor had I defeated Freyja's curse, it seemed.

I was aware of her presence before she stooped beside me, her engraved armour splattered in blood and a helm under one elbow.

"You're among the fallen."

"So it would appear. Where's your brother, then?"

Her lips quirked slightly but she pressed them together in a grave line.

"He'll join you in death soon."

"Then you can carry us both away."

"What makes you think you're worthy of my troops in Fólkvangr?"

I winced, another stab of pain bringing tears to my eyes.

"My charm and good looks?"

"You were never happy in Asgard."

"No. Which is why we're all here now."

"There's not long to go. Time runs short for you. Yggdrasil burns with Surtr's flames, Níðhöggr consumed the roots and Fenrir has torn apart the worlds in vengeance."

"Yet I've never felt greater freedom."

She looked at me quizzically. "Most of your internals are free from your body. You're dying, Loki."

"Gullveig cursed Óðinn all those eons ago. I know some of the secrets you, Angrboða and the other völva keep hidden."

"Do you know Gullveig never cursed Óðinn, then?"

"What?" I coughed, a trickle of blood running from my lips. "Then how?"

"What was Óðinn's greatest weakness?"

"He had many, but pride was one of them."

"In trying to avoid a fate where he must weaken his position or be devoured by a giant wolf, he chose this carnage."

"She never cursed him?"

"We are *völva*," Freyja said, standing and looking across the battlefield. "Curses were never a power we possessed, but prophecy has always been our gift. Óðinn feared what he didn't understand. It drove his actions, and it drove your reactions."

I stared at Freyja's pale face, her grim features as she scanned the battlefield, looking over the corpses with sorrow.

I closed my eyes, breathing shallowly against the pain. Exhaling deeply, I listened to my slowing heartbeat, waiting and wondering with each pulse whether it would beat once more. Sluggish and failing, that was death. Why did men worship battle, then? There was no glory or power in these moments, only a fading of life.

"Loki." A chill voice whispered above me.

I twitched, trying to move, but only gasped in fresh agony. Skuld, one of the Norns, stood above me, her wizened face a wrinkled horror of amusement. A few paces ahead, her sisters walked barefoot through the muddy, bloody battlefield. They held aloft between them a small but complex weaving of red threads. Their long fingers balanced the fates and lives of all who still breathed on the battlefield.

"Are you going to cut that thread?"

Urd stared up at the ruins of Yggdrasil, tears running down her youthful cheeks. The three sisters cared for Yggdrasil and managed the fate and life-force of everything. They'd known this moment would come but not acted to prevent it.

Skuld tilted her head, waggling a single thread with her little finger. A single red thread unravelled from the tapestry.

"Was it Frigg who opposed me all along?" I stared at the bloody thread that was my life made manifest.

Skuld didn't answer me, but she so rarely spoke. Instead, it was the middle sister, Verdandi, who knelt beside me. She smoothed my sweaty forehead as though calming a scared child.

"Frigg's weaving was a complex one. But her thread and yours have always been so closely bound. Both she and you shared Óðinn's trust and his fate."

"*She* banished me from the Nine Worlds? But Gullveig's curse was only Óðinn's paranoia—his own downfall."

"You both were each other's downfall." Skuld's voice sounded like cracking bones.

I coughed again, blood running into my beard. "Frigg never did like me."

Skuld smiled in condescension as she raised her shears. The sharp clack as she snipped my thread from the tapestry echoed in the sudden silence.

The Norns had vanished. I stared at the length of red yarn lying in the mud. Was that all that had ever bound my life to the Nine Worlds? *Is this death, then? Or is this a place in-between life?*

I relinquished my consciousness and let thought and memory flow uninhibited into the dark void of Ginnungagap. Nothing ever truly ended, of course. Gods and men were bound by the same laws and the same fragile constraints. *Will the Nine Worlds end in ice or flame?* I stared up at the growing darkness and smiled. Embers and bitter ash rained down on me. *Next time will it end in ice?*